The
VANISHING
HALF

Also by Brit Bennett
The Mothers

The VANISHING HALF

BRIT BENNETT

dialogue
books

DIALOGUE BOOKS

First published in the United States in 2020 by Riverhead Books
First published in Great Britain in 2020 by Dialogue Books

11

A CIP catalogue record for this book
is available from the British Library.

Hardback ISBN 978-0-349-70146-2
Trade paperback ISBN 978-0-349-70145-5

Book design by Lucia Bernard
Printed and bound in Great Britain by Clays Ltd, Elcograf S.p.A.

Papers used by Dialogue Books are from well-managed forests
and other responsible sources.

FSC
www.fsc.org

MIX
Paper from
responsible sources
FSC® C104740

Dialogue Books
An imprint of
Little, Brown Book Group
Carmelite House
50 Victoria Embankment
London EC4Y 0DZ

An Hachette UK Company
www.hachette.co.uk

www.littlebrown.co.uk

For my family

Part I

———

THE LOST TWINS

(1968)

One

The morning one of the lost twins returned to Mallard, Lou LeBon ran to the diner to break the news, and even now, many years later, everyone remembers the shock of sweaty Lou pushing through the glass doors, chest heaving, neckline darkened with his own effort. The barely awake customers clamored around him, ten or so, although more would lie and say that they'd been there too, if only to pretend that this once, they'd witnessed something truly exciting. In that little farm town, nothing surprising ever happened, not since the Vignes twins had disappeared. But that morning in April 1968, on his way to work, Lou spotted Desiree Vignes walking along Partridge Road, carrying a small leather suitcase. She looked exactly the same as when she'd left at sixteen—still light, her skin the color of sand barely wet. Her hipless body reminding him of a branch caught in a strong breeze. She was hurrying, her head bent, and—Lou paused here, a bit of a showman—she was holding the hand of a girl, seven or eight, and black as tar.

"Blueblack," he said. "Like she flown direct from Africa."

Lou's Egg House splintered into a dozen different conversations. The line cook wondered if it had been Desiree after all, since Lou was turning sixty in May and still too vain to wear his eyeglasses. The waitress said that it had to be—even a blind man could spot a Vignes girl and it certainly couldn't have been that other one. The diners, abandoning grits and eggs on the counter, didn't care about that Vignes foolishness—who on earth was the dark child? Could she possibly be Desiree's?

"Well, who else's could it be?" Lou said. He grabbed a handful of napkins from the dispenser, dabbing his damp forehead.

"Maybe it's an orphan that got took in."

"I just don't see how nothin that black coulda come out Desiree."

"Desiree seem like the type to take in no orphan to you?"

Of course she didn't. She was a selfish girl. If they remembered anything about Desiree, it was that and most didn't recall much more. The twins had been gone fourteen years, nearly as long as anyone had ever known them. Vanished from bed after the Founder's Day dance, while their mother slept right down the hall. One morning, the twins crowded in front of their bathroom mirror, four identical girls fussing with their hair. The next, the bed was empty, the covers pulled back like any other day, taut when Stella made it, crumpled when Desiree did. The town spent all morning searching for them, calling their names through the woods, wondering stupidly if they had been taken. Their disappearance seemed as sudden as the rapture, all of Mallard the sinners left behind.

Naturally, the truth was neither sinister nor mystical; the twins soon surfaced in New Orleans, selfish girls running from responsibility. They wouldn't stay away long. City living would tire them out. They'd run out of money and gall and come sniffling back to their mother's porch. But they never returned again. Instead, after a year, the twins scattered, their lives splitting as evenly as their shared egg. Stella became white and Desiree married the darkest man she could find.

Now she was back, Lord knows why. Homesick, maybe. Missing

her mother after all those years or wanting to flaunt that dark daughter of hers. In Mallard, nobody married dark. Nobody left either, but Desiree had already done that. Marrying a dark man and dragging his blueblack child all over town was one step too far.

In Lou's Egg House, the crowd dissolved, the line cook snapping on his hairnet, the waitress counting nickels on the table, men in coveralls gulping coffee before heading out to the refinery. Lou leaned against the smudged window, staring out at the road. He ought to call Adele Vignes. Didn't seem right for her to be ambushed by her own daughter, not after everything she'd already been through. Now Desiree and that dark child. Lord. He reached for the phone.

"You think they fixin to stay?" the line cook asked.

"Who knows? She sure seem in a hurry though," Lou said. "Wonder what she hurryin to. Look right past me, didn't wave or nothin."

"Uppity. And what reason she got to be uppity?"

"Lord," Lou said. "I never seen a child that black before."

IT WAS A strange town.

Mallard, named after the ring-necked ducks living in the rice fields and marshes. A town that, like any other, was more idea than place. The idea arrived to Alphonse Decuir in 1848, as he stood in the sugarcane fields he'd inherited from the father who'd once owned him. The father now dead, the now-freed son wished to build something on those acres of land that would last for centuries to come. A town for men like him, who would never be accepted as white but refused to be treated like Negroes. A third place. His mother, rest her soul, had hated his lightness; when he was a boy, she'd shoved him under the sun, begging him to darken. Maybe that's what made him first dream of the town. Lightness, like anything inherited at great cost, was a lonely gift. He'd married a mulatto even lighter than himself. She was pregnant then with their first child, and he imagined his children's children's children, lighter still, like a cup of coffee steadily diluted with cream. A more perfect Negro. Each generation lighter than the one before.

Soon others came. Soon idea and place became inseparable, and Mallard carried throughout the rest of St. Landry Parish. Colored people whispered about it, wondered about it. White people couldn't believe it even existed. When St. Catherine's was built in 1938, the diocese sent over a young priest from Dublin who arrived certain that he was lost. Didn't the bishop tell him that Mallard was a colored town? Well, who were these people walking about? Fair and blonde and redheaded, the darkest ones no swarthier than a Greek? Was this who counted for colored in America, who whites wanted to keep separate? Well, how could they ever tell the difference?

By the time the Vignes twins were born, Alphonse Decuir was dead, long gone. But his great-great-great-granddaughters inherited his legacy, whether they wanted to or not. Even Desiree, who complained before every Founder's Day picnic, who rolled her eyes when the founder was mentioned in school, as if none of that business had anything to do with her. This would stick after the twins disappeared. How Desiree never wanted to be a part of the town that was her birthright. How she felt that you could flick away history like shrugging a hand off your shoulder. You can escape a town, but you cannot escape blood. Somehow, the Vignes twins believed themselves capable of both.

And yet, if Alphonse Decuir could have strolled through the town he'd once imagined, he would have been thrilled by the sight of his great-great-great-granddaughters. Twin girls, creamy skin, hazel eyes, wavy hair. He would have marveled at them. For the child to be a little more perfect than the parents. What could be more wonderful than that?

THE VIGNES TWINS vanished on August 14, 1954, right after the Founder's Day dance, which, everyone realized later, had been their plan all along. Stella, the clever one, would have predicted that the town would be distracted. Sun-drunk from the long barbecue in the town square, where Willie Lee, the butcher, smoked racks of ribs and brisket and hot links. Then the speech by Mayor Fontenot, Father Cavanaugh blessing the food, the children already fidgety, picking flecks of crispy chicken skin from plates held by praying parents. A long afternoon of celebration while the band played, the night ending in a dance in the school gymnasium, where the grown folks stumbled home after too many cups of Trinity Thierry's rum punch, the few hours back in that gym pulling them tenderly toward their younger selves.

On any other night, Sal Delafosse might have peeked out his window to see two girls walking under moonlight. Adele Vignes would have heard the floorboards creak. Even Lou LeBon, closing down the diner, might have seen the twins through the foggy glass panes. But on Founder's Day, Lou's Egg House closed early. Sal, feeling suddenly spry, rocked to sleep with his wife. Adele snored through her cups of rum punch, dreaming of dancing with her husband at homecoming. No one saw the twins sneak out, exactly how they'd intended.

The idea hadn't been Stella's at all—during that final summer, it was Desiree who'd decided to run away after the picnic. Which should not have been surprising, perhaps. Hadn't she, for years, told anyone who would listen that she couldn't wait to leave Mallard? Mostly she'd told Stella, who indulged her with the patience of a girl long used to hearing delusions. To Stella, leaving Mallard seemed as fantastical as flying to China. Technically possible, but that didn't mean that she could ever imagine herself doing it. But Desiree had always fantasized about life outside of this little farm town. When the twins saw *Roman Holiday* at the nickel theater in Opelousas, she'd barely been able to hear the dialogue over the other colored kids in the balcony, rowdy and bored, tossing popcorn at the white people sitting below. But she'd pressed against the railing, transfixed, imagining herself gliding above the clouds to some far-off place like Paris or Rome. She'd never even been to New Orleans, only two hours away.

"Only thing waitin for you out there is wildness," her mother always said, which of course made Desiree want to go even more. The twins knew a girl named Farrah Thibodeaux who, a year ago, had fled to the city and it sounded so simple. How hard could leaving be if Farrah, one year older than they, had done it? Desiree imagined herself escaping into the city and becoming an actress. She'd only starred in one play in her life—*Romeo and Juliet* in ninth grade—but when she'd taken center stage, she'd felt, for a second, that maybe Mallard wasn't the dullest town in America. Her classmates cheering for her, Stella receding into the darkness of the gym, Desiree feeling like only herself for once, not a twin, not one half of an incomplete pair. But the next year, she'd lost the role of Viola in *Twelfth Night* to the mayor's daughter, after her father had made a last-second donation to the school, and after an evening sulking in the stage wing as Mary Lou Fontenot beamed and waved to the crowd, she told her sister that she could not wait to leave Mallard.

"You always say that," Stella said.

"Because it's always true."

But it wasn't, not really. She didn't hate Mallard as much as she felt trapped by its smallness. She'd trampled the same dirt roads her entire life; she'd carved her initials on the bottom of school desks that her mother had once used, and that her children would someday, feeling her jagged scratching with their fingers. And the school was in the same building it'd always been, all the grades together, so that even moving up to Mallard High hadn't felt like a progression at all, just a step across the hallway. Maybe she would have been able to endure all this if it weren't for everyone's obsession with lightness. Syl Guillory and Jack Richard arguing in the barber shop about whose wife was fairer, or her mother yelling after her to always wear a hat, or people believing ridiculous things, like drinking coffee or eating chocolate while pregnant might turn a baby dark. Her father had been so light that, on a cold morning, she could turn his arm over to see the blue of his veins. But none of that mattered when the white men came for him, so how could she care about lightness after that?

She barely remembered him now; it scared her a little. Life before he died seemed like only a story she'd been told. A time when her mother hadn't risen at dawn to clean white people's houses or taken in extra washing on the weekends, clotheslines zigzagging across their living room. The twins used to love hiding behind the quilts and sheets before Desiree realized how humiliating it was, your home always filled with strangers' dirty things.

"If it was true, then you'd do something about it," Stella said.

She was always so practical. On Sunday nights, Stella ironed her clothes for the entire week, unlike Desiree, who rushed around each morning to find a clean dress and finish the homework crushed in the bottom of her book bag. Stella liked school. She'd earned top marks in arithmetic since kindergarten, and during her sophomore year, Mrs. Belton even allowed her to teach a few classes to the younger grades. She'd given Stella a worn calculus textbook from her own Spelman days, and for weeks, Stella lay in bed trying to decipher the odd shapes and long strings of numbers nestled in parentheses. Once, Desiree flipped through the book, but the equations spanned like an ancient language and Stella snatched the book back, as if by looking at it, Desiree had sullied it somehow.

Stella wanted to become a schoolteacher at Mallard High someday. But every time Desiree imagined her own future in Mallard, life carrying on forever as it always had, she felt something clawing at her throat. When she mentioned leaving, Stella never wanted to talk about it.

"We can't leave Mama," she always said, and, chastened, Desiree fell silent. She's already lost so much, was the part that never needed to be said.

ON THE LAST DAY of tenth grade, their mother came home from work and announced that the twins would not be returning to school in the fall. They'd had enough schooling, she said, easing gingerly onto the couch to rest her feet, and she needed them to work. The twins were sixteen then and stunned, although maybe Stella should have noticed the bills that arrived more frequently, or Desiree should have wondered why, in the past month alone, their mother had sent her to Fontenot's twice to ask for more credit. Still, the girls stared at each other in silence as their mother unlaced her shoes. Stella looked like she'd been socked in the gut.

"But I can work and go to school too," she said. "I'll find a way—"

"You can't, honey," her mother said. "You gotta be there during the day. You know I wouldn't do this if I didn't need to."

"I know, but—"

"And Nancy Belton got you teachin the class. What more do you need to learn?"

She had already found them a job cleaning a house in Opelousas and they would start in the morning. Desiree hated helping her mother clean. Plunging her hands into dirty dishwater, stooping over mops, knowing that someday, her fingers would also grow fat and gnarled from scrubbing white folks' clothes. But at least there would be no more tests or studying or memorizing, no more listening to lectures, bored to tears. She was an adult now. Finally, life would really begin. But as the twins started dinner, Stella remained silent and glum, rinsing carrots under the sink.

"I thought—" she said. "I guess I just thought—"

She wanted to go to college someday and of course she'd get into Spelman or Howard or wherever else she wanted to go. The thought had always terrified Desiree, Stella moving to Atlanta or D.C. without her. A small part of her felt relieved; now Stella couldn't possibly leave her behind. Still, she hated to see her sister sad.

"You could still go," Desiree said. "Later, I mean."

"How? You have to finish high school first."

"Well, you can do that then. Night classes or somethin. You'll finish in no time, you know you will."

Stella grew quiet again, chopping carrots for the stew. She knew how desperate their mother was and would never fight her on her decision. But she was so rattled that her knife slipped and she cut her finger instead.

"Damn it!" she whispered loudly, startling Desiree beside her. Stella hardly ever swore, especially not where their mother might overhear. She dropped the knife, a thin red line of blood seeping out her index finger, and without thinking, Desiree stuck Stella's bleeding finger in her own mouth, like she'd done when they were little and Stella wouldn't stop crying. She knew they were far too old for this now, but she still kept Stella's finger in her mouth, tasting her metallic blood. Stella watched her silently. Her eyes looked wet, but she wasn't crying.

"That's nasty," Stella said, but she didn't pull away.

ALL SUMMER, the twins rode the morning bus into Opelousas, where they reported to a giant white house hidden behind iron gates topped with white marble lions. The display seemed so theatrically absurd that Desiree laughed when she first saw them, but Stella only stared warily, as if those lions might spring to life at any moment and maul her. When their mother found them the job, Desiree knew the family would be rich and white. But she'd never expected a house like this: a diamond chandelier dripping from a ceiling so high, she had to climb to the top of the ladder to dust it; a long spiraling staircase that made her dizzy as she traced a rag along the banister; a large kitchen she mopped, passing appliances that looked so futuristic and new, she could not even tell how to use them.

Sometimes she lost Stella and had to search for her, wanting to call her name but afraid to send her voice echoing off the ceilings. Once, she'd found her polishing the bedroom dresser, staring off into the vanity mirror adorned by tiny bottles of lotions, wistfully, as if she wanted to sit on that plush bench and rub scented cream onto her hands like Audrey Hepburn might. Admire herself for the sake of it, as if she lived in a world where women did such a thing. But then Desiree's reflection appeared behind her, and Stella looked away, ashamed, almost, to be seen wanting anything at all.

The family was called the Duponts. A wife with feathery blonde hair who sat around all afternoon, heavy-lidded and bored. A husband who worked at St. Landry Bank & Trust. Two boys shoving each other in front of the color television set—she'd never seen one before—and a colicky, bald baby. On their first day, Mrs. Dupont studied the twins a minute, then said absently to her husband, "What pretty girls. So light, aren't they?"

Mr. Dupont just nodded. He was an awkward, fumbling man who wore Coke-bottle glasses with lenses so thick his eyes turned into beads. Whenever he passed Desiree, he tilted his head, as if he were quizzing himself.

"Which one are you again?" he'd ask.

"Stella," she sometimes told him, just for fun. She'd always been a great liar. The only difference between lying and acting was whether your audience was in on it, but it was all a performance just the same. Stella never wanted to switch places. She was always certain that they would get caught, but lying—or acting—was only possible if you committed fully. Desiree had spent years studying Stella. The way she played with her hem, how she tucked her hair behind her ear or gazed up hesitantly before saying hello. She could mirror her sister, mimic her voice, inhabit her body in her own. She felt special, knowing that she could pretend to be Stella but Stella could never be her.

All summer, the twins were out of sight. No girls walking along Partridge Road or sliding into a back booth at Lou's or heading to the football field to watch the boys practice. Each morning, the twins disappeared inside the Duponts' house and in the evening, they emerged exhausted, feet swollen, Desiree slumping against the bus window during the ride home. Summer was nearly over and she couldn't bring herself to imagine autumn, scrubbing bathroom floors while her friends gossiped in the lunchroom and planned homecoming dances. Would this be the rest of her life? Constricted to a house that swallowed her as soon as she stepped inside?

There was one way out. She knew it—she'd always known it—but by August, she was thinking about New Orleans relentlessly. The morning of Founder's Day, already dreading returning to the Duponts', she nudged Stella across the bed and said, "Let's go."

Stella groaned, rolling over, the sheets knotted around her ankles. She'd always been a wild sleeper, prone to nightmares she never talked about.

"Where?" Stella said.

"You know where. I'm tired of talkin about it, let's just go."

She was beginning to feel as if an escape door had appeared before her, and if she waited any longer, it might disappear forever. But she couldn't go without Stella. She'd never been without her sister and part of her wondered if she could even survive the separation.

"Come on," she said. "Do you wanna be cleanin after the Duponts forever?"

She would never know for sure what did it. Maybe Stella was also bored. Maybe, practical as she was, Stella recognized that they could earn more money in New Orleans, send it home and help Mama better that way. Or maybe she'd seen that escape door vanishing too and realized that everything she wanted existed outside of Mallard. Who cared why she changed her mind? All that mattered was that Stella finally said, "Okay."

All afternoon, the twins lingered at the Founder's Day picnic, Desiree feeling like she might burst open from carrying their secret. But Stella seemed just as calm as usual. She was the only person Desiree ever shared her secrets with. Stella knew about the tests Desiree had failed, how she'd forged her mother's signature on the back instead of showing her. She knew about all the knickknacks Desiree had stolen from Fontenot's—a tube of lipstick, a pack of buttons, a silver cuff link— because she could, because it felt nice, when the mayor's daughter fluttered past, knowing that she had taken something from her. Stella listened, sometimes judged, but never told, and that was the part that mattered most. Telling Stella a secret was like whispering into a jar and screwing the lid tight. Nothing escaped her. But she hadn't imagined then that Stella was keeping secrets of her own.

Days after the Vignes twins left Mallard, the river flooded, turning all the roads to muck. If they'd waited a day longer, the storm would've flushed them out. If not rain, then the mud. They would've trudged halfway down Partridge Road, then thought, forget it. They weren't tough girls. Wouldn't have lasted five miles down a muddy country road—they would've returned home, drenched, and fallen asleep in their beds, Desiree admitting that she'd been impulsive, Stella that she was only being loyal. But it didn't rain that night. The sky was clear when the twins left home without looking back.

ON THE MORNING Desiree returned, she got herself half lost on the way to her mother's house. Being half lost was worse than being fully lost—it was impossible to know which part of you knew the way. Partridge Road bled into the woods and then what? A turn at the river but which direction? A town always looked different once you'd returned, like a house where all the furniture had shifted three inches. You wouldn't mistake it for a stranger's house but you'd keep banging your shins on the table corners. She paused in the mouth of the woods, overwhelmed by all those pine trees, stretching on endlessly. She tried to search for anything familiar, fiddling with her scarf. Through the gauzy blue fabric, you could barely see the bruise.

"Mama?" Jude said. "We almost there?"

She was gazing up at Desiree with those big moon eyes, looking so much like Sam that Desiree glanced away.

"Yes," she said. "Almost."

"How much more?"

"Just a little while, baby. It's right through these woods. Mama's just catchin her bearings, that's all."

The first time Sam hit her, Desiree started to think about returning home. They'd been married three years then, but she still felt like they were honeymooners. Sam still made her shiver when he licked icing off her finger or kissed her neck while she pouted into her lipstick. Washington, D.C., had started to feel like a type of home, where she might be able to imagine the rest of her life playing out without Stella in it. Then, one spring night, six years ago, she'd forgotten to sew a button on his shirt, and when he reminded her, she told him that she was too busy cooking dinner, he'd have to sew it himself. She was tired from work; it was late enough that she could hear *The Ed Sullivan Show* in the living room, Diahann Carroll trilling "It Had to Be You." She lowered the chicken into the oven, and when she turned, Sam's hand smashed hot against her mouth. She was twenty-four years old. She had never been slapped in the face before.

"Leave him," her friend Roberta told her over the phone. "You stay, he thinks he can get away with it."

"It ain't that simple," Desiree said. She glanced toward her baby's room, touching her swollen lip. She suddenly imagined Stella's face, her own but unbruised.

"Why?" Roberta said. "You love him? And he loves you so much, he knocked your head off your shoulders?"

"It wasn't that bad," she said.

"And you aim to stick around until it is?"

By the time Desiree found the nerve to leave, she hadn't spoken to Stella since she'd passed over. She had no way to reach her and didn't even know where she lived now. Still, weaving through Union Station, her daughter confused and clinging to her arm, she only wanted to call her sister. Hours earlier, in the middle of another argument, Sam had grabbed her by the throat and aimed his handgun at her face, his eyes as clear as the first time he'd kissed her. He would kill her someday. She knew this even after he released her and she rolled, gasping, onto her side. That night, she pretended to fall asleep beside him, then, for the second time in her life, she packed a bag in darkness. At the train station, she raced to the ticket counter with the cash she'd stolen from Sam's wallet, gripping her daughter's hand, breathing so hard her stomach hurt.

What now, she asked Stella in her head. Where do I go? But of course, Stella didn't answer. And of course, there was only one place to go.

"How much more?" Jude asked.

"A little bit, baby. We almost there."

Almost home, but what did that mean anymore? Her mother might cast her out before she even reached the front steps. She would take one look at Jude before pointing them back down the road. *Of course that dark man beat you. What you expect? A spite marriage don't last.* She stooped to pick up her daughter, hoisting her onto her hip. She was walking now without thinking, just to keep her body moving. Maybe it was a mistake to return to Mallard. Maybe they should have gone somewhere new, started over fresh. But it was too late now for regrets. She could already hear the river. She started toward it, her daughter hanging heavy around her neck. The river would right her. She would stand on the bank and remember the way.

In D.C., Desiree Vignes had learned to read fingerprints.

She had never even known that this was something you could learn until the spring of 1956, when walking down Canal Street, she spotted a flyer tacked outside a bakery window announcing that the federal government was hiring. She'd paused in the doorway, staring at the poster. Stella had been gone six months then, time falling in a slow, steady drip. She would forget sometimes, as strange as it sounded. She would hear a funny joke on the streetcar or pass a friend they once knew and she would turn to tell Stella, "Hey did you—" before remembering that she was gone. That she had left Desiree, for the first time ever, alone.

And yet, even after six months, Desiree still held out hope. Stella would call. She would send a letter. But each evening, she groped inside the empty mailbox and waited beside a phone that refused to ring. Stella had gone on to craft a new life without her in it, and Desiree was miserable living in the city where Stella abandoned her. So she'd written down the number from the yellow flyer pressed against the bakery window and she went to the recruitment office as soon as she got off from work.

The recruiter, skeptical that she'd find anyone of good character in that whole city, was surprised by the neat young woman sitting in front of her. She glanced at her application, stumbling where the girl had marked colored. Then she tapped her pen on the box labeled *hometown*.

"Mallard," she said. "I've never heard of the place."

"It's just a little town," Desiree said. "North of here."

"Mr. Hoover likes small towns. The best folks come from small towns, he always says."

"Well," Desiree said, "Mallard is as small town as it gets."

IN D.C., she tried to bury her grief. She rented a room from the other colored woman in the fingerprinting department, Roberta Thomas. More a basement than a room, actually—dark and windowless but clean, and most importantly, affordable. "It ain't much," Roberta told her on her first day of work. "But if you really need a place." She'd offered tentatively, as if she were hoping Desiree might turn her down. She was exhausted, three children and all, and honestly, Desiree just seemed like another to take care of. But she pitied the girl, barely eighteen, alone in a new city, so the basement it was: a single bed, a dresser, the radiator rattling her to sleep each night.

Desiree told herself that she was starting over but she thought of Stella even more now, wondering what she would make of this city. She'd left New Orleans to escape the memory of her but she still couldn't fall asleep without rolling over to feel for Stella in bed beside her.

At the Bureau, Desiree learned arches and loops and whorls. A radial loop, flowing toward the thumb, versus an ulnar loop, flowing toward the pinky. A central pocket loop whorl from a double loop whorl. A young finger from an old one whose ridges were worn down with age. She could identify one person out of a million by studying a ridge: its width, shape, pores, contour, breaks, and creases. On her desk each morning: fingerprints lifted from stolen cars and bullet casings, broken windows and door handles and knives. She processed the fingerprints of antiwar protesters and identified the remains of dead soldiers arriving home wedged on dry ice. She was studying fingerprints lifted from a stolen gun the first time Sam Winston walked past. He wore a lavender tie with a matching silk handkerchief, and she was shocked by the brightness of the tie and the boldness of the jet-black brother who'd found the nerve to wear it. Later, when she saw him eating lunch with the other attorneys, she turned to Roberta and said, "I didn't know there were colored prosecutors."

Roberta snorted. "Of course there is," she said. "This ain't that down poke town you come from."

Roberta had never heard of Mallard. Nobody outside of St. Landry Parish had, and when Desiree told Sam, he struggled to even imagine it.

"You're jivin," he said. "A whole town of folks as light as you?"

He'd invited her to lunch one afternoon, leaning over her cubicle after he'd stopped by to ask about a set of fingerprints. Later, he told her that he hadn't been so desperate about those prints at all, he'd just wanted to find a reason to introduce himself. Now they were sitting in the National Arboretum, watching ducks glide over the pond.

"Lighter even," she said, thinking about Mrs. Fontenot, who'd always boasted that her children were the color of clabber.

Sam laughed. "Well, you gotta bring me down there sometime," he said. "I gotta see this light-skinned city for myself."

But he was only flirting. He was born in Ohio and had never ventured south of Virginia. His mother had wanted to send him to

Morehouse but no, he was a Buckeye back before all the dormitories desegregated. He'd sat in classrooms where white professors refused to answer his questions. He'd scraped piss-yellow snow off his windshield each winter. Dated light girls who would not hold his hand in public. Northern racism, he knew. That southern kind, you could keep. As far as he was concerned, his folks had escaped the South for a reason and who was he to question their judgment? Those rednecks probably wouldn't even let him come home, he always joked. He might go down to visit and wind up chopping cotton.

"You wouldn't like Mallard," she told him.

"Why not?"

"Because. They funny down there. Colorstruck. That's why I left."

Not exactly, although she wanted him to believe that she was nothing like the place she'd come from. She wanted him to believe anything beside the truth: that she was only young and bored and she'd dragged her sister to a city where she'd lost herself. He was quiet a minute, considering this, then he tilted the bag of breadcrumbs toward her. He had been ripping up the crust of his sandwich so she could feed the ducks, the type of subtle gallantry she would learn to love about him. She smiled, dipping her hand inside.

She told him that she had never been with a man like him before, but the truth was, she had never really been with a man at all. So she was surprised and delighted by every little thing he did: Sam escorting her into restaurants with white tablecloths and ornate silverware; Sam inviting her to the theater, surprising her with tickets to see Ella Fitzgerald. When he brought her home the first time, she'd wandered around his bachelor's apartment, amazed by his neat linens, his colorcoded wardrobe, his big spacious bed. She'd nearly cried when she'd returned to Roberta's basement after that.

He would never again offer to visit home with her. She would never ask him to. She'd told him in the beginning that she hated Mallard.

"I don't believe you," he said. They were lying in his bed, listening to the rain.

"What's there to believe? I told you how I feel."

"Negroes always love our hometowns," he said. "Even though we're always from the worst places. Only white folks got the freedom to hate home."

He was raised in the projects of Cleveland and he loved that city with the fierceness of someone who hadn't been given much to love. She'd only been given a town she'd always wanted to escape and a mother who'd made it clear that she was not welcomed back. She hadn't told Sam about Stella yet—it seemed like another thing about Mallard that he wouldn't understand. But as rain splattered against the metal fire escape, she turned toward him and said that she had a twin sister who'd decided to become someone else.

"She'll get tired of all that playacting," he said. "Bet she comes running back, feeling foolish. You're way too sweet for anyone to stay away."

He kissed her forehead, and she held him tighter, his heart thumping against her ear. This was back in the beginning. Before his hands curled into fists, before he called her *uppity yellow bitch* or *crazy as your sister* or *off thinkin you white*. Back when she'd found herself starting to trust him.

MANY YEARS LATER, when her eyesight would begin to fade, she would blame the years she'd spent squinting at sheets of fingerprints and marking their ridges. Roberta told her once that soon the entire fingerprinting system would be operated by machines. The Japanese were already testing out the technology. But how could a machine study a fingerprint better than the trained eye? Desiree saw patterns that most people couldn't. She could read a person's life off his fingertips. During training, she'd practiced reading her own finger-prints, those intricate designs that marked her as unique. Stella had a scar on her left index finger from when she'd cut herself with a knife, one of many ways that their fingerprints were different.

Sometimes who you were came down to the small things.

ADELE VIGNES LIVED in a white shotgun house that lurked on the edge of the woods, a house first built by the founder and inhabited by generations of Decuirs ever since. When she'd first married, her new husband, Leon Vignes, had wandered down the hall, inspecting the ancient furniture. He was a repairman who wanted to be a wood-worker and he ran a finger along the slender table legs, admiring the craftsmanship. He'd never expected to one day live in a home imbued with so much history, but then again, he'd never expected to marry a Decuir girl. A girl with Heritage. He could trace his own family to a long line of French winegrowers who'd hoped to build a vineyard in the New World before discovering that Louisiana was too hot and humid for grapes and settled instead for sugarcane. Big thinking crushed by reality—that's what he'd inherited. His own parents had set their sights more reasonably; they'd run a speakeasy on the edge of Mallard called the Surly Goat. The more pious in Mallard would later trace the tragedies to that sinful business: four Vignes brothers, none of whom lived past thirty. Leon, the runt of the litter, the first to die.

The house had faded with time but, somehow, still seemed exactly as Desiree had remembered it. She stepped into the clearing, gripping her own daughter tighter, shoulders stinging with each step. Those brass columns, teal roof, the narrow front porch where her mother was sitting on a rocking chair, snapping green beans into a bowl of water. Her mother still slight, her hair trailing down her back, temples now tinted gray. Desiree paused, her daughter hanging heavy from her neck. The years pushing her back like a hand to her chest.

"Wonderin when y'all would make it out here. You know Lou already called, sayin he seen you." Her mother was talking to her but staring at the child in her arms. "Mighty big to be carried."

Desiree finally set her daughter down. Her back ached, but pain, at least, felt familiar. A hurting body kept you alert, awake, which was better than how numb she'd felt on the train, moving but trapped in place. She nudged her daughter forward.

"Go give your Maman a kiss," she said. "Go on, it's all right."

Her daughter clamped around her legs, too shy to move, but she nudged her again until the girl dutifully climbed the steps, hesitating a second before she put an arm around her grandmother. Adele pulled back to get a better look at her, touching her mussed braids.

"Go take a bath," she said. "Y'all smell like outside."

In the bathroom, Desiree knelt on the cracked tile to run her daughter a bath in the clawfoot tub. She tested the water feeling, somehow, as if she were dreaming. The mirror blackened in the top corner, the chipped scalloped sink, the wooden floors creaking in the places she'd learned to avoid if she wanted to sneak in past curfew. Her mother snapping green beans on the porch, as if it were a normal morning. And yet, they hadn't spoken since Stella left. Desiree had called home, gulping back tears, and her mother said, "You did this." What could she even say? She was the one who'd pushed Stella to leave home in the first place. Now her sister had decided she'd rather be white and her mother blamed her because Stella was no longer there to blame.

In the kitchen, she sank into a chair, realizing a moment later, that she'd sat in the same place she always had, Stella's chair empty beside her. Her mother was busying at the stove, and for a long moment, Desiree stared at her stiffened back.

"So that's what you been up to," her mother said.

"What do you mean?"

"You know what I mean." Her mother turned, her eyes brimming with tears. "You hate us that much, don't you?"

Desiree pushed away from the table.

"I knew I shouldn't have come here—"

"Sit down—"

"If that's all you got to say to me—"

"What do you expect? You come from God knows where, draggin some child that don't look one lick like you—"

"We'll go," Desiree said. "You can be mad at me all you want, Mama, but you not gonna be nasty to my girl."

"I said sit down," her mother said again, this time quieter. She slid a yellow square of cornbread across the table. "I'm just surprised. Can't I be surprised?"

All those times Desiree had imagined calling home. When she'd arrived in D.C., settling in Roberta's basement, her mother with no way to reach her. Or after Sam proposed, and they took engagement photographs under the cherry blossoms. She'd slid a picture into an envelope, even addressed it, but she couldn't bring herself to send it. Not because she was ashamed of him—that was how Sam took it— but because what was the point of sharing good news with someone who couldn't be happy for you? She already knew what her mother would tell her. *You don't love that dark man. You're only marrying him out of rebellion and the worst thing to give a rebelling child is attention. You'll understand someday when you have a child of your own.* After the wedding, after the cake had been cut, after their friends had wandered boozy and laughing into the streets, she'd slumped in the back of the reception hall in her frilly white dress and cried. She had never imagined that she might get married someday without her sister and mother by her side.

She'd even thought about calling after she'd given birth to a baby girl at Freedmen's Hospital. When Jude was born, the colored nurse had paused before wrapping her in a pink blanket. "It's good luck," she'd finally said, handing her over, "for a girl to look like her daddy." She smiled a little after, offering reassurance to a woman she believed would need it. But Desiree stared into her baby's face, enchanted. A different woman might have been disappointed by how little her own daughter resembled her, but she only felt grateful. The last thing she wanted was to love someone else who looked just like herself.

"Would've fixed more if you told me you was comin," her mother said.

"It was sort of last minute," Desiree said.

She'd barely eaten on the train, nibbling on crackers and gulping black coffee until the caffeine made her jittery. She needed to plan. Mallard, and then what? Where to next? They couldn't possibly stay here but she didn't know where else to go. Now she stared around the aging kitchen, missing her own apartment in D.C. Her job, her friends, her life. Maybe she'd overreacted—the riots had set everyone on edge. A week ago, she'd watched Sam cry as Walter Cronkite delivered the news, holding him on the couch as he trembled in her arms. The shooter was a madman, maybe, or a military operative, or perhaps even an agent in the Bureau acting on behalf of the government. They were culpable, perhaps, complicit Negroes working for the wrong side. He was rambling and she clutched him until the broadcast ended. That night they'd made love desperately, a strange way to honor the Reverend, maybe, but she didn't feel like herself that night, overwhelmed by grief over a man she didn't know.

In the morning, she passed ravaged storefronts with SOUL BROTHER scribbled on boarded shop windows, hasty claims of allegiance written in marker and pasted against glass. The Bureau dismissed early that day. On her walk home from the bus, a scared colored youth—scrawny as the baseball bat he was gripping—demanded her pocketbook.

"Come on, you white bitch!" he screamed, slamming the bat against the pavement, as if he could drill to the center of the earth. She fumbled with her leather strap, too afraid to correct him, recognizing herself in his terror and fury, when Sam leapt in front of her, arms raised, and said, "This my woman, brother." The teen ran off into the din. Sam swept her inside the apartment, holding her against the safety of his chest.

The city lit up four nights. And on the last night, Sam gripped her naked body and whispered, "Let's make another." It took her a moment to realize he meant a baby. She'd hesitated. She hadn't meant to, but the thought of another baby anchoring her to him, another baby to worry about every time Sam was in a rage—she could never have another baby with him. Of course she didn't tell him this, but her hesitation made it clear, and later, when he'd grabbed her throat, she knew exactly why. She'd wounded him while he was still grieving. No wonder he'd gotten angry. So he liked to throw his weight around a little. Who could blame him, living in a world that refused to respect him as a man? She didn't have to be so mouthy. She could try harder to make a peaceful home. Wasn't this the same man who'd stood between her and an angry boy's bat? The same man who'd loved her after her sister abandoned her and her mother refused her phone calls?

Maybe it wasn't too late. They'd only been gone two days. She could always call Sam, tell him that she'd made a mistake. She'd needed a little time to clear her head, that's all, of course she'd never seriously meant to leave. Her mother pushed the plate toward her again.

"What type of trouble you in?" she said.

Desiree forced a laugh. "There's no trouble, Mama."

"I ain't stupid. You think I don't know you runnin from that man of yours?"

Desiree stared down at the table, her eyes welling up. Her mother poured milk onto the cornbread and mushed it with a fork, the way Desiree had eaten it as a girl.

"He gone now," her mother said. "Eat your cornbread."

LATE THAT NIGHT, over a hundred miles southeast of Mallard, Early Jones received a job offer that would alter the course of his life. He didn't know this at the time. Any job was just that to him—a job—and when he stepped inside Ernesto's, craning his neck for Big Ceel, he was only worried about whether he could afford a drink. He jangled the loose change in his pocket. Could never keep a dollar on him. Two weeks ago, he'd run a job for Ceel, and somehow, he'd burned through the money already on everything a young man alone in New Orleans required, card games and booze and women. Now he was desperate for another job. For the money, of course, but also because he hated being in one place for too long, and two weeks in the same place was, for him then, far too long.

He wasn't a settling man. He was only good at getting lost. He'd mastered that particular skill as a boy rooted nowhere. Spent his childhood—if you could call it that—sharecropping on farms in Janesville and Jena, down south to New Roads and Palmetto. He'd been given to his aunt and uncle when he was eight, because they had no children and his parents had too many. He did not know where his parents lived now, if they still lived, and he said that he never thought about them.

"They gone," he said, when asked. "Gone folks is gone."

But the truth is that when he'd first started hunting hiding people, he'd tried to find his folks. His failure was swift and humiliating; he didn't know enough about his parents to even guess where to begin. Probably for the best. They hadn't wanted him as a boy—what on earth would they do with him as a grown man? Still, his defeat nagged at him. Since he'd started hunting, his parents were the only people he had never found.

The key to staying lost was to never love anything. Time and time again, Early was amazed by what a running man came back for. Women, mostly. In Jackson, he'd caught a man wanted for attempted murder because he'd circled back for his wife. You could find a new woman anywhere, but then again, the most violent men were always the most sentimental. Pure emotion, any way you look at it. What really got him were the men who returned for belongings. Too many goddamn cars to count, always some junk a man had driven for years and couldn't part with. In Toledo, he'd caught a man who'd returned to his childhood home for an old baseball.

"I don't know, man," he said, cuffed in the backseat of Early's El Camino. "I just really love that thing."

Love had never dragged Early anywhere. As soon as he left a place, he forgot it. Names faded, faces blurred, buildings smudged into indistinguishable brick slabs. He forgot the names of teachers at all the schools he'd attended, the streets where he'd lived, even what his parents looked like. This was his gift, a short memory. A long memory could drive a man crazy.

He'd been running jobs for Ceel, off and on, for seven years now. He never wanted anyone to think that he was working for the law. He caught criminals for one reason only—the money—and he didn't give two shits about the white man's justice. After he caught a man, he never wondered if the jury convicted him or if the man survived prison. He forgot him altogether. And though he'd been recognized in a bar once, and still wore the knife scars across his stomach as a souvenir, forgetting was the only way he could do his job. He liked hunting criminals. Each time Ceel approached him about a missing child or deadbeat father, Early shook his head.

"Don't know nothin bout none of those people," he said, tilting back his whiskey.

In Ernesto's, Ceel shrugged. He had a proper office in the Seventh Ward, but Early hated meeting him there, across the street from a church, all those sanctified folks staring at him as they trampled down the steps. This bar was Early's kind of place, a little shadowy and safe. Ceel was a hefty man, cardboard-colored with silky black hair. He carried a silver cigarette lighter that he twirled between his fingers while he talked. He'd been twirling that lighter the first time he'd approached Early, in a bar like this one, years ago. Early had listened half-heartedly, watching the light glint off the silver and dance along the bar.

"Son, how'd you like to make some money?" Ceel asked.

He didn't look like a gangster or pimp but he carried the sleaziness of someone who did barely legal work. He was a bail bondsman, looking for a new bounty hunter, and he'd noticed Early.

"You got a quiet way about you," he said. "That's good. I need a man to look and listen."

Early was twenty-four then, fresh out of prison, alone in New Orleans because he'd figured it as good a place to start over as any. He took the job because he needed the work. He'd never expected to be good at it, so good, in fact, that Ceel kept approaching him with jobs that had nothing to do with bail bonds.

"You know about 'em what I tell you," Ceel said. "And I ain't told you nothin yet."

"Well, I don't like to be caught up in folks' affairs. Don't you have nothin else for me?"

Ceel laughed. "You 'bout the only man I ever hear say that. Everybody else I talk to be glad not to hunt down some mean sonofabitch for a change."

But Early could, at least, understand how a wanted man thought. The exhaustion, the desperation, the sheer selfishness of survival. The otherwise disappeared baffled him. He certainly didn't understand married folks and had no desire to get in between them. Then again, a job was a job. Why wouldn't he take on something light? He'd just spent two weeks tracking a man halfway to Mexico; his car broke down in the desert and he'd wondered if he would die out there, hunting a man he didn't even care to see punished. If the money was all the same, why not say yes to an easy job for once?

"I'm not grabbin her," he said.

"Nothin like that. You just call when you find her. Her old man's lookin for her. She run off with his kid."

"What she run off for?"

Ceel shrugged. "None my concern. Man wants her found. She from some little town up north called Mallard. Ever heard of it?"

"Passed through as a boy," Early said. "Funny place. Highfalutin."

He remembered little about the town, except that everyone was light and uppity, and once, at Mass, a tall pale man had slapped him for dipping his finger into the holy water font before the man's wife. He was sixteen then, shocked by the sudden sting on his neck, as his uncle grabbed his shoulder, staring at the cracked tile floor, and apologized. He'd spent a summer in that place, working a farm on the edge of town and delivering groceries to earn extra cash. He didn't make a single friend, but he did nurse a futile crush on a girl he'd met carrying groceries up her porch steps. He didn't know how she even entered his mind. He was so young when they'd met; he'd barely known her; by fall, he'd moved on to another farm in another town. Still, he saw her standing barefoot in her living room, washing the windows. When Ceel slid him the photograph, Early's stomach lurched. He almost felt as if he'd willed it. For the first time in ten years, he was staring at Desiree Vignes's face.

Two

***

The Vignes twins left without saying good-bye, so like any sudden disappearance, their departure became loaded with meaning. Before they surfaced in New Orleans, before they were just bored girls hunting fun, it only made sense to lose them in such a tragic way. The twins had always seemed both blessed and cursed; they'd inherited, from their mother, the legacy of an entire town, and from their father, a lineage hollowed by loss. Four Vignes boys, all dead by thirty. The eldest collapsed in a chain gang from heatstroke; the second gassed in a Belgian trench; the third stabbed in a bar fight; and the youngest, Leon Vignes, lynched twice, the first time at home while his twin girls watched through a crack in the closet door, hands clamped over each other's mouths until their palms misted with spit.

That night, he was whittling a table leg when five white men kicked in the front door and hauled him outside. He landed hard on his face, his mouth filling with dirt and blood. The mob leader—a tall white man with red gold hair like a fall apple—waved a crumpled note in which, he claimed, Leon had written nasty things to a white woman. Leon couldn't read or write—his customers knew that he made all of his marks with an X—but the white men stomped on his hands, broke every finger and joint, then shot him four times. He survived, and three days later, the white men burst into the hospital and stormed every room in the colored ward until they found him. This time, they shot him twice in the head, his cotton pillowcase blooming red.

Desiree witnessed the first lynching but would forever imagine the second, how her father must have been sleeping, his head slumped, the way he nodded off in his chair after supper. How the thundering boots woke him. He screamed, or maybe had no time to, his swollen hands bandaged and useless at his sides. From the closet, she'd watched the white men drag her father out of the house, his long legs drumming against the floor. She suddenly felt that her sister would scream, so she squeezed her hand over Stella's mouth and seconds later, felt Stella's hand on her own. Something shifted between them in that moment. Before, Stella seemed as predictable as a reflection. But in the closet, for the first time ever, Desiree hadn't known what her sister might do.

At the wake, the twins wore matching black dresses with full slips that itched their legs. Days earlier, Bernice LeGros, the seamstress, had come by to pay her respects and found Adele Vignes trying to darn a pair of Leon's church pants for his burial. Her hands were shaking, so Bernice took the needle and patched up the pants herself. She didn't know how Adele would handle this on her own. Decuirs were used to soft things, to long, easy lives. The twins didn't even have funeral dresses. The next morning, Bernice carried over a bolt of black fabric and knelt in the living room with her tape measure. She still couldn't tell the twins apart and felt too embarrassed to ask, so she gave simple commands like "You, hand me them scissors" or "Stand up straight, honey." She told the fidgety twin, "Stop wigglin, girl, or you gonna get sticked," and the other twin grabbed her hand until she stilled. Unnerving, Bernice thought, glancing between the girls. Like sewing a dress for one person split into two bodies.

After the burial, Bernice gathered in Adele's crowded living room, admiring her handiwork as the twins scampered past. The fidgety twin, who she would later learn was Desiree, pulled her sister's hand as they wove past the grown folks who huddled and whispered. Leon couldn't have written that note—the white men must have been angered over something else and who could understand their rages? Willie Lee heard that the white men were angry that Leon stole their business by underbidding them. But how could you shoot a man for accepting less than what you asked for?

"White folks kill you if you want too much, kill you if you want too little." Willie Lee shook his head, packing tobacco into his pipe. "You gotta follow they rules but they change 'em when they feel. Devilish, you ask me."

In the bedroom, the twins sat, legs swinging over the mattress edge, and pinched at a piece of pound cake.

"But what did Daddy do?" Stella kept asking.

Desiree sighed, for the first time feeling the burden of having to supply answers. Oldest was oldest, even if by only seven minutes.

"Like Willie Lee say. He do his job too good."

"But that don't make sense."

"Don't have to. It's white folks."

As the years passed, their father would only come to her in flashes, like when she fingered a denim shirt and felt small again, pressed against the rough fabric spanning her father's chest. You were supposed to be safe in Mallard—that strange, separate town—hidden amongst your own. But even here, where nobody married dark, you were still colored and that meant that white men could kill you for refusing to die. The Vignes twins were reminders of this, tiny girls in funeral dresses who grew up without a daddy because white men decided that it would be so.

Then they grew older and just became girls, striking in both their

35

sameness and differences. Soon it became laughable that there had ever been a time when no one could tell the twins apart. Desiree, always restless, as if her foot had been nailed to the ground and she couldn't stop yanking it; Stella, so calm that even Sal Delafosse's ornery horse never bucked around her. Desiree starring in the school play once, nearly twice if the Fontenots hadn't bribed the principal; Stella, whip smart, who would go to college if her mother could afford it. Desiree and Stella, Mallard's girls. As they grew, they no longer seemed like one body split in two, but two bodies poured into one, each pulling it her own way.

THE MORNING AFTER one of her lost daughters returned, Adele Vignes woke early to make coffee. She'd barely slept the night before. Fourteen years living alone and anything besides silence sounded foreign. She'd jolted awake at every creaking floorboard, every rustled cover, every breath. Now she shuffled across the kitchen, tightening the belt of her housecoat. A breeze floated in through the front door—Desiree leaning on the porch rail, smoke trailing past her head. She always stood like that, one leg behind the other like an egret. Or was that Stella? In her memories, the girls had gotten mixed up, their details switching places until they overlapped into a single loss. A pair. She was supposed to have a pair. And now that one had returned, the loss of the other felt sharp and new.

She slid the pot of water onto the stove and turned to find the dark child standing in the doorway.

"Goodness!" she said. "You about gave me a heart attack."

"I'm sorry," the girl whispered. She was quiet. Why was she so quiet? "Can I have some water?"

"May I have," Adele said, but she filled the cup anyway. She leaned against the counter, watching the girl drink, searching her face for anything that reminded her of her daughters. But she could only see the child's evil daddy. Hadn't she told Desiree that a dark man would be no good to her? Hadn't she tried to warn her all her life? A dark man would trample her beauty. He'd love it at first but like anything he desired and could never attain, he would soon grow to resent it. Now he was punishing her for it.

The child set her empty cup on the counter. She looked dazed, as if she'd woken up in a foreign country. Her granddaughter. Lord, she had a granddaughter. The word seemed funny even in her own head.

"Why don't you go on and play?" Adele said. "I'll fix us some breakfast."

"I didn't bring nothin with me," the girl said, probably thinking of all the toys she'd left behind. City toys, like choo choo trains driven by real motors or plastic dolls with human hair. Still, Adele went into the twins' room, freezing a second at the sight of the mussed bed—Desiree slept on her old side—before opening the musty closet. In a cardboard box near the back, she found a corncob doll that Stella had made Desiree. The girl hesitated—the doll must have looked monstrous compared to her store-bought ones—but she carried Stella's doll carefully into the living room.

A pair. Adele used to have a pair. Healthy twin girls, her first pregnancy at that. She'd given birth in her bedroom, the snow falling so suddenly, she wasn't sure that the midwife would make it in time. When she arrived, Madame Theroux told her how fortunate she was. There hadn't been twins in either family line for three generations. If you'd been blessed with twins, the midwife told her, you had to serve the Marassa, the sacred twins who united heaven and earth. They were powerful but jealous child gods. You had to worship both equally—leave two candies on your altar, two sodas, two dolls. Adele, catechized at St. Catherine's, knew that she should have been scandalized, listening to Madame Theroux talking about her heathen religion at the birth of her children, but the stories distracted her from the pain. Then Desiree appeared, and seven minutes later Stella, and she held a girl in each arm, wrinkled and pink and needing nothing but her.

After the twins were born, Adele never built an altar. But later, after her girls disappeared, she wondered if she'd been arrogant. Maybe she should have just built the altar, no matter how foolish it sounded. Maybe then her daughters would have stayed. Or maybe, she alone was to blame. Maybe she'd failed to love the twins equally and that chased them away. She'd always been hardest on Desiree, who was most like her father, confident that as long as she willed good things to happen, nothing could harm her. You had to curb a willful child. If she hadn't loved Desiree, she would have abandoned her to her own stubbornness. But then Desiree felt hated and Stella felt ignored. That was the problem: you could never love two people the exact same way. Her blessing had been doomed from the beginning, her girls as impossible to please as jealous gods.

Leon was easy to love. She should have known that he wouldn't be with her long. All of her blessings had come so easily in the beginning of her life, and she'd spent the back half losing them all. But she wouldn't lose Desiree again.

She stepped onto the creaking porch, carrying two cups of coffee. Desiree quickly stubbed out her cigarette on the banister. Adele almost laughed—grown as she was, acting like a child stealing sweets.

"I thought I'd fix some breakfast," Adele said. She handed her the mug and caught another glance at Desiree's splotchy bruise, barely hidden behind that silly scarf.

"I'm not too hungry," Desiree said.

"You gonna fall out if you don't eat somethin."

Desiree shrugged, taking a sip. Adele could already feel her fighting to break away, like a bird beating its wings against her palms.

"I can take your girl by the school later," Adele said. "Get her all signed up."

Desiree scoffed. "Now why in the world you wanna do that?"

"Well, she oughta keep on with her studies—"

"Mama, we're not stayin."

"Where you expect to go? And how you expect to get there? I bet you don't have ten dollars in your pocket—"

"I don't know! Anywhere."

Adele pursed her lips. "You rather be anywhere than here with me."

"It's not like that, Mama." Desiree sighed. "I just don't know where we oughta be right now—"

"You oughta be with your family, cher," Adele said. "Stay. You safe here."

Desiree said nothing, staring out into the woods. Overhead, the sky was awakening, fading lavender and pink, and Adele wrapped an arm around her daughter's waist.

"What you think Stella's doin right now?" Desiree said.

"I don't," Adele said.

"Ma'am?"

"I don't think about Stella," she said.

IN MALLARD, Desiree saw Stella everywhere.

Lounging by the water pump in her lilac dress, slipping a finger down her sock to scratch her ankle. Dipping into the woods to play hide-and-seek behind the trees. Stepping out of the butcher's shop carrying chicken livers wrapped in white paper, clutching the package so tightly, she might have been holding something as precious as a secret. Stella, curly hair pinned into a ponytail, tied with a ribbon, her dresses always starched, shoes shined. A girl still, since that was the only way Desiree had ever known her. But this Stella flitted in and out of her vision. Stella leaning against a fence or pushing a cart down a Fontenot's aisle or perching on St. Catherine's stone steps, blowing a dandelion. When Desiree walked her daughter to her first day of school, Stella appeared behind them, fussing about the dust kicking up on her socks. Desiree tried to ignore her, squeezing Jude's hand.

"You gotta talk to people today," she said.

"I talk to people I like," Jude said.

"But you don't know yet, who you gonna like. So you gotta be friendly to everyone, just to see."

She straightened the ruffles on her daughter's collar. She'd spent the night before kneeling in the yard, scrubbing Jude's clothes in the washtub. She hadn't packed enough for either of them, and plunging her hands into the filmy water, she imagined her daughter cycling through the same four dresses until she outgrew them. Why hadn't she made a plan? Stella would have. She would have planned to run months before she actually did, squirreling away clothes slowly, one sock at a time. Set aside money, bought train tickets, prepared a place to go. Desiree knew because Stella had done it in New Orleans. Slipped out of one life into another as easily as stepping into the next room.

Near the schoolyard, beige children pressed against the fence, gawking, and Desiree gripped her daughter's hand again. She'd laid out Jude's nicest outfit, a white dress with a pink pinafore, socks with lace trim, and Mary Janes. "Don't you have something brown?" her mother had asked, lingering in the doorway, but Desiree ignored her, tying pink ribbons around Jude's braids. Bright colors looked vulgar against dark skin, everyone said, but she refused to hide her daughter in drab olive greens or grays. Now, as they paraded past the other children, she felt foolish. Maybe pink was too showy. Maybe she'd already ruined her daughter's chances of fitting in by dressing her up like a department store doll.

"Why they all lookin at me?" Jude asked.

"It's just cause you new," Desiree said. "They just curious about you."

She smiled, trying to sound cheerful, but her daughter glanced warily toward the schoolyard.

"How long we stayin out here?" she asked.

Desiree knelt in front of her. "I know it's different," she said. "But it's just for a little bit. Just until Mama figures some things out, okay?"

"How long's a little bit?"

"I don't know, baby," Desiree finally said. "I don't know."

THE SURLY GOAT rose lazily on stilts, moss trees dripping onto the reddened roof. Desiree carefully picked around the muddy pathway just to find the first dilapidated step. A small town in the shadow of an oil refinery, with no picture show or nightclub or ballpark nearby meant one thing: an abundance of bored, rough men. Marie Vignes was the only person in Mallard who hadn't seen a problem with this. Instead, she'd turned the farmhouse her parents left her into a bar, put her four sons to work cleaning glasses and hauling kegs, and on occasion breaking up fights. She'd planned to leave the bar someday to one of her sons, but by the time she died, they were all gone. The twins rarely saw her after their father's funeral. Their mother had never wanted anything to do with that speakeasy or the unrefined woman it belonged to. The two women had been polite enough when Leon was there to smooth things over, but now that he was gone, there was no space for both of them and their grief.

So the twins only heard stories about how Marie Vignes used to serve whiskey to the roughest men in Mallard, how she kept a shotgun under the bar that she named Nat King Cole, and when the roughnecks started shoving over a game of poker or fighting about a woman, she'd pull out ol' Nat and those angry men, normally unmoved by a woman in a housedress, turned as docile as altar boys. But when Desiree stepped inside the Surly Goat for the first time, she felt almost disappointed. She'd always imagined the bar as a magical place that would, somehow, remind her more of her father. Instead, it was nothing but a country dive.

She was at a bar in the middle of the afternoon because she couldn't think of anywhere else to go. She'd spent the morning jostling in the front seat of Willie Lee's truck all the way to Opelousas. She wanted to apply for a job, she told him when she'd spotted him outside his shop, loading his truck for deliveries. Could he give her a ride into town? As the meat truck pulled farther from Mallard, she was thinking still about her daughter, glancing back at her as she'd disappeared inside the schoolhouse. Those thin shoulders, hands clenched tight at her sides.

"Where you need me to drop you off?" Willie Lee had asked.

"Just at the sheriff's."

"The sheriff's?" He turned to look at her. "What business you got down there?"

"Told you. A job."

He grunted. "You can find cleanin work closer to Mallard."

"Not to clean."

"Then what you aim to do at the sheriff's?"

"Apply to be a fingerprint examiner," she said.

Willie Lee laughed. "So you just gonna walk in there and say what?"

"That I want a job application. I don't know why you're laughing, Willie Lee. I been examining fingerprints for over ten years now and if I can do it for the Bureau, I don't know why I can't do it here."

"I can think of a few reasons," Willie Lee told her.

But hadn't the world changed a little since she'd been gone? And hadn't she walked into the St. Landry Parish Sheriff's Department with all the confidence in the world? She had stepped right inside that grimy tan building, surrounded by a barbed-wire fence, and told the sheriff's deputy, a portly man with sandy blond hair, that she wanted to apply for a job. "The Federal Bureau, did you say?" he'd asked, raising an eyebrow, and she allowed herself to feel hopeful. She sat in the corner of the waiting room, racing through the latent print examiner test, grateful for a thinking activity for once, not the type of thinking she had done lately—logistics, like how long her money would last—but real analytical thinking. She'd finished quick, the deputy said, laughing a bit in amazement, might have been a record. He pulled out the answer guide from a manila folder to check her work. But first, he glanced at her full application, and when he saw her address listed in Mallard, his gaze frosted over. He slid the answer key back in the folder, returned to his chair.

"Leave that there, gal," he said. "No use wasting my time."

Now she stepped inside the Surly Goat, passing under the welcome sign—COLD WOMEN! HOT BEER!—and pressed past a row of men in greasy coveralls to find an empty booth.

"Well, look what the cat drug in," Lorna Hebert, the old barmaid, said. She dropped off a shot of whiskey that Desiree hadn't even asked for.

"You don't look too surprised to see me," Desiree said. She'd been in town two days by now, of course everyone knew.

"Got to come home sometime," Lorna said. "Now let me get a good look at you."

In the darkness of the bar, she was still wearing her blue scarf. If Lorna noticed anything, she didn't say so. She disappeared back behind the bar and Desiree downed the shot, comforted by the burn. She felt pathetic, drinking alone in the middle of the day, but what else could she do? She needed a job. Money. A plan. But those children staring at her daughter. The deputy dismissing her. Sam gripping her throat. She waved over Lorna again, wanting to forget it all.

One shot then another and she was already tipsy by the time she saw him. He was sitting at the end of the bar wearing a worn brown leather jacket, a dirty boot kicked up on the stool. The man beside him said something that made him smile into his whiskey. Those high cheekbones pierced her. Even after all those years, she would know Early Jones anywhere.

HER LAST SUMMER in Mallard, Desiree Vignes met the wrong sort of boy.

She'd spent her life, up until then, only meeting the right sort: Mallard boys, light and ambitious, boys tugging on her pigtails, boys sitting beside her in catechism, mumbling the Apostles' Creed, boys begging her for kisses outside of school dances. She was supposed to marry one of these boys, and when Johnny Heroux left heart-shaped notes in her history book or Gil Dalcourt asked her to homecoming, she could practically feel her mother nudging her toward them. Pick one, pick one. It only made her want to dig her heels into the ground. Nothing made a boy less exciting than the fact that you were supposed to like him.

Mallard boys seemed as familiar and safe as cousins, but there were no other boys around except when someone's nephew visited or when tenant farmers moved to the edge of town. She'd never spoken to one of these tenant boys—she only saw them when they passed through town, tall and sinewy and caked brown. They looked like men, these boys, so what could you talk to them about? Besides, you weren't supposed to speak to dark boys. Once, one had tipped his hat at her and her mother tutted, gripping her arm tighter.

"Don't even look his way," her mother said. "Boys like that don't want nothin good."

Dark boys in Mallard only wanted to go girl hunting, her mother always said. They wanted to give it to a white girl but couldn't, so they thought a light girl was the next best thing. But Desirce had never met a dark boy until one June evening when she was washing the living-room windows and spotted, through the hazy glass, a boy standing on the front porch. A tall boy, shirtless in overalls, his skin caramelized into a deep brown. He held a paper bag in one arm and took a bite from a purplish fruit, wiping his mouth with the back of his hand.

"You gonna let me in?" he said. He was gazing at her so directly, she blushed.

"No," she said. "Who're you?"

"Who you think?" he said. He turned the bag toward her so that she could see the Fontenot's logo. "Open the door."

"I don't know you," she said. "You could be an ax murderer."

"Look like I got an ax on me?"

"Maybe I can't see it from here."

He could've left the bag on the porch. When he didn't, she realized that they were flirting.

She dropped her rag on the windowsill, watching him chew.

"What you eatin anyway?" she asked.

"Come see."

She finally unlatched the screen door and stepped barefoot onto the porch. Early eased toward her. He smelled like sandalwood and sweat, and as he neared, she thought, for one breathless second, that he might kiss her. But he didn't. He lifted his fig to her lips. She bit where his mouth had been.

LATER, SHE LEARNED HIS NAME, which wasn't even a name at all, although it made her smile when she rolled it around her mouth. Early, Early, like she was calling out the time. All month, he left fruit like flowers. Each evening when the twins came home from the Duponts, she found a plum on the porch banister, or a peach, or a napkin filled with blackberries. Nectarines and pears and rhubarb, more fruit than she could finish, fruit she hid in her apron to savor later or bake into pies. Sometimes he passed by in the evening on his way to deliver groceries, lingering on her porch steps. He told her that he made deliveries part time; the rest of his days were spent helping his aunt and uncle on a farm near the edge of town. But when the harvest ended, he planned to skip off and find himself in a real city like New Orleans.

"Don't you think your folks'll miss you?" Desiree said. "When you go?"

He scoffed. "The money," he said. "They gonna miss that. That's all they thinkin about."

"Well, you got to think about money," Desiree said. "That's how all grown folks are."

Who would her mother be if she wasn't worried about money all the time? Like Mrs. Dupont, maybe, drifting around the house dreamily. But Early shook his head.

"It's not the same," he said. "Your mama got a house. All y'all got this whole dern town. We got nothin. That's why I give this fruit away. Don't belong to me nohow."

She reached for a blueberry in his napkin. By now, she'd already eaten so many, her fingertips were stained purple.

"So if all this fruit belonged to you," she said, "you wouldn't give me nothin?"

"If it belonged to me," he said, "I'd give you all of it."

Then he kissed the inside of her wrist, and her palm, and slipped her pinky inside his mouth, tasting the fruit on her skin.

A DARK BOY stepping through the meadow behind the house to leave her fruit. She never knew when Early would come, if he would come at all, so she began waiting for him, sitting along the porch rail as the sun faded. Stella warned her to be careful. Stella was always careful. "I know you don't wanna hear it," she said. "But you hardly know him and he sounds fresh." But Desiree didn't care. He was the first interesting boy she'd ever met, the only one who even imagined a life outside of Mallard. And maybe she liked that Stella distrusted him. She never wanted the two to meet. He would grin, glancing between the girls, searching for differences amongst their similarities. She hated that silent appraisal, watching someone compare her to a version that she might have been. A better version, even. What if he saw something in Stella that he liked more? It would have nothing to do with looks, and that, somehow, felt even worse.

She could never date him. He knew this too even though they never talked about it. He only came by the porch while her mother was still at work, always leaving as soon as the sky grew dark. Still, one evening her mother came home from work and caught her talking to Early. He leapt off the railing, the blackberries in his lap scattering to the deck like buckshot.

"Best be goin now," her mother said. "I don't have no courtin girls here."

He raised his hands in surrender, as if he too felt that he had done something wrong.

"I'm sorry, ma'am," he said. He shuffled off into the woods, not looking at Desiree. She miserably watched him disappear between the trees.

"Why'd you have to do that, Mama?" she said.

But her mother ushered her inside. "You'll thank me someday," she said. "You think you know everything? Girl, you don't know how this world can be."

And maybe her mother was right about the world's immeasurable cruelties. She had already been dealt her portion; she could see that Desiree's was on its way and did not want a dark boy to hasten it. Or maybe her mother was just like everyone else who found dark skin ugly and strove to distance herself from it. Either way, Early Jones never visited again. Desiree wondered about him while she cleaned at the Duponts. She lingered in Fontenot's on Saturday afternoons even though she had nothing to buy, hoping to catch a glimpse of him hauling groceries down the road. When she finally asked, Mr. Fontenot told her that the boy's family had moved on to another farm.

And what would she have told Early if she knew how to reach him? That she was sorry for what her mother said? Or for what she hadn't said in his defense? That she wasn't like the folks she'd come from, although she wasn't sure that was even true anymore. You couldn't separate the shame from being caught doing something from the shame of the act itself. If she hadn't believed, even a bit, that spending time with Early was wrong, why hadn't she ever asked him to meet her at Lou's for a malt? Or take a walk or sit out by the riverbank? She was probably no different from her mother in Early's eyes. That's why he'd left town without saying good-bye.

Now Early Jones was back in Mallard, no longer a reedy boy carrying fruit in his tattered shirt but a grown man. Before she could think, she was pushing unsteadily to her feet and starting toward him. He glanced over his shoulder, his brown skin shining under the dull light. He didn't seem surprised to see her, and for a second, he gave her a little smile. For a second, she felt like a girl again, unsure of what to say.

"I thought it was you," she finally said.

"Course it's me," he said. "Who else would it be?"

He was, in a way, exactly how she'd remembered him, tall and leanly muscled like a wild cat. But even in the hazy bar, she could read hard years in his eyes, and his weariness startled her. He scratched the scruff on his chin, waving over Lorna and pointing lazily to Desiree's glass.

"What on earth you doin here?" she said. Mallard was the last place she would ever have imagined seeing him again.

"I'm just in town for a spell," he said. "Got a little business to tend to."

"What type of business?"

"You know. This and that."

He smiled again, but there was something unsettling about it. He glanced down at her left hand.

"So which one is your husband?" he said, nodding toward the roomful of men.

She'd forgotten that she was still wearing her wedding ring and curled her hand closed.

"He ain't here right now," she said.

"And he fine with you sittin up in a place like this all alone?"

"I can handle myself," she said.

"I bet."

"I wanted to visit my mama, that's all. He couldn't make the trip."

"Well, he a brave man. Lettin you out his sight."

He was only flirting, she knew, for old time's sake, but she still felt her skin flush. She fiddled absently with her blue scarf.

"What about you?" she said. "I don't see no ring on your hand."

"You won't," he said. "Don't have the taste for none of that."

"And your woman don't mind?"

"Who said I got a woman?"

"Maybe more than one," she said. "I don't know what you been up to."

He laughed, tilting back the rest of his drink. She hadn't flirted with a strange man in years, although Sam often accused her of it. She was making eyes with the elevator operator, she was smiling too friendly at the doorman, she laughed too hard at that taxi driver's jokes. In public, he seemed flattered when other men noticed her. In private, he punished her for their attention. And what would Sam say now, finding her in a place like this, Early standing so close she could reach out and touch the buttons down his shirt?

"So when you headin back home?" he said.

"I don't know."

"You ain't got a return ticket or nothin?"

"You sure askin a lot of questions," she said. "And you still ain't told me what you do yet."

"I hunt," he said.

"Hunt what?" she said.

He paused a long moment, staring down at her, and she felt his hand along the back of her neck. Tender, almost, the way you might soothe a crying child. It was so surprising, so different from his brusque flirting, that she didn't know what to say. Then he tugged her scarf loose. It was beginning to fade, but still, even in the dim bar, he could see the bruise splotched across her neck.

Nobody had warned her of this as a girl, when they carried on over her beautiful light complexion. How easily her skin would wear the mark of an angry man.

Early was frowning and she felt as exposed as if he'd lifted up her skirt. She shoved him and he stumbled backward, surprised. Then she desperately wrapped her scarf around her neck before pushing her way out the door.

MALLARD BENT.

A place was not solid, Early had learned that already. A town was jelly, forever molding around your memories. The morning after

Desiree Vignes shoved him in a bar, Early lay in bed at the boarding-house, studying the photograph Ceel had given him. He'd stayed at the Surly Goat longer than he'd planned, but then again, he hadn't planned to run into Desiree at all. He'd only wanted to kill time, maybe ask around a little. For two days, he'd poked around New Orleans, even though he knew Desiree wouldn't be there.

"She's back there, I know it," her husband had told him over the phone. "That's where all her friends are. Where else would she go? Sister gone. She and her mama don't talk."

Early clutched the phone, working his bare toe over the wood.

"Where her sister gone off to?" he said.

"Shit, I don't know. Look, I wired you the first payment. You gonna find her or what?"

This was why Early stuck to hunting criminals: it was never personal between the criminal and the bondsman, only a simple dis-agreement over dollars and cents. But a man searching for his wife was different. Desperate. He'd almost felt Sam Winston pacing be-hind him. Maybe Desiree would return to her husband on her own. If Early had a dime for every time a woman had stormed out on him. But Sam was convinced she'd left for good.

"She just lit out," he said. "Packed a bag and took my kid too, man. Just lit out in the middle of the night. What I'm supposed to do about that?"

"Why you think she run off like that?" Early said.

"I don't know," Sam said. "We had a disagreement, but you know how married folks are."

Early didn't, but he didn't say this. He didn't want Sam to know anything about him. So he didn't tell Sam when he'd decided to head to Mallard instead. A hurt bird always returns to its nest, a hurting woman no different. She would go home, he felt sure of this, even though he knew nothing about her life. On the I-10, he kept fiddling with the photos that Ceel had given him. Studying them for clues, he told himself, although he knew he was just admiring her. A pretty girl flirting with him on her porch now a beautiful woman, smiling, kneeling in front of a Christmas tree, surrounded by glimmering lights. She looked happy. Not like the type who might pick up and run. So what had driven her to? Well, no use in wondering. None of his concern, either way. He'd find her, take a couple pictures as proof. The photos in the mail, his money on its way, and his business with Desiree Vignes would be through.

He hadn't expected to find her so quickly in a bar filled with refinery men. He certainly hadn't expected that bruise on her neck. When he'd pulled her scarf, he hadn't meant to offend her—he was just surprised, that's all. But she'd recoiled as if he'd been the one to grab her throat, then shoved him so hard, he backed into the man behind him and spilled his drink. He should've followed after her, but he was shocked and a little embarrassed, to tell the truth, all the other men whooping and laughing.

"What she do that for?" the old barmaid asked.

"I don't know." Early reached for a napkin, wiping down his jacket. "I ain't seen her in years."

"Y'all used to go together?" a thin man in a Stetson asked.

"Used to!" An old man laughed, clapping Early on the back. "Yeah, used to sounds right!"

"She ain't used to be that angry," Early said.

"Yeah, well I leave her alone if I was you," the Stetson man said. "That whole family got problems."

"What kind of problems?"

"You know her sister run off, get to thinkin she white now."

"Oh yeah," the old man said. "Out there livin real fine like a white lady."

"Then Desiree got that child of hers."

"What's the matter with the child?" Early asked.

"Nothin the matter," the Stetson man said slowly. "She just black as can be. Desiree went out and married the darkest boy she could find and think nobody round here knows he be puttin his hands on her."

"Come back to town with a big ol' bruise." The old man laughed. "Guess he be trainin her. He turn her into Joe Frazier, that's why she come after you!"

Early didn't believe in beating on women—a man ought to fight fair, and until he met a woman who could match him blow for blow, he'd settle his disputes with them otherwise. At the same time, a job was a job. He wasn't her minister or even her friend. He'd never really known her at all. Just a girl flirting with him on her porch. What happened between her and her husband was none of his business.

In the morning, he gave a boy a nickel to point him to Adele Vignes's house. He trampled over thick tree roots, slowly remembering the way, the camera bag bouncing at his side. Already, he felt seventeen again, wandering heartsick through these woods. How disgusted Adele Vignes looked, pointing him down the path. Desiree silent beside her, unable to even look at him. He'd stumbled home, humiliated, but when he told his uncle, the man only laughed.

"What you expect, boy?" he said. "Don't you know what you is around here? You a nigger's nigger."

He never spoke to Desiree after that. What was he supposed to say? A place, solid or not, had rules. Early mostly felt foolish for thinking that Desiree would ever ignore them for him.

Now he waited, hidden behind trees, focusing on the white house through his lens. Ten minutes, maybe, although he lost track of time, listening to swallows swoop overhead. Finally, Desiree stepped onto the front porch and lit a cigarette. Yesterday she'd startled him in the dark bar. He'd barely registered the reality of her. In the daylight, she reminded him of the girl he'd once met. Willowy, her dark tangled hair hanging down her back. She was pacing barefoot, brimming with a nervous energy that seemed to glow through her body to the tip of her cigarette. He finally raised the camera and snapped. Desiree reaching the end of the porch—*click*—then turning on her heels—another *click*. Once he started, he couldn't stop watching her through the tiny rectangle, how her blue dress shifted as she walked, drawing his eyes to her slender ankles. Then the screen door opened and a jet-black girl stepped onto the porch. Desiree turned, smiling, stooping to sweep the girl into her arms. Early lowered the camera, watching Desiree carry her daughter inside the house.

"What's the news?" Sam said when he called that evening. "You found her?"

Early leaned against the closet, imagining Desiree on the porch, holding her daughter. When he'd pulled down her scarf, she'd reached for the bruise, her fingers trailing along her skin as if she were adjusting a necklace. He'd wanted to touch it too.

"I need a little more time," he said.

Three

Leaving Mallard was Desiree's idea but staying in New Orleans was Stella's, and for years, Desiree would puzzle over why. When the twins first arrived in the city, they found work together in the mangle room at Dixie Laundry, folding sheets and pillowcases for two dollars a day. At first, the smell of clean laundry reminded Desiree so much of home, she nearly cried. The rest of the city was filthy—urine-splattered cobblestone, garbage cans overflowing onto streets, and even the drinking water tasting metallic. It was the Mississippi River, Mae, their shift supervisor, said. Who knew what they dumped in there? She was born and raised in Kenner, not far out of the city, so she was amused to witness the twins' disorienting welcome. When they'd appeared at Dixie Laundry one morning—breathless and late after the annoyed streetcar driver left them fumbling for change on the curb—Mae pitied those poor country girls. She hired them on the spot, even though they were underage.

"Your tail, not mine," she said. When the inspectors came, always by surprise, she rang the lunch bell four times and the other laundry girls laughed as the twins darted into the bathroom until the inspection was over. Later, when she remembered Dixie Laundry, Desiree only pictured herself balancing on the toilet lid, pressed hard against Stella's back. She hated working like this, always looking over her shoulder, but what else could she do?

"I don't care how many toilets I got to jump in," she said. "I ain't goin back to Mallard."

She was willful enough to make declarations like this. In truth, she wasn't so sure. She still felt guilty about leaving their mother. Stella told Desiree that she couldn't be mad at them forever—when they found better jobs, they'd start sending money home and Mama would see that leaving was the kindest thing they could have done. For a moment, the thought assuaged her guilt, and Desiree felt so relieved, she didn't even find it strange that the Stella she'd dragged to New Orleans seemed intent on staying. Had Stella begun to change already? No, that came later. Back then, in the beginning anyway, she was the same Stella she had always been. Fastidious at work, stacking crisp pillowcases quietly, while Desiree always drifted toward the gossiping girls planning nights out. Stella tracking each penny they both earned, Stella sleeping beside her, still occasionally caught in nightmares until Desiree gently nudged her awake.

As the weeks turned into months, their sudden jaunt into the city began to feel more permanent. The thought was thrilling and terrifying. They could do this foolish thing. And if so, then what? What could they not do?

"The first year is the hardest," Farrah Thibodeaux told them. "You do a year, you can make it."

For the first month, the twins slept on a pile of blankets on Farrah's floor. They'd looked her up in the phone book when they arrived in the city, bleary-eyed and bedraggled and hungry. Farrah leaned against the doorway, laughing at the sight of them. She laughed at them often, like when they gawked at burlesque dancers posing in club windows or jolted away from drunk bums lurching down the sidewalk, or seemed every bit like two country girls who'd never been anywhere.

"These are my twins," she always said, introducing them to her friends, and Desiree only felt embarrassed. Her own awkwardness multiplied by her sister's. Farrah waited tables at a little jazz club called the Grace Note. On nights she closed, she snuck the twins in through the alley and smuggled them food from the kitchen. Her Dominican boyfriend played the saxophone and wore a shiny silver shirt unbuttoned to his navel; in between songs, he hung over the stage, asking the twins what they wanted to hear. Then the twins spent the night on the dance floor, giddy, twirled by big-eared boys. They started to befriend the regulars: a shoeshine boy who danced with Desiree until her feet ached; a soldier who kept begging to buy Stella drinks; a bellhop at Hotel Monteleone who always let Desiree blow his whistle to hail cabs.

"I bet you're not thinkin about Mallard now," Farrah said one night as the twins skittered, laughing and tired, onto the backseat.

Desiree laughed. "Never," she said.

She was good at pretending to be brave. She would never admit to Farrah that she was homesick and worried always about money. Soon Farrah would tire of the twins sprawling out on her floor, taking up time in her bathroom, eating her food, always being around, an unwanted guest doubled. Then what? Where would they be? Maybe they were just silly country girls in over their heads. Maybe Desiree was foolish to ever believe she could be more than that. Maybe they should just go back home.

"But you been talkin about comin out here forever," Stella said. "You wanna go back already? For what? So everyone can laugh at you?"

Only later, Desiree realized that each time she'd wavered, Stella had known exactly what to say to dissuade her from returning home. But if Stella herself wanted to stay, why hadn't she just said so? Why hadn't Desiree even asked? She was sixteen and self-centered, terrified that her impulsiveness would land her and her sister out on the streets.

"I shouldn't have brought you," she said. "I should've just left alone."

Stella looked as shocked as if Desiree had struck her.

"You wouldn't," she said, like it had suddenly become a possibility.

"No," Desiree said. "But I should've. I shouldn't have dragged you into this."

This was how Desiree thought of herself then: the single dynamic force in Stella's life, a gust of wind strong enough to rip out her roots. This was the story Desiree needed to tell herself and Stella allowed her to. They both felt safe inside it.

BY THE END OF Desiree Vignes's first week back in Mallard, everyone had already heard about the shove, which by then had become a slap, punch, or even a full-out brawl. The Vignes girl dragged, kicking and screaming, out of the bar. Those not too holy to admit that they'd been at the Surly Goat that afternoon said that they'd seen her leave, of her own volition, right after she attacked a dark man. Who was he and what had he said to anger her? Some thought he might have been her husband, come to fetch her. Others argued that he was a stranger who'd gotten fresh—she was just defending herself. Desiree had always been the prideful one; of course she'd lash out when wounded, unlike Stella, who'd rather die than make a scene. At the barber shop, Percy Wilkins slowly scraped his razor against the leather strop, listening to the men debate which twin had been the prettiest. In hindsight, Stella became more exotic, all the more beautiful now that she disappeared. But Desiree's stock rose since she'd come home. Still a firecracker, anyone could see that. At least three men joked that she could shove them around all she wanted.

"They never been right," the barber said. "After they daddy."

Little girls weren't supposed to witness what the Vignes twins had seen. At the funeral, he'd glanced at the twins, searching for some sign that they had been altered. But they just looked like girls to him, the same girls he'd seen skipping with Leon around town, each tugging on one of his arms. No way those girls could have turned out halfway normal. As far as he was concerned, both were a little crazy, Desiree perhaps the nuttiest of all. Playing white to get ahead was just good sense. But marrying a dark man? Carrying his blueblack child? Desiree Vignes had courted the type of trouble that would never leave.

AT LOU'S EGG HOUSE, Desiree Vignes learned how to balance plates of scrambled eggs and bacon and toast. Grits swirled with butter, thick pancakes sopping with syrup. She learned how to navigate around tiny tables, turn a sharp corner without losing a coffee cup, memorize orders. She learned quickly because when she applied for the job, she told Lou that she'd waited tables for three years.

"Three years, you say?" he asked on her first morning, when she struggled to take down an order.

"A long while ago, but yes," she said, smiling, "back in New Orleans." Other times, she told him she'd waitressed in D.C. She lost track of her lies, and even though Lou noticed, he never confronted her about it. He didn't believe in accusing ladies of lying, and besides, he knew that Desiree needed work, even if she was too proud to admit it herself. Imagine that—the founder's great-great-great-granddaughter waiting tables, not for white folks either but right in Mallard. Whoever thought they'd live to see the day? The Decuirs had lived free for generations, then Adele married a Vignes boy; now her daughter was serving coffee to refinery men and bringing pecan pie to farm boys. Once you mixed with common blood, you were common forever.

"She not much of a waitress," Lou told the line cook. "But she don't hurt much."

If he were honest, he'd admit that hiring Desiree had, in fact, boosted business. Old schoolmates, seized by curiosity, sat at the counter sipping coffee they ordinarily may have gone without. Even those too young to remember her, teenagers now, crowded in the back booths, whispering behind her back with the fervor of those witnessing the casual appearance of a minor celebrity. She noticed, of course she did. Still, each morning, she took a deep breath, tied her apron, fixed her face into a smile. She thought of her daughter and swallowed her humiliation. She bit her tongue even during her first week, when she'd stepped out of the kitchen to find Early Jones sitting at the counter. For a moment, she faltered, fingering her apron. She would draw more attention to herself by not serving him. Head down then, and get on with it.

He was wearing that leather jacket again, scratching at his beard as she slid over a coffee cup. A worn bag sat on an empty stool beside him. She reached over with the pot of coffee but he covered the cup with his hand.

"That fella that done that to you," he said. "He know where your mama stay?"

Her bruise had faded to a sick yellow by then, but still, she gingerly touched it.

"No," she said.

"She ever sent you a letter or nothin?"

"We wasn't in touch."

"Good." He slid his finger inside the smooth handle of his empty cup. "What about your sister?"

"What about her?"

"When's the last time you heard from her?"

She scoffed. "Thirteen years."

"Well, what happened to her?" he said.

"She took a job," she said. It all sounded so simple when she said it aloud, and of course, it had started that way. Stella needed to find a new job, so she'd responded to a listing in the newspaper for secretarial work in an office inside the Maison Blanche building. An office like that would never hire a colored girl, but they needed the money, living in the city and all, and why should the twins starve because Stella, perfectly capable of typing, became unfit as soon as anyone learned that she was colored? It wasn't lying, she told Stella. How was it her fault if they thought she was white when they hired her? What sense did it make to correct them now?

A good job for Stella, then a good job for her, that was the plan. So Stella would have to pretend a little but a little pretending to keep them off the streets seemed worth it. Then one evening, a year later, Desiree came home from Dixie Laundry to find an empty apartment. All of Stella's clothes, all of her things, gone. Like she'd never been there at all.

There was a note left behind in Stella's careful hand: *Sorry, honey, but I've got to go my own way.* For weeks, Desiree carried it with her until one night, in a fit of fury, she ripped it up, scattered it outside the window. She regretted that now, wished she still had something as small as a scrap of paper with Stella's handwriting on it.

Early was quiet a moment, then he finally pushed his empty cup toward her.

"What if I help you find her?" he said.

She frowned, pouring the coffee slowly.

"What you mean?" she said.

"Got a new job out in Texas, then I'm headin back this way," he said. "We could drive into New Orleans. Ask around."

"Why you wanna help me anyway?" she said.

"Cause I'm good at it," he said.

"Good at what?"

He slid a worn manila envelope onto the countertop. It was addressed to a man named Ceel Lewis, but she recognized Sam's handwriting.

"Huntin," he said.

IN A LITTLE TOWN outside Abilene, Texas, Early dreamed about Desiree Vignes.

Beneath the setting sun, he sprawled along the backseat of his El Camino, cradling a photograph of her. He'd given all of Ceel's pictures back to her except for one, which he'd already slid into the inside pocket of his leather jacket, feeling its corners poke his chest. He wasn't sure why he kept that picture. Wanted something to remember her by, maybe, if she decided to never speak to him again. She'd looked so shaken when she learned his true purpose in finding her, which he couldn't blame; he didn't stick around to find out if she could forgive him. Off to Texas, where he was hunting a mechanic charged with assault and attempted murder—his wife, her lover, a torque wrench. The blood-splattered garage made the front page in the *Times-Picayune*. On his drive west, Early imagined the mechanic swinging that wrench like Samson hurling a donkey jaw, blinded by his own righteousness and betrayal. Once, he might have been excited to hunt a man accused of such a sensational crime. But he was distracted now; when he closed his eyes, he imagined only Desiree.

At the truck stop, he bought a Coke and stepped into the phone booth to tell Sam Winston that his wife wasn't in New Orleans.

"Probably lit out east," he said. "New York, New Jersey, somethin like that."

"Why on earth she go out there, man?" Sam said. "No, I'm telling you, she's back in New Orleans. You just ain't looked hard enough."

"Ask Ceel how hard I look. If she was here, I woulda found her already."

"What if I send you more money?"

"Then I tell you the same thing," Early said. "She ain't here. Try someplace else."

He hung up the phone, leaning against the booth. His mind started to unspool backward; he knew how to find a hiding man but how to hide a woman so that she would never be found? Plant misinformation, scatter the trail so that any other man Sam hired wouldn't even know where to start. He fished in his pockets for a cigarette, his hands trembling. He'd never walked away from a job before. Exposed his camera film under the sunlight, the photographs of Desiree on her porch blackening. Money disappearing from his pockets. When he told Ceel that he'd come up empty and needed another job, quick, Ceel just shrugged, handing him the mechanic's photograph.

"Can't believe that little lady got the best of you," he'd said, laughing, as he pushed away from the bar.

She had, Early was starting to admit. He didn't know what it was about her but she'd hooked into him like a burr. He couldn't shake her. Didn't want to. In the phone booth, he pulled out a crumpled receipt from his pocket and dialed Lou's Egg House. When he heard her voice, he felt so nervous that he thought, for a second, about hanging up. Instead, he cleared his throat and asked how she was getting on.

"Oh fine," she said. "You know how it is. Where you off to right now?"

"Eula, Texas," he said. "You ever been to Eula?"

"No," she said. "What's it like?"

"Dry," he said. "Dusty. Lonesome. I feel like the only man alive out here. Like I fallen off the edge of the earth. You ever know that feeling?"

He imagined her on the other end, clutching the phone as she leaned against the kitchen door. The diner would be emptying now, near closing. Maybe she was all alone, willing the time to pass. Thinking about her sister, or maybe even thinking about him.

"I know it exactly," she said.

IF YOU'D ASKED BACK THEN, nobody believed that Desiree Vignes would stay in Mallard. The bet around town was that she wouldn't last a month. She'd tire of the crude whispers about her daughter, whispers she must have sensed, even if she could not hear them, each time the two walked around town. Some hoped, watching Desiree hold the hand of the little dark girl, that the two wouldn't even stay that long. They weren't used to having a dark child amongst them and were surprised by how much it upset them. Each time that girl passed by, no hat or nothing, they were as galled as when Thomas Richard returned from the war, half a leg lighter, and walked around town with one pant leg pinned back so that everyone could see his loss. If nothing could be done about ugliness, you ought to at least look like you were trying to hide it.

Still, a month passed, startling everyone. If Desiree didn't leave because of her daughter, surely boredom alone would root her out. After all her city adventures, how could she endure small-town living? The endless carousel of church bake sales, bazaars, talent shows, birthday parties and weddings and funerals. She'd never cared much for participating even before she'd left—that was the other one, Stella, who'd baked pecan pies for St. Catherine's bake sale, or sang dutifully in the school choir, or stayed two hours to celebrate Trinity Thierry's seventieth birthday. Not Desiree, who only attended the party after Stella dragged her, then looked so bored you wished you hadn't even invited her before she skipped out while you cut the cake.

Somehow that same Desiree was back, kneeling between her mother and daughter during Sunday Mass. She was as surprised as anyone to realize, one morning, that she had been home for an entire month. By then, she'd fallen into a routine, walking Jude to school, cleaning the house, working the sedate dinner crowd at Lou's as Jude read books at the counter. Each evening, she waited for Early Jones to call. She never knew where he would be calling from, or if he would call at all, but when Lou's phone rang near closing, she always answered. The shrill bell jolted her from mindlessly refilling sugar canisters or wiping down tabletops.

"Just checkin in on you," Early always said. How was her day? Her mama? Her daughter? Fine, fine, fine. Sometimes he asked about her shift and she told him that she'd had to send back three orders of eggs because the line cook, distracted as all get out, gave her scrambles instead of over easys. Or she asked about his drive and he told her that he'd been caught in a dust storm in Oklahoma, couldn't see his own hand in front of him, and he'd had to inch slowly down the road, hoping he wouldn't get hit. His stories excited her, even the dull ones. His life seemed so different from hers. Over time, he started to talk about the past, like how he'd been raised by his aunt and uncle after his parents dropped him off one night. She'd heard of children like this who had been given away. After her father died, her mother's sister offered to take one of the twins.

"It's too much," Aunt Sophie had said, clasping their mother's hands. "Let us lighten your load."

The twins pressed against their bedroom door, listening hard, each wondering if she would be the one to go. Would Aunt Sophie take her pick, like choosing a puppy out of a basket? Or would their mother decide which daughter she could live without? Eventually, their mother told Aunt Sophie that she could not separate her girls, but later, Desiree learned that her aunt had asked for her. Aunt Sophie lived in Houston, and Desiree used to imagine her life there, a city girl whisking around in starched dresses and shiny leather shoes, not the faded calico her mother salvaged from the church bin.

After Mallard, Early said, he was sick of farming other people's land, so he set off to Baton Rouge to try his luck. Well, the only luck he found was the hard kind. He spent a year there, stealing car parts in order to feed himself, until he got caught and shipped off to Angola State Prison. He was twenty then, already a man in the eyes of the law and truth telling, he'd felt like a man since the night his parents left him without saying good-bye. The world worked differently than he'd ever imagined. People you loved could leave and there was nothing you could do about it. Once he'd grasped that, the inevitability of leaving, he became a little older in his own eyes.

He spent four years in prison, a time he leapt over and would never, in all his life, talk much about.

"Does that change anything?" he asked her.

She imagined him in a phone booth somewhere, his boot kicked up on the glass.

"What would it change?" she said.

He was quiet a minute, then said, "Oh, I don't know."

But she knew what he meant: would she think about him differently now? She wasn't sure what she thought about him at all. She'd had a crush on him once, long ago, but she didn't know the man he'd grown up to be. She had no idea what he wanted from her. Weeks before, he'd offered to find Stella, and when she told him that she couldn't pay him right away, he said, "That's all right."

"What you mean that's all right?" she said.

"I mean, I don't need it right off. We can work somethin out."

She'd never met a working man who was so casual about his money, but then again, she'd never met a working man who did what Early did for a living. He hunted bail jumps who'd disappeared without a trace, hoping to start over somewhere new. But there was always a trail if you looked closely enough—no one disappeared completely. Again, she thought about the envelope of photographs he'd given her. In the diner, she'd held the package, her heart thudding.

"Don't worry," he'd said. "I'll send that sonofabitch far away from here." She must have looked unsure because he said, "Trust me. I won't give you up."

But why wouldn't he? He barely knew her and Sam had offered him good money. What reason did he have to be loyal to her? For weeks, she'd wondered if she and Jude should move on again. If Sam was looking, wouldn't he eventually find her? Wouldn't he just travel to Mallard himself? But maybe now, Mallard was the safest place to be. Sam's hired man told him she wasn't in Louisiana, and what reason would Sam have to doubt him? Maybe she could trust Early—if he'd wanted to hurt her, Sam would have found her already. But just because she could trust him didn't mean that he didn't want anything.

"He just tellin you what you wanna hear," her mother said one night, handing her a wet plate. "That man don't know where Stella is any more than you do."

Desiree sighed, reaching for the dish rag.

"But he knows how to look," she said. "Why shouldn't we try?"

"She don't want to be found. You gotta let her go. Live her life."

"This ain't her life!" Desiree said. "None of it woulda happened if I didn't tell her to take that job. Or drag her to New Orleans, period. That city wasn't no good for Stella. You was right all along."

Her mother pursed her lips. "It wasn't her first time," she said.

"Ma'am?"

"Bein white," her mother said. "New Orleans was just her chance to do it for real."

HERE WAS THE STORY her mother had been keeping:

A week after Stella disappeared into the city, Willie Lee came by the shotgun house, hangdog. He had something to tell Adele— something he should've told her weeks before Founder's Day. One afternoon he'd driven Stella into Opelousas. She helped him around the butcher shop on weekends because she was quick at adding figures in her head. She could eyeball a pound of ground chuck more accurately than him, and whenever he weighed her measurements, she was never off. She was a smart, careful girl, but that last summer, he'd noticed something different about her. She seemed sadder, wrapped up in herself. Because she'd dropped out of school, he figured, although he didn't quite understand it, having flunked out of ninth grade himself. A girl who could eyeball a pound of ground chuck would do fine in life, college or not. But not everybody was practical minded like him, so when Stella sullenly stood behind the cash register, he figured that she was still disappointed that she wouldn't be off to Spelman someday like she'd hoped.

So he'd invited her to Opelousas one afternoon. He had to make deliveries and figured, hell, she might want to get out of town for a bit. He'd given her a nickel to buy a Coke, and when he'd finished unloading, he found her standing beside his truck, breathless and flushed. She'd gone inside some shop called Darlene's Charms, where the shopgirl mistook her for white.

"Isn't it funny?" she'd said. "White folks, so easy to fool! Just like everyone says."

"It ain't no game," he told her. "Passin over. It's dangerous."

"But white folks can't tell," she said. "Look at you—you just as redheaded as Father Cavanaugh. Why does he get to be white and you don't?"

"Because he *is* white," he said. "And I don't wanna be."

"Well, neither do I," she'd said. "I just wanted to look at that shop. You won't tell my mama, will you?"

In Mallard, you grew up hearing stories about folks who'd pretended to be white. Warren Fontenot, riding a train in the white section, and when a suspicious porter questioned him, speaking enough French to convince him that he was a swarthy European; Marlena Goudeau becoming white to earn her teaching certificate; Luther Thibodeaux, whose foreman marked him white and gave him more pay. Passing like this, from moment to moment, was funny. Heroic, even. Who didn't want to get over on white folks for a change? But the *passe blanc* were a mystery. You could never meet one who'd passed over undetected, the same way you'd never know someone who successfully faked her own death; the act could only be successful if no one ever discovered it was a ruse. Desiree only knew the failures: the ones who'd gotten homesick, or caught, or tired of pretending. But for all Desiree knew, Stella had lived white for half her life now, and maybe acting for that long ceased to be acting altogether. Maybe pretending to be white eventually made it so.

———

"Finishin up," Early said, two nights later, calling outside of Shreveport. "Headin back your way, if you still wanna look for your sister."

She had never imagined that Stella kept big secrets from her. Not Stella, who'd slept beside her, whose thoughts ran like a current between them, whose voice she heard in her own head. How could she have spent that whole summer not knowing that Stella had already decided to become someone else? She didn't know who Stella was anymore, and maybe she'd never quite known her at all.

She twirled her finger tighter around the phone cord. Inside the empty diner, Jude sat at the counter, reading a book. She was always reading, always alone.

"Yes," Desiree said. "I suppose so."

THE MORNING EARLY JONES ARRIVED, the sky hung heavy and hot with rain. From the edge of the couch, Desiree listened to the spring storm as she braided Jude's hair, remembering those first weeks in New Orleans, ducking with Stella under eaves when the showers caught them unaware. She eventually grew used to the capricious rain, but back then she'd shrieked at every sudden storm, laughing with Stella as they pressed against the side of a building, water splattering against their ankles. On the rug in front of her, Jude squirmed, pointing at the porch.

"Mama, a man," she said, and there was Early standing on the front steps, jacket collar flipped up, his beard flecked with raindrops. Desiree scrambled to her feet, feeling strangely nervous, and she didn't realize until she opened the door that they were standing exactly where they'd first met a lifetime ago.

"You can come in," she said.

"You sure?" he said. "Don't wanna make no mess."

He looked as nervous as she felt, which emboldened her. She beckoned him inside, and he kicked his boots against the porch, shucking off mud. Then he followed her, standing in the doorway, one hand balled up in his jacket pocket.

"This is Jude," she said. "Jude, come say hi to Mr. Early. I'm goin on a little drive with him, remember?"

"It's just Early," he said. "I ain't nobody's mister."

He smiled, holding out his hand. Jude slid hers into his for a second, then darted off into the bedroom to fetch her book bag. Later, on the interstate, Early asked if Jude was always so quiet.

Desiree gazed out the window, watching the sunlight glint off Lake Pontchartrain.

"Always," she said. "She ain't like me at all."

"Like her daddy, then?"

She didn't like talking about Sam to Early, didn't even want to imagine both men existing within the same expanse of her life. Besides, Jude wasn't like Sam either. She was, in a way, like Stella. Private, like if she told you anything about herself, she was giving away something she could never get back.

"No," she said. "Not like anybody but herself."

"That's good. For a girl to be herself."

"Not in Mallard," she said. "Not a girl like Jude."

Early touched her hand, surprising her, then remembering himself, he pulled away.

"Won't be easy," he said. "Wasn't easy for me. You know a man smacked me once at church? Right on the back of my neck. All because I put my finger in the holy water before his wife. Like I ruined it somehow. I thought my uncle was gonna stick up for me. I don't know why, I just thought. But he told the man sorry like I done somethin wrong."

He let out a bitter laugh. On the other side of the interstate, a freight train rumbled along, rainwater sloughing off the tracks. She turned back to him, eyes also wet.

"I should've said somethin," she said. "When my mama run you off like that."

He shrugged. "Long time ago."

"So why you helping me then? Why really."

"Oh, I don't know," he said. "Guess it make me sad, thinkin about you and your sister." He stared ahead, refusing to look at her. "And I guess I just like talkin with you. Ain't talked to no woman so much in all my life."

She laughed. "You ain't said but two words at a time."

"It's enough," he said.

She laughed again, touching the back of his neck, and later, he would tell her that was the first time he knew. That gentle hand on the back of his neck as he steered the car across the bridge.

THEY WERE CHASING THE PAST, searching for Stella down streets and stairwells and alleyways.

Trampling up the steps of the twins' three-story walk-up, where an elderly colored couple now lived. Desiree asked, as politely as she could, if they might have received any mail intended for a Desiree or Stella Vignes, but they'd only lived there for two years. The lives of the twin girls had already faded into the apartment walls long before they'd arrived. Sisters cooking together, listening to the little transistor radio that had been their first luxury purchase. Sisters staying up until dawn, feeling finally like the grown women they believed themselves to be. Sisters signing the lease to that first apartment, although maybe even then, Stella had known that the arrangement would be temporary. Maybe she had already started searching for a way out.

All afternoon, they hunted Stella in the old spots. They asked after her in Dixie Laundry and the Grace Note. Desiree searched for old friends in the phone book but nobody had heard from Stella. Farrah Thibodeaux, married now to an alderman, laughed when Desiree called.

"I can't believe little Stella's run off," she said. "Now you, I would've thought . . ."

"Thanks anyway," Desiree said, starting to hang up.

"Wait a minute," Farrah said. "I don't know what your hurry is. I was going to tell you I saw your sister."

Her heart quickened. "When?"

"Oh, a long time ago. Before you left. She was walkin down Royal Street, just as carefree as she could be. Arm in arm with a white man too. Looked right at me, then looked the other way. I swear she saw me."

"You sure it was her?"

"As sure that it wasn't you," Farrah said. "It's all in her eyes, honey. Her white man was handsome too. Must've been why she was smiling like that."

Stella leaving her to chase after some man. Stella secretly in love. Stella, who had never been boy crazy, who had rolled her eyes at Desiree mooning over Early, who had never even had a boyfriend before. The frigid twin, the boys called her. But Early told her that the simplest explanation is often the right one.

"You be surprised by what emotion make people do," he said.

"But I know her," she said, then stopped herself. She couldn't assume anything about Stella anymore. Hadn't she learned that already?

She was exhausted by the time Early suggested she try the Maison Blanche building. She'd only ventured inside once before, days after Stella first disappeared. She'd told herself, riding the streetcar down Canal, that Stella couldn't be gone for good. This was Stella, fallen into one of her bad moods. Stella playing hide-and-seek, ducking behind the drying sheets. She told herself lots of reassuring things she didn't believe. Stella would pop back up. She would appear on their apartment stoop and explain herself. She wouldn't walk away from the best job she'd ever had. She wouldn't leave her sister behind.

Inside the department store, Desiree had wandered, walking slowly down the perfume aisle. She knew that Stella worked in an office on one of the top floors but she didn't know which one. In the lobby, she studied the directory so long, the brusque security guard asked what her business was. She'd faltered, afraid to expose Stella, and he finally shooed her away.

"Too pushy," Early said. "You gotta have a soft touch. You come across too desperate, folks sense it. Clam up."

They were sitting in a café across the street from Maison Blanche. She'd barely touched her espresso. She was still thinking about the white man Farrah saw Stella with. How happy she'd looked. She didn't want to be found. What was Desiree doing, trying to drag her back into a life she no longer wanted?

"You gotta go in there like somebody they tell things to," he said. "Somebody that gets what she wants."

"Be white, you mean."

He nodded. "Easier that way," he said. "I can't go in with you. Give you away. But you just go in, say you lookin for somebody. An old friend. Not your sister, that raise too many questions. Tell 'em you lost touch, somethin like that. Just keep it light, breezy. Like a white lady with no worry on her mind."

So she imagined herself as Stella—not the Stella she once knew but Stella as she was now. Pushing past the giant brass MB door handles, stepping inside the department store. She passed through the perfume aisle with the confidence of a woman who could buy any bottle she wished. She stopped to smell a few, as if she were considering a purchase. Admired the jewelry in the display case, glanced at the fine handbags, demurred when salesgirls approached her. In the lobby, the colored elevator operator gazed at the floor when she stepped on. She ignored him, the way Stella might have. She felt queasy at how simple it was. All there was to being white was acting like you were.

When she entered the first office level, a white security guard hurried over to help her. She played back Early's words. Light, breezy, no worry on her mind. She told him that she was looking for an old friend who used to work in marketing.

Of course he couldn't find a Stella Vignes in the building directory, but he gave her directions to the department. She rode the elevator to the sixth floor, and when she stepped inside the office, she braced herself for someone to mistake her for Stella. But the redheaded secretary just smiled at her pleasantly.

"I'm lookin for an old friend," Desiree said. "She used to be a secretary here."

"And what's the name?"

"Stella Vignes." She glanced around the quiet office, as if by speaking her name, she might have conjured her.

"Stella Vignes," the secretary repeated, turning to a file cabinet behind her. She hummed to herself as she searched, the only other sounds the gentle clacking of typewriters. Desiree tried to imagine Stella in a place like this. Joining the ranks of other polite white girls sitting at their desks.

The secretary returned to her seat holding a file folder.

"No current address, I'm afraid," she said. "Our last few Christmas cards returned to sender."

She was so apologetic, so sorry that she could only give Desiree the most recent address she had on file, a card filled out in Stella's careful handwriting with a forwarding address leading her to Boston, Massachusetts.

"AIN'T NO SMOKIN GUN," Early said that night. "But it's a start."

They were sitting together in a darkened booth at the Surly Goat, Early sipping his whiskey slowly. In the morning, he'd be gone again, a new job carrying him off to Durham. But after that, he would go to that address in Boston, see what he could dig up there. She couldn't imagine how Stella found herself in that city of all places, but it didn't matter. That scrap of paper held more new information about Stella than Desiree had ever learned.

She felt, again, overwhelmed by Early's help, unsure of how she could ever manage to thank him. After they finished their drinks, she walked him to the boardinghouse. He tucked her hand under his arm as they climbed up the muddy steps and she didn't pull away, not even once they were inside his room. She wasn't drunk but the room suddenly felt hot. She hadn't undressed in front of a strange man in years.

Slowly, then. He was leaning against the worn dresser, waiting, and she pressed against him, trailing her hand down his stomach. He stopped her at his belt.

"It's just a start," he said. "I ain't no closer to findin her."

He held on to her hand, as if he understood that this was a condition for them to go any further.

"All right," she said.

"I might not. She might just be gone. You know that, right?"

She paused. "I know."

"I'll look as long as you want me to," he said. "Tell me to stop and I'll stop."

She wrested her hand free, slipping it under his black T-shirt. Her fingers brushed against a rough scar stretching across his stomach. He shivered.

"Don't stop," she said.

Part II

MAPS

(1978)

Four

In the autumn of 1978, a dark girl blew into Los Angeles from a town that existed on no maps.

She rode a Greyhound all the way from this unmapped place, her two suitcases rattling in the undercarriage. A girl from nowhere and nothing, and if you'd asked any of the other passengers, they would have noticed nothing interesting about her except that she was so, well, black. Aside from that, quiet. Flipping through a worn detective novel that her mother's boyfriend had given her for her seventeenth birthday, which she was reading for the second time to find all the clues she'd missed. At rest stops, she clamped that book under her arm, walking in slow circles to stretch her legs. Twitchy. She reminded the Italian bus driver of a cheetah pacing around a cage. He wouldn't have been surprised at all to learn that she was a runner—that lean, boyish body, those long legs. He smoked his cigarette, watching her make another lap around the bus. Too bad, those legs with that face. That skin. Jesus, he'd never seen a woman that black before.

She didn't notice the bus driver watching her. She barely noticed anyone staring at her at all anymore, or if she did, she knew exactly why they were looking. She was impossible to miss. Dark, yes, but also tall and rangy, just like her father, whom she had not seen or heard from in ten years. She took another slow lap, trying to find her place in that dog-eared book with the cracked spine. She'd loved detective stories ever since she was little; she used to sit on the porch while her mother's boyfriend cleaned his gun and told her about the men he hunted.

Later, it'd seem like a strange bonding activity for a grown man and a little girl, but she'd already learned that Early Jones was a strange man. Not her father but the closest to it she would ever come. She liked watching him slowly disassemble the gun while she peppered him with questions. You could find just about anybody if you were good at lying, he told her. Half of hunting was pretending to be somebody else, an old friend searching for his buddy's address, a long-lost nephew trying to find his uncle's new phone number, a father inquiring about the whereabouts of his son. There was always someone close to the mark that you could manipulate. Always a window in if you couldn't find a door.

"Ain't that exciting," he told her, chewing on a toothpick. "Most of it just sweet-talkin old ladies on the phone."

He made finding the lost sound so easy that once, she'd asked if he could search for her daddy. He didn't look up at her, swabbing his brush inside the gun barrel.

"You don't want me to go lookin for him," he said.

"Why not?"

"Because," he said. "He's not a nice man."

He was right, of course, but she hated how certain he was. How could he possibly know? He'd never even met her daddy.

She'd always imagined her father driving up in his shiny Buick to rescue her. She'd step out of school one day and find him waiting. Her father, tall and handsome, smiling at her, arms open. The other kids would gawk. Then he'd bring her back to D.C., and she'd go to school and make friends and date boys and run track and go off to college in a place so unlike Mallard that she would hardly believe that Mallard even existed, that she hadn't just imagined it.

But ten years passed, no phone calls or letters. In the end, she rescued herself. She won a gold medal in the 400 meters at the state championship meet, and miracle of miracles, college recruiters saw her. She'd run as hard as she could and now she was getting the hell out. At the bus station, she'd stood at the base of the metal steps while Early loaded her suitcases. Her grandmother slipped her rosary over her neck before her mother pulled her into a hug.

"I still don't know why you wanna go all the way out to California," she said. "There's some perfectly good schools right here."

She laughed a little, as if she were kidding, as if she hadn't been trying to convince Jude to stay. They both knew that she couldn't. She'd already accepted the track scholarship from UCLA—as if she could even think about turning it down—and now she was standing in front of a bus, waiting to climb on.

"I'll call," she said. "And write."

"You better."

"It'll be fine, Mama. I'll come back and see you."

But they both knew that she'd never come back to Mallard. On the bus, she fiddled with the rosary beads, imagining her mother traveling away from Mallard on a bus like this. Except she hadn't been alone, Stella beside her staring out into the dark. Jude held the worn paperback in her lap, pressing against the filmy window. She'd never seen a desert before—it seemed to stretch on forever. Another mile ticked by, carrying her further from her life.

THEY CALLED HER TAR BABY.

Midnight. Darky. Mudpie. Said, Smile, we can't see you. Said, You so dark you blend into the chalkboard. Said, Bet you could show up naked to a funeral. Bet lightning bugs follow you in the daytime. Bet when you swim it look like oil. They made up lots of jokes, and once, well into her forties, she would recite a litany of them at a dinner party in San Francisco. Bet cockroaches call you cousin. Bet you can't find your own shadow. She was amazed by how well she remembered. At that party, she forced herself to laugh, even though she'd found nothing funny at the time. The jokes were true. She *was* black. Blueblack. No, so black she looked purple. Black as coffee, asphalt, outer space, black as the beginning and the end of the world.

At first, her grandmother tried to keep her out of the sun. Gave her a big gardening hat, tied the straps tight around her chin even though it choked her. She couldn't run with the hat on, and she loved to run, which couldn't be helped, although Adele begged her to wait, at least, until the sun went down. She'd spent her summers reading indoors, or when she felt like she was going crazy from being cooped up, she chased shade around the yard, wearing the big choking hat, long sleeves clinging to her sweaty arms. She would get no darker, although she seemed to the longer she lived in Mallard. A black dot in the school pictures, a dark speck on the pews at Sunday Mass, a shadow lingering on the riverbank while the other children swam. So black that you could see nothing but her. A fly in milk, contaminating everything.

In homeroom, she sat in front of Lonnie Goudeau, the varsity pitcher, who threw paper balls at her back all period. He was gray-eyed with auburn hair licking up the back of his neck, his cheeks splashed with freckles. A beautiful boy. So she prickled when she imagined him staring at her, rolling up his sleeves, his forearms so light you could see the brown hair, and flexing, the paper pinched between his fingers. Then she felt the soft pat against her neck, the boys behind her snickering. She never turned around. Once,

Mr. Yancy caught Lonnie and sentenced him to detention. On her way out, Jude passed him wiping down the chalkboard and he smirked at her, sliding the eraser through the dust. She replayed that moment her whole walk home. His lips, caught between a grimace and a smile.

Lonnie Goudeau was the first person to call her Tar Baby. A month after she moved to Mallard, he found a copy of *Brer Rabbit* in the class bin and gleefully tapped the shiny black blob on the cover. "Look, it's Jude," he said, and she was so startled that he knew her name, she didn't realize that he was making fun of her until the whole class dissolved into laughter. He was chastened for disrupting silent reading, the book quickly removed by their blushing teacher, but that night after dinner, Jude asked her mother what a tar baby was. Her mother paused, dipping their dirty plates into the sink.

"Just an old story," she said. "Why?"

"A boy called me that today."

Her mother slowly dried her hands on the towel, then knelt in front of her.

"He just wants to get a rise out of you," she said. "Ignore him. He'll get bored and cut all that out."

But he didn't. Lonnie flecked mud at her socks and threw her books into the trash. Jostled her chair leg during exams, yanked the ribbons in her hair, sang "Tutti-frutti, dark Judy" as soon as she was in earshot. On the last day of fifth grade, he tripped her down the school steps and she scraped her knee. At the kitchen table, her grandma pulled her leg onto her lap, gently swabbing the blood with a cotton ball.

"Maybe he likes you," Maman said. "Little boys always act real mean to girls they like."

She tried to imagine Lonnie holding her hand, carrying her books home from school, kissing her, even, his long eyelashes tickling her cheeks. Sitting beside him in a movie theater, or on the top of the Ferris wheel at the carnival, Lonnie's arm around her. But all she could picture was Lonnie splashing her in a mud puddle or sticking chewing gum in her hair or calling her a dumb bitch, Lonnie punching her until her lip burst open and her eye swelled shut. After, her father would always storm out while her mother sobbed on the floor, her face buried in the couch cushion. Once, he didn't leave right away. Instead, he pulled her mother's face into his stomach, petting her hair. Her mother whimpered but didn't pull away, as if she were comforted by his touch.

Better to picture Lonnie beating on her. That other thing—that soft part—terrified her even more.

BEFORE THE INSULTS AND JOKES, before the taunting, the muddied socks, the kicked chairs, the empty lunch bench, before all of that, there were questions. What was her name? Where'd she come from and why was she here? On her first day of school, Louisa Rubidoux leaned across their shared desk and asked who was that lady walking with her earlier.

"My mama," Jude said. Wasn't it obvious? She'd walked her to school, held her hand. Who else would she be?

"But not your real mama, right?" Louisa said. "Y'all don't look nothin alike."

Jude paused, then said, "I look like my daddy."

"Well, where's he at?"

She shrugged, even though she knew. Back in D.C., where they'd left him. She missed him already even though she could still see that bruise on her mother's neck, even though she could remember all the bruises she'd seen on her body over time, dark splotches on that strange topography. Once, at the swimming pool, she'd stared as her mother started to change in their stall before stopping, midway, when she discovered a fading bruise on her thigh. She quietly put her clothes back on, then told Jude she'd decided to just sit by the pool today and watch her. When they arrived home, her father greeted her mother with a kiss, and Jude realized that if she tried, she could pretend that the bruises came from someplace else. Her relationship with one parent magically untethered to the other. So when she thought of her daddy, he was sprawled beside her on the rug, flipping through the comics. Not dragging her mother by her hair into the bedroom—no, that was some other man. And after the broken glass was swept, the blood wiped off the tile, after her mother retreated into the bathroom, a bag of ice pressed against her face, her real daddy returned, smiling, stroking her cheek.

"How come I don't look like you?" she asked her mother that night. She was sitting on the worn rug in front of the couch while her mother braided her hair so she couldn't see her face but felt her hands still.

"I don't know," her mother finally said.

"You look like Maman."

"It just work that way sometimes, baby."

"When are we going home?" she asked.

"What'd I tell you?" her mother said. "We got to be here a little while. Now stop wigglin around and let me finish."

She was beginning to realize what she would soon know for sure: there was no plan to go back home or to go anywhere else, even, and her mother was lying each time she pretended that there was. The next day, she was sitting alone during lunch when Louisa cornered her, flanked by three beige girls.

"We don't believe you," Louisa said. "About that bein your mama. She too pretty to be your mama."

87

"She's not," Jude said. "My real mama's somewhere else."

"Where at?"

"I don't know. Somewhere. I haven't found her yet."

She was thinking, somehow, of Stella—a woman who resembled her just as little but would be a better version of her mother. Stella wouldn't make Daddy so angry that he beat on her. She wouldn't wake Jude in the middle of the night and force her onto a train to a little town where other children taunted her. She would keep her word. Stella wouldn't promise that they would leave Mallard again and again, only to stay.

"You gotta watch your mama," her father had warned her once. "She still like those folks."

"What folks?" She was lying on the rug beside him, watching him catch jacks, his large hands blurring in front of her eyes.

"The folks she come from," he said. "Your mama still got some of that in her. She still think she better than us."

She didn't understand exactly what he meant, but she liked being part of an us. People thought that being one of a kind made you special. No, it just made you lonely. What was special was belonging with someone else.

BY HIGH SCHOOL, the names no longer shocked her but the loneliness did. You could never quite get used to loneliness; every time she thought she had, she sank further into it. She sat by herself at lunch, flipping through cheap paperbacks. She never received visits on the weekends, or invitations to Lou's for lunch, or phone calls just to see how she was doing. After school, she went running alone. She was the fastest girl on the track team, and on another team in another town, she might have been captain. But on this team in this town, she stretched alone before practice and sat by herself on the team bus, and after she won the gold medal at the state championship, no one congratulated her but Coach Weaver.

Still, she ran. She ran because she loved it, because she wanted to be good at something, because her father had run himself at Ohio State, and when she laced up her cleats, she thought about him. Sometimes, when she circled behind the baseball dugout, she felt Lonnie Goudeau staring. She ran with a hitch in her gait—ungraceful and uneven, a bad habit Coach tried and failed to correct. Lonnie probably thought she ran funny or maybe he just liked laughing at her, that white top and white shorts against all that black skin. She never felt darker than when she was running, and at the same time, she never felt less black, less anything.

She ran in a pair of gold running shoes she'd begged Early for one Christmas. Her mother had sighed.

"Wouldn't you like a nice dress?" she asked. "Or new earrings?" Each year, she shoved the box across the rug as if she could barely stand to touch it. "Gym shoes again," she said glumly, as Jude pulled out the tissue paper. "I swear I'll never understand how one girl could want so many pairs of gym shoes."

When she was eleven, Early had bought her first pair of running shoes, white New Balance sneakers he'd found in Chicago. The next year, he was off working a job in Kansas, so he didn't come for Christmas at all, then the next, he was back as if he'd never left, bearing a new pair, and by then she'd long gotten used to his coming and going, which felt as regular as the seasons.

"That man sniffin around again," her grandmother always said. She never called Early by his name—always "that man" or sometimes just "him." She didn't approve of her daughter shacking up with a man, even though Early was never around long enough for his visits to constitute shacking up, which either made it better or worse. Still, each Early season, as Jude began to think of it, her mother started to change. First, the house transformed, her mother balancing on chairs, ripping down the curtains, beating dust out of the rugs, washing the windows. Then her clothes: her mother springing for a new pair of nylons, finishing the dress she'd started sewing months ago, shining her shoes until they gleamed. The final, and most embarrassing part: her mother preening in the mirror like a vain schoolgirl, flipping her long hair onto one shoulder, then the other, trying a new shampoo that smelled like strawberries. Early loved her hair, so she always paid it special attention. Once, Jude had seen him ease up behind her mother and bury his face in a handful of her hair. She didn't know who she wanted to be in that moment—Early or her mother, beautiful or beholding—and she'd felt so sick with longing that she turned away.

Her mother never acknowledged the beginning of an Early season, but Maman knew. This, too, was a feature of Early season: she and her grandmother, tentative allies, forging clearer allegiance.

"All those men," Maman said, "all those men around town and she's still out here chasin after him."

In her grandmother's bedroom, Jude maneuvered around the bed, reaching for the bottle of eye drops Dr. Brenner prescribed after her grandmother complained about dryness. Each night before bed, her grandmother rested her head in Jude's lap, her graying hair spread out like a fan, while Jude carefully placed a drop in each eye.

"You should have seen," her grandmother said. "All the boys who loved them."

She still did this sometimes, talked about Jude's mother as *them*. Jude never corrected her. She slowly released the drop, her grandmother blinking up at her.

———————

WHEN DESIREE VIGNES waved at her daughter's bus from the terminal, she waited until the Greyhound disappeared around the corner to wipe the tears from her eyes. She didn't want the last thing for her daughter to see, if she had in fact been staring out the back window, to be her silly mother, crying as if she'd never see her again. Early handed her a handkerchief and she laughed, dabbing her eyes. "I'm fine, I'm fine," she said, although nobody had asked and she wasn't. After he dropped her by Lou's Egg House for her shift, she realized, tying her apron, that she was starting her day the same way she'd started it for the past ten years, except that this time, she did not know when she would see her daughter again.

Ten years. She had been home ten years. Sometimes she glanced around the house, shaking her head, as if she still didn't understand how she'd found herself back. As if she were in *The Wizard of Oz*, but instead of a house dropping on her, she'd fallen through the roof and awakened, years later, dazed to realize that she was still there. When she'd first decided to stay, she gave herself practical reasons. She didn't earn enough at Lou's to live anywhere else. She couldn't abandon her mother again. She still hoped that Stella might return home on her own. And even if Stella didn't, Desiree felt closer to her here, wandering around Stella's old things. The chair where Stella sat at the table, a cornhusk doll Stella named Jane. Everywhere around the house, a door handle or blanket or couch cushion that Stella had once touched, bearing the invisible remnants of her fingerprints.

She'd made a sort of life for herself here, hadn't she? With her mother and her daughter and Early Jones, who left and continued to leave but also continued to return. When he visited, Desiree felt like a girl again, the years falling away like meat off the bone. His arrivals always seemed a little miraculous. Once, she was carrying a country-fried steak and eggs to a table and found Early sitting at the end of the counter, chewing on a toothpick. Another time, she locked up the diner and turned to see Early leaning against the phone booth across the road. She was exhausted but still laughed at the sight of him, as unexpected as the sudden coming of spring. One day there was frost, and the next, bloom.

"I was just thinkin about you," he'd say, as if he had stopped by on his way home, not driven all the way from Charleston, pressing on through the night, bleary-eyed, to get to her sooner. "Wonderin what you was up to."

She was never up to anything, of course, her days blending to-gether into a sameness that she later found comforting. No surprises, no sudden anger, no man holding her one moment, then hitting her the next. Now life was steady. She knew what each day would bring, except when Early appeared. He was the only thing in her life she wasn't prepared for. He never stayed longer than a day or two before he was gone again. Once, he'd convinced her to call in sick to Lou's so that he could take her fishing. They didn't catch anything but half-way through the afternoon, he kissed her, slipping his fingers under her dress, stroking her as they floated on the glassy lake. It was the most thrilling thing that had happened to her in months.

When Early came to town, her mother grew grim and tightlipped, glaring at the door when Desiree slipped out to meet him at the boardinghouse.

"I don't know why you foolin around with that man," she said. "Can't stick around, find no decent work."

"He works," Desiree said.

"Nothin decent!" her mother said. "Probably got all type of women out there runnin after him—"

"Well, that's his business, not mine."

She didn't ask who Early spent his nights with outside of Mallard. He didn't ask her either. Each time he left, she missed him, but she wondered if his leaving was the only reason why they worked. He wasn't a settling man, and maybe she wasn't a settling woman either. When she thought about marriage, she felt trapped with Sam in an airless apartment, bracing herself, through each calm moment, for his inevitable rage. But Early was easy. He had no hidden sides. They didn't argue, and if she ever grew annoyed with him, she was comforted by the fact that soon enough he would be gone again. He couldn't trap her because he refused to trap himself. She'd had to convince him to stay at the house when he visited.

"Aw, I don't know, Desiree," he'd said, rubbing his jaw slowly.

"I'm not askin for a ring," she said. "I'm not really askin for anything. It just don't make sense, me runnin out to the boardinghouse all the time. And I think with Jude, it would be better if—" But she paused here. She never wanted Early to think that she expected him to be a father to her daughter. He didn't owe the two of them anything. Owing was never part of their arrangement.

"What about your mama?" he said.

"Don't worry about her. I'll take care of all that. I just think . . . well, it don't make sense, that's all. We two grown people. I'm tired of sneakin around."

"Well, all right," he said.

The next time he came to town, he met her at her mother's house. He stood on the porch, carefully unlacing his dirty boots, and moved inside the house as if it were a fancy store and he was afraid he'd break something. He'd brought, ridiculously, flowers for the table and she filled a vase with water, feeling like they were playing a married couple, Early carrying on like a television husband, honey-I'm-home-ing her from the doorway. He'd also brought gifts from his travels: a new purse for her, a bottle of perfume her mother refused to thank him for, and a book for Jude. She had explained to her daughter that Early would come to stay with them.

"All the time?" Jude asked.

"No, not all the time," Desiree said. "Just sometimes. When he's in town."

Her daughter paused, then said, "Well, maybe he shouldn't come here. Maybe we should go with him."

"We can't, baby. He don't even have a real house. That's why we gotta stay here. But he'll come visit and bring you nice things. Wouldn't you like that?"

She knew better, of course. Her daughter only wanted to leave. She'd wanted to leave Mallard since they'd arrived and Desiree, ashamed, kept promising that they would. She couldn't promise Jude that the other children would be kind or eat lunch with her or invite her over to play, so when another birthday party arrived without Jude receiving an invitation, Desiree told her daughter that none of this would matter once they'd left town. Leaving was the only thing she could offer. But, she thought, watching Early and Jude read together on the carpet, maybe staying wasn't the worst thing for Jude. She had family here, at least. She was loved. At night, Desiree held her daughter and told her stories about her own childhood. At first she said, I have a sister named Stella, then, you have an aunt, then, once upon a time, a girl named Stella lived here.

FOR YEARS, Early tracked Stella Vignes until she was no longer Stella Vignes.

She'd been Stella Vignes in New Orleans and Boston, then the trail ran cold—she'd married, he figured, but he couldn't find a marriage license for a Stella Vignes in any place he knew she'd been. So she'd married someplace else. She was still, he assumed, Stella. A new first name was too difficult to get used to. Only a professional con man could assume a completely new identity and Stella was nobody's professional. Why worry about carefulness if you didn't expect anyone to come looking for you? She'd been sloppy enough that he found her apartment in Boston.

"Oh, she was real nice," the landlady said when he called. "Quiet. Worked somewhere downtown. A department store, maybe. Then upped and left. But she was real nice. Never caused no trouble."

He imagined Stella behind a perfume counter, spraying pink bulbs toward ladies passing by, or gift wrapping dolls during Christmas. He'd had one or two dreams where he was chasing her through a Sears and Roebuck, Stella ducking behind dress carousels and shoe racks.

"She have a boyfriend?" he asked.

The landlady grew silent after that, then said she had to go. A colored man asking after a white woman—she'd already said too much. But not enough for Early, who hadn't even found a forwarding address. Stella sprinkled breadcrumbs, which was almost worse than nothing. Almost, because he didn't want to find Stella at all.

There'd been a time in the beginning—at least, he told himself this—when he'd wanted to find her in earnest. Now, looking back, he wasn't so sure. Maybe it had always been Desiree's will, tugging him along. He'd wanted to please her, that was why he'd offered to hunt for Stella in the first place. He wanted to find Stella because Desiree wished her found; those wishes overlapped into a single desire, one that kept him on the trail for years. But Stella did not want to be found, and that desire seemed even stronger. Desiree pulled, then Stella pulled harder. Early, somehow, had been caught between.

Now time had fallen right out of his pockets when he wasn't looking. One morning, he climbed out of Desiree Vignes's bed and found a gray hair in his beard. He spent ten minutes in front of the bath-room mirror, rooting around for others, startled, for the first time, by his own face. He was, he suspected, beginning to look more and more like his own father, which was as unsettling as transforming into a stranger. Then he felt arms around his waist, Desiree pressing against his back.

"You about done starin at yourself?" she asked.

"I found a gray hair," he said. "Look. Right here."

She laughed suddenly. After all those years, he still felt delighted by that laugh, stunned to be caught in its blast.

"Well, I hope you didn't think you'd be young and cute forever," she said, ushering him to the side so that she could brush her teeth. He leaned against the doorway, watching her. Most mornings, she opened Lou's at four, so she was gone by the time he woke up. Then again, most mornings, he woke up someplace other than this bed. He would lie in the backseat of his car or sprawl across the stained mattress in some rundown motel, imagining Desiree's room. The dark wooden walls, the dresser lined with photographs, the calico blue bedspread. Her childhood room, the bed she'd once shared with Stella. Early had learned to sleep on Stella's side, and sometimes, when they made love, he felt shy, like Stella was perched on the dresser, watching.

Desiree splashed water on her face. He wanted to pull her back into bed. There was never enough of her. He could never love her the way he wanted to. Full. A full love would scare her. Each time he re-turned to Mallard, he thought about bringing a ring. Her mother, at least, would finally respect him; she might even begin to think of him like a son. But Desiree never wanted to marry again.

"I've been through all that already," she said, with the same weari-ness of a soldier talking about war.

It had been a war, in a sense, one that she could never win and only hope to survive. She'd told him about all the ways Sam had hurt her:

slamming her face into the door, dragging her by her hair across the bathroom floor, backhanding her mouth, his hand streaked with lipstick and blood. She touched Early's mouth gently, and he kissed her fingertips, trying to reconcile that quiet voice he'd heard over the phone ten years ago with the man she described. She didn't know where Sam lived now, but Early, of course, had traced him already. He lived in Norfolk with his new wife and three boys. Exactly what the world didn't need, three boys growing up to be spiteful men. But he'd never told Desiree this. What good would it do?

"Jude called last night," Desiree said.

"Yeah?" he said. "How she gettin on?"

"You know her. She never tell me much. But I think she good. She likes it out there. She said to tell you hi."

He grunted. Doubtful, thousands of miles away, that she was even thinking about him at all. He only reminded her of the father who wasn't there.

Desiree patted his stomach. "You take a look at that leaking sink, baby?"

At least she asked nice. Not like Adele, who barely looked at him across the table. Called out "chair's wobbly" when she passed him on her way to work. Treated him like a glorified handyman. And maybe he was. He was the man of a house he barely lived in. He was the father to a daughter who didn't even like him.

In the kitchen, he squeezed under the sink, his back aching. Everything was catching up with him now, nights spent sleeping in his car, hours hiding in some crawl space. He wasn't young anymore, not the same young man who'd felt a jolt of energy each time he set out on a new job. Now it was only tiredness, boredom even. He'd hunted every type of man there was. He'd still never found the people he'd searched for the longest.

On the best nights, he settled in Desiree Vignes's bed, rubbing her feet. He watched her brush out her hair, listened to her hum. He shucked off his pants and she climbed in bed in her nightgown, and even then it felt like too many layers—a lie, really, that they were telling themselves—because as soon as she turned out the light, his boxer shorts were around his ankles, her nightgown pushed up to her waist. They tried to be quiet, but after a while, he didn't care about anyone hearing, not when there were too few nights like this. On the road, he tried to remember how to fall asleep alone.

"Gets harder, you know," he told Desiree one night. "More time goes by. Sometimes folks slip up, but—"

"I know," she said. Her skin looked silvery in the moonlight. He rolled toward her, touching her hip. She was so slender, he forgot sometimes, the longer he was away.

"She might come back on her own," he said. "Homesick. Maybe she gets older, figures none of this is worth it."

He reached over, touching Desiree's soft curls. He was so hungry and so full of her, he could hardly stand it. But she rolled away from him.

"It's too late," she said. "Even if she comes back. She's already gone."

In Los Angeles, no one had ever heard of Mallard.

All freshman year, Jude delighted in telling people that her hometown was impossible to find on a map, even though few believed her at first, especially not Reese Carter, who insisted that every town had to be on a map somewhere. He was more skeptical than the Californians who easily believed that some Louisiana town might be too inconsequential to warrant a cartographer's attention. But Reese was a southerner also. He grew up in El Dorado, Arkansas, a place that sounded even more fantastical than her hometown yet still existed on maps. So one April evening, she dragged him to the library and flipped through a giant atlas. They'd just stepped in from the rain, Reese's wet hair looping across his forehead in loose curls. She wanted to push his drooping hair back, but instead, she pointed at a map of Louisiana, below where the Atchafalaya River and the Red River met.

"See," she said. "No Mallard."

"Goddamn," he said. "You're right."

He leaned over her shoulder, squinting. They'd met at a track-and-field party her roommate, Erika, had dragged her to last Halloween. Erika was a stout sprinter from Brooklyn who complained about Los Angeles endlessly, the smoggy air, the traffic, the lack of trains. Her grievances only made Jude realize how grateful she felt. Gratitude only emphasized the depth of your lack, so she tried to hide it. On move-in day, Erika had glanced at Jude's two suitcases and asked, "Where's the rest of your stuff?" Her own desk was cluttered with records, photographs of friends taped to the walls, her closet stuffed with shimmery blouses. Jude, quietly unpacking everything she owned, said that her other things were still in storage. She knew that she liked Erika when she never brought it up again.

On Halloween, Erika draped herself in a sparkly purple dress and tiara, Jude reaching for a lazy pair of cat ears. In the bathroom, she sat on the toilet lid while Erika hunched in front of her, powdering electric blue on her eyelids.

"You know, you could look real pretty if you tried a little," she said.

But the bright blue only made her look darker, so Jude dabbed at her eyes during the whole ride over. Later, Reese would tell her that the blue eyeshadow was the first thing he noticed about her. In the cramped apartment, she'd stumbled after Erika, squeezing past witches and ghosts and mummies. When Erika fished in the ice-filled bathtub for beers, Jude ducked into a doorway, overwhelmed by it all. She'd never been invited to a stranger's party before, and she was so nervous, she didn't even notice, at first, a cowboy sitting on the couch. He was golden brown and handsome, his jaw covered in stubble. He wore a rawhide vest over a blue plaid shirt and faded jeans, a red bandanna tied around his neck. She felt him watching her, and not knowing what else to do, said, "Hi, I'm Jude."

She tugged at the fringe of her skirt, already embarrassed. But the cowboy smiled.

"Hi Jude," he said. "I'm Reese. Have a beer."

She liked how he said it, more of a command than an offer. But she shook her head.

"I don't drink beer," she said. "I mean, I don't like the taste. And it makes me feel slow. I'm a runner."

She was rambling now, but he tilted his head a little.

"Where you from?" he said.

"Louisiana."

"Whereabouts?"

"A little town. You haven't heard of it."

"How you know what I've heard of?"

"Trust me," she said. "I know."

He laughed, then tilted his beer toward her. "You sure you don't want a sip?"

Maybe it was his accent, southern like hers. Maybe his handsomeness. Maybe because, in a room full of people, he'd chosen to talk to her. She took a step toward him, then another and another, until she was standing inside his legs. Then a loud group of boys jostled into the room with a keg, and Reese reached out, pulling her into safety. His hand cupped the back of her knee, and for weeks after, when she thought about that party, she only remembered his fingers lingering at the edge of her skirt.

Now, in the damp library, she flipped through the atlas, past Louisiana to the United States to the world.

"When I was little," she said, "like four or five, I thought this was just a map of our side of the world. Like there was another side of the world on some different map. My daddy told me that was stupid."

He'd brought her to a public library, and when he spun the globe, she knew that he was right. But she watched Reese trace along the map, a part of her still hoping that her father was mistaken, somehow, that there was still more of the world waiting to be found.

Five

On the road from El Dorado, Therese Anne Carter became Reese. He cut his hair in Plano, hacking off inches in a truck stop bathroom with a stolen hunting knife. Outside of Abilene, he bought a blue madras shirt and a leather belt with a silver stallion buckle; the shirt he still wore, the buckle he'd pawned in El Paso when he ran out of money but mentioned wistfully, still feeling its weight hanging at his waist. In Socorro, he began wrapping his chest in a white bandage, and by Las Cruces, he'd learned to walk again, legs wide, shoulders square. He told himself that it was safer to hitchhike this way, but the truth was that he'd always been Reese. By Tucson, it was Therese who felt like a costume. How real was a person if you could shed her in a thousand miles?

In Los Angeles, he found a cleaning job at a gym near UCLA, where he met body builders who told him where to get the good stuff. At Muscle Beach, he lingered on the edge of the crowd as men bulging out of tank tops preened under the afternoon sun. Ask for Thad, someone said, and there he was, a giant of a man, hairless except for his scraggly beard. When Reese finally mustered the nerve, Thad brushed him aside with a big paw.

"Boy, come back with fifty dollars," he said. "Then we got somethin to talk about."

All month he scrimped and saved until he raised the money and found Thad at a bar off the boardwalk. Thad steered him into the men's room and pulled out a vial.

"You ever shot up before?" he asked.

Reese shook his head, staring wide-eyed at the needle. Thad laughed.

"Christ, kid, how old are you?"

"Old enough," Reese said.

"This shit ain't nothin to play with," Thad said. "Make you feel different. Make your baby makers slow. But I guess you ain't worried about none of that yet."

"No sir," Reese said, and Thad showed him what to do. Since then, he'd bought plenty of steroids off plenty of Thads, each time the transaction feeling as grimy as when he'd first stood in that dirty bar bathroom. He met meatheads in dark alleys, felt vials pressed into his palm during handshakes, received nondescript paper bags in his gym locker. Now, seven years later, Therese Anne Carter was only a name on a birth certificate in the offices of Union County Public Records. No one could tell that he'd ever been her, and sometimes, he could hardly believe it either.

He said this matter-of-factly, under the glowing red light of the darkroom, not looking at Jude as he lowered the blank photo into the developer. Weeks after the Halloween party, they'd started meeting here. She hadn't expected to ever see him again, and might not have, if, on the ride home, Erika hadn't mentioned that she'd seen that cute cowboy before, working at the gym nearby. Jude began to run there even though she hated running indoors—no sky, no air, just running in place, staring at her own reflection. She hated every part of it except for when Reese eased up beside her, wiping down a stationary bike. He leaned against the handlebars and said, "Where's your ears?"

She glanced into the mirror, confused, until she realized he was referring to her dull costume. She laughed, surprised he even remembered her from that party. But of course he did. Who on this campus—who in all of Los Angeles—was as dark as her?

"Must have forgot them," she said.

"Too bad," he said. "I liked them."

He wore a slate gray T-shirt, a silver dumbbell emblazoned across his chest. Sometimes, during a shift, he grew bored, hoisting himself onto the bars to do a few pull-ups. He'd applied for the job because he could use the gym for free and the manager didn't care that he had arrived from out of town with no identification. But his real dream was to be a professional photographer. He offered to show her his work sometime, so they started meeting on Saturdays in the campus darkroom. Now, as he watched the photo, she watched him, trying to picture Therese. But she couldn't. She only saw Reese, scruffy face, shirtsleeves rolled up to his elbows, that loop of hair always falling onto his forehead. So handsome that when he glanced up, she couldn't look into his eyes.

"What do you think of all this?" he said.

"I don't know," she said. "I've never heard anything like it."

But that wasn't exactly true. She'd always known that it was possible to be two different people in one lifetime, or maybe it was only possible for some. Maybe others were just stuck with who they were. She'd tried to lighten her skin once, during her first summer in Mallard. She was still young enough then to believe that such a thing was possible, yet old enough to understand that it would require a degree of alchemy that she didn't quite understand. Magic. She wasn't foolish enough to hope that someday she might be light, but a deep brown maybe, anything better than this endless black.

You couldn't force a magic like this but she tried her best to conjure it. She'd seen a Nadinola ad in *Jet*—a caramel woman, dark by Mallard's standards but light by her own, smiling, red-lipped, as a brown man whispered into her ear. *Life is more fun when your complexion is clear, bright, Nadinola-light!* She ripped the ad out of the magazine and folded it into a tiny rectangle, carrying it with her for weeks, opening it so many times that white creases cut across the woman's lips. A jar of cream. That was all she needed. She'd slather it on her skin, and by fall, she would return to school, lighter and new.

But she didn't have the two dollars for the cream and she couldn't ask her mother, who would only scold her. Don't let those kids get to you, she would say, but it was more than her classmates. Jude wanted to change and she didn't see why it should be so hard or why she should have to explain it to anyone. Strangely, she felt that her grandmother might understand, so she handed her the worn ad. Maman stared at it a moment, then passed it back to her.

"There are better ways," she said.

All week, her grandmother created potions. She poured baths with lemon and milk and instructed Jude to soak. She pasted honey masks on her face, then slowly peeled them off. She juiced oranges, mixed them with spices, and applied the mixture to Jude's face before she went to bed. Nothing worked. She never lightened. And at the end of the week, her mother asked why her face looked so greasy, so Jude rose from the dinner table, washed Maman's cream off her face, and that was that.

"I always wanted to be different," she told Reese. "I mean, I grew up in this town where everybody's light and I thought—well, none of it worked."

"Good," he said. "You got beautiful skin."

He glanced at her, but she looked away, staring down at the photo paper as an abandoned building shimmered into view. She hated to be called beautiful. It was the type of thing people only said because they felt they ought to. She thought about Lonnie Goudeau kissing her under the moss trees or inside the stables or behind the Delafosse barn at night. In the dark, you could never be too black. In the dark, everyone was the same color.

BY SPRINGTIME, she spent every weekend with Reese, so inseparable that you began to ask for one if you saw the other. Sometimes she met him downtown, wandering beside him while he shot pictures, his camera bag slung across her shoulder. He taught her the names of different lenses, showed how to hold the reflector to bounce the light. He'd been given his first camera by a man at his church—a local photographer—who'd let him borrow it once to take pictures at the picnic. The man had been so shocked by Reese's raw talent, he gave him an old camera to play around with. Reese spent all of high school with a camera in front of his face, shooting football games and school plays and marching band practice for the yearbook. He snapped dead possums in the middle of the road, sunlight streaking through the clouds, toothless rodeo stars gripping bucking horses. He loved taking pictures of anything but himself. The camera never saw him the way he did.

Now he spent his weekends shooting abandoned buildings shuttered behind wood boards, graffitied bus stops, paint chipping off stripped car husks. Only dead, decaying things. Beauty bored him. Sometimes he snapped pictures of her, always candids, Jude lingering in the background, staring off into space. She didn't realize until she was developing them. She always felt vulnerable seeing herself through his lens. He gave her one photo of herself standing on a boardwalk, and she didn't know what to do with it so she sent it home. On the telephone, her grandmother marveled.

"Finally," she said. "One good picture of you."

In all of her school pictures, she'd either looked too black or over-exposed, invisible except for the whites of her eyes and teeth. The camera, Reese told her once, worked like the human eye. Meaning, it was not created to notice her.

"There you go again," Erika said sleepily, each time Jude slipped out early Saturday morning. "Off to see that fine man of yours."

"He's not my man," Jude said, again and again. Which was techni-cally true. He'd never asked her on a date, escorted her into a restau-rant, pulled out her chair. He didn't kiss her or hold her hand. But didn't he shield her with his jacket when they were caught in a rain-storm, leaving himself dripping wet? Didn't he attend all of her home track meets, cheering during her heat and, after, pulling her into a hug outside the girls' locker room? Didn't she talk to him about her mother and father, Early, even Stella? On the Manhattan Beach pier, she leaned against the turquoise rail while Reese aimed at three fishermen. Biting his lip, the way he always did when he was concentrating.

"What do you think she's like?" he asked.

She fiddled with the strap of his camera bag. "Oh, I don't know," she said. "I used to wonder. Now I don't think I wanna know. I mean, what kind of person just leaves her family behind?"

She realized, all too late, that this was, of course, exactly what Reese had done. He'd shed his family right along with his entire past and now he never talked about them at all. She knew not to ask, even as he wanted to know more about her life. Once, he asked about her first kiss and she told him that a boy named Lonnie had grabbed her outside a barn. She was sixteen then, sneaking out for a late-night run; he was tipsy from a stolen bottle of cherry wine that he'd passed, back and forth, amongst friends all night on the riverbank. She would always wonder if that empty bottle was the only reason he'd kissed her, why he'd even wandered over to her, climbing unsteadily over the fence, as she finished her lap behind the Delafosse barn. She stopped hard, her knee stinging.

"W-what you doin out here?" he'd asked.

Stupidly, she glanced over her shoulder and he laughed. "You," he said. "Ain't nobody here but us." He'd never spoken to her before outside of school. She'd seen him, of course, goofing around with his friends in a back booth at Lou's or hanging out the side of his father's truck. He always ignored her, as if he knew that his teasing was out of place beyond the school halls, or maybe because he realized that ignoring her was even crueler, that she preferred his taunting to the absence of his attention. But she only felt irritated that he'd decided to speak to her now, when she was panting and dirty, her skin misted with sweat.

He told her that he was on his way home, cutting through the Delafosse farm. He tended Miss Delafosse's horses after school. Did she want to see them? They were old as dirt but still pretty. The horses were locked in the stable for the night but he could use his key to get in. She didn't know why she followed him. Maybe because the whole night was unfolding so strangely—Lonnie catching her, Lonnie speaking to her decently—that she had to see where it would end. In the stables, she followed Lonnie blindly, overwhelmed by the smell of manure. Then he stopped, and through the streaming moonlight, she saw two horses, brown and gray, taller than she'd imagined, their powerful bodies sleek with muscles. Lonnie touched the gray one's neck and she slowly touched him too, stroking his soft hair.

"Pretty, huh?" Lonnie said.

"Yes," she said. "Pretty."

"You should see 'em run. R-reminds me of you. You don't run like no person I ever seen. Got a hitch in your gait like a pony."

She laughed. "How you know that?"

"I notice," he said. "I notice everything."

Then the brown horse stamped his hoof, spooking the gray horse, and Lonnie pulled her out of the stable before Miss Delafosse's light flickered on. They skittered behind the barn, laughing at the nearness of getting caught, then Lonnie leaned in and kissed her. Around them, the night hung heavy and damp like soaked cotton. She tasted the sugar off his lips.

"JUST LIKE THAT?" Reese said.

"Just like that."

"Well, goddamn."

They were standing on the rooftop of his friend Barry's apartment. Earlier that night, Barry had performed as Bianca at a club in West Hollywood called Mirage. For seven electrifying minutes, Bianca strutted onstage, a purple boa wrapped around her broad shoulders, and belted out "Dim All the Lights." She wore ruby red lipstick and a big blonde wig like Dolly Parton.

"It's not enough to be a woman," Reese had joked during the show. "He's gotta be a white woman too."

Barry's apartment was lined with wig heads covered in hair of every color, realistic and garish: a brown bob, a black pageboy, a straight Cher cut dyed pink, the bangs slicing across the forehead. At first, she'd thought that Barry might be like Reese, but then she arrived at his apartment to find him wearing a polo shirt and slacks, scratching his bearded cheek. During the week, he taught high school chemistry in Santa Monica; he only became Bianca two Saturdays a month in a tiny dark club off Sunset. Otherwise, he was a tall, bald man who looked nothing like a woman, which was part of the delight, she realized, watching the enraptured crowd. It was fun because everyone knew that it was not real.

Downstairs, the apartment was loud and hot, a new Thelma Houston record radiating out the windows. The girls had come over. The girls, Barry always said, when he meant the other men who performed alongside him at his drag nights. By spring, Jude had been to enough of Barry's parties to know what everyone looked like without makeup: Luis, who sang Celia Cruz in pink fur, was an accountant; Jamie, who wore a Supremes wig and go-go boots, worked for the power company; Harley transformed himself into Bette Midler—he was a costume designer for a minor theater company and helped the others find their wigs. The girls took Jude in until she felt, almost, like one of them. She'd never belonged to a group of friends before. And they'd only accepted her because of Reese.

"What about you?" she said. "Who was your first kiss?"

He leaned against the railing, lighting up a joint. "It's not that interesting."

"So? It doesn't have to be."

"Just this girl from church," he said. "She was friends with my sister. It was before."

Before he was Reese, he meant. He never talked about Before. She didn't even know that he had a sister.

"What was she like?" she asked. His sister, the girl he'd kissed. Therese. It didn't matter, she just wanted to understand his old life. She wanted him to trust her with it.

"I don't remember," he said. "So what happened to the horse boy?" He smirked, offering her the joint. He sounded almost jealous, or maybe she just wanted him to.

"Nothing," she said. "We kissed a few times but we didn't talk after that."

She was too ashamed to tell him the truth: that she'd spent weeks meeting Lonnie in the stables at night. In the dark corner, he'd spread a blanket, prop up a flashlight, call it their secret hideaway. It was too dangerous, meeting in the middle of the day. What if someone saw them? At night, nobody would catch them. They could be truly alone. Didn't she want that?

He wasn't her boyfriend. A boyfriend would hold her hand, ask about her day. But in the stables, he only touched her, palming her breasts, slipping his fingers up her shorts. In the stables, she swallowed him dripping into her mouth, breathing manure through her nose. But around town, he looked right past her. And yet, she would have kept meeting him each night if she hadn't been caught by Early. Early hearing her creep out one night, tracking her through the woods, banging on the door until Lonnie, yanking frantically at his pants, shoved her outside. She was crying before she even stepped through the doorway. Early hooked a hand around her arm, unable to look at her.

"What's the matter with you?" he said. "You want a boyfriend, you tell him to come by the house. You don't go off meetin no boy in the middle of the night."

"He won't talk to me nowhere else," she said.

She started crying harder, her shoulders shaking, and Early pulled her into his chest. He hadn't held her like that in years; she hadn't wanted him to. He wasn't her father and never would be, a man whose violence had not yet reached her, whose anger pointed everywhere but at her. Her father made her feel special, and she hadn't felt that way until Lonnie kissed her behind the barn.

He wasn't her boyfriend. She'd never been foolish enough to think that he might be. But she couldn't imagine any boy loving her; it was enough that Lonnie noticed her at all.

A breeze drifted past and she shivered, hugging herself. Reese touched her elbow.

"You cold, baby?" he said.

She nodded, hoping that he might wrap his arm around her. But he offered his jacket instead.

"I DON'T UNDERSTAND IT," Barry said. "It's like a sexless marriage."

Backstage at Mirage, he perched in front of the vanity mirror, swiping blush across his cheeks. It was an hour before the show, and soon, the dressing room would be crowded with queens jostling in front of the mirrors, swapping eyeshadow, the air clouded with hairspray. But now, Mirage was dark and quiet, and she sat on the floor watching Barry, a chemistry textbook balanced on her knees. They had an arrangement. He helped with her chemistry homework and she joined him at the Fox Hills Mall, where she pretended to buy the makeup he wanted. He guided her down the aisles, her arm looped through his; to strangers, they might have passed as lovers, a tall man in gray slacks, a young woman reaching for face powder. When he paid for everything at the counter, the clerks thought he was a gentleman. No one imagined his bathroom counter covered in tiny bottles of scented lotions, palettes of eye shadow, gold tubes of lipstick. Or that the girl at his side had no interest in any of this, despite his plea to teach her how to wear makeup. She doubted that she would find any shade to match her skin and besides, she knew what people called dark girls wearing red lipstick. Baboon ass.

No, she had no interest in sorting through Barry's bottles and tubes, which seemed as mysterious to her as the test tubes in her chemistry lab. Weeks into the semester and she was already falling behind. Barry had only agreed to tutor her because Reese asked him to, and he could never tell Reese no. When they'd first met seven years ago at a disco, he thought that Reese was gorgeous and, after too many drinks, finally worked up the nerve to tell him so.

"What did you say?" she asked.

"What do you think?" he said. "I invited him home! And you know what he told me? 'No thank you.'" Barry laughed. "Can you believe it? He said no thank you, like I was offering him a cup of coffee. Oh, I always like those country boys. Country and sweet, that's exactly how I like 'em."

She tried to imagine being so bold, walking up to Reese and telling him what? That she thought about him relentlessly, even now, while she was staring at a textbook filled with confusing symbols and talking to a man applying lipstick?

"We're friends," she said. "What's so wrong with that?"

"Nothing's *wrong* with it." He glanced at her through the mirror. He was trying a new look—classic Hollywood, Lana Turner—but the blush was too pink, tinting his skin orange. "I've just never seen Reese with no friend like you."

Once, carrying her groceries up the stairs, Reese had joked that he sometimes felt like her boyfriend, and she'd laughed, unsure of what was funny. That he wasn't? That he would never be? That in spite of this, he had, somehow, found himself playing this role? What she didn't say: she felt like his girlfriend sometimes too, and the feeling scared her. A big feeling. It took up all the space in her chest, choking her.

"We're friends," she said again. "I don't know why you can't see that."

"I don't know why you can't see that you're not." He sighed, turning to face her. One cheek was covered in full makeup, the other half of his face still clean. "I don't know why you're fighting it neither.

What could be better than being eighteen and in love? Oh, you don't
even know. If I could go back, I'd do everything different."

"Like what?" she said.

"Oh, everything." He turned back to the mirror. "This big ol'
world and we only get to go through it once. The saddest thing there
is, you ask me."

THAT SUMMER, she moved out of the dormitories and into Reese's
apartment.

She gave herself a list of logistical reasons why it made sense: she
was working on campus, which was the obvious choice even though
she hated how disappointed her mother had sounded when she told
her she wasn't coming home. She hadn't found an apartment yet for
next year and she could save money, splitting rent and groceries. She
could make a foolish decision if she pretended it was based on thrift
alone. So when Reese asked, she said yes, and soon, the two were carrying her boxes up the narrow stairwell. Reese told her that he would
sleep on the couch.

"Trust me, I've slept worse places," he said, and she thought of
him hitchhiking from Arkansas. Sleeping at truck stops or squatting
in abandoned buildings like the ones he'd photographed, over and
over again.

At first, she felt strange in Reese's apartment, like a guest overstay-
ing her welcome. Then she started to feel at home. Tiptoeing through
the living room on her way out to her morning run, Reese curled
under a blanket, hair falling in front of his closed eyes. Sharing a
bathroom counter, running a finger along the handle of his razor.
Returning in the evening to find him boiling hot dogs for dinner, or
ironing his shirts along with her own, or listening to records with him

on the couch, her foot pressed against his thigh. He taught her how to drive, surprisingly patient as she slowly guided his creaking Bobcat around an empty mall parking lot.

"You know how to drive, you can go anywhere," he told her. "You get tired of this city, you just head off for another one."

He smiled over at her, an arm hanging out the window, as she made another slow lap. He made it sound so easy, leaving.

"I'll never get tired of this city," she said.

During the week, she reported to her job at the music library, where she pushed a heavy cart down the aisles and slid thin scores onto the shelves until her fingers dried from touching their dusty covers. When she returned home, West Hollywood felt so different from that idyllic campus, the brick buildings she still felt cowed to enter, always lowering her voice as if stepping inside church, those endless green lawns, the bicycles constantly whisking past. In the dormitories, she'd been surrounded by the relentlessly ambitious, but in that West Hollywood apartment building, all of the neighbors she met were people whose dreams of fame had already been dashed. Cinematographers working at Kodak stores, screenwriters teaching English to immigrants, actors starring in burlesque shows in seedy bars. The people who did not make it were ingrained in the city; you walked on stars emblazoned with their names and never realized it.

On the weekends, she and Reese wandered Santa Barbara beaches, or explored the National History Museum, and even once went whale watching in Long Beach. They'd only seen dolphins, but what she remembered was how she'd lost her balance on the deck and he stepped behind to steady her. She stood like that for the rest of the boat ride, leaning back against his chest.

Some Saturday nights, they passed under the cascade of rainbow flags and ducked inside Mirage to catch Barry's show. Other times, they saw a movie at the Cinerama Dome, where, in the darkness of the theater, she thought Reese might reach for her hand. But he never did. At Barry's Fourth of July party, everyone crowded on his rooftop, watching fireworks crackle across the sky. All around them, boys drunk and kissing, and she thought Reese might even kiss her—a friendly kiss, right on her cheek. But instead, he stepped inside to get a drink, leaving her alone washed under red and blue light. What did he want from her? It was impossible to tell. Once after Barry's show at Mirage, Reese asked her to dance. The night was nearly over; the DJ had already started playing slow songs to usher lovers out the door. He held out his hand and she allowed him to guide her onto the dance floor. She'd never been held so closely by anyone before.

"I love this song," she said.

"I know," he said. "I hear you singin it."

She wasn't drunk but she felt lightheaded, swept up in Smokey Robinson's voice, Reese's arms around her. Then the lights flipped on rudely, all the couples groaning, and Reese let her go. She hadn't realized until then how depressing Mirage looked with the lights on: the exposed pipes, peeling paint, wood floors sticky with beer. And Reese, laughing as their friends drifted toward the door, as if dancing with her had been as casual as helping her into a jacket. Somehow she felt closer to him and further away than ever.

Then one evening in July, she came home early from work and found Reese shirtless through the open bathroom door. His chest was wrapped in a large bandage, but there were red bruises peeking out, and he was gingerly feeling his ribcage. Her first thought was her stupidest thought: someone had attacked him. When he glanced up, their eyes met in the mirror, and he quickly yanked on his shirt.

"Don't creep up on me like that," he said.

"What happened?" she said. "That bruise—"

"Looks worse than it feels," he said. "I'm used to it."

She slowly realized what he was trying to tell her: that no one had attacked him, that it was the bandage he wore that was digging into his ribcage, bruising him.

"You should take that thing off," she said. "If it hurts you. You don't have to wear it here. I don't care what you look like."

She thought he might be relieved, but instead, a dark and unfamiliar look passed across his face.

"It's not about you," he said, then he slammed the bathroom door shut. The whole apartment shook, and she trembled, dropping her keys. He had never yelled at her before.

She left without thinking. She had never seen him so angry. He swore at bad drivers, he griped about his co-workers, he shoved a white man in a bar once who kept calling her darky. His anger flared and waned and then he was back to himself again. But this time he was angry at her. She shouldn't have looked at him—she should have turned as soon as she saw him through the open door. But the bruises shocked her and then she'd said something so idiotic and now she couldn't even apologize because he was angry. He'd slammed a door, not her face, but maybe that was out of convenience. Maybe, if she had been closer, he would have slammed her against the wall just as easily.

She was crying by the time she reached Barry's. He just pulled her into a hug.

"He hates me," she said. "I did this stupid thing and now he hates me—"

"He doesn't hate you," Barry said. "Come sit down. It's gonna be all right in the morning."

IT WAS NO BIG DEAL, Barry said. Just a little fight.

But all her life, she would hate when people called arguments fights. Fights were bloody events, punctured skin, bruised eye sockets, broken bones. Not disagreements over where to go to dinner. Never words. A fight was not a man's voice raised in anger, although it would always make her think of her father. She would wince a little when she heard raucous men leaving bars or boys screaming at televisions during football games. The sound of slamming doors. Broken plates. Her father had punched walls, he smashed dishes, and even once his own eyeglasses, hurling them across the living room at the door. To be so angry that you'd make yourself blind. Strange, and yet so normal to her then in a way she wouldn't fully realize until she was older.

She spent the night on Barry's couch, staring up at the ceiling. At half past three, she heard a knock on the door. Through the peephole, she found Reese under the glowing porch light. He was breathing hard, his fists balled in the pockets of his jean jacket, and he started to knock again when she finally unlatched the deadbolt.

"You're gonna wake everyone up," she whispered.

"I'm sorry," he said. His breath smelled sweet like beer.

"You're drunk," she said, more surprised than anything. She'd never known him to disappear into a bar when he was upset, but here he was now, swaying on his feet.

"I shouldn't have hollered at you like that," he said. "I didn't mean to—goddamnit, you know I wouldn't hurt you. You know that, don't you, baby?"

You could never know who might hurt you until it was too late. But he sounded desperate, pleading with her from the step, and she cracked the door a little more.

"There's this doctor," he said. "Luis told me about him. You gotta pay him upfront for the surgery but I been savin up."

"What surgery?" she said.

"For my chest. Then I won't have to wear this damn thing at all."

"But is it safe?"

119

"Safe enough," he said.

She stared at the shallow rise and fall of his chest.

"I'm sorry too," she said. "I just don't want you to hurt. I didn't mean—oh, I don't even know. I wasn't trying to act like I'm somebody special."

"Don't say that," he said.

"Say what?"

He was quiet a moment, then he leaned in and kissed her. By the time she realized it, he was already pulling away.

"That you're not special to me," he said.

IN THE MORNING, she wandered through the bright campus, dazed. She hadn't slept a second after Reese departed down the darkened sidewalk. Even now, thinking about him, her stomach twisted with dread. Maybe he'd been so drunk he wouldn't even remember kissing her. He'd awakened at home, vaguely recalling that he had done something embarrassing. Or maybe he'd sobered up and regretted it. She was the type of girl that boys only kissed in secret and, after, pretended that they hadn't.

That night, the girls threw a party. In Harley's crowded living room, she squeezed onto the windowsill, nursing a rum and Coke. She wasn't in a partying mood but she still felt too embarrassed to go home and face Reese; of course, he then arrived at the party, wearing a black T-shirt and jeans, his hair still wet from the shower. He'd waved to her when he first walked in but he didn't come over to say hello. Maybe he pitied her. He'd only kissed her because he felt so bad about yelling at her. He knew that she hoped that kiss meant more so he was avoiding her, standing so far on the other side of the room that Harley asked what was wrong.

"Nothing," she said, tilting more rum into her cup.

"Then why're you both acting so damn funny?" he said.

He had blond feathered bangs like Farrah Fawcett that he kept sweeping out of his eyes. She shrugged, staring out the window. She couldn't continue like this, pretending that everything was normal. She needed air. But the room suddenly fell into complete darkness. The music cut off, the silence as jarring as the black. Then voices ringing out, Barry asking where to find a flashlight, Harley offering that there might be candles in the bathroom, and Luis, leaning over by the window, calling everyone over. All around the block, all the other buildings descended into darkness too.

She said that she would look for candles and groped her way down the dark hallway toward the bathroom when Reese grabbed her hand.

"It's me," he said.

"I know," she said.

In the dark, you could be anybody, but she knew him before he even spoke. His cologne, his rough palms. She could find him in any darkened room.

"I can't see shit," he said, laughing a little.

"Well, I'm trying to find the candles."

"Wait. Can we just talk?"

"We don't have to talk," she said. "I know you don't like me. Not like that. And it's okay. We just don't have to talk about it."

He dropped her hand. At least she didn't have to look at him. Maybe she would never find the candles and she wouldn't have to see his face. She inched farther down the hall, finally feeling the tile on the bathroom wall, but when she opened the medicine cabinet, Reese pressed it shut. Then he was kissing her against the bathroom sink.

Down the hall, their friends were gamely calling each other's names, laughing at their own blindness. But in the bathroom, they were kissing desperately, as if both knew that the moment couldn't possibly last. The lights would flicker on, someone would come searching for them, they would wrench apart at the sound of footsteps, guilty, caught. But by the time Barry returned from the kitchen, triumphantly waving a flashlight, they'd already slipped out the door. They felt their way down the stairwell until they emerged on the sidewalk, still holding hands, fading into the blackened city. Overhead, traffic lights blinked uselessly. Cars crept along the street. The skyline above them disappeared, and for the first time in nearly a year, she saw stars.

Somewhere, across the vast city, a grandmother listened to children tell ghost stories in front of the black television screen. A man sat on his porch, petting a dog's graying muzzle. A dark-haired woman lit a candle in her kitchen, staring out at her swimming pool. A young man and young woman walked home, climbing the silent steps, shutting the door on the rest of the city. She held his lighter as he searched the cabinets for candles. He couldn't find any and they both felt relieved. She wasn't afraid of the dark; he felt safer inside it.

In bed, he tugged off her shirt, kissing down her neck to her breasts. Only once he was kissing between her thighs did she realize that he hadn't undressed at all.

All over the city, couples doing what they were doing. Teenagers kissing on blankets at a beach, the ocean rolling in black. Newlyweds fumbling in a hotel room. A man whispering into his lover's ear. A woman holding a match to a slender candle, her face glowing off the kitchen window. Across the city, darkness and light.

Six

There's something different about you," Desiree Vignes told her daughter over the phone.

By late August, a heat wave had rolled through Los Angeles, and even with all the windows open, you couldn't catch a breeze. Outside, the pavement shimmered like a pond. Big brown crickets searched the pipes for water, and every morning, Jude always found one or two in the shower; she grew so paranoid that they would blend into the beige carpet that she refused to walk around barefoot. The heat was maddening but life could be worse, she thought, watching Reese slide an ice cube between his lips. He was wearing blue swim trunks and a black T-shirt, his collarbone glistening with sweat. She twirled the phone cord around her finger.

"Ma'am?" she said.

"Oh, don't ma'am me. You heard what I said. There's somethin different. I can hear it in your voice."

"Mama, there's nothing wrong with my voice."

"Not wrong. Different. You think I can't tell?"

They were meeting the girls at Venice Beach; she'd just started packing a picnic basket when the phone rang. She hadn't called home

in a month, so she felt too guilty to ask to talk later, but now she regretted answering. What did her mother mean, different? And how could
she even tell? Jude hated the idea of being so transparent to anyone,
even her own mother. Then again, hadn't Barry noticed right away?
Two days after the blackout, she'd met him by the fountain outside
the May Company and before she'd even walked over, he was suspicious, squinting at her.

"What happened?" he demanded. "Why do you look like that?"

"Like what?" she said, laughing.

Then it dawned on him. "You didn't," he whispered. "Oh, I can't
believe you! You sat right there on my couch and told me you had
some big fight—"

"We did! I mean, nothing had happened then, I swear—"

"Why didn't you tell me?" he said. "I don't know why neither of
you called me."

But after the blackout, she hadn't told anyone. She wasn't even sure
how to explain what had happened between her and Reese. One night
they'd been friends, the next lovers. He'd left for work by the time she
awoke in the morning. She'd reached across the wrinkled sheets, still
warm from his body. In the light of day, the previous night seemed
like a fever dream. But those still-warm sheets. Her panties on the
floor. His cologne on the pillow. She rolled over, burying her face in
the smell of him. All day, she imagined how he would tell her that the
previous night had been a mistake, but he climbed into her bed that
night and kissed the back of her neck.

"What're we doing?" she said.

"I'm kissing you," he said.

"You know what I mean."

She rolled over to face him. He was smiling, playing with the
fringe of her T-shirt.

"Do you want me to go?" he said.

"Do you?"

"Hell no, baby."

He kissed her neck again. When he tugged off her pajamas, she reached for his belt and he squirmed away.

"Don't," he said softly, and she froze, not knowing what to do. Lonnie had never been shy about what he'd wanted. Shoving her hand down his boxers, pushing her face toward his lap. But there were rules to loving Reese and over time, she learned them. Lights off. No undressing him. She could touch his stomach or arms but never his chest, his thighs but not between them. She wanted to touch him as freely as he touched her but she never complained. How could she? Not now, not when she was so happy Barry noticed it radiating off her from across a shopping mall, so happy that her mother could even hear it through the phone.

At the beach, she sat on her towel, watching Barry and Luis and Harley splash around in the water. They'd been stuck in traffic for an hour, slowly creeping toward the coast; when they finally arrived at Venice, the girls shucked their shirts, tossing them in a careless pile, and ran yelping toward the shore. Reese rested his head in her lap, watching as they dipped into the water, slick under the sunlight. She raked her fingers through his hair.

"Don't you want to swim?" she said.

He smiled, squinting up at her. "Maybe later," he said. "Aren't you gonna get in?"

She told him that she didn't like to swim. But she'd loved going to the city pool in D.C. In Mallard, she never dared to swim in the river—imagine showing so much of yourself. She wasn't in Mallard anymore, but somehow, the town wouldn't leave her. Even now at Venice Beach, she pictured sunbathers laughing as soon as she tugged off her shirt. Snickering at Reese, too, wondering what on earth is he doing with that black thing?

That night, when they came home from the beach, Reese slid on top of her and she asked if she could flip on the light. He laughed a little, burrowing his face into her neck.

"Why?" he murmured.

"Because," she said, "I want to see you."

He stilled for a moment, then he rolled off her.

"Well, I don't want you to," he said.

For the first time in weeks, he slept on the couch. He came back to bed the next night but she still remembered the loneliness of sleeping without him, only a wall apart. Sometimes she felt as if that wall had never quite fallen. She never felt what she wanted to feel, his skin on hers.

"I'm seeing someone," she told her mother the next time she called.

Her mother laughed. "Of course you are," she said. "I don't know why you think I don't know anything."

"He's . . ." Jude paused. "He's nice, Mama. He's so sweet to me. But he's not like other boys."

"What you mean?"

She thought, for a second, about telling her mother Reese's story. Instead, she just said, "He keeps me out."

"Well," her mother said, "I'm sorry to tell you but he's just like other boys. Exactly like all the rest of 'em."

The door unlocked, and Reese shuffled inside, tossing his jacket on the back of the chair. He smiled as he walked past, reaching over to stroke her ankle.

"Jude?" her mother said. "You still there?"

"Yes ma'am," she said. "I'm here."

A JOB. She would find a new job.

The answer seemed so simple once it arrived one night as she watched Reese climb out of bed in his sweaty T-shirt. He wanted a new chest. Carried in his wallet a worn business card from Dr. Jim Cloud, a plastic surgeon with an office on Wilshire. Dr. Cloud, a patron at Mirage, had worked on friends of friends, but his price was steep. Three thousand dollars cash up front. Fair, if you thought about the risks he was incurring even performing such procedures. The medical board could revoke his license, shutter his practice, call for his arrest. The shadiness unnerved Jude, although Reese insisted the doctor was legit. Still, she'd done the math, unfurling the faded gray sock in his drawer and dumping the crumpled bills onto the bedspread. Two hundred dollars. He would never save enough by himself.

"I need a new job," she told Barry.

Autumn had arrived, along with the Santa Ana winds. At night, angry hot gusts rattled their windowpanes. They were celebrating Barry's thirtieth birthday, everyone crowded in his apartment.

Barry shrugged, running a hand over his shaven head.

"Well, don't look at me," he said. He was on his third martini and already fresh. "I need a new job too. Those white people don't hardly pay me as it is."

"You know what I mean," she said. "A real job. One that pays real money."

"I wish I could help, sweet thing, but I don't know nobody who's hiring. Well, my cousin Scooter drives a catering van but you don't wanna do nothing like that, do you?"

Scooter picked her up the next afternoon in an old silver van that read, in peeling purple cursive, CARLA'S CATERING. Inside, the van was crumbling, a chunk of yellow foam gaping from the passenger's seat, the roof cloth hanging like a canopy, a faded air freshener dangling from the rearview mirror. Not much to look at, but the fridge worked, Scooter said, thumbing at the wall separating the cooled food. He was lanky like Barry but yellower, wearing a purple Lakers cap.

"Let me tell you," he said, "don't believe none of what you hear about the economy and all that. It don't matter one bit. White folks always wanna throw a party."

He laughed, the van lurching onto Fairfax, and she quickly reached for her seat belt. He drove with an arm hanging out the window, chatting amiably the whole time, always starting midway into a conversation as if he were responding to a question she hadn't actually asked.

"Yeah, I had my own spot once," he said. "Nice little joint, off Crenshaw. But I couldn't hang it. Never been all that good with money, you know. I get a penny, I spend a penny, you know how that go. I was good with the food but I ain't no businessman, that's for sure. But it turned out all right. Now I'm Carla's right-hand man."

Carla Stewart, he explained, as they crawled along the Pacific Coast Highway toward Malibu, was tough but fair. You had to be both if you were a woman in the food world. She'd built the catering company after her husband died. A smart business in a city where there was never a shortage of people wanting to host events while exerting as little effort as possible. He tossed a black polo shirt onto her lap.

"You gotta put this on," he said. When she hesitated, he laughed. "Not now, when we get inside! I ain't no pervert. Don't worry, Barry said you like a little sister to him and he better not hear I tried to flirt with you or nothin."

It was the nicest thing Barry had ever said about her, and of course, he never intended her to hear it.

"Barry's funny," she said.

"He is," Scooter said. "He's a funny boy, but I love him. I love him all the same."

Did Scooter know about Bianca? Barry prided himself on his

ability to keep his lives separate. "It's like the Good Book says," he told her once, "don't let your right hand know what your left hand is doing." He was Bianca on two Saturday nights a month, and otherwise, he pushed her out of sight, even though he thought about her, shopped for her, planned for her eventual return. Barry went to faculty meetings and family reunions and church, Bianca always lingering on the edge of his mind. She had her role to play and Barry had his. You could live a life this way, split. As long as you knew who was in charge.

"WHERE YOU BEEN?" Reese asked when she climbed into bed that night.

He sounded worried; she never stayed out late without calling. But she'd catered a party for a real estate agent who'd sold homes to Burt Reynolds and Raquel Welch. She'd wandered through the house, admiring the long white couches and marble countertops and the giant glass windows that faded into a view of the beach. She couldn't imagine living like this—hanging on a cliff, exposed by glass. But maybe the rich didn't feel a need to hide. Maybe wealth was the freedom to reveal yourself.

The party had ended at one and she'd had to clean up after. By the time Scooter dropped her back off, the morning sky was tinting lavender.

"Malibu," she said.

"What you doin all the way out there?"

"I got a new job," she said. "With this catering company. Barry helped me find it."

"Why?" he said. "I thought you said you were gonna focus on school."

She couldn't tell him the real reason; he didn't even like her to pay for dinner, always reaching for his wallet as soon as the check came. He would never agree to let her pay for an expensive surgery. And what if he misunderstood? What if he thought she wanted him to have the surgery because she wanted him to change? She could never tell him, not until she'd saved so much money that he would be foolish to refuse it. She slid into the crook of his arm, touching his face.

"I just thought it'd be nice to have some extra cash," she said, "that's all."

THAT SEMESTER, she thought of bodies.

Once a week, she sat on the edge of the bathtub, holding a hypodermic needle while Reese rolled up his plaid boxers. On the counter, a glass vial filled with a liquid that was yellowy clear like chardonnay. He still hated needles; he never looked when she flicked the tip before squeezing the fat part of his thigh. Okay, she always whispered after, sorry that she'd hurt him.

Each month, he paid out of pocket for a vial small enough to fit in his palm. She barely understood how hormones worked, so on a whim, she enrolled in an anatomy class that she enjoyed far more than she'd expected. The rote memorization that bored the rest of the class thrilled her. She left flash cards labeled with body parts strewn all over the apartment: *phalanges* by the bathroom sink, *deltoids* on the kitchen table, *dorsal metacarpal veins* squeezed between couch cushions.

Her favorite organ was the heart. She was the first person in her class to properly dissect the sheep heart. It was the most difficult dissection, the professor said, because the heart isn't perfectly symmetrical but so close to it that you cannot tell which side is which. You have to orient the heart correctly to find the vessels.

"You really must experience the heart with your hands," he told the class. "I know it's slippery but don't be shy. You have to use your fingers to feel your way through the dissection."

At night, she placed her flash cards on Reese to quiz herself. He stretched out on the couch, reading a novel, trying to remain still while she propped a card against his arm. She traced a finger along his biceps, chanting the Latin terms to herself quietly until he tugged her into his lap. Skin tissue and muscles and nerves, bone and blood. A body could be labeled but a person couldn't, and the difference between the two depended on that muscle in your chest. That beloved organ, not sentient, not aware, not feeling, just pumping along, keeping you alive.

IN PACIFIC PALISADES, she carried platters of bacon-wrapped dates around a mixer for booking agents. In Studio City, she served cocktails at the birthday party of an aging game-show host. In Silver Lake, a guitarist hovered over her shoulder to ensure that the crab salad was made from real crab, not imitation. By the end of her first month, she could pour a martini without measuring. At the laundromat, she found crushed water crackers in her pockets. She could never wash the smell of olives off her hands.

"Why don't you see if the library's hiring again?" Reese said.

"Why?"

"Because you're always gone. I barely see you anymore."

"I'm not gone that much."

"Too much for me."

"It's better money, baby," she said, wrapping her arms around him.

"And I get to see the city. More fun than being stuck in some old library all day."

She worked jobs from Ventura to Huntington Beach, Pasadena to Bel Air. In Santa Monica, she carried a tray of oysters through the home of a record producer, pausing in the foyer to admire the pool that spilled endlessly toward the skyline. From here, Mallard felt farther away than ever. Maybe, in time, she would forget it. Push it away, bury it deep inside herself, until she only thought of it as a place she'd heard about, not a place where she'd once lived.

"I just don't like it," her mother told her. "You oughta be focusin on your studies, not servin white folks. I didn't send you all the way to California to do that."

But it wasn't the same, not really. She wasn't her grandmother, cleaning after the same family for years. She didn't wipe the snotty noses of children, she didn't listen to wives complain about cheating husbands as she mopped the floor, she didn't take in laundry until her home crowded with other people's dirty underwear. There was no intimacy here. She swept through their parties, carrying trays of food, and never saw them again.

Late one night, she lay in bed holding Reese, too hot to fall asleep so close to him but unable to let go.

"What you thinkin about?" he asked.

"Oh, I don't know," she said. "Just this house in Venice. You know they had centralized air? And didn't even need it. So close to the beach, they could just crack open a window and cool down. But I guess that's how rich folks are."

He laughed and then climbed out of bed to bring her a cup of ice. He slipped a cube through her lips and she swirled the ice around her mouth, surprised by how normal this all felt. Months ago, she couldn't even admit that she had a crush on Reese, and now she was lying naked in his bed, chewing ice. She peeked through the blinds at a police helicopter whirring overhead and turned back to find him staring.

"What?" she said, laughing. "Stop that."

He was still wearing a T-shirt and boxers, and she suddenly felt self-conscious, tugging the sheet over her breasts.

"Stop what?" he said.

"Looking at me like that."

"But I like looking at you."

"Why?"

"Because," he said, "you're nice to look at."

She scoffed, turning back to the window. He didn't mind that she was dark, maybe, but he couldn't possibly like it. Nobody could.

"I hate when you do that," he said.

"What?"

"Act like I'm lying," he said. "I ain't those people back home. Sometimes you act like you're still back there. But you're not, baby. We're new people here."

He'd told her once that California got its name from a dark-skinned queen. He'd seen a mural of her in San Francisco. She hadn't believed him until he showed her a photograph he'd taken and there the dark queen was, seated at the top of the ceiling. Flanked by a tribe of female warriors, looking so regal and imposing that Jude was heartbroken to discover that she wasn't even real. She was a character from a popular Spanish novel, an art history book said, about a fictional island ruled by a black Amazon queen. Like all colonizers, the conquistadors wrote their fiction into reality, their myths transforming into history. What remained was California, a place that still felt like a mythical island. She was in the middle of the ocean, sealed away from everyone she'd once known, floating.

———————

PERHAPS THE STRANGEST part of that fall was that she started to dream about her father.

Sometimes she was walking beside him along the street, holding his hand as they passed through a busy intersection; she jolted awake as the cars whizzed past. Other times, he was pushing her on a playground swing, her legs stretching in front of her. In one dream, he was walking in front of her on a track, and she ran to catch up but could never reach him. She awoke, gasping.

"You're shaking," Reese whispered, pulling her closer.

"It was just a dream," she said.

"About what?"

"My daddy." She paused. "I don't even know why. We haven't talked in so long. I used to think he'd come looking for me. He's not even a good man. But part of me still wants him to find me. Isn't that stupid?"

"No." He was staring up at the ceiling. "It's not stupid at all. I ain't talk to my folks in seven years but I still think about them. My mama used to like my pictures. She showed everybody in church. I took so many photos of her but I left them behind. I left everything."

"What happened?" she said. "I mean, why'd you leave?"

"Oh, it's a long story."

"Then tell me some of it. Please."

He was quiet a long moment, then he told her that his father had caught him fooling around with his sister's friend. He'd been home alone, pretending to be sick while his family went to a tent revival, rifling instead through his father's closet. He tried on crisp dress shirts, practiced Windsor knots, walked around in slick leather wingtips. He had just splashed himself with cologne when Tina Jenkins appeared on the lawn and tapped on the windowpane. What was he doing? Was he in some type of play? His costume wasn't bad, he just needed to do something with his hair. She'd pinned his ponytail to the back of his neck.

"There," she said. "Now you look more mannish, see? What's the play? And do you have anything to drink?"

He ignored the first question and tended to the second. Later, Tina would tell her parents that the gin made her do it. The gin that he'd poured in two big glasses, replacing his mother's Seagram with water. She did not tell her parents that she'd kissed him first, or that they'd only stopped because his family had come home early.

"My daddy had one of those belts with the big silver buckle," he said. "He told me if I wanted to be a man, he'd treat me like one."

She clenched her eyes.

"I'm so sorry," she said.

"Long time ago."

"I don't care," she said. "It wasn't right. He had no right to do that to you—"

"I used to think about drivin down to El Dorado," he said. "Tell him to try me now. It ain't right to feel that way about your own daddy. Chokes me, like I can't even breathe through it. Then other times, I think about just walkin around town. No one recognizin me. It'd be like showin up to your own funeral. Just watchin life go on without you. Maybe I knock on the door. Say, Hi Mama, but she'd know already. Even though I look different, she'd still know me."

"You could do it," she said. "You could go back."

"Would you go with me?"

"I'd go anywhere with you," she said.

He kissed her, pushing up her shirt, and she reached unthinkingly for his. He stiffened, and she shrank when he pulled away. But he disappeared into the bathroom, and when he came back out, he was shirtless, bending over her in the bandage wrapped around his chest.

"I need it," he said.

"Okay," she said. "Okay."

She pulled him on top of her, her fingers trailing up his smooth back, touching skin and skin and cotton.

FROM THE BEGINNING, Reese Carter had thought about the end.

Like when he'd first arrived in Los Angeles—homeless, shorn like a baby lamb, already imagining himself leaving a city that would certainly destroy him. Or when he first saw Jude Winston at a Halloween party, a party that he'd only attended because a boy he spotted for at the gym invited him and he thought, hell, why not. She was standing alone, fidgeting with her skirt, dark as anything he'd ever seen and pretty enough that he felt like a heavy hand was pinning him to that couch. Leave it alone, Reese. Easy now. He already knew how that would end, how she would leave him once she reached for his lap and only felt him pushing away.

In the beginning, he never thought about staying in Los Angeles. He'd only wanted to put as many miles between himself and El Dorado as possible. He would've kept going into the ocean, if he could. For weeks, he'd spent his nights touching men in dark alleys, sometimes using his mouth, which he hated, although those men were kinder after, more grateful. They pet his head and called him a pretty boy. He carried his father's hunting knife as protection, and sometimes, glancing up at those heads thrown back against the wall, he imagined slicing their bobbing throats. Instead, he pocketed their crumpled bills and searched for shelter, sleeping on park benches or beneath freeway overpasses, which reminded him, strangely, of camping with his father. Sitting on a hollowed log, watching his daddy slice open a rabbit with a knife he told Reese to never touch. A knife handed down from his own father, a knife he would have passed on to his son, if he'd had one, which was why, when Reese left, he took it.

He met men to touch at nightclubs and bars, men who grabbed his hand as he passed through the crowds, men who foisted drinks toward him and begged him to dance. He never went to the same club twice, always terrified that someone might notice his smooth neck or small hands or the rolled-up sock in his underpants. Once, an angry white man in Westwood discovered his secret and gave him a black eye. He quickly learned the rules. To be honest about the past meant that he would be considered a liar. The only safety was in hiding.

The night he met Barry, he was dizzy with hunger, sipping on a whiskey soda and almost desperate enough to follow him home. But he'd never been with a man outside of the alleys; he felt safer there in the darkness. So he told Barry no, which was why he was surprised when, later that night, Barry grabbed his arm and asked if he wanted dinner. Reese shook himself free, startled.

"I fucking said no—"

"I know what you said," Barry told him. "I'm asking if you want food. You look hungry. There's a spot right there."

He was pointing to a late-night diner a block away. The neon sign washed the concrete in purple and blue light. Barry ordered pecan pie, and Reese ate two cheeseburgers and a basket of fries so quickly that he almost choked. He would have to pay for the meal somehow, or maybe not, he thought, feeling the knife in his pocket. Barry watched him, trailing his fork through the whipped cream.

"How old are you?" he said.

Reese wiped his mouth with the back of his hand, then, feeling uncivilized, reached for the napkin dispenser.

"Eighteen," he said, although he wouldn't be for two more months.

"Lord." Barry laughed. "You a baby, you know that? I got students as old as you."

He was a teacher, he said, which was maybe why he'd decided to be kind. In another life, Reese might have been one of his students, not some boy he picked up in a nightclub. But Reese never finished high school, which he didn't regret at first, not until he fell in love with a smart girl. School seemed like just another way she would eventually leave him behind.

"So where'd you come from?" Barry said. "Seems like everybody in this city's from somewhere else."

"Arkansas."

"Long way, cowboy. What you doin all the way out here?"

He shrugged, dipping his fries into a puddle of ketchup. "Startin over."

"You got people out here?"

Reese shook his head. Barry lit a cigarette. His fingers were lovely and long.

"You need people," he said. "Too big a city to be out here by yourself. You need a place to stay? Oh, don't look at me like that. I don't want nobody who don't want me. I'm asking if you need a place to sleep. What, you too good for my couch?"

Reese didn't know why he said yes. Maybe he was just sick of sleeping in abandoned buildings, stamping his feet to keep away the rats. Maybe he saw something in Barry that he trusted, or maybe he felt the knife banging against his thigh and knew that, if he had to, he could. Either way, he followed Barry home. When they stepped inside, he paused, glancing around at the wigs lining the countertops. Barry stiffened.

"It's just a thing I do sometimes," he said, but he touched a wig gingerly, looking so vulnerable that Reese turned away.

"I'm not what you think I am," Reese said.

"You're a transsexual," Barry said. "I know exactly what you are."

Reese had never heard the word before—he hadn't even known that there was a word to describe him. He must have looked surprised because Barry laughed.

"I know plenty boys like you," he said. He took a step closer, eyeing him. "Of course, they all got better haircuts. You do this yourself?"

In the bathroom, he wrapped a towel around Reese's neck and reached for his clippers. He gently pushed Reese's head forward, and Reese closed his eyes, trying to remember the last time another man had touched him so tenderly.

BY DECEMBER, the city had finally cooled but the sun still hung high and unnaturally bright; it felt wrong to even call it wintertime. In the catering van, Jude stuck her arm out the window, enjoying the breeze. She'd picked up a last-minute shift to work a retirement party in Beverly Hills, and the money was too good to turn down even though Reese had sulked watching her slip out the door.

"I wanted to take you to dinner," he said.

"Tomorrow, baby," she said. "I promise."

She'd kissed him, already imagining the tips she would pocket once the night was over. A company party was always good money. Big wigs, Scooter told her, as they coasted into Beverly Hills. The van glided up winding roads that grew more secluded until they finally reached a black iron gate. Scooter snorted.

"Big money they pay to live like this," he said, the gate slowly creaking open. "Can you imagine?"

The next century would be like this, he told her. The rich moving away from cities, locked behind giant gates like medieval lords building moats. They drove slowly down the quiet tree-lined streets until they reached the house—a white two-story hidden behind Roman columns. Carla let them in. She rarely appeared during their jobs but the party was important and she was short-handed.

"The Hardison Group is a very loyal client," she said, "so on our best behavior tonight, yes?"

Her mere presence made Jude jittery. She could feel Carla appraising her as she chopped celery and pureed tomatoes, as she swept through the party balancing trays of rolled prosciutto or mixed cocktails at the bar. The retiring man was Mr. Hardison—he was stocky and silver-haired, wearing a gray suit that looked expensive, his young blonde wife hanging on to his arm. The crowd, all white and middle-aged and moneyed, toasted his career and raised a glass afterward to his successor, a handsome blond man in a navy suit. A girl lingered by his side. She looked eighteen maybe, leggy with wavy blonde hair, and she wore a shimmery silver dress cut scandalously above her knees. Halfway through the party, she stepped away from the man and sauntered over to the bar, tilting her empty martini glass.

"I'm not supposed to serve anyone under twenty-one," Jude said.

The girl laughed, pressing a hand against her collar.

"Well, I'm twenty-one then," she said. Her eyes were so blue, they looked violet. She tipped her glass again. "This party's a drag anyway. Of course I need a drink."

"Your dad doesn't care?"

The girl glanced over her shoulder, back to the handsome man.

"Of course not," she said. "He's too busy trying to distract himself from the fact that Mother isn't here. Isn't that something? I came all the way in from school because he got some big promotion, and she couldn't even bother to show up. Now isn't that a bitch?"

She wiggled the glass again. She clearly didn't plan on leaving until she got her way, so Jude poured her a fresh drink. The girl turned toward the party, slipping the olive through her pink lips.

"So do you like being a bartender?" she asked. "I bet you get to meet all sorts of fascinating people."

"I'm not a bartender. Not all the time. I'm a student mostly." Then Jude added, a little too proudly, "At UCLA."

The girl raised an eyebrow. "How funny," she said. "I go to Southern California. Guess we're rivals."

It wasn't hard to tell which part seemed funny to her: that a stranger happened to attend her crosstown rival or that the black girl serving drinks had, somehow, managed to attend a school like UCLA. A white man in a tweed jacket asked for wine and Jude uncorked the bottle of merlot, hoping the girl might leave. But as she began to pour, she heard exclamations filtering in from the foyer. The girl turned to her glumly.

"Fun's over," she said, and drained her martini in a gulp.

Then she set her empty glass on the bar and started toward the entrance, where a woman had just walked in. Mr. Hardison was helping her out of her fur coat, and when she turned, passing a hand through her dark hair, the bottle of wine shattered on the floor.

Part III

HEARTLINES

(1968)

Seven

The night one of the lost twins returned to Mallard, a notice was pinned to the front door of every house in the Palace Estates, calling for an emergency Homeowners Association meeting. The Estates, the newest subdivision in Brentwood, had only called one emergency meeting before, when the treasurer was accused of embezzling dues, so that night, the neighbors gathered in the clubhouse, whispering hotly, expecting the hint of a scandal. What they did not expect was this: current president Percy White standing in front of the room, his face beet red as he delivered regretful news. The Lawsons on Sycamore Way were selling their house and a colored man had just placed an offer to buy it. The room sputtered to life, and Percy threw up his hands, suddenly finding himself in front of a firing squad.

"Just the messenger," he kept saying, although no one could hear him. Dale Johansen asked what the hell was the point of having a Homeowners Association if not to prevent such a thing from happening. Tom Pearson, determined to outbluster him, threatened to withhold his dues if the association did not start doing their jobs. Even the women were upset, or perhaps, especially the women were upset. They did not shout like the men but each had made a certain sacrifice in marrying a man who could afford a home in the most expensive new subdivision in Los Angeles County and she expected a return on that investment. Cath Johansen asked how they ever expected to keep the neighborhood safe now, and Betsy Roberts, an economics major at Bryn Mawr before she'd married, complained that their property values would plummet.

But years later, the neighbors would only remember one person speaking up in the meeting, a single voice that had, somehow, risen above the noise. She hadn't yelled—maybe that's why they'd listened. Or perhaps because she was ordinarily so soft-spoken, everyone knew that if she was standing to her feet in the middle of a raucous meeting, she must have had something urgent to say. Or maybe it was because her family currently lived on Sycamore Way, in a cul-de-sac across from the Lawsons, so the new neighbors would affect her most directly. Whatever the reason, the room quieted when Stella Sanders climbed to her feet.

"You must stop them, Percy," she said. "If you don't, there'll be more and then what? Enough is enough!"

She was trembling, her light brown eyes flashing, and the neighbors, moved by her spontaneous passion, applauded. She never spoke up in their meetings and hadn't even known that she would until she'd already clambered to her feet. For a second, she'd almost said nothing—she hated feeling everyone watch her, had wanted to run shrinking at her own wedding. But her shy, faltering voice only gripped the room more. After the meeting, she couldn't even make it out the door without neighbors wanting to shake her hand. Weeks later, yellow flyers flapping on trees and light posts read in big block letters: PROTECT OUR NEIGHBORHOOD. ENOUGH IS ENOUGH. When she found one stuck in the windshield of her car, she was startled to see her own words reflected back to her, as foreign as if they'd come from a stranger.

FOR WHAT IT'S WORTH, Blake Sanders had been as surprised as anyone that his wife had spoken in that meeting. She wasn't one for demonstrating. He'd never seen her riled up enough about any issue to do more than sign a petition, and even then it was usually because she was too polite to shove a clipboard back into some college kid's face like he would've done. Sure, he wanted to keep the planet clean. He thought the war was rotten. But that didn't mean that screaming in the faces of decent, hardworking people was the right way to go about any of it. But Stella indulged these idealists, listened to their speeches, signed their petitions, all because she was too sweet to tell them to bug off. Yet here she was now, somehow, as fervent as any of those young protesters in the middle of the association meeting.

He could have laughed. His shy Stella making a scene! Although maybe he shouldn't have been surprised. A woman protecting her home came from a place more primal than politics. Besides, in all the time he'd known her, she'd never spoken kindly of a Negro. It embarrassed him a little, to tell the truth. He respected the natural order of things but you didn't have to be cruel about it. As a boy, he'd had a colored nanny named Wilma who was practically family. He still sent her a Christmas card each year. But Stella wouldn't even hire colored help for the house—she claimed Mexicans worked harder. He never understood why she averted her gaze when an old Negro woman shuffled past on the sidewalk, why she was always so curt with the elevator operators. She was jumpy around Negroes, like a child who'd been bit by a dog.

That night, as they slipped out of the clubhouse, he smiled, offering his arm to her cheekily. It was a brisk April night. They passed slowly under the jacaranda trees beginning to bloom lavender over their heads.

"I didn't know I'd married such a rabble-rouser," he said.

He was a banker's son who'd left Boston to attend college, he'd told her when they first met, although he didn't mention then that the bank at which his father was an executive was Chase National, and the college he'd left to attend, Yale. She would later realize that these were signs that he truly came from wealth: how rarely he wore expensive clothes even though he could afford to, how little he talked about his father or his inheritance. He'd studied finance and marketing, and instead of heading to Madison Avenue, he'd followed his fiancée back to her hometown of New Orleans. The relationship fizzled, but by then he'd fallen in love with the city. That's how he'd ended up working in the marketing department at Maison Blanche, and that was why he was hiring her, Stella Vignes, as his new secretary.

Even after eight years of marriage, Stella still felt a little squeamish when people asked how they'd met. A boss, his secretary, a tale as old as time. It made you picture a greasy-haired potbelly in suspenders chasing a young girl around his desk.

"I wasn't some old lech," Blake had said once, laughing, at a dinner party, and it was true. He was twenty-eight then, hard-jawed with ruffled blond hair and blueish-gray eyes like Paul Newman. And maybe that was what made his attention different. Back then, she'd withered when a white man noticed her. Under Blake's gaze, she'd blossomed.

"Did I make a fool out of myself?" she asked later. She was sitting in front of her vanity, brushing out her hair. Blake eased behind her, unbuttoning his white shirt.

"Of course not," he said. "But it'll never happen, Stel. I don't know why everyone's getting all worked up."

"But you saw Percy up there. He looked plumb scared."

Blake laughed. "I love when you say things like that."

"Like what?"

"Your country talk."

"Oh, don't make fun. Not right now."

"I'm not! I think it's cute."

He stooped to kiss her cheek, and in the mirror, she watched his fair head bend over her dark one. Did she look as nervous as she felt? Would anybody be able to tell? A colored family in the neighborhood. Blake was right, it would never happen. The association would put a stop to it. They had lawyers on hand for such a thing, didn't they? What was the purpose of having an association if not to stop undesirables from moving in, if not to ensure the neighborhood exists precisely as the neighbors wished? She tried to steady that flutter in her stomach but she couldn't. She'd been caught before. Only once, the second time she'd ever pretended to be white. During her last summer in Mallard, weeks after venturing into the charm shop, she'd gone to the South Louisiana Museum of Art on an ordinary Saturday morning, not Negro Day, and walked right up to the main entrance, not the side door where Negroes lined up in the alley. Nobody stopped her, and again, she'd felt stupid for not trying this sooner. There was nothing to being white except boldness. You could convince anyone you belonged somewhere if you acted like you did.

In the museum, she'd glided slowly through the rooms, studying the fuzzy Impressionists. She was listening distractedly as an elderly docent intoned to a circle of listless children, when she noticed a Negro security guard in the corner of the room staring. Then he'd winked, and, horrified, she rushed past him, head down, barely breathing until she stepped back into the bright morning. She rode the bus back to Mallard, her face burning. Of course passing wasn't that easy. Of course that colored guard recognized her. We always know our own, her mother said.

And now a colored family moving across the street. Would they see her for what she was? Or rather, what she wasn't? Blake kissed the back of her neck, slipping his hand inside her robe.

"Don't worry about it, honey," he said. "The association will never allow it."

IN THE MIDDLE OF THE NIGHT, her daughter woke up screaming, and Stella stumbled into the girl's room to find her in the throes of another nightmare. She crawled into the tiny bed, gently shaking her awake. "I know, I know," she said, dabbing at her tears. Her own heart was still pounding, although by now, she should have been used to scrambling out of bed, following her daughter's screams, always fearing the worst, only to find Kennedy twisted in her covers, clenching the sheets. The pediatrician said that nothing was physically wrong; the sleep specialist said that children with overactive imaginations were prone to vivid dreams. It probably just meant that she was an artist, he'd said with a chuckle. The child psychologist examined her drawings and asked what she dreamt about. But Kennedy, only seven, never remembered, and Blake dismissed the doctors as a waste of money.

"She must get it from your side," he told Stella. "A good Sanders girl would be out like a light."

She told him that she used to have nightmares when she was young, too, and she never remembered them either. But that last part wasn't true. Her nightmares were always the same, white men grabbing her ankles and dragging her screaming out of the bed. She'd never told Desiree. Each time she'd snapped awake, Desiree snoring beside her, she felt stupid for being afraid. Hadn't Desiree watched from that closet too? Hadn't she seen what those white men had done? Then why wasn't she waking up in the middle of the night, her heart pounding?

They never talked about their father. Whenever Stella tried, Desiree's eyes glazed over.

"What you want me to say?" she said. "I know just as much as you do."

"I just wish I knew why," Stella said.

"Nobody knows why," Desiree said. "Bad things happen. They just do."

Now Stella gently brushed back the silken blonde hair from her daughter's forehead.

"It's all right, darling," she whispered. "Go back to sleep."

She held her daughter closer, pulling the covers over the both of them. She hadn't wanted to be a mother at first. The idea of pregnancy terrified her; she imagined pushing out a baby that grew darker and darker, Blake recoiling in horror. She almost preferred him thinking that she'd had an affair with a Negro. That lie seemed kinder than the truth, momentary unfaithfulness a gentler deception than her ongoing fraud. But after she'd given birth, she felt overwhelmed with relief. The newborn in her arms was perfect: milky skin, wavy blonde hair, and eyes so blue they looked violet. Still, sometimes, Kennedy felt like a daughter who belonged to someone else, a child Stella was borrowing while she loaned a life that never should have been hers.

"Where are you from, Mommy?" Kennedy asked her once during bath time. She was nearly four then and inquisitive. Stella, kneeling beside the tub, gently wiped her daughter's shoulders with a washcloth and glanced into those violet eyes, unsettling and beautiful, so unlike the eyes of anyone else she'd ever known.

"A little town down south," Stella said. "You won't have heard of it." She always spoke to Kennedy like this, as if she were another adult. All the baby books recommended it, said it helped with developing language skills. But really, she just felt silly babbling like Blake.

"But where?" Kennedy asked.

Stella poured warm water over her, the bubbles dissolving. "It's just a little place called Mallard, darling," she said. "It's nothing like Los Angeles."

She'd been, for the first and final time, completely honest with her daughter, only because she knew the girl was too young to remember. Later, Stella would lie. She'd tell Kennedy, as she'd told everyone, that she was from Opelousas, and beyond that, she would barely talk about her childhood at all. But Kennedy still asked. Her questions always felt like a surprise attack, as if she were pressing her finger into a bruise. What was it like when you were growing up? Did you have brothers and sisters? What did your house look like? Once, during bedtime, she asked Stella what her mother was like and Stella nearly dropped the storybook.

"She's not here anymore," she finally said.

"But where is she?"

"Gone," she said. "My family is gone."

She'd told Blake the same lie years ago in New Orleans: that she was an only child who'd moved to New Orleans after her parents died in an accident. He'd touched her hand and she saw herself, suddenly, through his eyes. A lowly orphan, alone in the city. If he pitied her, he wouldn't be able to see her clearly. He would refract all of her lies through her mourning, mistake her reticence about her past for grief. Now what began as a lie felt closer to the truth. She hadn't spoken to her sister in thirteen years. Where was Desiree now? How was their mother? She'd slid the book back on the shelf before she even reached the end, and later that night, brushing her teeth, she heard Blake speaking to Kennedy.

"Mommy doesn't like talking about her family," he murmured. "It makes her sad."

"But why?"

"Because. They aren't here anymore. So don't ask her anything else, okay?"

In Blake's mind, her life before him had been tragic, her whole family swallowed up. She preferred him to think of her that way. Blank. A curtain hung between her past and present and she could never peek behind it. Who knows what might scuttle through?

A COLORED FAMILY in the neighborhood. It would never happen.

And yet, the morning after the association meeting, Stella floated for hours in her swimming pool, still thinking about it. Clouds drifted overhead, rain, maybe, on the way. She wore a red bathing suit that matched her plastic raft, and she was sipping on a gin and soda that she'd poured secretly as soon as she'd seen her daughter off to school and hoped, sipping again, that it looked like water to Yolanda, bustling around in the kitchen. Obviously it was too early for gin, but she was trying to steady that uneasiness creeping inside her since last night. Blake said that there was no chance the bid for the Lawson house would be approved, but why would Percy have even called the meeting unless it was possible? Why had he looked so shaken, standing in the front of the room, as if he'd already known that there was nothing he could do? The country was changing every day, she read all about the marches in the newspapers. Restrooms and universities and public pools desegregating, which was why when they'd first moved to Brentwood, Blake insisted on building one in the backyard. A private pool seemed too lavish to her, but Blake said, "You don't want Ken in the city pool, do you? Swimming around with whoever they let in there now."

He'd grown up in Boston, swimming in whites-only pools. She'd swum in the river or, occasionally, at the Gulf beach where the white lifeguards instructed them to keep to the colored side of the red flag.

Of course the water mixed from one side to another, and if you peed on the colored side—which Desiree, giggling, always threatened to do—it would eventually make its way to the white side. But Stella agreed that Blake was right, they couldn't send their daughter to a city pool. The only solution was to build their own.

Over the years, she'd come to appreciate the pool and everything else Blake insisted they needed in Los Angeles: her red Thunderbird, her maid, Yolanda, and all the other little creature comforts he provided. She loved that phrase, loved imagining comfort as a plush Pomeranian curling around her ankles. Before Blake, she'd never felt comfortable. She didn't realize this until after she'd met him, marveling as he ordered an entire steak for himself, remembering the nights she'd fallen asleep, her stomach hollowed. Or watching Blake try to decide between two neckties and, in the end, purchasing both, when she used to walk to school, toes cramped against her shoes. Or stepping into the kitchen to see Yolanda polishing the silverware, when, years earlier, she'd been staring at her own reflection in the Duponts' forks.

Back then, she was responsible for cleaning a home filled with expensive things that she would never be able to afford. Picking up after those bratty boys and dodging Mr. Dupont, who followed her into the pantry, shut the door, and stuck his hand up her dress. Three times he'd touched her and himself too, panting, his breath thick with brandy, while she tried to get away, but the pantry was too small and he was too strong, pressing her against the shelves. Then it was over, as quick as it started. Soon her fear of him became worse than the touching. All the days she worried that he might creep up behind her ruined the ones when he didn't. After the first time, she'd asked Desiree, that night in bed, what she thought of him.

"What's there to think about him?" Desiree said. "He's just a skinny ol' white man. Why? What you think about him?"

Even in their darkened bedroom, even to Desiree, Stella couldn't bring herself to say. She always wanted to believe that there was something special about her but she knew that Mr. Dupont only picked her because he sensed her weakness. She was the twin who wouldn't tell.

And she didn't. Her whole life, she would never tell anyone. But when Desiree came up with the plan to leave after Founder's Day, Stella felt Mr. Dupont shoving her against the pantry shelf and knew she had to go too. In New Orleans, when Desiree began to waver, Stella felt his fingers worming inside her underwear and found the strength to stay for the both of them.

But that was a lifetime ago. She slipped a toe over the edge of her raft, skimming her foot along the water. Now this was comfort—a languid morning spent floating across a swimming pool, a two-story house with cabinets always filled with food, a chestful of toys for her daughter, a bookshelf that held an entire encyclopedia set. This was comfort, no longer wanting anything.

She was growing sleepy in the midmorning haze, lulled by gin, so she forced herself out of the water. When she padded, still dripping, onto the kitchen tile, Yolanda glanced up from dusting the dining-room furniture. Her feet were still damp, and she realized, a moment too late, that Yolanda had already mopped.

"I'm sorry," she said. "Look at me, dirtying your floor."

She still spoke to Yolanda like this sometimes, as if Stella were the visitor in her home instead of the other way around. Yolanda only smiled.

"It's okay, miss," she said. "Your tea."

Stella sipped her sweet tea, the towel draping lazily across her shoulders, as she headed to the shower. At least the pool would be good exercise, she'd told herself at first. But most mornings, she didn't swim at all, only floated on the raft. On the best mornings, she floated with a cocktail, sipping slowly as she drifted beneath the sunrise. It felt deliciously wrong, enjoying a drink so early, but at the same time, it was pitiful that this passed as excitement. Her days blended together, refracting each other, as if she were trapped in a hall of mirrors like the one Desiree once led her to at a fair. As soon as they'd entered, she'd skittered off, Stella calling hopelessly after her. At one point, she'd seen Desiree behind her, but when she turned, no one was there. She was only staring at her own face reflected strangely back to her.

Life felt like this now, her days duplicating one another, but how could she complain? Not to Blake, who'd worked so hard in New Orleans and Boston, until he'd earned the attention of a firm in Los Angeles, of all places, a major international market. He worked endless hours, traveled constantly, fell asleep in bed studying colorful charts. Her days probably seemed like a dream to him, especially if he knew how little she actually did. How often the cakes she iced when he arrived home came from a box, how the sheets he climbed into at night were washed by Yolanda, how even her daughter's life sometimes seemed like another area of the household she'd delegated to someone else.

That afternoon, she sat in the multipurpose room at Brentwood Academy, slowly trailing her celery sticks through ranch. At the head of the room, Betsy Roberts was scribbling down volunteers for the spring dance. Stella knew she should raise her hand—when's the last time she'd volunteered to do more than bring a punch bowl?—but instead, she stared out the window at the perfectly manicured lawn. She always grew listless during these meetings, listening to debates about which color streamers to hang. Which flavor brownies to bake, which end-of-the-year gift to give to Principal Stanley. God, if she had to listen to another conversation about some kid she didn't know— how Tina J. stole the stage at the talent show or Bobby R. won the tee ball game or any other number of inane accomplishments. Her daughter never managed to accomplish anything special, but even if she did, Stella, at least, had the decency not to force everyone to hear about it.

She knew what the other mothers thought of her—there goes that Stella Sanders, a snooty you-know-what. Well, fine, let them think that. She needed to keep her distance. Even after all these years, she still felt nervous around white women, running out of small talk as soon as she opened her mouth. When the meeting wrapped up, Cath Johansen scooted over and thanked Stella for speaking up last night.

"It's high time someone stood up for what's right," Cath said.

The Johansens were native Angelenos. Dale's family owned acres of orange groves in Pasadena, and once, he'd invited her and Blake to tour the farm, as he called it, as if it were a humble little homestead, not a million-dollar estate. Stella suffered his pretentiousness only by breaking off from the group and wandering alone between the rows of trees. On the drive home, Blake suggested that she and Cath might make good friends. He was always doing that, trying to coax her further outside herself. But she felt safe like this, locked away.

A WEEK AFTER the association meeting, Stella started to see the signs that her worst fear had come true. First, the literal one: a red SOLD sign on the Lawsons' lawn. She didn't know the Lawsons well; she rarely spoke to them, beyond the expected pleasantries at the neighborhood potluck, but she still forced herself to wave down Deborah Lawson in her driveway one morning. Deborah glanced back at her, harried, as she ushered her two tow-headed boys into the backseat of her sedan.

"The new family," Stella said. "Are they nice people?"

"Oh, I don't know," Deborah said. "I haven't met them. The broker handles all that."

But she wouldn't look directly at Stella the whole time, brushing past her to climb into the car, so Stella knew that she was lying. Later, she would learn the full story about Hector Lawson's gambling problem, which submerged his family in debt. Half the neighbors would pity him, the other half blaming his irresponsibility for their current predicament. You might feel sorry for a man who'd lost so much, but not when his bad luck hurt the entire neighborhood. Still, Stella held out hope that her suspicions were wrong, until Blake came home from racquetball, wiping his sweaty face with his T-shirt, and told her that the association had rolled over.

"The colored fellow threatened to sue if he wasn't let in," Blake said. "Hired a big lawyer too. Got old Percy running scared." He noticed her fallen face and squeezed her hip. "Aw, don't look like that, Stel. It'll be fine. I bet they won't last a month here. They'll see they're not wanted."

"But there'll be more after them—"

"Not if they can't afford it. Fred told me the man paid for that house in cash. He's a different breed."

He almost sounded as if he admired the man. But what type of person threatened to sue his way into a neighborhood where he would not be welcomed? Why would anyone insist on doing such a thing? To make a point? To make himself miserable? To end up on the nightly news like all those protesters, beaten or martyred in hopes of convincing white people to change their minds? Two weeks ago, she'd watched from the arm of Blake's chair as cities across the country lit up in flames. A single bullet, the newscaster said, the force of the gunshot ripping off King's necktie. Blake stared mystified at devastated Negroes running past flaming buildings.

"I'll never understand why they do that," he said. "Destroy their own neighborhoods."

On the local news, police officials urged calm, the city still roiling from the Watts riots three years ago. She'd stepped into the powder room, a hand clasped over her mouth to muffle her crying. Was Desiree feeling hopeless on a night like this? Had she ever felt hopeful at all? The country was unrecognizable now, Cath Johansen said, but it looked the same as it ever had to Stella. Tom Pearson and Dale Johansen and Percy White wouldn't storm a colored man's porch and yank him out of his kitchen, wouldn't stomp his hands, wouldn't shoot him five times. These were fine people, good people, who donated to charities and winced at newsreels of southern sheriffs swinging billy clubs at colored college students. They thought King was an impressive speaker, maybe even agreed with some of his ideas. They wouldn't have sent a bullet into his head—they might have even cried watching his funeral, that poor young family—but they still wouldn't have allowed the man to move into their neighborhood.

"We could threaten to move out," Dale said at dinner. He was rolling a cigarette between his fingers, peering out the window like a sentry on lookout. "How'd the association like that, huh? All of us, just up and leave."

"Why should we be the ones to leave?" Cath said. "We've worked hard, paid our dues."

"It's just a tactic," Dale said. "A negotiating tactic. We leverage our collective power—"

"You sound like a Bolshevik," Blake said, smirking. Stella hugged herself. She had barely touched her wine. She wanted to think about anything other than the colored family moving in, which was, of course, the only thing that anyone could talk about.

"I'm glad you're having a big laugh about all of this," Dale said. "Just wait until the whole neighborhood looks like Watts."

"I'm telling you it'll never happen," Blake said, leaning over to light Stella's cigarette. "I don't know why you all are getting so worked up."

"It better not," Dale said. "I'll see to that."

She couldn't tell what unnerved her more, picturing a colored family moving in or imagining what might be done to stop them.

DAYS LATER, a yellow moving van crept slowly up the winding streets of the Palace Estates, halting at each intersection, in search of Sycamore Way. From her bedroom window, Stella peered through the blinds as the van parked in front of the Lawsons' house. Three lanky colored men climbed out the back in matching purple shirts. One by one, they unloaded a leather couch; a marble vase; a long, furled rug; a giant stone elephant with a flared trunk; a slender floor lamp. An endless parade of furniture and no family in sight. Stella watched as long as she could until her daughter sidled up behind her and whispered, "What's happening?" As if they were playing some spy game. Stella jolted away from the blinds, suddenly embarrassed.

"Nothing," she said. "Want to help Mommy set the table?"

After weeks of worrying, her first encounter with the new neighbors was both accidental and unremarkable. She ran into the wife early the next morning while ushering her daughter out the door for school. She was distracted, trying to balance a diorama as she locked the door, and she almost didn't notice, at first, the pretty colored woman standing across the street. She was neat and slender, pecan-colored, her hair bobbed like one of the Supremes. She wore a golden-rod dress with a scooping neckline, and she held the hand of a little girl in a pink dress. Stella paused, clutching the shoebox diorama against her stomach. Then the woman smiled and waved, and Stella hesitated before finally lifting her hand.

"Nice mornin," the woman called. She had a slight accent—midwestern, maybe.

"Yes, it is," Stella said.

She should introduce herself. None of the other neighbors had, but her house was right across the street—she could practically see into the woman's living room. Instead, she nudged Kennedy toward the car. She gripped the wheel tightly during the whole drive to school, rewinding the conversation in her head. That woman's easy smile. Why did she feel so comfortable speaking to Stella in the first place? Did she see something in her, even across the street, that she felt like she could trust?

"I met the neighbor," she told Blake that night. "The wife."

"Mmm," he said, climbing into bed beside her. "Nice, at least?"

"Yes, I suppose."

"It'll be fine, Stel," he said. "They'll keep to themselves, if they know what's best."

The room fell dark, the mattress creaking as Blake rolled over to kiss her. Sometimes when he touched her, she saw the man who'd dragged her father onto the porch, the one with the red-gold hair. Tall, gray shirt partially unbuttoned, a scab on his cheek as if he'd nicked himself while shaving. Blake pressed open her thighs and the man with the red-gold hair was on top of her—she could almost smell his sweat, see the freckles on his back. Then it was Blake's clean Ivory soap again, his voice whispering her name. It was ridiculous— the men looked nothing alike and Blake had never hurt her. But he could, which made her grip him even tighter as she felt him sink inside.

Eight

The new neighbors were Reginald and Loretta Walker, and when the news spread that Sergeant Tommy Taylor himself was moving onto Sycamore Way, even the most belligerent faltered in their protest. Sergeant Taylor was, of course, a beloved character on *Frisk*, the hottest police drama on television. He played the straitlaced partner of the rowdy hero, always nagging him about paperwork and protocol. "File that form!" was his signature phrase, and for months, when Blake spied him across the cul-de-sac, he called it out to him in greeting. Reg Walker, mowing his lawn or plucking a newspaper from the driveway, always started before flashing his trademark smile, shrugging a little, as if he figured it the least offensive thing a white man might holler at him from across the street.

Blake loved it, like they were in on a joke together. He couldn't see how patiently Reg Walker tolerated him. But it always embarrassed Stella, who hurried him inside. She barely watched television at all beyond the news, and she certainly had no interest in cop shows, so when she'd learned about the Walkers, she didn't care at all that Reg was on some program that Blake liked. Maybe the husbands would be won over by this; if they had to live next to a Negro, he might as well be a famous one. A trusted one, even, a character they never saw onscreen out of his uniform. Imagine their surprise when they first saw Reg Walker: tall, lean, his hair picked out in a short natural. He wore green plaid pants with silk shirts that hugged his broad chest. A gold watch glinted on his wrist, bouncing the sunlight as he climbed into his shiny black Cadillac.

"Flashy," Marge Hawthorne called him, in the same dramatic way she might have said, "Dangerous."

On Friday nights, Stella watched the Walkers climb into their car, Reg wearing a black suit, Loretta draped in a royal blue dress. On their way to a party, maybe. Crowding with movie stars in a Hollywood Hills mansion, piling into a nightclub on Sunset with ballplayers. For a moment, Stella felt stupid for distrusting them. Bob Hawthorne was a dentist. Tom Pearson owned a Lincoln dealership. Perhaps, to the Walkers, the rest of them seemed like the undeserving neighbors. Glancing down at herself, already in her pajamas, she couldn't disagree.

"Well?" Cath asked breathlessly, plopping beside her at the next PTA meeting. "What're they like?"

Stella shrugged. "I don't know," she said. "I've only seen them once or twice."

"I heard the husband is all right. But that wife of his is something else."

"What do you mean?"

"Well, she's uppity as I don't know what. Barb told me that she wants to put her daughter at our school next year. It's crazy, if you ask me! I mean, there's perfectly good schools all over the city with plenty of colored children. They have buses and everything."

Loretta Walker didn't look like the type to start trouble, but what did Stella know about her at all? She kept her distance, only peeked out at her through the blinds. Reg Walker leaving for early-morning

164

shoots in his Cadillac, Loretta wrapped in a silky green robe and waving at him from the porch. Loretta returning from the grocery store on
Mondays, always Mondays, unloading her trunk. Once a tan Buick
pulled into the driveway and three colored ladies piled out, carrying
wine and cake. Loretta came down the driveway to greet them, laughing, her head thrown back. A big smile that made Stella smile too.
When was the last time she'd seen anyone smile like that?

Through her blinds, she watched the Walkers as if their lives were
another program on her television set. But she never saw anything
alarming until the morning when she spotted her daughter playing
dolls in the cul-de-sac with the Walker girl. There was no time to
think. Before she knew it, she'd stormed across the street and grabbed
her daughter's arm, both girls gaping as she dragged Kennedy back
into the house. She was shaking, fumbling to lock the door behind
her as her daughter whined about the doll she'd left in the street. She
already knew she'd overreacted—hadn't she played with white girls
when she was Kennedy's age? Nobody cared when you were young
enough. The twins used to follow their mother to work, playing with
the white girl who lived there, until one afternoon the girl's mother
had suddenly yanked her out of their circle. Stella told her daughter
the same thing she'd heard that mother say.

"Because we don't play with niggers," she said, and maybe it was
her harsh tone, or the fact that she'd never said that word to her
daughter before, but that was the end of it.

Or at least, she'd thought, until after dinner, when the doorbell
rang and she found Loretta Walker on her welcome mat, holding
Kennedy's doll. For a moment, under the soft glow of the porch lights,
hugging that blonde doll against her stomach, Loretta almost looked
like a girl herself. Then she thrust the doll into Stella's hands and
walked back across the street.

FOR THREE WEEKS, Stella avoided Loretta Walker.

Forget spying out of her own curiosity—now she glanced through the blinds before fetching the mail, just to ensure that she wouldn't run into Loretta. She went to the grocery store on Tuesdays, never Mondays, terrified that they might bump into each other down the milk aisle. So far there'd been only one accidental pileup on Sunday morning, when both couples left for their churches at the same time. The husbands had been pleasant but the wives didn't even speak, each helping her girl into the car.

"She's not too friendly," Blake grumbled, backing out of the driveway, and Stella said nothing, plucking at her gloves.

She had nothing to be embarrassed about, really. She'd behaved exactly as Cath Johansen or Marge Hawthorne might have. Still, she didn't tell Blake. What if he wondered why she'd overreacted? Or thought she was behaving like the Louisiana swamp trash his mother had always said she was? He believed in a moderate country. What he wanted most, he always said, watching policemen club protesters on the news, was for everyone to get along. So he would be embarrassed, as if she weren't enough already. Because even though she knew she hadn't done anything wrong, she still felt sick each time she pictured Loretta standing on her porch, hugging that doll. It would've been better if Loretta had sworn at her. Called her a backward, small-minded bigot. But she wouldn't. She was decent because she had to be, which only made Stella feel more ashamed.

"Did you know that Walker woman sent a letter to the school?" Cath asked her one Sunday, squeezing next to her on the pew.

"A letter?" Stella said. She felt too exhausted to keep up with Cath's breathless innuendo. Even here, at church, she couldn't avoid Loretta Walker.

"A legal letter," Cath said. "From some big lawyer, saying that if they don't let her girl come here in the fall, she'll sue. Can you imagine that? A whole lawsuit over that one little girl? I swear, some people just love the attention—"

"She doesn't seem that way to me," Stella said.

"And how would you know?" Cath said. She folded her arms across her chest. Stella raised her hands, surrendering.

"You're right," she said. "I don't know."

In June, she baked her guilt into a lemon cake with vanilla frosting. The idea arrived suddenly—before she could second-guess, she was tugging a bag of flour out of the cupboard, hunting through the re-frigerator for eggs. She would go crazy skulking around her own home, glancing out the window each time she wanted to venture outside. She was tired of her stomach clenching when she imagined the Walker girl abandoned on the sidewalk by the strewn dolls, star-ing back at her with those big eyes. She had to apologize. She wouldn't feel better until she did. She'd bake a cake to bring over as a house-warming gift. At least then she could be cordial to the woman. Decent. Hospitality wasn't the same as friendliness, and if anyone asked, she would say that she'd been raised to be hospitable. Nothing more, nothing less. One lemon cake for her peace of mind felt like an easy trade.

In the afternoon, she let out a deep breath before starting across the street, the cake balanced on a glass platter. The tan Buick was parked in the Walkers' driveway. Good, Loretta was entertaining. All the easier to bring the cake, apologize, and go.

Loretta answered the door in a shimmery green dress, a golden scarf draped around her neck. Already, Stella felt embarrassed in her ordinary blue dress, holding her slumping cake.

"Hi there, Mrs. Sanders," Loretta said. She was leaning against the doorway, holding a glass of white wine.

"Hello," Stella said. "I just wanted to—"

"Why don't you come in?"

Stella paused, not expecting this. A peal of laughter escaped the living room, and she felt a sharp pang. When was the last time she'd sat around, laughing with girlfriends?

"Oh no, I couldn't," she said. "You have company—"

"Nonsense," Loretta said. "No reason for us to be talkin out here on the porch."

Stella paused in the entrance, startled by the palatial decor: the living room floor adorned with a white fur rug, a floor lamp topped by a gilded shade, the tiled vase on the mantel. Her own home was simple, a marker of good taste. Only the low class lived like this, furniture covered in gold, knickknacks crowded everywhere. On the long leather couch, three colored women sat drinking wine and listening to Aretha Franklin.

"Ladies, this is Mrs. Sanders," Loretta said. "She lives across the street."

"Mrs. Sanders," one of the women said. "We've heard so much about you."

Stella flushed, knowing, from the women's smiles exactly what they'd heard. Why had she agreed to come inside? No, why had she brought the cake over in the first place? Why couldn't she just be like the rest of the neighbors and keep her distance? But it was too late now. Loretta steered her toward the kitchen, where Stella set the cake on the counter.

"Would you like a drink, Mrs. Sanders?" Loretta asked.

"It's Stella," she said. "And I couldn't, I just wanted to stop by and—well, welcome you all to the neighborhood. And also, about what happened—"

She hoped that Loretta might meet her halfway, spare her the shame of repeating the incident. Instead, the woman raised an eyebrow, reaching for an empty wineglass.

"You sure you don't want a drink?" she said.

"I just wanted to apologize," Stella said. "I don't know what came over me. I'm not normally like that."

"Like what?"

Loretta knew exactly what she meant, but she was having too much fun toying with her. Stella blushed again.

"I mean, I don't normally—" She paused. "This is all new to me, you see."

Loretta eyed her for a second, then took a sip of wine.

"You think I wanted to move here?" she said. "But Reg got his mind set on it and by then . . ."

She trailed off, but Stella could fill in the rest. When she'd first passed over, it seemed so easy that she couldn't believe she'd never done it before. She felt almost angry at her parents for denying it to her. If they'd passed over, if they'd raised her white, everything would have been different. No white men dragging her daddy from the porch. No laundry baskets filling the living room. She could have finished school, graduated top of her class. Maybe she would have ended up at a school like Yale, met Blake there proper. Maybe she could have been the type of girl his mother wanted him to marry. She could have had everything in her life now, but her father and mother and Desiree too.

At first, passing seemed so simple, she couldn't understand why her parents hadn't done it. But she was young then. She hadn't realized how long it takes to become somebody else, or how lonely it can be living in a world not meant for you.

"Maybe the girls can play some time," Stella said. "There's a nice little park one street over."

"Yes, maybe." Loretta's smile lingered a second too long, as if there were more she wanted to say. For a second, Stella wondered if she'd realized her secret. She almost wished Loretta had. It scared her, how badly she wanted to belong to somebody.

"It's funny," Loretta finally said.

"What is?"

"I didn't know what to expect when we moved here," Loretta said. "But I never imagined no white woman showing up in my kitchen with the most lopsided cake I ever seen."

LORETTA WALKER DID NOT KNOW how she'd ended up in Los Angeles. That's how she said it, too, with an exhausted sigh, taking another drag of her cigarette. She sat on the park bench, watching the girls play on the swings. Early summer still, but the morning was already so warm, Stella dabbed at her damp forehead with a handkerchief. She'd been pushing Kennedy on the swings when the little colored girl came running into the park, Loretta trailing behind. The girl eyed Stella warily, reaching for her mother's hand, and for a moment, Stella thought about leaving. Instead, she took a deep breath and stayed.

Now Loretta gazed up moodily at the cloudless sky.

"All this sun," she said. "Unnatural. Like being in a picture show all the time."

She was born in St. Louis, but she'd met Reg at Howard. He was a theater major, obsessed with August Wilson and Tennessee Williams; she studied history, hoped to become a professor someday. Neither had imagined that Reg would become famous for playing a boring police officer. When he'd practiced long soliloquies, impressing Loretta with his elocution, he hadn't expected that years later, his most well-known line would be "File that form!"

"How'd you like it?" Stella asked. "Howard. It's a colored school, isn't it?" As if she hadn't saved all the college pamphlets Mrs. Belton had given her, cracking the Howard one open so often it fell apart down the center. All those colored students lounging on the lawn, flipping through books. It seemed like a dream to her then.

"Yes," Loretta said. "I liked it fine."

"I always wanted to go to college," Stella said.

"You still could."

Stella laughed, gesturing around the neighborhood. "Why would I?"

"I don't know. Because you want to?"

Loretta made it sound so simple, but Blake would laugh. A waste of time and money, he'd tell her. Besides, she'd never even finished high school.

"It's too late for all that," she finally said.

"Well, what's it you like to study?"

"I used to like math."

Now Loretta laughed. "Well, you must be some big brain," she said. "Don't nobody just like math for fun."

But she loved the simplicity of math, a number growing or shrinking depending on which function you performed. No surprises, just one logical step leading to another. Loretta leaned forward, watching the girls play. She didn't seem at all like the uppity wife everyone gossiped about, the one who wanted to force her way into the Brentwood Academy. She didn't even seem like she wanted to live in Los Angeles at all. After college, she'd planned to return to Missouri, maybe earn her master's. Then she'd fallen for Reg and gotten swept up in his dreams.

"So why did you move here?" Stella asked. "The Estates, I mean."

Loretta raised an eyebrow. "Why did you?"

"Well, the schools. It's a nice neighborhood, don't you think? Clean. Safe."

She gave the answers she ought to, although she wasn't so sure. She'd moved to Los Angeles for Blake's job and sometimes she felt like she'd had no say in the matter. Other times, she remembered how thrilling the possibility of Los Angeles had seemed, all those miles between there and her old life. Foolish to pretend that she hadn't chosen this city. She wasn't some little tugboat, drifting along with the tide. She had created herself. Since the morning she'd walked out of the Maison Blanche building a white girl, she had decided everything.

"Then don't you think I'd want those same things too?" Loretta said.

"Yes, but don't you—I mean, it's got to be easier, isn't it, if you—"

"Stuck to my own kind?" Loretta lit another cigarette, her face shining like bronze.

"Why, yes," Stella said. "I just don't know why anyone would want to do it. I mean, there are plenty of fine colored neighborhoods and folks can be so hateful."

"They're gonna hate me anyway," Loretta said. "Might as well hate me in my big house with all of my nice things."

She smiled, taking another drag of her cigarette, and that sly smile reminded Stella of Desiree. She felt like a girl again, sneaking a smoke on the porch while their mother slept. She reached for Loretta's cigarette, leaning into the glow.

You had the Johansens, of course, on Magnolia Way—Dale worked downtown in finance, Cath served as secretary of the Brentwood Academy PTA, even though she hardly took minutes at all during the meetings, you couldn't guess how many times Stella had glanced at her notepad and found it blank. Then the Whites over on Juniper—Percy worked in accounting at one of the studios, she couldn't remember which, Blake would know. He was also association president, but he'd only run because his wife kept pushing him to be more ambitious. Lynn was from Oklahoma, an oil family, and God only knew how she'd found herself saddled with Percy White. You'd understand if you took a look at him, but let's just say he wasn't what she had in mind when she'd dreamt of marrying a man who worked in Hollywood. Then the Hawthornes on Maple—Bob had about the whitest teeth she'd ever seen in her life.

"I think I've seen him," Loretta said. "Big ones too? Kind of like Mister Ed?"

Stella laughed, nearly dropping the ball of blue yarn. Across the leather couch, Loretta smirked the way she always did when she knew she'd said something funny. Which was often, now that they were on their second glass of wine.

"You'll see them all soon," Stella said. "They're all nice enough people."

"To you," Loretta said. "You know you're the only one who's darkened my door."

Stella did know, but she tried not to dwell on that fact. She watched the yarn slip out in front of her, Loretta's crochet hook winding through the air. When she'd called Loretta earlier and asked if the girls might want to play again, she figured they would meet up at the park. She did not expect Loretta to invite her over or for herself to accept. Now the girls were playing in the Walkers' backyard—you could hear their yelps through the screen door—and she was tipsy from the wine, listening to Loretta talk about witnessing Reg's acting career finally take off. How even though he found *Frisk* stultifying, he was grateful to play a cop for once, not another street hood snatching some lady's purse in the opening credits. Loretta went to set with him from time to time, but found the whole business so dreadfully boring, she usually ended up in a corner somewhere, crocheting. It amazed Stella, how deeply unimpressed Loretta seemed by every fantastic aspect of her life. Whenever Loretta asked her a question, Stella grew embarrassed, aware of how little she had to offer.

"I told you," she said. "I'm really not that interesting."

"Oh, I don't believe that for a second," Loretta said. "I bet there's all sorts of fascinating things swirling around inside that head of yours."

"I assure you, there isn't," she said. "I'm as plain as they come."

She'd done one interesting thing in her whole life, but she would spend the rest of her days hiding it. When Loretta asked about her childhood, she always hedged. She couldn't share any memory of her youth without also conjuring Desiree; all of her memories were cleaved in half, her sister excised right out of them, and how lonely they seemed now, Stella swimming by herself at the river, wandering through sugarcane fields, running breathlessly from a goose chasing her down the road. A lonely past, a lonely present. Until now. Somehow, Loretta Walker had become the only person she could talk to.

All summer, she waited for Loretta's phone calls. She might be watching her daughter paint watercolors in the backyard when the kitchen phone rang, and just like that, she'd pack up the paint set, glancing carefully down the street before ushering Kennedy across. Or she might be on her way to the public library for storytime when Loretta phoned, and suddenly the overdue books were no longer as important as venturing across the cul-de-sac. When they returned home, she told her daughter not to mention the playdate to Blake.

"Why?" Kennedy asked. Stella knelt in front of her, untying her shoes.

"Because," she said, "Daddy likes us to be at home. But if you don't say anything, we can keep going across the street. You'd like that, wouldn't you?"

Her daughter put her hands on her shoulders, as if she were giving her a stern talking-to, but she was only balancing herself as she stepped out of her tennis shoes.

"Okay," she said, so simply it stung.

Like anything, lying to her daughter became easier over time. She was raising Kennedy to lie too, although the girl would never know it. She was white; she would never think of herself as anything else. If she ever learned the truth, she would hate her mother for deceiving her. The thought flashed through her head each time Loretta called. But each time, she steeled her nerve, took her daughter by the hand, and stepped across the street.

ON WEDNESDAY AFTERNOONS, the tan Buick pulled into the Walkers' driveway just past lunchtime, and Cath Johansen called Stella to gossip. "I knew there wouldn't be just one," she said. She was convinced the colored women were there to scout out the neighborhood to plan their own eventual arrival. Stella clamped the phone against her cheek, peering through the kitchen blinds as Loretta's girlfriends climbed out. The tall one was Belinda Cooper—her husband composed movie scores for Warner Bros. Mary Butler in the cat-eyed glasses was married to a pediatrician. She was sorority sisters with Eunice Woods, whose husband had just sold a screenplay to MGM. Stella knew basic things about the ladies that Loretta had told her, but she'd never expected to meet any of the women until one Wednesday when Loretta called to tell her that Mary was sick. Would she like to be their fourth hand?

"I'm not much of a bid whist player," Stella said. She was terrible at cards, at any game that relied on chance.

"Honey, that's all right," Loretta said. "Sometimes we don't even take out the cards."

Playing bid whist, she learned, was mostly a guise for what the women really wanted to do, which was drink wine and gossip. Belinda Cooper, halfway through her second glass of Riesling, kept going on about a movie actor having a sloppy affair with one of the secretaries at Warner, a pretty young thing but bold as you know what, taking messages from his wife, then slipping down to his trailer to deliver much more than a missed call.

"These girls are gettin bolder today," Loretta said. She took another drag of her cigarette, not even touching her cards. "You know me and Reg went out to Carl's the other day and ran into Mary-Anne—"

"How is she?"

"Pregnant. Again."

"Lawd!"

"And you know what she had to say? Euny, it's your hand, baby."

"Mary-Anne never liked me," Eunice said. "You remember that time at Thelma's wedding?"

All of their conversations went like this, around and around in loops that Stella couldn't follow. She wasn't meant to understand their shorthand or glean complicated backstories from the cast of characters they introduced. To be there at all, really. But she was happy to sit quietly, fiddling with her cards, listening. If Belinda and Eunice had a problem with her being there, they didn't say. But they spoke around her, never directly to her, as if to tell Loretta, this is your responsibility. Still, the afternoon passed pleasantly enough, until the girls rushed in for snacks. It always struck Stella how natural Loretta seemed around Cindy. The girl clambered to her side, rubbing against her like a cat, and Loretta, without even breaking the conversation, reached for her. She seemed to know what Cindy wanted before she even asked for it. When the girls ran back upstairs, Eunice took a drag of her cigarette and said, "I still don't know why you so set on doin it."

"Doin what?" Loretta said.

"You know what. I know this is your new life now—"

"Oh please—"

"But your girl's gonna be miserable and we all know it. It's not worth it, just to make a point."

"It's not about making a point," Loretta said. "The school's right down the street and Cindy's just as smart as all those other kids—"

"We know, honey," Belinda said. "It's not about being right. You can be right til the cows come home. But this is your one child and this is her one life."

"You think I don't know that?" Loretta said. Her eyes flashed, and then, remembering herself, she laughed a little, stubbing out her cigarette. "Thank God all of us don't think like you two."

"Let's ask your new friend," Eunice said. "What do you make of all of this, Mrs. Sanders?"

Stella stared down at the card table, her neck already hot.

"Oh, I don't know," she said.

"Surely you have some opinion."

Eunice was giving Stella a smile that reminded her of a hunting dog with a rabbit in his teeth. The more you twitched away, the tighter those jaws fastened around you.

"I wouldn't do it," she finally said. "Those other parents will make her life hell, they'll want to make an example out of her. You don't know how they talk when you're not around—"

"And I bet you jump right to her defense too," Eunice said.

"That's enough," Loretta said softly, but she didn't have to. By then, the mood had soured. Belinda and Eunice left before the game even finished. Stella washed the wineglasses while the girls cleaned up their toys upstairs. It was getting late, nearly four. Blake would almost be home. Beside her, Loretta silently dried the glasses with a plaid dishtowel.

"I'm sorry," Stella said. For what exactly, she didn't know. Sorry for coming over, for ruining the card game, for being exactly who

177

Eunice Woods accused her of being. She didn't defend Loretta, not even to silly Cath Johansen. She conscripted her own daughter to lie, afraid her husband would find out she socialized with the woman.

Loretta gave her a strange smile.

"You think I want your guilt?" she said. "Your guilt can't do nothin for me, honey. You want to go feel good about feelin bad, you can go on and do it right across the street."

Stella set the wet glass on the countertop, dried her hands on the towel. So this is what Loretta really thought about her—a white woman swarming around to assuage her guilt. And wasn't it true? She did feel guilty, but if anything, spending time with Loretta only made her feel even worse. Her real life seemed even more fake by comparison. And yet, she didn't want to stay away, not even now, not when Loretta was angry at her. Loretta reached for the wet glass and knocked it off the counter, the glass shattering at their feet. She stared up at the ceiling, suddenly exhausted. She was too young to look this tired, but she must be, fighting all the time. Stella never fought. She always gave in. She was a coward that way.

Loretta bent to pick up the glass, but not thinking, Stella jutted her arm out and said, "Don't, baby, you'll cut yourself." Then she was kneeling on the tile, cleaning up the mess she'd made.

First Martin Luther King Jr. in Memphis, then Bobby Kennedy in downtown Los Angeles. Soon it felt like you couldn't open a paper without seeing the bleeding body of an important man. Stella started switching off the news when her daughter came bounding into the kitchen for breakfast. Loretta said that, a couple months ago, Cindy asked her what *assassination* meant. She told her the truth, of course—that an assassination is when someone kills you to make a point.

Which was correct enough, Stella supposed, but only if you were an important man. Important men became martyrs, unimportant ones victims. The important men were given televised funerals, public days of mourning. Their deaths inspired the creation of art and the destruction of cities. But unimportant men were killed to make the point that they were unimportant—that they were not even men—and the world continued on.

Sometimes she still had dreams that someone was breaking into her house. More than once, she'd prodded Blake out of bed to check. "I told you it's a safe neighborhood," he grumbled, climbing back under the covers. But hadn't she felt safe once, years ago, hidden in a little white house surrounded by trees? Now she slept with a baseball bat behind the headboard. "What're you gonna do with that, Slugger?" Blake said, squeezing her tiny bicep. But when he traveled for business, she could never fall asleep without touching the worn handle, just to remind herself that it was there.

"YOU NEVER TALK ABOUT your family," Loretta said.

In her backyard, she stretched out on a lawn chair, her face half hidden behind sunglasses. She wore a purple bathing suit, her legs still speckled with water from the pool. Stella craned her neck, watching the girls splash around. In two weeks, school was starting again, Kennedy back at the Brentwood Academy, Cindy off to St. Francis in Santa Monica. A good school, only half an hour away, Loretta said, and Stella felt relieved. She wanted to tell Loretta that it was for the best—there was nothing wrong with putting your head down and trying to survive—but she would only have made Loretta feel even more like she'd given in. Now Loretta was complaining about her in-laws flying in from Chicago—they planned to stay ten whole days, and Reg, of course, said yes, because he could never tell them no, and because, of course, she would have to do most of the entertaining while he was off to set.

"What about you?" Loretta said. "Does your husband get along with your parents?"

The pointed question caught Stella off guard; she was distracted, already wondering what she would do with the ten days when she wouldn't see Loretta at all.

"My folks are long gone," she said. "They're . . ."

She trailed off, unable to finish. Loretta's face fell.

"Oh honey, I'm sorry," she said. "Look at me, bringin up bad memories—"

"It's all right," Stella said. "It happened so long ago."

"You were young, were you?"

"Young enough," she said. "It was an accident. Nobody's fault." Bad things happen, they just do.

"What about brothers or sisters?" Loretta said.

"No brothers." Stella paused, then said, "I had a twin sister. You remind me of her a little."

She hadn't planned to say this, and as soon as she did, she regretted it. But Loretta only laughed.

"How so?" she said.

"Oh, I don't know. Little ways. She was funny. Bold. Nothing like me, really." She felt herself tearing up, hurried to dab her eyes. "I'm sorry, I don't know why I'm going on like this—"

"Don't be sorry," Loretta said. "You lost your whole family! If anything's worth boo-hooing about, it's that. And a sister too. Have mercy."

"I still think about her," Stella said. "I didn't know I would still think about her like this—"

"Of course you do," Loretta said. "Losing a twin. Must be like losing half of yourself."

Sometimes she imagined picking up the phone and calling Desiree, just to hear her voice. But she didn't know how to reach her and besides, what would she even say? Too many years had passed. What good would looking back do? She was tired of justifying a choice she'd already made. She didn't want to be pulled back into a life that was no longer hers.

"Twins," Loretta said, as if the word itself contained magic. "You know what my mama used to say? She could always tell if a woman will have twins, right from her palm."

Now Stella laughed. "What?"

"Oh yeah, you never had your palm read? Look, I'll show you." Loretta reached, suddenly, for Stella's hand. "See this line right here? That's your child line. If it forks out, it means you'll have twins. But you got just the one. And this here, this is your love line. See how it goes deep and straight? That means you'll be married a long time. And this one's your life line. Look how it splits."

"And what's that mean?"

"It means your life's been interrupted."

Loretta smiled, and again, Stella wondered if she knew. Maybe the whole time, Loretta had just been playing along. The thought was humiliating but strangely liberating. Maybe Stella could tell her the whole story now and maybe Loretta would understand. That she hadn't meant to betray anyone but she'd just needed to be new. It was her life, why couldn't she decide if she wanted a new one? But Loretta laughed. She was only joking. You couldn't read a person's life off her hand, let alone a life as complicated as Stella's. Still, she liked sitting here, Loretta tracing a fingernail along her palm.

"Okay," Stella said. "What else does it say?"

Nine

I n New Orleans, Stella split in two.

She didn't notice it at first because she'd been two people her whole life: she was herself and she was Desiree. The twins, beautiful and rare, were never called the girls, only *the twins*, as if it were a formal title. She'd always thought of herself as part of this pair, but in New Orleans, she splintered into a new woman altogether after she got fired from Dixie Laundry. She'd been daydreaming during her shift, thinking, again, about the morning she'd visited the museum as a white girl. Being white wasn't the most exciting part. Being anyone else was the thrill. To transform into a different person in plain sight, nobody around her even able to tell. She'd never felt so free. But she was so distracted by her own remembering, she almost caught her hand in the mangle. The near accident was dangerous enough for Mae to fire her. Any workplace injury would be bad, but an accident involving a girl illegally hired was too much of a risk.

"You lucky you just fired," Mae told her. Lucky because she'd only lost a job, not a hand, or lucky because she'd only been let go, Desiree offered a stern warning? Either way, she needed a new job. For weeks, she reported to the temp agency and spent all afternoon in crowded waiting rooms, leaving with the promise that she could try again in the morning. She dreaded facing Desiree each evening she returned home to find their money jar dwindling. Then, the Sunday before rent was due, she spotted a job listing in the paper. Maison Blanche was looking for young ladies with fine handwriting and proficient typing skills to fill an opening in the marketing department, no office experience necessary. She'd always gotten good marks for her typing, but a department store would never hire a colored girl to do more than put away shoes or spray perfume at the counters. Still, Desiree told her she had to apply.

"This'll pay way more than Dixie Laundry," she said. "You have to go down there and see."

She almost said no. Told Desiree, forget it. So what if she could type? Why subject herself to the humiliation of some prim white secretary telling her that colored girls need not apply? Still, she woke up the next morning, put on her nice dress, and rode the streetcar to Canal Street. It was her fault that they were running out of money in the first place; she had to at least try. The elevator carried her to the sixth floor, where she stepped into a waiting room filled with white girls. She halted in the doorway, wondering if she should just turn back. But the blonde secretary waved her over.

"I need your typing sample, dear," she said.

Stella could have left. Instead, she carefully filled out the application and typed up the sample paragraph. Her hands trembled as she pressed the keys. She was terrified of being discovered, but almost more afraid that she wouldn't be. And then what? This wasn't the same as sneaking into the art museum. If she was hired, she would have to be white every day, and if she couldn't sit in this waiting room without her hands shaking, how could she ever manage that? When the secretary announced that the position was filled, she felt relieved. She'd applied; at least, she could tell Desiree that she'd done her best. She quickly gathered her coat and her pocketbook, heading toward the elevator when the secretary asked if Miss Vignes could start tomorrow.

AT MAISON BLANCHE, Stella addressed envelopes for Mr. Sanders. He was the youngest associate in the marketing department and movie-star handsome, so all the other girls in the building envied her. Carol Warren, a busty blonde from Lafayette, told Stella she didn't know how lucky she was. Carol worked for Mr. Reed, who was nice enough, she supposed, even though she couldn't stop staring at the gray hairs sprouting out his ears when he dictated messages. But what it must be like to work for Mr. Sanders! Carol chewed her salad eagerly, waiting for Stella to share some delicious detail about him, but she didn't know what to say. She hardly spoke to the man at all, except in the mornings when he dropped his coat and hat on her desk, and when he returned from lunch and she passed on his messages. "Thanks dear," he always said, reading the scraps of paper as he started back into his office. She didn't think he even knew her name.

"A real dish, isn't he?" Carol whispered once after she'd caught Stella staring.

She flushed, shaking her head quickly. The last thing she needed was to get caught up in the office gossip. She kept to herself, arrived on time, left when she was supposed to. She ate lunch at her desk and spoke as little as possible, certain that she'd say the wrong thing and make somebody wonder about her. She certainly tried not to speak around Mr. Sanders, only offering a soft hello when he greeted her. One morning, he paused in front of her desk, his briefcase swinging at his side.

"You don't talk much," he said.

It wasn't a question, but she still felt compelled to answer.

"I'm sorry, sir," she said. "I've always been quiet."

"I'll say." He started toward his office, then suddenly turned. "Let me take you out to lunch today. I like to get to know the girls who work for me." Then he patted the desk as if she'd said yes, to show that it had been decided.

All morning, she was so rattled, she kept misaddressing her envelopes. By lunchtime, she hoped that Mr. Sanders would forget about his offer. But he emerged from his office and beckoned her to follow him, so off they went. In Antoine's, Blake ordered oysters and, when she stared silently at the menu, an alligator soup for both of them.

"You're not from around here, are you?" he asked.

She shook her head. "No, sir," she said. "I was born . . . well, it's a little town north of here."

"Nothing wrong with little towns. I like little towns."

He smiled at her, lifting the spoon to his mouth, and she tried to smile back. Later that evening, when Desiree demanded details from her, Stella wouldn't remember the emerald green wallpaper, the framed photographs of famous New Orleanians, the taste of the soup. Nothing but that smile Mr. Sanders had given her. No white man had ever smiled at her so kindly.

"Here's what we'll do," he said. "Anything you want to know about the city—anything at all—you ask me. Don't feel silly about it. I know how strange a new city can be."

She paused. "How do you eat those?" she asked, pointing to the oysters.

He laughed. "You've never had oysters? I thought all you Louisiana people love them."

"We never had much money. I always wondered."

"I didn't mean to poke fun," he said. "I'll show you. It's very simple." He reached for the fork, glancing up at her. "You belong here, Stella. Don't ever think you don't."

At work, Stella became Miss Vignes or, as Desiree called her,

White Stella. Desiree always giggled after, as if she found the very idea preposterous, which irritated Stella. She wanted Desiree to see how convincingly she played her role, but she was living a performance where there could be no audience. Only a person who knew her real identity would appreciate her acting, and nobody at work could ever know. At the same time, Desiree could never meet Miss Vignes. Stella could only be her when Desiree was not around. In the morning, during her ride to Maison Blanche, she closed her eyes and slowly became her. She imagined another life, another past. No footsteps thundering up the porch steps, no ruddy white man grabbing her father, no Mr. Dupont pressing against her in the pantry. No Mama, no Desiree. She let her mind go blank, her whole life vanishing, until she became new and clean as a baby.

Soon she no longer felt nervous as the elevator glided skyward and she stepped into the office. You belong here, Blake had told her. Soon she thought of him as Blake, not Mr. Sanders, and she began to notice how he lingered at her desk now when he said good morning, how he invited her to lunch more often, how he began walking her to the streetcar after work.

"It's not safe out here," he said once, pausing at the crosswalk, "a pretty girl like you walking alone."

When she was with Blake, no one bothered her. The leering white men who'd tried to flirt with her at her stop now fell suddenly silent; the colored men sitting in the back didn't even look in her direction. At Maison Blanche, she once overheard another associate refer to her as "Blake's girl," and she felt as if that distinction covered her even beyond the office building. As if just by venturing into the world as Blake's girl, she had been changed somehow.

Soon she began to look forward to stepping through the glass doors, ambling slowly down the sidewalk with Blake. Soon she noticed how when he blinked, his eyelashes were dark and full like a baby doll. How on days when he had a big presentation, he wore bull-dog cuff links, which he admitted, almost bashfully, were a gift from his ex-fiancée. The relationship had failed but he still considered them lucky.

"You're observant, Stella," he said. "I don't think anybody's ever asked me about these before."

She noticed everything about him, but she didn't tell this to any-one, especially not Desiree. This life wasn't real. If Blake knew who she truly was, he would send her out of the office before she could even pack her things. But what had changed about her? Nothing, really. She hadn't adopted a disguise or even a new name. She'd walked in a colored girl and left a white one. She had become white only because everyone thought she was.

Each evening, she went through the process in reverse. Miss Vignes climbed onto the streetcar where she became, again, Stella. At home, Stella never liked to talk about work, even when Desiree asked. She didn't like to think about Miss Vignes when she wasn't her, although, sometimes, the other girl appeared suddenly, the way you might think about an old friend. An evening lying about the apartment, and she might think, I wonder what Miss Vignes would be doing right now. Then there she was, Miss Vignes lounging in her lush home, a fur rug peeking between her toes, not this cramped studio she shared with a sister who always smelled like starch. Or one night, when they'd stood outside a restaurant waiting to be served at the colored window, she thought, Miss Vignes would not receive her food out an alley window like a street dog. She couldn't tell if she was offended, or if Miss Vignes was on her behalf.

Sometimes she wondered if Miss Vignes was a separate person al-together. Maybe she wasn't a mask that Stella put on. Maybe Miss Vignes was already a part of her, as if she had been split in half. She could become whichever woman she decided, whichever side of her face she tilted to the light.

No one in the Estates knew what to make of it: Stella Sanders crossing the street to visit with that colored woman. Marge Hawthorne swore she saw her venture over months ago, Stella ducking her head as she carried a cake in her arms. "Welcoming that woman here, can you believe it?" Marge asked, and nobody did believe her, not at first. Marge was always imagining things; she'd sworn twice that she had seen Warren Beatty at the car wash. But then Cath Johansen spotted Stella and Loretta at the park, sitting side by side on a bench. Their shoulders rounded, casual and easy. Loretta said something that made Stella laugh, and Stella actually reached for Loretta's cigarette and took a drag. Put that colored woman's cigarette in her own mouth! This detail—specific and odd—made the story stick, not to mention the fact that Cath was telling it. She'd always been a little enamored with Stella, orbiting around her like a satellite planet happy to be washed in her light.

But when she told the other ladies about Stella and Loretta, Cath said that she'd never known Stella well, not really, and besides, there was always something a little strange about that woman. Betsy Roberts interrupted to tell the group that just that Monday, she'd seen Stella walking across the street with her daughter.

"That's the shame of it," she said. "To bring that little girl into all of this."

But what all of this meant was anybody's guess. No one said a word to Blake Sanders, who'd noticed Stella's strangeness but had already accepted that his wife was the type of woman who fell into moods he could not decipher. His mother had warned him about her, said she wouldn't be worth the trouble. He'd just started dating Stella then, but she'd been his secretary for two years already; he spoke to her more than to anyone else in his life. He could sense by the shape of her shoulders if she was in a bad mood; he could read in the slant of her handwriting when she was hurried. But dating Stella felt like unfolding an entirely new mystery. He never met anyone else in her life. No family, no friends, no former lovers. Back then, her distantness seemed dreamy. Romantic, even. But his mother said that Stella was hiding something.

"I don't know what," she'd said, "but I'll tell you this—her family's still alive."

"Then why would she say they aren't?"

"Because," his mother said, "she probably comes from some backwoods Louisiana trash and she doesn't want you to find out about it. Well, you'll find out soon enough."

His mother had wanted him to marry a different girl, one who came from a certain pedigree. In college, he'd escorted that type of girl to dozens of formals—society girls who bored him to tears. Maybe that's why he was drawn to the pretty secretary who came from nowhere and had nobody. He didn't mind her secrets. He would learn them in good time. But years had passed and she was as inscrutable as ever. He came home early from work one afternoon, calling her name, and found the house empty. When his wife and daughter finally returned, an hour later, Stella, surprised to see him, bent to give him a kiss.

"Sorry, darling," she said. "We were at Cath's and I lost track of time."

Another time, he'd beaten her home because she'd stayed too late at Betsy Roberts's house.

"What were you two talking about?" he asked later.

She was sitting in front of her vanity mirror, brushing her hair.

One hundred strokes each night before bed; she'd read it in *Glamour* once. The red brush blurred, mesmerizing him.

"Oh, you know," she said. "The girls. Little things like that."

"I've just never known you to be like this."

"Like what?"

"Well, friendly."

She laughed. "I'm just being neighborly. Aren't you the one who's always telling me to get out more?"

"But you're gone all the time now."

"What am I supposed to do?" she said. "Tell Kennedy she can't have friends?"

He'd been a shy child, so he never had many friends, colored or otherwise. But he did play with Jimbo, an ugly black rag doll with a plastic head and queer red lips. His father hated his son running around with a doll, a nigger doll at that, but Blake carried him everywhere, whispering all of his secrets into those plastic ears. This was a friend, someone who guarded your feelings behind that frozen red smile. Then one day, he stepped into the yard and saw clumps of cotton scattered all over the grass. On the dirt pathway, there was Jimbo, gutted, arms and legs strewn, his insides spilling out. The dog must've got to it, his father told him, but Blake always imagined him tossing that doll into the dog's snapping jaws. He'd knelt, picking up one of Jimbo's arms. He'd always wondered what the inside of the doll might look like. For some reason, he'd thought the cotton would be brown.

By CHRISTMASTIME, Stella had spent so many afternoons at Loretta's house that, out of habit, she told Loretta one Monday that she'd see her tomorrow. "It's Christmas Eve, honey," Loretta said, laughing, and Stella laughed too, embarrassed that she'd forgotten. She always dreaded the holidays. She could never stop thinking about her family, even though their celebrations were nothing like hers now. A tree so tall the star brushed against the ceiling, so much food for dinner that she got sick of leftovers, and mountains of presents awaiting Kennedy. Each December, she piled into the department store with the other mothers, clutching the letter to Santa, and tried to imagine a childhood like this. The twins always received one present apiece, something useful like a new church dress. One year, Stella received a piglet from the Delafosse farm that she named Rosalee. For months, she'd fed Rosalee, running when the pig chased her around the yard. Then Easter Sunday came and her mother killed the pig for supper.

"And I ate every single bite," she told her daughter once. She thought the story might teach Kennedy to be a little more grateful; she hadn't expected the girl to burst out crying, staring at her as if she were some monster. Maybe she was. She didn't remember crying for that pig at all.

"You all doing anything exciting for the holidays?" Loretta asked.

"Just a few people coming over," Stella said. "A small thing, we do it every year."

The party was not a small event; they'd hired caterers and a string quartet, invited the entire neighborhood. But of course, she couldn't tell this to Loretta. She'd known, licking the invitations shut, that she could never invite the Walkers.

On Christmas Eve, the Johansens arrived first, bearing a brick-hard fruit cake, then the Pearsons carrying bourbon for the eggnog. The Robertses, deeply Catholic, brought a tiny blonde angel for the tree. Then the Hawthornes waving from the front steps with homemade fudge, the Whites with an ironic beach snow globe, and soon the living room crowded with company. Stella felt hot from all the people, or the mulled wine, or maybe even from knowing that, across the street, Loretta could probably hear the music. She must have seen that endless parade of neighbors climbing up the steps. Or maybe not. Her own parents had arrived that evening; Stella had watched the elderly couple climb out of the Cadillac, Reg hefting the suitcases from the trunk, Loretta wrapping her arms around their backs as they glanced around the neighborhood, as dazed as if they'd stumbled into another country. Wouldn't her own mother look at her new life the same way? At least Loretta's parents would be proud. She had come upon her nice things the honest way, not by stealing a life not meant for her. Then again, she and Loretta had both wound up in the Estates by marrying well. Maybe there wasn't such a big difference between the two after all.

Blake swapped her empty glass with another mulled wine, bending to kiss her cheek. He loved hosting parties, even though it only made Stella want to find a corner and hide. Betsy pulling her into a conversation about linens, Cath asking where she'd purchased an end table, Dale dangling mistletoe over her head. She was lingering on the edge of a circle, wondering if her daughter was still spying through the bannister, always afraid that she was missing something exciting. Then the circle of neighbors lit up with laughter, smiling at her, awaiting a response.

"I'm sorry," she said. "What was it again?"

She was so easily embarrassed at these parties. She'd catch herself on the edge of a political discussion—the Vietnam situation, perhaps, or an upcoming election—and someone would ask what she thought. Even though she read the newspapers and had her opinions like anyone else, her mind went blank. She was always afraid that she'd say the wrong thing. Now Dale Johansen was smirking at her.

"I said I'm wondering when your new friend might show up," he said.

"Oh I don't know," she said. "I think everyone's here by now."

When the others exchanged amused glances, she blushed. She hated being the butt of a joke.

"What're you talking about, Dale?" she said.

Dale laughed. "I'm just asking if your friend from across the street is coming. I'm sure she can hear the music out there."

Stella paused, her heart thrumming.

"She's not my friend," she said.

"Well, people are saying that you've been calling on her," Cath said.

"So?"

"So is it true? Have you been visiting with her?"

"I don't think that's any of your goddamn business," Stella said.

Betsy Roberts gasped. Tom Pearson laughed uncomfortably, as if he were willing it to become a joke. Suddenly, Stella felt as if she had transformed into a totally new creature in their eyes. Something wild and feral. Cath stepped back, her cheeks pink.

"Well, everyone's talking," she said. "I just thought you should know."

THE NERVE OF THAT WOMAN.

In front of the bathroom mirror, Stella fumed, splashing water on her face. Where did Cath Johansen get off anyway? Storming into her house with that dry slab of fruit cake and telling her, to her face, in her own home, in front of everyone, that the entire neighborhood was judging her. Dale grinning dumbly beside her, Blake watching with that confused look on his face like he'd woken up from a nap to find all these strangers standing around in his living room. She'd stormed upstairs and smoked a cigarette hanging out the bedroom window. She could hear the quiet murmuring of the party downstairs, Blake, no doubt, making excuses for her. Oh don't mind, Stella, she's always a little testy this time of the year. Yes, her holiday blues, who knows, who can understand that woman half the time anyway? Then the Johansens and the Hawthornes and the Pearsons stepping carefully down the walkway, past the manicured lawns, behind their identical front doors to whisper about her. If only they knew. The thought ran through her head deliciously, the same way she always thought, driving on an overpass, of turning her wheel and sending herself careening over the rail. There was nothing more tantalizing than the possibility of total destruction.

"I mean, can you believe it?" she told Blake. "In my own home! Talking to me like that. I mean, where does she find the nerve?"

She furiously spread night cream on her face. Blake lingered behind her, unbuttoning his shirt.

"Why didn't you tell me?" he said. He didn't look angry, only worried.

"There's nothing to tell," she said. "The girls like playing together—"

"Then why wouldn't you tell me? Why would you lie about going to Cath's—"

"I don't know!" she said. "I just thought—it seemed easier that way, all right? I knew you would have all your questions—"

"Can you blame me?" he said. "You've never been like this. You didn't even want them to move in—"

"Well, the girls like playing! What was I supposed to do?"

"Not lie to me," he said. "Not tell me you're doing one thing then sneaking over there all the time—"

"It's not all the time."

"Cath said it was twice this week!"

Stella laughed. "You can't be serious," she said. "You can't truly be taking Cath Johansen's side over mine."

"It's not about sides!" he said. "I've been noticing it too, you know. You're not yourself. You've been walking around like you've got your head in the clouds. And now you're chasing after that Loretta woman.

It's not normal. It's—" He eased up behind her, cupping her shoulders. "I understand, Stella, I do. You're lonely. That's right, isn't it? You never wanted to move to Los Angeles in the first place and now you're lonely as all hell. And Kennedy's getting older. So you probably . . . well, you should take a class or something. Something you've always wanted to do. Like learn Italian or make pottery. We'll find you something good to do, Stel. Don't worry."

One night, long ago in New Orleans, Blake had invited her to a work banquet. "I'd hate to go alone," he told her, "you know how these things are," and she'd nodded, even though, of course, she didn't. She told Desiree she had to work late and instead borrowed a dress from one of the other secretaries. Blake met her in the lobby of the banquet hall, as dashing as any leading man. "Aren't you a sight for sore eyes?" he whispered into her hair. All evening, he never left her side, his hand always lingering at the small of her back. At the end of the night, he brought her to a café for coffee, and halfway through her cherry pie, he told her that he was moving back to Boston. His father was sick, and he wanted to be closer to home.

"Oh," she said, dropping her fork. She hadn't realized how desperately she wanted more nights with him like tonight until she realized that there would never be another. But he surprised her, touching her hand.

"I know it's crazy," he said, "but I've got a job offer in Boston and—" He faltered a second, then laughed. "It's crazy, Stella, but would you join me? I'll need a secretary there and I just thought . . ."

They hadn't even kissed yet but his question sounded as serious as a marriage proposal. "Just say yes," he said, and the word tasted like cherries, sweet and tart and easy. Yes, and just like that, she could become Miss Vignes for good. She didn't give herself a chance to second-guess. She didn't plan how she would leave her sister, how she would settle in a new city on her own. For the first time in her life, she didn't worry about any of the practical details when she told Blake Sanders yes. The hardest part about becoming someone else was deciding to. The rest was only logistics.

Now she glanced at him through the mirror, Blake watching her with those soft, worried eyes. She'd created a new life with a man who could never know her, but how could she walk away from it now? It was the only life she had left.

ON CHRISTMAS MORNING, she leaned against Blake's chest, watching their daughter squeal and dive into her pile of gifts. A Talking Barbie that spoke when you pulled her cord, a Suzy Homemaker oven set, a red Spyder bicycle. Look at this, look at that, she must have been such a good girl this year! Unlike all those rotten poor children staring at empty trees who must have deserved it, bad because they were poor, poor because they were bad. She'd never wanted to participate in the Santa mythmaking, but Blake said that it was important to preserve Kennedy's innocence.

"It's just a little story," he said. "It's not like she'll hate us when she figures it out."

He couldn't even bring himself to say the word *lie*. Which was a lie in itself.

Scraps of wrapping paper littered the carpet, Kennedy collapsing in a blissful haze. Stella opened each of Blake's boxes to reveal another gift she hadn't asked for: a floor-length mink coat, a diamond tennis bracelet, an emerald necklace he fastened as they stood together in front of the bedroom mirror.

"It's too much," she whispered, fingering the gem.

"Nothing is too much for you, my sweet," he said.

She was one of the lucky ones. A husband who adored her, a happy daughter, a beautiful home. How could she complain about any of it?

Who was she to want more, when she'd already taken so much? She would have to stop playing these foolish games with Loretta Walker. Stop pretending the two had anything in common, that they existed in the same universe. That they could ever be friends. She would have to tell Loretta that she couldn't visit her anymore.

In the kitchen, she mashed potatoes until her arms burned. She slid pineapple wedges into the folds of the ham and pushed it into the oven. Blake, watching the Lakers wallop the Suns, told her that Kennedy had gone outside to play with the other neighborhood kids. But when she stepped out, she didn't see the Pearson boys racing bicycles past or the Johansen girls tugging their wagons or anyone tossing a football. No children at all, their cul-de-sac empty except for Kennedy and Cindy on the Walkers' lawn, both girls crying. Loretta kneeling between them—frazzled, still in her apron. Stella ran across the street, grabbed her daughter, searched her skin for cuts and scrapes. But she didn't find any, so she pulled Kennedy in for a hug instead.

"What's the matter?" she asked Loretta. "Did something happen?"

A fight over a new toy, maybe. Talking Barbie was lying in the dirt between them. But Loretta stood, grabbing her daughter's hand.

"You should know," she said.

Her voice was strangely cold. Maybe she had heard the music from the party last night, maybe she was still sore about not being invited. Stella stroked her daughter's hair.

"You have to share, honey," she said. "What did Mommy tell you about that? I'm sorry, Loretta, she's an only child, you know—"

"Oh, she shared plenty," Loretta said. "Keep her away from my girl."

"What?" Now Stella stood, gripping Kennedy's shoulder protectively. "What're you talking about?"

"You know what she said to Cindy? Well, the girls were playing some game and Kennedy was losing so she said, 'I don't want to play with a nigger.'"

Her stomach sank.

"Loretta, I—"

"No, I understand," Loretta said. "I don't blame her. It all comes from the home, see. And like a fool, I let you into mine. The loneliest goddamn woman in this whole neighborhood. I should've known. You stay away from me."

Loretta quivered, powerless in her anger and all the angrier for it. Stella felt numb. She guided her daughter back across the street. As soon as she shut the door, she grabbed Kennedy and slapped her. The girl yelped.

"What'd I do?" she asked, crying again.

Behind her, the crowd on the television roared, Blake cheering along. Stella stared into her daughter's face, seeing everyone that she had ever hated, then she was looking at her daughter again, gazing at her with watery eyes, a hand covering her reddened cheek. Stella fell to her knees, pulling her daughter close, kissing her damp face.

"I don't know," she said. "I don't know. Mommy's sorry."

YEARS LATER, Stella would only remember speaking to Reg Walker three times: One morning when she stepped out to collect the newspaper as he was leaving for the set, and he paused on the driveway and said, "Lovely day, ain't it?" She agreed that it was, watched him climb into his sleek black car. The second time, when he came home to find her sitting on the couch with his wife and paused a little in the doorway, as if he'd walked into the wrong house. "Hi there," he'd said, suddenly shy, and Loretta laughed, reaching for her glass of wine. "Sit with us awhile, baby," Loretta said. He didn't, but before he left, he leaned over to light her cigarette, their eyes meeting in a glance that felt so intimate, Stella looked away. And the third time, when Reg helped Stella unload her groceries. She should've recoiled as he came near but she let him carry her bags inside, the walk from the driveway to the kitchen counter feeling unnaturally long. Even Loretta hadn't been inside her home before. She walked with him down the lonely, sterile hallways, where he set the bags on the counter.

"There you go," he said. He didn't even look at her. But a week after Christmas, sitting around her sewing circle, she told Cath Johansen and Betsy Roberts that he made her uncomfortable.

"I don't know," she said, plucking at her misplaced stitch. "I just never liked the way he looked at me."

Three days later, someone threw a brick through the Walkers' living-room window, shattering that tiled vase Loretta had bought in Morocco. Tom Pearson and Dale Johansen both claimed credit, although it was neither of them—instead, Stella later discovered, it was beet-faced Percy White, who'd taken the new neighbors as a personal slight, as if they had only moved in to mar his presidential term. Some applauded him, although it made others uneasy.

"This is Brentwood, not Mississippi," Blake said. Tossing bricks through windows seemed like something the gap-toothed trash did. But a week later, a different man, desperate to prove himself one, left a flaming sack of dog shit on the Walkers' front steps. Days later, another brick sailed through the living-room window. According to the newspaper, the daughter was watching television at the time. The doctor had to remove glass shards from her leg.

By March, the Walkers left the Estates as suddenly as they'd arrived. The wife was miserable, Betsy Roberts told Stella, so they'd bought a new house in Baldwin Hills.

"I don't know why they didn't just do that from the start," Betsy said. "They'll be so much happier there."

By then, Stella hadn't spoken to Loretta since Christmas Day. But she still watched, through the blinds, as the yellow moving van pulled up, and a pack of young colored men slowly carried cardboard boxes out of the house. She imagined marching across the street to explain herself. Standing in Loretta's cavernous living room, Loretta balanced on one moving box while taping another shut. Loretta wouldn't look angry to see her—she wouldn't look like anything at all, and her blank face would hurt even more. Stella would tell her that she'd only said those terrible things about Reg because she was desperate to hide.

"I'm not one of them," she would say. "I'm like you."

"You're colored," Loretta would say. Not a question, but a statement of blunt fact. Stella would tell her because the woman was leaving; in hours, she'd vanish from this part of the city and Stella's life forever. She'd tell her because, in spite of everything, Loretta was her only friend in the world. Because she knew that, if it came down to her word versus Loretta's, she would always be believed. And knowing this, she felt, for the first time, truly white.

She imagined Loretta pushing off the box and stepping toward her. Her face frozen in awe, as if she'd seen something beautiful and familiar.

"You don't have to explain anything to me," she would say. "It's your life."

"But it's not," Stella would say. "None of it belongs to me."

"Well, you chose it," Loretta would tell her. "So that makes it yours."

Part IV

THE STAGE DOOR

(1982)

Ten

If you went to the Park's Korean Barbecue on Normandie and Eighth, during the fall of 1982, you'd probably find Jude Winston wiping down one of the high tables, staring out the foggy window. Sometimes before her shift started, she sat in a back booth reading. The noise never distracted her, the other waiters didn't understand it. She told Mr. Park on her first day that she'd practically grown up in a restaurant—a diner, really—even though she'd never waitressed before. She did not tell him that most of that time had been spent reading, not watching her mother run the place, but maybe as a father himself, he was sympathetic to restaurant kids. Maybe he respected her eagerness to find a job—barely a week after her college graduation, and she wasn't lazing about on the beach like his own sons would have done. Or maybe he just remembered her from the past spring, always sitting at a high top studying a worn MCAT book she'd borrowed from a teammate. When he'd brought her pork belly and asked how she was doing, she always got a dazed look in her eyes, as if he'd asked in Korean. She was a smart girl, he could tell. Plenty dull boys wanted to go to medical school but only smart girls found the nerve to apply. He'd finished two years of medical school himself, back in Seoul, so he understood her anxiety and wished her luck. He was always wishing her luck now, even though she told him she wouldn't hear back from any schools for months. Ah well, good luck, then.

"You don't need luck," Reese said. "You're gonna get in."

He stole a shrimp off her plate with his chopsticks. He visited sometimes during her dinner break, but Mr. Park never minded. He was a fair boss; she was lucky to work for someone like him. And still, she could only think about the letters that would arrive in the spring. Rejections mostly, but maybe one yes. You only needed one yes to be happy—medical school was like love in that regard. Some days her chances seemed promising, and other days she hated herself for clinging to this ridiculous dream. Hadn't she muddled her way through chemistry? Struggled in biology? You needed more than a good GPA to get into medical school. You had to compete against students who'd grown up in rich families, attended private schools, hired personal tutors. People who had been dreaming since kindergarten of becoming doctors. Who had family photos of themselves in tiny white coats, holding plastic stethoscopes to teddy bear bellies. Not people who grew up in nowhere towns, where there was one doctor you saw only when you were puking sick. Not people who'd stumbled into the whole idea of medical school after dissecting a sheep's heart in an anatomy class.

Seven schools were reading her application right now and would, in a few months, decide her future. Made her sick to even think about.

"I figured out how to fix that ceiling," Reese said. "I know it's been drivin you crazy."

It was November, and already unreasonably wet. Every morning this week, they'd driven through deep pockets of rainwater on Normandie, worried the car would stall. At home, they nudged a silver bucket underneath the leaking ceiling, which Reese dumped on the sorry patch of grass behind the Gardens Apartments. The Edenic name of their building always made him laugh. Why not call this building the Brick Slab, or the No Hot Water, or the Hole in the Roof? But Jude didn't find that funny. She glanced back at the clock, only five minutes left of her break.

"Why don't you just call Mr. Song?" she said.

"You know he's too old to be climbin up that ladder."

"He should hire someone, then."

"Too cheap," he said, squeezing her hip.

He'd found a new job at the Kodak store, selling cameras and developing photographs. He missed the camaraderie of the gym, but the Kodak store offered an employee discount on film. Not that he'd needed any lately. He hadn't taken a new photograph in six months. He spent his free time helping Mr. Song mop up water from the basement or plant mouse traps or whatever little chores he could do around the building to earn reduced rent. He unclogged the Parks' toilet, fixed the Shaws' broken pantry shelf, fished into the kitchen sink for Mrs. Choi's fallen wedding ring. If he came across a job he didn't know how to do, he called Barry for help.

"I told you that place was a dump," Barry said. But what were they supposed to do? Their old landlord had jacked up the rent, so off to Koreatown it was. In a way, it was an adventure. The new foods to try, the signs you couldn't read, the language spoken around you, on the bus or the street, that allowed you to drift off into your own thoughts. The neighbors in the Gardens, mostly elderly like the Chois and the Parks and the Songs, who pitied those two young people living in the apartment with the leaky ceiling and brought them sticky rice cakes for Christmas. But the ceiling. The cramped bedroom. The tiny kitchen. Reese said that if he helped enough around the Gardens, maybe they'd save so much on rent they could find a new place. But by then, Jude hoped that she would be gone.

"You worryin about nothin," her mother told her once over the phone. "You a smart girl."

"Plenty of people are smart, Mama."

"Not like you," her mother said.

Whenever they hung up, Jude always felt a little guilty knowing that the life she most feared was the one her mother was already living. Waiting tables forever, living in a cramped home. At least she had Reese. At least she wasn't in Mallard. She could be grateful for that, even if she couldn't stop herself from projecting into the future. Each time she mentioned spring, Reese shifted a little, a distant look falling over his face, like he didn't want to talk about it.

That night, after she closed Park's, they walked home, Reese's arm around her shoulders. On the corner outside the Gardens, a pale dark-haired woman passed and Jude held her breath. But it was just a white woman gliding underneath the streetlights.

IT COULDN'T BE STELLA. For years after that Beverly Hills party, Jude had thought of little else.

Sometimes the woman in the fur coat looked exactly like her mother, down to the curve in her smile. Other times, she was only slender and dark-haired, a passing resemblance at best. After all, she'd only caught a glimpse of the woman before the wine splashed against her leg. Then she was scrambling to pick up the shattered glass while the whole party gawked. This, of course, stayed with her too. How she'd groped along the table for cocktail napkins before Carla pushed her out of the way, frantically blotting the ruined rug. By the time she'd dumped the wine-bloodied napkins into the trash, Carla told her to leave and never come back. She'd quietly gathered her purse, too embarrassed to glance around the room lest she lock eyes with one of the many witnesses to her humiliation. She looked up once as she shut the door behind her and she didn't see the woman at all, only the girl with the violet eyes watching her leave, pink lips curled into a smirk.

A dark-haired woman who could have been anyone. Maybe she just missed her mother so much, she'd convinced herself of the resemblance. Maybe she felt guilty about not going home, about never going home, and this woman was a projection of her subconscious. Or maybe—no, she wouldn't even consider that possibility. That she had been in the same room with Stella, that she'd caught eyes with her even, before she'd dropped that wine bottle and shattered everything.

"What's wrong, baby?" Reese had asked later that night. "You're shaking."

They were walking to meet Barry at Mirage. She hadn't said much since she'd returned home early but Reese looked worried, pausing under the stoplight, and she knew that she had to tell him the truth.

"I lost my job," she said.

"What? What happened?"

"It's stupid. I saw Stella. I mean, I thought it was her. I swear she looked just like her—"

She felt even crazier saying it aloud. That she'd gotten herself fired because she'd caught a glimpse, through a crowded party, of a woman who may have resembled her mother.

"I can't believe I was so stupid," she said.

He pulled her into a hug.

"Aw, it's all right," he said. "You'll find another job."

"But I wanted to help you. I thought if we both put money away—"

He groaned. "That's why you were workin so crazy?"

"I just thought if the both of us—"

"But I didn't ask you to do that," he said.

"I know," she said. "I just wanted to. Don't be mad, baby. I just wanted to help."

She wrapped her arms around him and after a moment, he held her back.

"I'm not mad," he said. "I just don't like feelin like some charity case."

"You know I don't think of you like that."

"You gotta tell me things," he said. "You're so hidden away sometimes."

Maybe that was what drew them together. Maybe this was the only way they knew how to love, drawing near, then ducking away. He touched her cheek and she tried to smile.

"Okay," she said. "No more hiding."

FOR YEARS, Stella drifted through her dreams. Stella draped in mink, Stella perched on a ledge, Stella shrugging, smiling, slipping in and out of doors. Always Stella, never her mother, as if, even asleep, she could tell the difference. She always awoke shaken. She was tired all the time. She found a new job dishwashing in a campus cafeteria for two dollars an hour, where she spent her shift alone, steaming piles of cruddy plates clean. Each evening, she came home with pruned fingers, her shoulders stooped. At one point, she was three weeks behind on a history paper and her GPA was teetering so dangerously, her track coach called her into his office.

"You're smarter than this," he said, and she nodded, chastened, springing from the claustrophobic office as soon as he dismissed her. Yes, yes, she would work harder, apply herself more. Of course she took school seriously, of course she wanted to compete in the spring. Of course she couldn't lose her scholarship. She was just a little distracted at the moment, nothing too serious. She would shake out of it. But she didn't, because every time she tried to study, she only imagined Stella.

"Do you still think about her?" she asked her mother one afternoon.

"Who?"

Jude paused, wrapping her finger around the telephone cord. "Your sister," she finally said.

She couldn't bring herself to say Stella's name, like it would conjure her again. Stella strolling by on the sidewalk outside, Stella appearing in the fogged window.

"Now why you askin about all that?" her mother said.

"I don't know, I'm just wondering. Can't I wonder?"

"No use in wonderin," her mother said. "I stopped wonderin long ago. I don't think she's even here anymore."

"Living?" Jude said. "But what if she is? I mean, what if she's just out there somewhere?"

"I would feel her," her mother said quietly, and Jude began to think of Stella as a current running under her mother's skin. Under her own skin, dormant until that party when she'd locked eyes with Stella across the room. Then a leap, a spark, her arm jolting from her side. Now she was trying to forget that charge. She thought, once or twice, about telling her mother about the woman at the party, but what good would that do? It was Stella, it wasn't, she was dead, she was alive, she was in Omaha, Lawrence, Honolulu. When Jude stepped outside, she imagined bumping into her. Stella pausing on the sidewalk, admiring a purse through a shop window. Stella on the bus, hanging on to the vinyl strap—no, Stella in a smooth black limousine, hiding behind the tinted glass. Stella everywhere, always, and nowhere at the same time.

IN NOVEMBER 1982, a musical comedy called *The Midnight Marauders* opened in a nearly abandoned theater in downtown Los Angeles. The playwright, a thirty-year-old still living at home in Encino, was determined to make it in a city where, he claimed to friends, no one valued theater. He'd written *The Midnight Marauders* as a joke, and of course, the joke always being on him, it was his only success. The play ran at the Stardust Theater for four weekends, was nominated for a local award, and earned tepid praise in the *Herald-Examiner.* But Jude would have never heard about it if Barry hadn't landed a spot in the chorus line. For weeks leading up to the audition, he was a nervous wreck, bouncing on his heels as he practiced "Somewhere Over the Rainbow." He had never sung in front of anyone before dressed only as himself.

"I felt naked out there," he told her after the audition. "I was sweatin like a hog on Easter Sunday."

She was happy for him when he earned his spot in the company. He sent her tickets for opening night, but she told Reese that she had to work.

"Ask for the night off," he said. "We gotta support him. And we never go out anymore. We should have a little fun."

The previous month, his car engine had died and he'd emptied his savings to fix it. All those crumpled bills in his sock drawer, gone. He'd started working the door at Mirage to make extra cash on the weekends. The muscle, technically, although he was mostly just a handsome face greeting the customers. So far, he'd only broken up one drunk fight and earned a cut on that handsome face as gratitude. In the bathroom, he'd winced as Jude dabbed the cut with alcohol, missing those weekends they used to spend chasing sunlight across the marina in search of the perfect shot. Reese biting his lip as the shutter clicked. Now on Friday and Saturday nights, he left in a black T-shirt and black jeans and came home at dawn, his hands flecked with glitter from helping the go-go dancers onto the stage. Then off to the Kodak store, or helping Mr. Song. Some days, she barely saw him at all, only feeling him drop into bed beside her.

She couldn't afford to miss a night of work in order to sit in a damp theater, enduring three hours of amateur acting in hopes of catching a glimpse of Barry in the chorus line. Still, she agreed, running her fingers through Reese's hair. They needed a night out, one night where she didn't think about spring decisions, where he didn't obsess over money, where they wouldn't worry about anything at all.

On opening night, she slipped into a purple dress and glided panty hose up her legs as Reese, tying his tie, smiled at her through the mirror. They were overdressed because they never had anywhere nice to go; tonight was an excuse to pretend otherwise. They could pretend to be anything: a young couple on a first date, newlyweds sneaking away from the children, a pair of sophisticated theatergoers who never worried about money, never clipped coupons, never counted change.

"Fancy, fancy," Luis teased, when they all met up in the lobby with a dozen of the other boys she used to see scrambling around backstage in bustiers. Soon they were all laughing, clambering into the mildewed theater, everyone giddy as the lights dipped.

"This better be good," Reese stage-whispered, but he was so good natured about it, she could tell he didn't care. He kissed her as the orchestra began to play a jaunty overture. The curtains parted, and she leaned forward, straining to see Barry. He was high kicking with the other dancers, wearing a fringed leather vest and cowboy hat. She giggled, watching him twirl a redhead. Then the dancers receded and the show lead appeared center stage, a blonde girl in a long, hooped dress. Her singing voice was pretty if plain; still, she was charming enough, delivering her lines with a wryness so familiar that, in the darkness, Jude reached for her *Playbill*. And there she was, the blonde girl with the violet eyes.

AFTER THE CURTAIN FELL, after a beaming Barry took his bow, after the audience slowly trampled across the fading red carpet into the lobby, dissecting plot holes and glaring miscues, Jude circled with her friends outside the stage door. The group was chatty, debating drink plans while they waited for Barry to emerge so that they could embarrass him with thunderous applause. But she hugged herself, shifting from foot to foot, staring down the alley, expecting, at any moment, her mother's ghost to appear.

She'd slipped out of the theater during intermission, certain that in the darkness, she had mistaken the girl in the *Playbill* for the girl at the Beverly Hills party. But there she was, in full light. *Born in Brentwood, Kennedy Sanders studied at USC but left early to pursue a career in acting. She recently played Cordelia* (King Lear)*, Jenny* (Death of a Salesman) *and Laura* (The Glass Menagerie). *This is her first appearance at the Stardust Theater, though hopefully not her last.* In her headshot, the girl smiled, her wavy blonde hair falling angelically to her shoulders. She looked innocent here, nothing like the sassy girl who'd demanded a martini from her at a party, and she might have believed that this was a different white girl altogether if not for those eyes. She could never forget them.

If that girl was in the show, did that mean that the woman in the fur coat was here too? What if it was Stella? What if it wasn't? She'd wandered around the lobby until the house lights flickered but she never saw a woman who looked like her mother. Now she felt even crazier than before.

"You all right, baby?" Reese asked.

She nodded, trying to smile.

"I'm just cold," she said. He wrapped his arms around her, warming her up. Then the stage door opened, but instead of Barry wandering out, Kennedy Sanders stepped into the alley, fumbling with a pack of Marlboros. She looked startled to see the crowd waiting, and for a second, she smiled expectantly before realizing that no one was there to see her. Then her eyes flickered to Jude. She smirked.

"Oh," she said. "It's you."

She remembered her, three years later. Of course she did. Who would forget a dark girl who'd spilled wine all over an expensive rug?

"My friend's in this show," Jude said.

Kennedy shrugged, shaking a cigarette into her palm. She was wearing a tattered Sex Pistols T-shirt that stopped above her navel, jean shorts over ripped fishnet tights, and black leather boots—she looked nothing like the Beverly Hills princess from that party. She started walking down the alley, and Jude scrambled after her.

"Barry," she said. "He's in the chorus?"

"Is that your boyfriend?" Kennedy asked.

"Barry?"

"No, silly. Him." She jerked her head back toward the group. "The one with the curly hair. He's a doll. Where'd you find him?"

"At school," she said. "Well, really at this party—"

"You have a light?" Kennedy slid a cigarette into her mouth. When Jude shook her head, she said, "Just as well. Bad for the singing voice, you know."

"I thought you were amazing tonight," Jude said. She didn't really, but she would have to flatter this girl to get anything out of her. "Your folks must be proud."

Kennedy scoffed. "Please. They hate that I'm doing this."

"Why?"

"Because they sent me to school to do something practical, you know. Not drop out and throw my life away. At least that's what my mother says. Hey, do you have a light?" She flagged down a shaggy-haired white man smoking on the corner. "Well, so long!"

She hurried over to the man on the corner, who smiled as he leaned in to light her cigarette. A flicker in the darkness, then she was gone.

BARRY SAID THAT Kennedy Sanders was a rich bitch.

"You know the type," he told Jude. "A couple of solos in the high school choir and now she thinks she's Barbra Streisand." He was putting on his face in the backstage of Mirage for the Sunday brunch show, the only time slot available now that *The Midnight Marauders* had taken over his evenings. He hated the early call time and the thinner crowds but he loved being Bianca too much to wait three weeks until the play closed. He gestured behind him and Jude yanked the hairbrush jutting out of his gym bag.

"So what do her parents do?" she asked.

"Who knows?"

"They haven't been by the theater?"

"Hell, no," Barry said. "You think they'd come around that dump? No ma'am, she comes from real money. Some hoity-toity folks, big house in the hills, all that. Why you asking about her anyway?"

"No reason," she said.

But that afternoon, she rode the bus downtown to the Stardust Theater. The Sunday matinee was starting in a half hour; the teenage usher wouldn't let her inside without a ticket, so she paced on the sidewalk under the green eaves. She already felt foolish riding down in the first place. What would she even say to Kennedy? She tried to think of what Early might do. The key to hunting, he'd told her, is pretending to be someone else. But she'd never been able to be anyone but herself, so when the usher shooed her away, she slunk off to the sidewalk. Of course right then she bumped into Kennedy hustling toward the entrance. She wore jean shorts so short, the pocket flaps were showing, and a pair of worn cowboy boots.

"Sorry," they both said, then Kennedy laughed.

"Well, goddamn," she said. "You following me or something?"

"No, no," Jude said quickly. "I'm looking for my friend but they won't let me inside. I don't have a ticket."

Kennedy rolled her eyes. "Like Fort Knox in here," she said. Then she told the usher, "She's with me," and like that, Jude was fumbling after her through the lobby, past backstage, and into her dressing room. The room was barely bigger than a closet, the yellow paint chipping off the walls.

Under the dim mirror lights, Kennedy plopped into the worn leather chair.

"Donna wanted to skin you alive," she said.

"What?" Jude said.

"After you ruined her rug. God, you should've seen her, running around like you'd slaughtered her firstborn. My rug! My rug! It was a riot. Well, not for you, probably." She spun in her chair, eyeing herself in the mirror. "What's your name anyway?"

"Jude."

"Like the song?"

"Like the Bible."

"I like it," Kennedy said. "Hey Jude, not to be a bitch or anything, but I've gotta change."

"Oh," Jude said. "I'm sorry."

She started to back out the door but Kennedy said, "Don't go. You can help me. I can never get into this thing on my own." She was tugging the big hooped dress from the opening number out of the closet. Jude smoothed the wrinkles out of the orange fabric as Kennedy yanked her T-shirt over her head. She was slender and tan, wearing a matching pink bra and panty set. Jude tried not to watch, staring instead at the cluttered countertop covered in palettes of makeup, a curling iron, gold earrings, a crumpled candy wrapper.

"So where you from, Hey Jude?" Kennedy said. "Bring that over, will you? Jesus, I hate this thing. It always makes me sneeze." She lifted her arms and Jude stared into the smoothness of her armpits as she helped lift the dress over her head. True to her word, Kennedy let out one dainty sneeze before slipping her arms into the sleeves.

"Louisiana," Jude said.

"No kidding. So's my mother. I'm from here. Well, I don't know if you can say you're from a place if you've never left. Can you? I don't know how anything works. Zip me?"

She spoke so quickly, Jude felt dizzy following along.

"Which part?" she asked.

"Hey, can you hurry? Curtain's in twenty and I haven't done my makeup yet." She pulled her blonde hair off her shoulder. Jude stepped behind her, tugging the zipper.

"What's your mother's last name?" she said. "Maybe I know her people."

Kennedy laughed. "I doubt that."

What was she doing? She'd seen a woman who may have looked like her mother and now she'd ended up stalking a white girl and helping her into a ridiculous costume? What did she care, anyway? She'd never even met Stella. Kennedy leaned into the mirror, powdering her face. For the first time, she was quiet and focused, like Barry right before a performance. "I have to get into my zone," he always said, shooing Jude before his curtain call. Sometimes she lingered in the doorway and watched as a veil seemed to drop before his face. One moment he was Barry, the next, Bianca. She could see a similar moment passing through Kennedy right now. It felt more intimate to witness than seeing the girl in her underwear. She turned to leave.

"You don't know anyone named Vignes, do you?" Kennedy called after her. "That's my mother's name. Or was her name." She glanced over her shoulder. "Estelle Vignes. But everyone calls her Stella."

Eleven

Statistically speaking, the likelihood of encountering a niece you'd never met at a Beverly Hills retirement party was improbable but not impossible. Which Stella Sanders might have, at least intellectually, understood. Improbable events happened all the time, she tried to explain to her students, because improbability is an illusion based on our preconceptions. Often it has nothing to do with statistical truth. After all, it's wildly improbable that any one person is alive. A particular sperm cell fertilizing a particular egg, producing a viable fetus. Twins are more likely to be stillborn, identical twins more vulnerable than fraternal twins, yet here she was, teaching Introduction to Statistics at Santa Monica College. Likely does not mean certain. Improbable does not mean impossible.

She'd discovered statistics unexpectedly in her second year at Loyola Marymount University. She didn't call herself a sophomore then; she was ten years older than everyone else in the class, so the title felt silly. She didn't even know what she wanted to study, only that she liked numbers. Statistics entranced her because so many people misunderstood it. In Las Vegas, she'd sat beside Blake in a smoke-filled casino as he lost four hundred dollars at the craps table, staying in the game longer than he should have because he was convinced that he was due. But dice owed you nothing.

"It doesn't matter what's already rolled," she finally told him, exasperated. "Each number is equally likely if the dice are fair. Which they're not."

"She takes one class," Blake told the man sitting next to them.

The man laughed, puffing at his cigar. "I always stay on," he said. "Rather lose than know I would've won if I hadn't played it safe."

"Well said." Blake and the man clinked their glasses. Statistical truth, like any other truth, was difficult to swallow.

For most people, the heart decided, not the mind. Stella was like everyone else in this regard. Hadn't her decision to follow Blake from New Orleans been an emotional one? Or her choice to stay with him over the years? Or her agreement to, say, attend Bert Hardison's retirement party, even cajoling her daughter to appear, because, Blake claimed, they needed to show a united front? One big happy family—it mattered to the rest of the partners. Blake was a marketing man who understood the value of his own brand, Stella and Kennedy merely an extension of it. So she'd agreed to go to that party. In spite of everything, she'd whisked around the living room, playing the dutiful wife even as Bert Hardison, smelling like brandy, crowded near her all night, his hand on her waist (as if she wouldn't notice!). But Blake, of course, didn't see, huddling in the corner with Rob Garrett and Yancy Smith, while Stella tried to make small talk with Donna Hardison, keeping an eye on her daughter, who kept inching near the bar, and avoiding the red stain on the white rug that a lanky black man was feebly blotting with soda water.

There'd been a disturbance earlier, a black girl spilling wine on the rug, which had, for a few moments, stolen the attention of everyone at the party. Stella had just arrived, so she'd only seen the aftermath. A charcoal girl frantically mopping an expensive merlot out of the even more expensive rug before Donna shrieked that she was only making it worse. Even after the girl was dismissed, the party continued to discuss her.

"I just can't believe it," Donna told Stella. "What's the point of hiring waiters if they can't hold on to a damn bottle of wine?"

The topic bored Stella, to tell the truth. The type of minor skirmish that people fixated on during a party where there was nothing more interesting to discuss. Unlike the math department mixers, where conversations leapt from one topic to another—inscrutable, pretentious, but never boring. She always felt lucky to be in the presence of such brilliant people. Thinkers. Blake's colleagues viewed intelligence as a means to an end, and the end was always making more money. But in the mathematics department at Santa Monica College, no one expected to be rich. It was enough to know. She was lucky to spend her days like this, knowing.

That night, driving home from the party, she'd found herself thinking about Loretta Walker. Stella was wearing the mink coat Blake had surprised her with that Christmas and maybe the luxurious fur brushing against her calves reminded her. Or maybe because that morning, when she'd told Blake that she would be late to the party, they'd fought again about the job that she only had because of Loretta. For months after the Walkers left, she'd fallen into a depression that was deep even by her own standards. She was grieving for reasons that she could never explain. Like she'd lost Desiree all over again. Blake suggested she take a class, which he later regretted because she brought it up each time he complained about her working.

"You said it yourself," she said, during their last argument. "I was going crazy in that house."

"Yes, but—" He paused. "I thought you'd, I don't know, take a flower-arranging class or something."

But she'd always felt ashamed of being a high school dropout. She felt stupid when someone used a term she didn't understand. She hated asking for directions even when she was lost. She dreaded the day when her daughter would know more than her, when she would stare at Kennedy's homework, unable to help. So she'd told Blake that she wanted to take a GED class.

"I think that's great, Stel," he'd said. He was pacifying her, of course, but she signed up for classes anyway. Two nights in a row, she sat in the parking lot outside the public library, afraid to venture inside. She would feel stupid, staring blankly at the chalkboard. When was the last time she'd done any math more complicated than balancing her checkbook? But when she finally went inside, the teacher began to explain an algebra problem and slowly, she felt sixteen again, acing Mrs. Belton's tests. This was what she loved about math: it was the same now as it had been then, and there was always a correct answer, whether she knew it or not. She found that comforting.

Blake seemed happy for her when she finally received her diploma in the mail. But he was less thrilled when she announced that she wanted to take classes at Santa Monica College to earn her associate's degree, or when she transferred to Loyola Marymount for her bachelor's, or when, last year, Santa Monica College hired her as an adjunct for an Introduction to Statistics class. The job paid next to nothing, but she felt invigorated during her sections, standing at the chalkboard in front of a dozen undergraduates. Her faculty mentor, Peg Davis, was encouraging her to enroll in a master's program next, even to start thinking about her PhD. She could become a full professor, earn tenure someday. Dr. Stella Sanders had a nice ring, didn't it?

"It's that women's libber," he complained, whenever Stella worked late on campus. "She's the one putting all those ideas into your head."

"Surprisingly, I have thoughts of my own," she said.

"Oh, that's not what I meant—"

"It's exactly what you meant!"

"She's not like you," he said. "You have family. Obligations. She just has her politics."

But when had Stella based her decisions on an obligation to family? That was heart space. And maybe it had always been her head guiding her. She had become white because it was practical, so practical that, at the time, her decision seemed laughably obvious. Why wouldn't you be white if you could be? Remaining what you were or becoming something new, it was all a choice, any way you looked at it. She had just made the rational decision.

"I've told you already, you don't have to do this," Blake always said, gesturing to the stacks of tests under her arm. "I've always provided for this family."

But she hadn't accepted the job because she was worried about money. She'd just chosen her brain over her heart, and maybe that was what Loretta had seen, tracing that long line down her palm.

"You missed my toast," Blake said when they'd returned from the Hardisons. He was tugging off his tie in the doorway to their closet.

"I told you I had to enter grades," she said.

"And I told you tonight was important."

"What do you want me to say? I tried my best."

He sighed, staring out the darkened window.

"Well, it was a nice toast," he said. "A nice party."

"Yes," she said. "The party was lovely."

"I KNOW WHY YOU'RE HERE," Kennedy said.

In the half-crowded restaurant, one week after *The Midnight Ma-rauders* opened, she smiled at Stella across the table, playing with the white tablecloth. She always showed all of her teeth when she smiled, which unnerved Stella. Imagine, revealing so much of yourself. One table over, an Asian woman was grading term papers in between spoonfuls of split pea soup. Two young white men were arguing quietly about John Stuart Mill. Stella said that she had chosen a restaurant near USC's campus because it was convenient, although that wasn't, of course, true. She'd hoped the university crowd might prompt her daughter to rethink her own choices, or, at the very least, to feel embarrassed about them.

Stella unfurled her napkin, spreading it across her lap.

"Of course you do," Stella said. "I'm here to have lunch with you."

Kennedy laughed. "Sure, Mother. I'm certain that's the only reason you drove all across the city—"

"I don't know why you have to turn everything into some big conspiracy. I can't go to lunch with my daughter?"

She hadn't driven near campus in years, and even then she'd visited just a handful of times: the college tour, where she'd trailed behind her daughter, gazing skeptically at the trellises climbing the red brick, wondering how a girl with her grades would ever get in; move-in day, since lackluster test scores were nothing that family donations could not fix; a few shameful weeks later, to plead with the freshman dean after the resident assistant caught Kennedy smoking pot in her room. The drugs bothered Stella less than the indiscretion. Only a lazy girl would get caught, and her daughter was clever but lazy, blissfully unaware of how hard her mother worked to maintain the lie that was her life.

Now Kennedy smirked, slowly stirring her soup.

"Fine," she said. "We'll just save your lecture for dessert."

There would be no lecture, Stella had promised Blake. She would only nudge Kennedy to do what was right. The girl knew that she needed to go back to school. She'd only missed a semester so far—she could go to the registrar's office, explain that she'd had a mental lapse, and beg her way back in. She would be one term behind her peers— maybe she could graduate after summer school. Stella worked out various scenarios in her head, each time unable to land anywhere besides her own anger. Quitting school to become an actor! The idea was so idiotic, she could barely restrain herself from saying so as soon as she reached for the menu.

The most shocking part? She'd thought Kennedy had already been through her hell years. High school teachers calling because she cut class again, the awful report cards, the nights Stella heard the door creaking open at some ungodly hour and reached for her baseball bat before realizing that it was only her drunk daughter sneaking home. The mangy boys always hanging out of cars in front of the house, honking their horns.

"She's my wild child," Blake said once, chuckling, as if it were something to be proud of.

But her wildness only scared Stella, disrupting the careful life she'd built. In the mornings, she'd stared across the breakfast table at a child she no longer recognized. Gone was her sweet-faced girl, and in her place, a tawny, long-limbed woman who changed her mind daily about the person she wanted to be. One morning, a faded Ramones T-shirt hung off her gaunt shoulders, the next, a plaid miniskirt inched up her thighs, and the next, a long dress flowed to her ankles. She'd dyed her hair pink, twice.

"Why can't you just be yourself?" Stella asked once.

"Maybe I don't know who that is," her daughter shot back. And Stella understood, she did. That was the thrill of youth, the idea that you could be anyone. That was what had captured her in the charm shop, all those years ago. Then adulthood came, your choices solidifying, and you realize that everything you are had been set in motion years before. The rest was aftermath. So she understood why her daughter was searching for a self, and she even blamed herself for it. Maybe something in the girl was unsettled, a small part of her realizing that her life wasn't right. As if she'd gotten older and started touching the trees, only to find that they were all cardboard sets.

"There's no lecture," Stella said. "I just want to make sure we're thinking about next semester—"

"There it is."

"You didn't miss much time, sweetie. I know you're excited about that play—"

"It's a musical."

"Whatever you call it—"

"Well, you'd know if you actually came to opening night."

"How about this?" Stella said. "I'll come to your play if you go down to the registrar—"

"Emotional blackmail," she said. "That's a new one for you."

"Blackmail!" Stella leaned into the table, then dropped her voice. "Wanting what's best for you is blackmail? Wanting you to get an education, to better yourself—"

"Your best isn't necessarily mine," her daughter said.

But what was Kennedy's best, then? Stella had been shocked, and a little embarrassed, to learn that her daughter had spent the last semester on academic probation. "She's young, she'll figure it out," Blake said, but Stella balked. She was some poor colored girl from nowhere Louisiana and even she'd managed a better showing than two C-minuses, two Ds, and a lone B-minus coming from a drama class. Drama wasn't even a class—it was a hobby! A hobby that, months after that dismal semester, her daughter decided she was leaving school to pursue full time. What was the point, then, of giving a child everything? Buying books for her, enrolling her in the finest schools, hiring tutors, pleading her way into college—what was the point of any of it, if the result was only this, one bored girl gazing around a restaurant filled with some of the nation's finest minds and playing idly with her soup?

"College isn't for everyone, you know," Kennedy said.

228

"Well, it is for you."

"And how do you know that?"

"Because. You're a smart girl. I know you are. You just don't try. We don't even know what you're capable of when you try your hardest—"

"Maybe this is it! I'm not some big brain like you."

"Well, I don't believe that's your best."

"And how would you know?"

"Because I gave up too much for you to flunk out of school!"

Kennedy laughed, throwing up her hands. "Here we go again. It's not my fault you grew up poor, Mother. You can't blame me for shit that happened before I was born."

A young black waiter leaned in to refill her water glass and Stella fell silent. She had chosen her own life, years ago; Kennedy had only cemented her into it. Recognizing this wasn't the same as blaming her. She'd sacrificed for a daughter who could never learn what she'd lost. The time for honesty between the two of them had passed long ago. Stella dabbed her mouth with the white napkin, folding it back onto her lap.

"Lower your voice," she said. "And don't swear."

"IT'S NOT THE end of the world," Peg Davis said. "Lots of students take time off."

Stella sighed. She was sitting across the desk in Peg's cluttered office, which was always so messy that Stella had to slide books off the chair or spend ten minutes searching for Peg's reading glasses, which were tucked under a pile of midterms. Peg could hire someone to help her organize. Stella had even volunteered to help. The office reminded her of living with Desiree, who'd spent far more time searching for lost things than she would have spent keeping her side of the room neat, but whenever Stella told her this, Desiree had rolled her eyes and said to stop mothering her. Peg was just as dismissive.

"Oh, they're around here somewhere," she said, each time she misplaced her keys, and like that, another meeting turned into a scavenger hunt.

You could be a bit of a wreck when you were a genius. Peg taught number theory, a field of mathematics that seemed so complicated, it might as well have been magic. Theoretical mathematics shared little in common with mathematical statistics, but Peg had offered to advise Stella anyway. She was the only tenured female professor in the math department, so she took on all the female students. Their first advising meeting, Peg had leaned back in her chair, studying her. The professor had long, graying blonde hair and wore round eyeglasses that covered half her face.

"So tell me," she'd said. "What's your story?"

Stella had never been caught so squarely in the gaze of such a brilliant woman before. She fidgeted, twisting her wedding ring around her finger.

"I don't know," she said. "What do you mean? I don't have a story. I mean, nothing that interesting."

She was lying, of course, but she was startled when Peg laughed.

"Like hell," she said. "It's not every day a housewife suddenly decides she wants to take up math. You don't mind if I call you that, do you?"

"Call me what?"

"A housewife."

"No," Stella said. "It's what I am, isn't it?"

"Is it?"

Conversations with Peg always went like this: twisting and turning, questions sounding like answers, answers seeming like questions. Stella always felt like Peg was testing her, which only made her want to prove herself. The professor gave her books—Simone de Beauvoir, Gloria Steinem, Evelyn Reed—and she read them all, even though Blake rolled his eyes when he glanced at the covers. He didn't see what any of that had to do with mathematics. Peg invited her to protests and even though Stella was always too nervous to stand in a crowd of shouting people, she always read about them afterward in the paper.

"What are Peggy's girls up to this time?" Blake would ask, peeking over her shoulder at the local section. There they were, protesting the Miss America pageant, a sexist advertisement inside *Los Angeles Magazine*, the opening of a new slasher movie that glorified violence against women. Peggy's girls were all white, and when Stella asked once if there were any Negro women in the group, Peg prickled.

"They have their own concerns, you know," she said. "But they're welcome to join us in the fight."

Who was Stella to judge? At least Peg stood for something, fought for something. She went to war with the university over everything: paid maternity leave, sexist faculty hiring, and exploitation of adjunct labor. She argued about these things even though she had no children and had already secured tenure—she argued even though her advocating wouldn't benefit her at all. It baffled Stella, protesting out of a sense of duty, or maybe even amusement.

Now, sitting in Peg's office, she reached for a volume on prime numbers and said, "It's only time off if you eventually go back."

"Well, maybe she will," Peg said. "On her own. You did."

"That's different."

"How?"

"I didn't have a choice," she said. "I had to leave school. When I was her age, the only thing I wanted was to go to college. And she just throws it away."

"Well, she isn't you," Peg said. "It's unfair for you to expect her to be."

It wasn't that either, or at least, it wasn't only that. Her daughter felt like a stranger, and maybe, if she was still in Mallard, she would be amused by all the ways that they were different. By all the ways her daughter reminded her of Desiree, even—she might laugh with her sister about it. Are you sure she's not yours? But here in this world, her daughter felt like a stranger and it terrified her. If her daughter didn't feel like she was really hers, then nothing about her life was real.

"Maybe you're actually upset at yourself," Peg said.

"Myself? Why?"

"All those years you've been talking about graduate school. Then nothing."

"Yes, but—" Stella stopped. That was a different matter altogether. Each time she talked to Blake about applying to a master's program, he reacted as childishly as she expected. More school? Christ, Stella, how much more school do you need? He accused her of abandoning the family, she accused him of abandoning her, both fell asleep angry.

"I mean, of course that husband thinks he can still push you around," Peg said. "You frighten him. A woman with a brain. Nothing scares them more."

"I don't know if that's true," Stella said. Blake was still her husband; she didn't like hearing anyone talk about his faults.

"I just mean it's all about power," Peg said. "He wants it, and he doesn't want you to have it. Why else do you think men fuck their secretaries?"

Again, she regretted telling Peg how she and Blake met. Their story, romantic at the time, only became crasser over the years. She was so young, her daughter's age; she'd never met a man like Blake before. Of course she hadn't been able to resist his pull. Their first time in bed, she was only nineteen, along with Blake on a work trip to Philadelphia. By then, she'd learned that being a secretary was a little like being a wife; she memorized his schedule, hung his hat and coat, poured him a Scotch. She brought him lunch, managed his moods, listened to him complain about his father, remembered to send his mother flowers for her birthday. This was why he'd invited her to Philadelphia, she'd thought, until the final night of the trip when he leaned in at the hotel bar and kissed her.

"You don't know how long I've been wanting to do that," he said. "Since Antoine's. You looked so sweet and so lost. I knew I was in trouble then. I told them, find me a girl with the nicest handwriting, it doesn't matter if she isn't much to look at. I hoped you wouldn't be. I didn't need the distraction. I'm not that sort of man, you see. But of course, the prettiest handwriting belonged to the prettiest girl. And you've been torturing me ever since."

He laughed a little but he was gazing at her so seriously, she felt her neck flush.

"I didn't mean to," she said. "Torture you, I mean."

"Do you hate me for telling you all of this?" he said.

His nervousness settled her. She'd gone on a few dates with white men before but never made it past kissing in their cars. She was always afraid that they might be able to read her lie, somehow, on her naked body. Maybe against white sheets, her skin would look darker, or maybe she would just feel different once he was inside of her. If nakedness would not reveal who you were, then what would?

In the hotel room, Blake slowly undressed her. He unzipped her skirt, unclipped her bra, bent to unfurl her nylons. He was straining against his white briefs and she felt embarrassed for him, embarrassed for all men, really, forced to wear their desire so openly. She could think of nothing more horrifying than not being able to hide what she wanted.

She couldn't have said no to him, she'd since realized, but she didn't want to. And maybe that was the difference, or maybe, the difference was in thinking that there was one at all.

"Don't look at me like that," Peg said.

"Like what?"

"Like your cat just died." Peg leaned across the desk. "I just hate to see you make yourself small for him. Just because he'll never see you the way you see yourself."

Stella glanced away.

"You don't understand," she said. "When I think about who I was before him. It's like being a whole other person."

"So who were you then?" Peg said.

Sometimes being a twin had felt like living with another version of yourself. That person existed for everyone, probably, an alternative self that lived only in the mind. But hers was real. Stella rolled over in bed each morning and looked into her eyes. Other times it felt like living with a foreigner. Why are you not more like me? she'd think, glancing over at Desiree. How did I become me and you become you? Maybe she was only quiet because Desiree was not. Maybe they'd spent their lives together modulating each other, making up for what the other lacked. Like how at their father's funeral, Stella barely spoke, and when someone asked her a question, Desiree answered instead. At first it unnerved Stella, a person speaking to her and Desiree responding. Like throwing her own voice. But soon she felt comfortable disappearing. You could say nothing and, in your nothingness, feel free.

She stared out the window at students biking past, then back to the professor.

"I can't even remember," she said.

Twelve

By the end of Jude's first two weeks as the newest usher at the Stardust Theater, she'd already learned two main things about Kennedy Sanders: she wanted to be a Broadway star, and she carried herself like every aggrieved actress, a little prideful, a little wounded. The pride was impossible to miss; she delighted in making others wait for her, sauntering through every held door. She argued with the director over the delivery of lines, often, it seemed, for fun. She parked her red sports car on the far side of the garage because, she claimed, it had once been keyed by a jealous understudy. She liked to invent stories about her life, as if the reality were too dull to repeat. Sometimes she revised herself in the middle of a conversation, like when she told Jude that her car had been a high school graduation gift.

"No, more like a 'we can't believe you graduated' gift," she said. "I was a little shit in high school. But weren't we all? I mean, maybe not. You don't look like a little shit to me."

"I wasn't," Jude said.

"I know you weren't. See, I can always tell. Who ate their broccoli and listened to daddy and who was a fucking hell-raiser. Hey, be a doll and throw this away, will you?"

In her dressing room, she dropped crumpled candy wrappers into Jude's waiting hands. For the past two weekends, Jude had ridden the bus downtown to the decrepit theater, where she swept popcorn off the floors, scrubbed the bathroom sinks, and cleaned out the dressing rooms. In time, her supervisor promised, she would work her way up to ticket taking and seat directing. Little did he know, she was exactly where she wanted to be. But of course she didn't tell him that. She'd only given him the simple story: that she was a recent college graduate looking to earn extra money on the weekends. She could work Friday and Saturday nights, Sunday afternoons. *The Midnight Marauders* shifts. He told her to come back for the Sunday matinee dressed in all black.

"I don't like it," Reese said. He leaned against the kitchen countertop, Mr. Song's worn tool belt still around his waist, looking so worried, she wished she hadn't said anything in the first place.

"It's just a little side job," she said lightly. "We could use the money."

"It's not and you know it."

"Well, what am I supposed to do? Just go on pretending she ain't Stella's daughter? I can't do that. I have to know her. I have to meet Stella."

"And how you plan on doin that?"

But she had no plan beyond the Stardust Theater. Before each show, she met Kennedy in her dressing room and helped lift the big dress over her head. She did other little favors for her too: brought her hot water with lemon, fetched her sandwiches from a nearby diner, ran for Cokes from the lobby vending machine. She always felt foolish, standing outside the dressing room holding a steaming mug of tea, until Kennedy whisked in, breathless and unapologetic.

"You're a lifesaver," she'd say, or, "I owe you one." Never just, thank you.

During the first act, before preparing the concession stand for intermission, Jude slipped into the wing to watch a play that became sillier the more times she saw it. A western musical about a spunky girl who arrives in a ghost town to find it occupied by actual ghosts.

"I think it's very clever," Kennedy said. "Sort of like *Hamlet* when you think about it." The play was nothing like *Hamlet*, but she said it with such conviction that you almost believed her. It was the first starring role she'd landed since dropping out of school two months ago, she told Jude one evening after a show. They were sitting together at a diner across the street, Kennedy dipping fries into a puddle of ranch.

"My mother still hasn't been to a show," she said. "She's so pissed at me for leaving school. She thinks I'm gambling away my future. And maybe I am. Hardly anyone makes it, right?"

For the first time, she dropped the bravado, looking so genuinely unsure of herself that Jude almost squeezed her hand. The sudden rush of empathy startled her. Was that what it was like to be this girl? An unwise choice earning you sympathy, not scorn, a single moment of doubt forcing a practical stranger to affirm that you were, in fact, special?

"No one gets into med school either," Jude said.

"Oh, it's not the same. My mother would love if I were going to be a doctor, trust me. I suppose most mothers would. They all want us to live better lives than they did, right?"

"What was hers like?"

"Rough. You know, real white trash, *Grapes of Wrath*. Walked ten miles each day just to get to school, all that."

"She come from a big family?"

"Oh no. Just her. But her mother and father died years ago. She's the only one left."

Sometimes you could understand why Stella passed over. Who didn't dream of leaving herself behind and starting over as someone new? But how could she kill the people who'd loved her? How could she leave the people who still longed for her, years later, and never even look back? That was the part that Jude could never understand.

"I don't know how you put up with her," Barry said. "That girl never stops talking! I'd shove that bonnet in her mouth."

Like the rest of the cast, he found Kennedy insufferable. But Jude needed to hear her talk. She was searching all of her stories for Stella. So she lifted that dress over her head, listening to Kennedy go on about how she wanted to visit India over the summer, but she was worried, you know. You can't even drink the water in a place like that, and she had a friend—well, not really a friend, a childhood neighbor, Tammy Roberts—who went on a mission trip there and came back sick from eating fruit. Can you imagine it, fruit? She'd rather die with a needle jabbed in her arm than let a mango kill her. Another time, Kennedy told her that an old fling would be in the audience, a married surfer who lived in her apartment building. She'd slept with him once after he brought a bottle of absinthe back from France.

"We saw some trippy shit," she said, stretching out barefoot on the lumpy couch.

Curtain was in fifteen, and she still wasn't even dressed yet. She was never focused, never prepared. When Jude arrived to help her dress, she always answered the door a little surprised, as if she hadn't been the one to ask Jude in the first place. She always mentioned her mother suddenly, like when she told Jude before a show that she had first started acting when she was eleven. Her mother had placed her in all of these different activities because that's what parents do in Brentwood, cast their children out like a fishing net and hope that they catch a talent. So she'd taken tennis lessons and ballet classes and clarinet and piano—enough instruments to start her own symphony, really. But nothing stuck. She was horribly mediocre. Her mother was embarrassed.

"She never said as much but I could tell," Kennedy said. "She really wanted me to be special."

So on a whim, she'd auditioned for a school play about the gold rush and earned a small role as a Chinese railroad worker. Only seven lines, but her mother helped her memorize them, holding the script in one hand, stirring pasta sauce with the other. Kennedy dragging her invisible pick across the kitchen floor.

"I mean, it was completely ridiculous," she said. "Here I am, playing some coolie in one of those straw hats. You couldn't even see my face. But my mother told me I did a good job. She was . . . I don't know, she seemed excited for once."

She spoke about her mother wistfully, the way everyone talked about Stella. That was the only part that felt real.

FOR THE REST OF NOVEMBER, Jude Winston worked *The Midnight Marauders* shift. She refilled the popcorn machines, passed out *Playbills* at the door, helped old ladies to their seats. At night, she fell asleep, still hearing the overture. She closed her eyes and saw Kennedy at center stage, glowing in light. They couldn't be cousins. Each time the blonde swept into the theater, her face hidden behind sunglasses, the idea seemed even more preposterous. A long-lost relative— you'd have something in common, wouldn't you? Maybe you couldn't spot it at first, but in time, you'd feel, somehow, your shared blood. But the longer she spent around Kennedy, the more foreign the girl seemed.

One Friday night, the cast went out for a nightcap. Barry tugged Jude's arm to convince her to stay, but before she could tell him that she was exhausted, Kennedy jogged out beside her. So of course she'd stayed. She never told her no. She felt desperate around her. The play was nearly over and she'd barely learned anything about Stella. In the dim bar, the pianist found a dusty upright in the back and started picking around chords. Slowly the cast migrated over, a little tipsy and still eager to perform. But Kennedy sat with Jude at the worn end of the table, their knees touching.

"You don't have many friends like me, do you?" she asked.

"What do you mean?"

White people, probably, although Kennedy surprised her by saying, "Girlfriends. You were with a whole bunch of boys when I saw you."

"No," Jude said. "I don't have any girlfriends, really."

"Why not?"

"I don't know. I never really had any growing up. It's the place I come from. They don't like people like me."

"Blacks, you mean."

"Dark ones," she said. "The light ones are fine."

Kennedy laughed. "Well, that's silly."

They both found each other's lives inscrutable, and wasn't that the only way it could be? Didn't Jude wonder what it would be like to care so little about your education, to know that even if the worst happened, you would be all right? Didn't she hate the loud punk rock screeching out the speakers when Kennedy peeled into the parking garage? Yes, and she rolled her eyes each time Kennedy arrived late. She resented when Kennedy demanded lemon tea. She felt defensive when Barry called her a spoiled brat even though she was one, of course she was. The girl was maddening sometimes, but maybe this was who Jude would have been if her mother hadn't married a dark man. In this other life, the twins passed over together. Her mother married a white man and now she slipped out of mink coats at fancy parties, not waited tables in a country diner. In this reality, Jude was fair and beautiful, driving a red Camaro around Brentwood, her hand trailing out the window. Each night, she strutted onstage, beaming, tossing back her golden hair while the world applauded.

The boy on the piano started banging out "Don't Stop Me Now," and Kennedy shrieked, grabbing Jude by the hand. Jude never sang in front of anybody. But somehow, she found herself singing along with the giddy group, annoying the other patrons, until the bartender kicked them out. She climbed into bed that night after three, her head buzzing, still feeling Kennedy's arm around her shoulders. They weren't real family, and they weren't real friends, but they were something. Weren't they?

"Where'd you go?" Reese asked. They were kissing in bed but she was distracted, her head still swimming with music.

"I'm sorry," she said. "I'm just thinking."

"About that white girl?" He sighed. "Baby, you gotta stop. You're playin a dangerous game."

"It's not a game," she said. "It's my family."

"Those people ain't your family. They don't wanna be and you can't make them."

"I'm not trying to—"

"Then why are you sniffin around that girl? You can't make nobody be what they don't wanna be. And if your aunt wants to be a white woman, it's her life."

"You don't understand," she said.

"You're right," he said, throwing up his hands. "I don't understand you at all—"

"That's not what I meant," she said, but wasn't it? He hadn't watched her mother spend years pining after Stella, or Early driving thousands of miles searching for her. He didn't see the mornings Jude had spent digging through the crates in the back of the closet, sifting through Stella's things. Junk, mostly, a few old toys or an earring or a sock. She couldn't tell if her grandmother chose to keep these mementos or if she'd forgotten the boxes were even there. But she'd sort through them, trying to discover what made Stella different. How

241

had she found a way to leave Mallard when her mother only knew how to stay?

All November, she reported to Kennedy Sanders's dressing room to help lift the big dress over her head. Then each evening, she stood in the wing of the theater, searching the audience for Stella. She did not see her once. Still, she looked for her as the overture faded and Kennedy finally took the stage. Somehow, as soon as the show started, she lost that smart-alecky tone that made the crew roll their eyes. When the lights hit, she was no longer the sarcastic girl chain-smoking in the alley. She became Dolly, the sweet, carefree nobody lost in an abandoned town.

"I don't know," she said. "I've just always loved the stage. Everyone watching you. Sort of thrilling, isn't it?"

After a Saturday night show, she'd offered to drive Jude home. She glanced across the car, smiling at her, and Jude, fidgeting, stared out the window. She hated how directly Kennedy looked at her, as if she were daring her to look away.

"No," Jude said. "I'd hate everyone staring at me like that."

"Why?"

"I don't know. It makes me feel . . . exposed, I guess."

Kennedy laughed.

"Yes, but acting is different," she said. "You only show people what you want to."

Thirteen

By December, *The Midnight Marauders* poster outside the Stardust Theater had already been tacked over with an advertisement for *West Side Story*. Jude must have looked so glum that the man changing the marquee glanced down his ladder and said, "Sometimes they bring 'em back for a second run." But she wasn't thinking about the show—she was only thinking about Stella, who still had not appeared. Now the play was over and what did she even have to show for it? A few old stories about a woman she would never know.

On the night of the final performance, she stepped into the empty theater to sweep the floors and found Kennedy standing alone on the dim stage. She was never early, so Jude asked if something was wrong. Kennedy laughed.

"I always come early to the last show," she said. "It's the one people will remember you by, you know. You're only as good as your last performance."

She was wearing ripped jeans and a big floppy purple hat that hid half her face. She always dressed like that, like a child ripping clothes out of a costume chest.

"Why don't you come on up?" Kennedy said.

Jude laughed, glancing around the empty theater. "What're you talking about?" she said. "I'm working."

"So? No one's here. Just come up for a second, just for fun. I bet you've never even been on a stage like this before."

She hadn't, although she'd thought about trying out for the school play every year. Her mother had starred in *Romeo and Juliet*—learned all that funny English, had to let Ike Goudeau kiss her in front of the whole school. But what a time she'd had, taking her final bow to thunderous applause. Her mother would have been thrilled to see Jude star in anything. And she'd almost found the nerve to audition, not because she wanted the role but because acting was something her mother once loved. She wanted to prove to herself that they were alike. But she'd barely stepped into the theater for tryouts before she imagined the whole town laughing at her, and she slipped out the wing before the drama teacher called her name.

She propped her broom against the front-row seats.

"I almost tried out for a play once," she told Kennedy, climbing the steps. "But I chickened out."

"Well, maybe that's your problem," Kennedy said. "You tell yourself no before anyone even says it to you."

The theater did look different from the stage—the house lights dimmed, so you couldn't see the faces of all the people watching you. How strange that must be, to not know what the people looking at you were thinking.

"I used to have these terrible nightmares," Kennedy said. "When I was little. I mean, awful ones."

"About what?"

"That's the thing, I could never remember. But when I started acting, they stopped. It was the strangest thing. Like there was something bad inside me trying to get out and I could only get rid of it here." She tapped the stage floor. "But that doesn't make any sense, does it? The doctors said that creative people have the most vivid dreams. I don't know why. Maybe you'll figure it out when you're a doctor."

She didn't want to be a psychologist, but she was grateful for Kennedy's confidence. When you're a doctor. It sounded so easy when she said it.

"Yes," she said. "Maybe."

She followed her down off the stage. She could hear the rest of the company arriving, giddy as they raced around backstage, dressing for the final time. She would sweep the theater floor, then take her place in the dark one last time. And after the final curtain, for the first time since she'd realized who Kennedy Sanders was, she had no idea when she might see her again.

"You should come to the cast party," Kennedy said. "Bring your boyfriend. I bet the theater'll pay him to take some pictures."

The suggestion was surprisingly thoughtful; she'd told Kennedy once that Reese was a photographer but she never expected her to remember.

"Thanks," she said. "I'll give him a call."

Kennedy started toward backstage, then paused. "I don't know what happens after this."

"What do you mean?"

Maybe, to an actor, the dark wing of a theater felt as intimate as church; either way, Kennedy began to confess. She didn't know what she would do tomorrow—no, literally, what she would do when she woke up in the morning, because this play was the only thing that had given her any sense of purpose in months. It was the only thing she was good at, acting. She'd left school because she was shit at it, she was shit at everything else. And maybe her mother was right—maybe she had made a big mistake. Maybe acting was a waste of time. Maybe her parents argued so much because they were splitting up. Maybe her mother would rather grade math assignments than talk to her. Maybe all those things were true. And maybe she had only landed her biggest role yet because the boy she was sleeping with told her one night, while they were stoned, that his big brother had written a hilariously bad play that some company was putting on downtown. And even though it was bad, she'd wept when she read the script. A lonely girl living in a world surrounded only by ghosts. Nothing reminded her of her own life more.

Maybe the director, Doug, sensed this, or maybe he just liked looking at her tits, or maybe the boy told his brother to pull some strings, to do whatever he had to do to make sure that her name was at the top of the call sheet. Either way, she won the starring role.

"But I could never tell my mother any of this," she said. "She'd just say that she was right. She cares more about being right than being my mother. Sometimes I don't even think she likes me very much. Isn't that something? To think your own mother can't even stand you."

She was smiling but her violet eyes filled with tears.

"I'm sure that's not true," Jude said.

"Well, you don't know her, do you?" Kennedy said.

THAT NIGHT, for the final time, she witnessed Kennedy Sanders transform under the spotlight.

Kennedy strutting out for the opening number in the town square, singing her contemplative solo in the cemetery, high-kicking on the bar during the act-closing dance with a chorus of drunk ghosts. Onstage, you couldn't tell the girl had just been crying. She became new each time she stepped under the lights. After the first act ended, applause ringing in the theater, Jude waded through the crowd to the concession stand. She was shoveling lukewarm popcorn into a paper bag when she saw, finally, Stella.

Her mother, but not. That's the only way she could think of her. Like her mother's face transplanted onto another woman's body. Stella wore a long green dress, her hair pulled into a low bun. Diamond earrings, black pumps. She was fiddling with a leather pocketbook as she glided through the lobby, rolling her neck a little before she smiled at a tall man holding open the door. For a second, in that smile, she was Mama. Then the mask slid back on, another woman taking over.

There was no time to think. Jude abandoned the popcorn station and followed, pushing through the crowded lobby to the door. Outside, she found Stella standing under the eaves, fumbling for a cigarette. She glanced over, startled by the sudden intrusion, and Jude froze. Her first stupid thought was that Stella might recognize her. She'd see something familiar in her face—her eyes, or her mouth even—and then she would gape, her pocketbook falling open on the sidewalk. But Stella's eyes glazed over and she stared moodily into the street. Jude alone with the pounding heart.

"Hi," Jude said. "I'm friends with your daughter."

She couldn't think of anything else to say. Stella paused, then lit her cigarette.

"From school?" she said. Her voice was smoother, softer.

"No, from the play."

"Oh. Lovely," Stella said.

It was a word her mother would have never used. *Lovely.* Stella gave a little smile, then she took a drag, glancing up at the eave.

"Did you want a cigarette?" she asked.

Jude almost said yes. At least then she'd have a reason to be standing there.

"No," she said. "I don't smoke."

"Good girl," Stella said. "They say it's awful for your health."

"I know. My mother's trying to quit."

Stella glanced at her. "It's terribly difficult to quit," she said. "All the best things are."

Intermission was nearly over; soon Stella would head back inside, disappearing into the darkness of the theater. When the play ended, she would join the crowd surging out onto the street. She would go home, and maybe later that night, in a quiet moment, she would think about that dark girl who'd interrupted her smoke break, and then she'd never remember the moment again.

"Kennedy said you're from Louisiana," Jude finally said. "I am too. I'm from Mallard."

Stella glanced at her, an eyebrow slightly arched. Nothing in her body changed, nothing suggested that she'd even heard except for that tiny lift of her eyebrow.

"All right," she said. "I'm sorry, I don't know it."

"My mama—" Jude took a breath. "My mama's name is Desiree Vignes."

Now Stella turned toward her.

"Who the hell are you?" she said quietly.

"I told you, my mama—"

"Who are you? What're you doing here? I don't understand."

She was partly smiling but she held the cigarette away from her body, warning Jude not to come closer. She was angry—Jude hadn't expected that. Stella would be confused. Startled, even. But maybe once the surprise wore off, she'd thought, Stella might be glad to meet her. She might even marvel at all the works of chance that had drawn them together. Instead, Stella shook her head, as if trying to wake herself from a nightmare.

"I wanted to meet you," Jude said.

"No no no, I don't understand. Who are you really? You look nothing like her."

Through the window, the lobby lights flickered. She was supposed to be guiding people back to their seats. Her supervisor was probably going crazy, looking for her. And what would he find if he stepped outside right now—a black girl pleading for a white woman to recognize her.

"She told me how you used to hide in the bathroom," Jude said. "At that laundry place in New Orleans. She said you almost cut your hand off." She was rambling now, willing to say anything to keep Stella from leaving. Stella took a shaky drag, then stomped out her cigarette on the sidewalk.

"She would never go back to Mallard," she said.

"Well, we had to. To get away from my daddy. He kept beating on her."

"Beating on her?" Stella paused, softening. "I mean, is she still—is my mama still—"

"They're still down there. My mama works at the diner."

"Lou's? My God. I haven't thought about Lou's in—" Stella stopped. "Well, it must've been awful for you."

Jude glanced away. She hated the thought of Stella pitying her.

"My mama kept looking for you," she said.

Stella's mouth curved, like she was going to smile or cry, her face, somehow, caught in between. Like a sun shower. The devil beating his wife, her mother used to say, and Jude imagined it every time she heard her father rage. The devil could love the woman he beat; the sun could burst through a rainstorm. Nothing was as simple as you wanted it to be. Without thinking, she reached toward her aunt but Stella jutted her arm out. Her eyes were shining.

"She shouldn't have," Stella said. "She should've forgotten all about me."

"But she didn't! You can call her. We can call her right now. She would be so glad—"

"I've got to go," Stella said.

"But—"

"It's too much," she said. "I can't go back through that door. It's another life, you understand?"

Headlights washed over them, and for a second, bathed in yellow light, Stella looked panicked, as if she might run into the car's path. Then she clutched her purse tightly and disappeared into the night.

AT THE CAST PARTY, all of the actors and musicians gathered around to watch their show lead get hammered and complain, to anyone who might listen, that her mother hadn't shown. "Can you believe it?" she kept saying. "Closing night and all she gave me is that she would try. Not too hard, apparently!" No one had ever seen her in such a nasty mood. She'd barely lingered onstage past the curtain call, ignored the cast members who tried to congratulate her, dumped the roses the director had given her into the trash. She hadn't even offered to sign *Playbills* at the stage door. Now she was spending the first half hour of the cast party pounding tequila alone at the bar.

"My first big show," she told Jude. "All she had to do was sit through it. And she couldn't even do that."

Across the bar, Reese was roving, snapping candid photos of the cast. She should have been happy for him, behind the camera again, but instead, she was standing at the bar beside a surly drunk girl, still shaken. She'd met Stella but Stella didn't want to know her. It shouldn't have been surprising. She hadn't wanted anything to do with the family for decades, so nothing had changed. But why did Jude feel as if she'd lost someone? Again, she saw herself reaching toward Stella, Stella pushing her away. She felt as if she'd reached for her mother and only felt her shove her back.

"I have to go," she said. She felt too hot in that crowded party, desperate for air.

"What're you talking about?" Kennedy said. "The party just started."

"I know. I'm sorry. I can't stay."

"Come on," she said. "Just have a drink with me. Please."

She sounded so vulnerable, Jude nearly said yes. Almost. But she imagined Stella disappearing into the night, glancing over her shoulder, panicked, as if she were being hunted, and she shook her head.

"I really can't," she said. "My boyfriend's ready to go."

Across the room, Reese was packing up his camera and chatting with Barry. Kennedy glanced over, watching the two for a second.

"You're really lucky, you know," she said. She was still smiling but meanness wedged inside her voice.

"What do you mean?" Jude said.

"Nothing. But you know. Nobody really expects someone like him to be with you, do they?" Kennedy laughed. "You know I don't mean anything by it. I'm just saying. Your men usually like the light girls, don't they?"

Years later, she would always wonder what exactly pushed her. That sly smile, or the way she'd said *your men* so casually, as if it didn't include her. Or maybe it was because Kennedy was right. She knew how lucky Jude felt to be loved. She knew, even though Jude tried to hide it, exactly how to hurt her.

For weeks, she'd followed Kennedy around the Stardust Theater. She'd helped her dress, brought her tea, listened to her trill notes in the hallway. She'd cleaned toilets to talk to her, wondering always how this strange girl could be related to her. But she finally saw it: Kennedy Sanders was nothing but an uppity Mallard girl who believed the fiction she'd been told.

"You're so stupid," Jude said. "You don't even know what you are."

"And what's that?"

"Your mother's from Mallard! Where mine's from. They're twins. They look exactly alike and even you would see it—"

Kennedy laughed. "You're crazy."

"No, your mother's crazy. She's been lying to you your whole life."

She regretted the words as soon as they left her mouth, but by then, it was too late. She had rung the bell, and all her life, the note would hang in the air.

MR. PARK BROUGHT BULGOGI on the house, setting the dish on the table. "So sad," he said. "Never seen you so sad." What a sight they must have been—Jude dabbing at her puffy eyes, Reese somber beside her, looking as helpless as he always did whenever she cried. He squeezed her shoulder and said, "Come on, baby, eat." But she wasn't hungry. On the ride over, she'd told him about the whole terrible night. She told him everything except what Kennedy had said to hurt her, because it cut too close to share, even with him.

"You were right," she said. "You were right about everything. I should've never gone looking—"

"It's okay," he said. "You wanted to know them. Now you do. Now you can move on."

"I can't tell Mama," she said.

She'd never kept a secret like this from her mother before. But if it was cruel to not tell her that Stella was alive—that she'd met her, even—then wasn't it even worse to tell her that Stella wanted nothing to do with her? What good would come of her mother discovering that the sister she'd spent years searching for wouldn't even call her? Maybe her mother would realize that losing her was for the best. Maybe, over time, she would just forget Stella, the way Jude had already started to lose her father's face. Not all at once, but slowly, her memories disintegrating. Eventually remembering turned into imagining. How slight the difference was between the two.

Her mother would never forget Stella. She would stare into the mirror for the rest of her life, reminded of her loss. But Jude wouldn't add to her grief. She would talk to her mother on the phone, days later, and not say a word about Stella. Maybe she was like her aunt in that way. Maybe, like Stella, she became a new person in each place she'd lived, and she was already unrecognizable to her mother, a girl who hoarded secrets. A liar.

THE MORNING AFTER THE PLAY, Stella awoke with a pounding heart.

She'd barely opened her eyes before the previous night returned to her: that awful play she'd finally attended, even though she knew acting was a waste of her daughter's time and talents. But she'd gone because it was closing night—she'd sat through the dreadful thing, delighted and a little surprised that her daughter was the only bright spot. At intermission, she'd applauded as loudly as anyone, hoping her daughter would see her. But the girl ducked backstage with the rest of the cast, and Stella slipped out for a smoke. She was thinking, leaving the dingy theater, about how she could make things right. She could take Kennedy to dinner after the show, apologize for not attending sooner. Suggest that she take more drama classes, as long as she went back to school. And that was when that dark girl had emerged from the shadows. After, Stella charged into the street, not even thinking about where she was going. She'd stumbled two blocks downtown before remembering where she'd parked.

The dark girl couldn't be Desiree's daughter. She looked nothing like her. Pure black, like Desiree had never even touched her. She could be anyone. But how, then, had she known those stories about New Orleans? Who else would know but Desiree? Well, maybe she'd told someone. Maybe this girl thought she could come to California and threaten to expose Stella. Blackmail her, even! The possibilities grew more lurid in her head, none of them making sense. How had the girl even found her? And if she'd wanted to blackmail her, why hadn't she named her price? Instead of withering on the sidewalk, as if her feelings were hurt. As if Stella had disappointed her somehow.

"Your heart's racing," Blake said. He lifted his head, smiling sleepily at her. He liked to fall asleep with his head on her breasts, and she let him because it was sweet.

"I had a strange dream," she said.

"A scary one?"

She ran her fingers through his graying blond hair.

"I used to have these nightmares," she said. "That these men would drag me out of bed. It felt so real. I could feel their hands on my ankles, even after I woke up."

"That's not why you keep that bat here, is it?"

She started to respond but instead turned away, her eyes filling with tears.

"Something happened," she said. "When I was young."

"What happened?"

"I saw something—" But her voice cracked, and she couldn't say any more. Blake kissed her cheek.

"Oh honey, don't cry," he said softly. "I don't know what you're so afraid of. I'll always keep you safe."

She kissed him before he could say anything else. They made love desperately, the way they had when she was nineteen, touching Mr. Sanders for the first time. The image would have made her younger self blush. Two middle-aged people gripping each other's bodies, knocking off the covers, as sunlight cracked through the blinds, the alarm clock blaring, calling each to a separate day. Her body changed, his body changing, familiar and foreign at the same time. When you married someone, you promised to love every person he would be. He promised to love every person she had been. And here they were, still trying, even though the past and the future were both mysteries.

That morning, she was late for class. A quick shower, then she was pulling a blouse onto her damp shoulders, Blake smiling at her through the mirror as he shaved. "I do believe I made you late to work, Mrs. Sanders," he said, which didn't have as nice a ring to it as Dr. Sanders, but maybe that was okay. Maybe it was enough to be Mrs. Sanders, maybe it was enough to have her Introduction to Statistics class, and her house, and her family. That dark girl. She saw her again, tried to shake her out of her mind. She'd been arrogant, that was her problem. So focused on what was next that she didn't appreciate what she'd already gotten away with. She couldn't let herself slip up like that again. She'd have to focus. Stay alert.

She was running out the door when she bumped into her daughter, lugging a bag of laundry up the steps. Both women jolted, then Kennedy flashed the disarming smile she'd inherited from her father. It was impossible to ever be angry at that smile, and Kennedy had tested it often: when she'd begged for a puppy but left Yolanda to care for him, when she'd failed ninth-grade geometry in spite of Stella's attempts to help her, when she'd crashed her first Camaro and, somehow, convinced Blake to buy her a second one.

"Well, she's got to have a way to get around," he said, and Stella, tired of being the difficult one, finally agreed. Not that she'd had much say. Kennedy learned long ago that if she wanted anything, she ought to ask her father. Telling Stella was a mere formality.

"I was hoping to speak to you," Stella said. "Listen, about last night—"

"I know, I know, you're sorry. But if you weren't going to come, you could've just told me. I would've given the ticket to someone else—"

"I did see your play! I just had to slip out early, that's all. I wasn't feeling well—something I ate, probably. But I promise I was there. I thought it was very clever. The ghosts and all. And that song you did in the saloon. I loved it all. Really."

Her daughter was wearing big shiny sunglasses so Stella couldn't see her eyes, only her own face reflected back at her. She looked calm, natural. Not like a woman who had awakened with her heart racing.

"Did you really like it?" Kennedy asked.

"Of course, darling. I thought you were marvelous."

She pulled her daughter into a hug, running a hand along her thin shoulder blades.

"All right," she said. "I'm running late. Have a good day."

She fumbled with her attaché case, searching for her keys, when she heard her daughter call, over her shoulder, "You've never been to a place called Mallard, have you?"

Stella never expected to hear that word fall out of her daughter's mouth, and for the first time all morning, she faltered.

"What do you mean?" she said.

"I met this girl from there—she said she knows you."

"I've never even heard of the place. Mallard, did you say?"

That disarming smile again. Kennedy shrugged.

"That's okay," she said. "Maybe she was thinking of someone else."

WHEN BLAKE CAME HOME from work that evening, Stella told him about the dark girl.

All afternoon, she'd debated whether to say anything before deciding that she should. A preemptive strike. She didn't want him to think that she had anything to hide, and she preferred him to hear the story from her. She hated the idea of her husband and daughter whispering about her. So while he undressed for bed, she told him that a dark girl, claiming to be a cousin, had cornered Kennedy after her play. She watched his face the entire time, waiting to see it change. A flicker of recognition, maybe. Relief that a question he'd always wondered had finally been answered. But he just scoffed, unbuttoning his dress shirt.

"It's the Camaro," he said. "I'm sure she saw it and thought, boom. Payday."

"Exactly," Stella said. "That's exactly right. That's what I've been trying to tell her."

"This city, I swear, sometimes."

They'd been talking recently about leaving Los Angeles. Moving to Orange County, maybe, or even farther north to Santa Barbara. She'd resisted at first, not wanting to leave her job, but now she kept imagining that dark girl creeping up to her again, poking her head in doorways, tapping on the windows. Or worse, the girl following Kennedy around the city, appearing at her shows, stalking her between auditions. What could she possibly want? Again, her face flashed through Stella's mind. How she'd stood under that eave, wounded.

Stella's mistake had been to think that she could settle anywhere. You had to keep moving or the past would always catch up to you.

"You know those people downtown," she said. "High out their minds, half of them."

"Hell, more than half," Blake said, sliding in bed beside her.

The first time she'd ever been white, Stella couldn't wait to tell Desiree what she'd done. Desiree would never believe it—she didn't think Stella was capable of doing anything surprising. But that evening, when Stella returned home, she passed her sister in the hallway and said nothing. A secret transgression was even more thrilling than a shared one. She had shared everything with Desiree. She wanted something of her own.

She was forty-four now; she'd spent more of her life without Desiree than with her. Still, as the weeks passed, she felt Desiree's pull on her tighten, like a hand gripping her neck. Sometimes it felt like a gentle rub; other times, it choked her. She blamed the dark girl, although she hadn't seen her since that night outside the Stardust Theater. The city was large; the girl would never find her again. Stella never thought of her as a niece. *Niece* didn't seem the right word for a girl you didn't know, a girl who looked nothing like you. Then again, wouldn't Desiree feel the same way about Kennedy? Sometimes even Stella stared at her daughter and saw a stranger. It wasn't Kennedy's fault that Stella had decided, long ago, to become someone else. Now her whole life had been built on that lie and the other lies Stella stacked in order to maintain it, until one dark girl appeared, threatening to send them all tumbling down.

"Did you ever have a sister?" Kennedy asked one night. Stella, bending over to sweep crumbs off the table, stiffened.

"What do you mean?" she said. "You know I didn't."

"I just thought—"

"You're not still thinking about that black girl, are you?"

But her daughter bit her lip, staring out the darkened window. She was—she just hadn't said anything about it, which felt like an even bigger betrayal.

"My God," Stella said. "Who do you believe? Some crazy girl or your own mother?"

"But why would she lie? Why would she say those things to me?"

"She wants money! Or maybe she just wants to poke fun at you. Who knows why crazy people do things?"

Blake wandered into the kitchen, pausing, like he always did before stepping into one of their arguments, as if to remind himself that it wasn't too late to disengage and pretend this had nothing to do with him. He hadn't been interested enough in the dark girl to say much else about it, except that if Kennedy saw her again, she ought to call the police. Now he squeezed his daughter's shoulder.

"Just drop it, Ken," he said. "You can't let that girl get to you."

"I know, but—"

"We love you," he said. "We wouldn't lie to you."

But sometimes lying was an act of love. Stella had spent too long lying to tell the truth now, or maybe, there was nothing left to reveal. Maybe this was who she had become.

IN JUNE, Stella and Blake surprised their daughter with the keys to a new apartment in Venice. They'd pay the rent for one year while she went on auditions, and after, she'd have to go back to school or find a job. Technically it wasn't a bribe, but when Stella handed her ecstatic daughter the keys, she felt so awash in relief that it seemed like one. Maybe now her daughter would stop barraging her with questions about her past. She'd always worried about Kennedy discovering her secret and rejecting her, Blake leaving, her whole life disintegrating in her hands. What she hadn't pictured was doubt. It would almost have been better if Kennedy just believed that dark girl. Instead, she seemed to mull over her claims, sometimes considering them, sometimes rejecting them, and Stella never knew where she would land. She couldn't predict what she might ask, or what she believed, and the uncertainty made her crazy. The new apartment would at least be a distraction. Maybe even a solution.

On a Saturday morning, she and Blake helped their daughter move in. Blake assembled furniture in the bedroom, and Stella wiped down the kitchen drawers, remembering the apartment she and Desiree had shared in New Orleans. The walls were paper thin, the floorboards always creaking, a water splotch growing across the ceiling. And yet, in spite of that, she'd loved that place. She'd been so grateful to leave Farrah Thibodeaux's floor that she hadn't even cared how tiny and cramped this new apartment was. It was hers and it was Desiree's, and she'd felt as if they were both on the cusp of lives too big to even imagine. She teared up, and Kennedy startled her, hugging her from behind.

"Don't get all sappy," she said. "I'll still come by for dinner."

Stella laughed, dabbing her eyes.

"I hope you like this place," she said. "It's a nice little apartment. You should've seen mine in New Orleans."

"What was it like?"

"Well, it could've fit in here, twice over. We were always on top of each other—"

"Who was?"

Stella paused. "I'm sorry?"

"You said 'we.'"

"Oh. Right. My roommate. This girl I lived with, she was from my town."

"You never told me that before," Kennedy said. "You never tell me anything about your life."

"Kennedy—"

"It's not about that," she said. "It's not about that girl at all. It's just like, it's impossible to know anything about you. I have to beg you just to tell me about some roommate you had and you're my mother. Why don't you want me to know you?"

She'd imagined, more than once, telling her daughter the truth, about Mallard, and Desiree, and New Orleans. How she'd pretended to be someone else because she needed a job, and after a while, pretending became reality. She could tell the truth, she thought, but there was no single truth anymore. She'd lived a life split between two women—each real, each a lie.

"I've just always been this way," Stella said. "I'm not like you. Open. It's a good way to be. I hope you stay that way."

She handed her daughter a sheet of shelf paper, and Kennedy smiled.

"I don't know any other way to be," she said. "What do I have to hide?"

Part V

PACIFIC COVE

(1985/1988)

Fourteen

In 1988, exhausted from her pursuit of artistic seriousness and, more importantly, pushing thirty, Kennedy Sanders would begin to appear on a series of daytime soap operas, and a month after she turned twenty-seven she would finally land a three-season arc on *Pacific Cove*. It would be her longest acting job ever, and even decades later, she would sometimes be stopped in the mall by some gooey-eyed fan who called her Charity Harris. It was the role she was born to play, the director told her, she just had a face for the soaps. She must have frowned because he laughed, touching her arm way too close to her tits.

"It's not a knock, babe," he said. "I just mean—well, I can tell you have a flair for the dramatic."

There was nothing wrong with melodrama, she told her parents when she'd called to share the news. In fact, some of the greatest classic actresses—Bette Davis, Joan Crawford, Greta Garbo—trafficked in it from time to time. Her father was glad that she was moving back to California. Her mother was glad that she was working. After she hung up, she wandered around a Burbank shopping mall where, a year later, she would be stopped by a middle-aged woman outside a shoe rack and asked for an autograph. She was jolted each time someone approached her in public. They recognized her? Just as she was, before costumes, before hair and makeup? At first, she was thrilled, then it unsettled her, the idea of anyone noticing her before she noticed them.

AN INCOMPLETE LIST OF characters she played in the soap world before landing *Pacific Cove*: a conniving candy striper who steals a baby; a teacher who seduces her student's father; a stewardess who spills water on the lead, maybe accidentally, maybe intentionally, the script was unclear; the mayor's daughter who gets seduced by the show rogue; a nurse who gets strangled in a car; a florist who hands the star a rose; a stewardess who survives a plane crash to later be strangled in a car. She wore black wigs, brown wigs, red wigs, and eventually, when she played Charity Harris, her own blonde waves. She only played white girls, which is to say, she never played herself.

On the set of *Pacific Cove*, the cast and crew referred to her as Charity, never her real name, and later, in an interview with *Soap Digest*, she would tell a reporter that it helped her stay in character. She preferred readers to think that she was a method actor than know the truth: that no one had bothered to learn her real name because they did not expect her to stick around. Three seasons in the soap world was like three seconds anyway, and when the show ended in 1994, Charity Harris would appear in the finale for a millisecond as the camera swept over photographs on the wall. Only the most passionate fans would remember her most prominent arc, the nine months she'd been kidnapped by her lover's stalker and tied up in a basement. For months, she'd twisted in the chair—screaming, pleading, begging—and not until years later would she realize that her biggest storyline was not being a real part of the show.

She brought her mother to set once. She'd warned her beforehand that the soundstage could get chilly, so ridiculously, her mother had worn a bright blue sweater in spite of the ninety-degree heat in Burbank. Kennedy gave her a little tour around the sets, pointing out the exterior of the Harris house, the town hall, the surf shack where Charity worked. She even brought her to the basement where Charity was currently trapped, only three months into her abduction.

"I sure hope they let you out of there soon," her mother said, collapsing Kennedy and Charity like the rest of the crew. It was the most her mother had ever validated her as an actor. Strange that the greatest compliment an actress could receive was that she had disappeared into somebody else. Acting is not about being seen, a drama teacher told her once. True acting meant becoming invisible so that only the character shone through.

"You should just change your name to Charity," the *Pacific Cove* director told her. "No offense but when I hear your name, I just think about a guy getting shot in the head."

HERE'S SOMETHING she hadn't thought about in forever:

Once, when she was seven or so, she was sitting in the kitchen on a step stool, watching her mother frost a cake. She was wedged in a corner, trying to learn a new yo-yo trick so halfheartedly that she was just flinging the toy, sending it clattering to the tile, waiting for her annoyed mother to tell her to stop. She did things like that often—desperate things, too small to get her in trouble but irritating enough to earn attention. But her mother wasn't even looking at her—she wasn't the type to transform a chore into a bonding opportunity. Honey, let me show you how to knead bread. Or come here, baby, this is how you make frosting. Her mother seemed relieved once Kennedy aged out of asking to help in the kitchen.

"It's not that I don't want your help," her mother always said. "But

I can do it faster on my own." As if that last part contradicted the first one, not justified it.

Why was she baking a cake in the first place? She wasn't the type to bake for no reason. She contributed store-bought cookies to bake sales, transferring them into a tin so nobody would notice. Her father's birthday, maybe. But it was summer, not spring, or else she wouldn't have been home from school in the middle of the day, bored, watching her mother smooth the tiny ripples of frosting.

"How'd you learn to do that?" she asked.

Her mother, concentrating hard, like she was restoring a damaged oil painting.

"I don't know," she finally said. "Picked it up over time."

"Did your mom show you?" She'd thought her mother might say yes, call her over and hand her a knife. But she didn't even look up.

"We didn't have money for cakes," she said.

Later, Kennedy would realize how often her mother used money to avoid discussing her past, as if poverty were so unthinkable to Kennedy that it could explain everything: why her mother owned no family photographs, why no friends from high school ever called, why they'd never been invited to a single wedding or funeral or reunion. "We were poor," her mother would snap if she asked too many questions, that poverty spreading to every aspect of her life. Her whole past, a barren pantry shelf.

"What was she like?" Kennedy asked. "Grandma."

Her mother still didn't turn around, but her shoulders tightened.

"It's strange to think of her like that," she said.

"Like what?"

"A grandmother."

"Well, she is. Even if you're dead, you're still somebody's grandma."

"I suppose so," her mother said.

Kennedy should've dropped it there. But she was angry, her

mother so focused on that damn cake, as if it were the important thing, as if talking to her daughter was the dreaded chore. She wanted her mother to stop what she was doing, to notice her.

"Where did she die?" she said.

Now her mother turned around. She was wearing a peach apron, her hands speckled with vanilla frosting, and she was frowning. Not angry, exactly, but confused.

"What type of question is that?" she said.

"I'm just asking! You never tell me anything—"

"In Opelousas, Kennedy!" she said. "The same place I grew up. She never left and never went anywhere. Now don't you have something else you could be doing right now?"

Kennedy almost cried. She cried easily and often back then, embarrassing her mother, who only cried during the occasional sad movie, always laughing at herself after, apologizing as she swept tears from the corners of her eyes. Kennedy cried on the supermarket floor if she wanted a pink bouncy ball that her mother, dragging her down the aisle, refused to buy. On the playground when she lost at tetherball. At night, when she woke from nightmares she couldn't remember. And she blinked back tears then, even as her mother said something that she knew was wrong.

"That's not where you're from," she said.

"What're you talking about? Of course it is."

"No, it's not. You told me you were from a little town. It starts with an *M*. M-something. You told me when I was little."

Her mother was quiet for so long that Kennedy started to feel crazy, like Dorothy at the end of *The Wizard of Oz*. And you were there, and you were there too! But the story about the town was real, she just couldn't remember all the particulars, except that she'd been in the bathtub, her mother leaning over her. But now, her mother only laughed.

"And when was I supposed to have told you this?" she said. "You're little now."

"I don't know—"

"You must have remembered wrong. You were still a baby." Her mother stepped forward, the cake behind her smoothed on the top and edges. "Come here, honey. Want to lick the spoon?"

This was the first time Kennedy realized that her mother was a liar.

THE TOWN CLUNG.

She couldn't shake it, even though she didn't remember its name. Because she didn't remember its name, even. For years, she never mentioned it to her mother again. But one night in college, a little high, she'd pulled an encyclopedia off her boyfriend's shelf. "What're you doing?" he asked halfheartedly, more interested in the joint he was rolling, so she ignored him, flipping until she landed on Louisiana. Down, down the page to the list of cities and towns in alphabetical order. Mansfield, Marion, Marksville.

"Hey," he said, "put that shit down, you're not supposed to be fucking studying right now."

Mer Rouge, Milton, Monroe.

"Come on, man, that book can't be more interesting than me."

Moonshine, Moss Bluff, Mount Lebanon. She would know its name when she saw it, she was sure. But she scanned the whole list and not one of them seemed familiar. She slid the book back on the shelf.

"Sorry," she said. "I don't know what came over me."

After that night, she never tried to search for the town again. It would be something that she would always know she was right about but could never prove, like people who swore they'd seen Elvis wandering around the grocery store, knocking on the melons. Unlike those loons, she wouldn't tell anyone. A private crazy—she was okay with that. Until she met Jude Winston. That night, at the cast party, Jude spoke the word *Mallard* and it sounded like a song Kennedy hadn't heard in years. Ah, that's how it goes.

IN 1985, nearly three years after *The Midnight Marauders* closed, she saw Jude again in New York.

She was still new to the city then, half surviving her first winter. All her life, she'd never imagined living outside of Los Angeles, but the city had started to feel smaller by the second. She hadn't seen Jude since the cast party, but she imagined bumping into her whenever she turned a corner. She saw her sitting in the windows of restaurants. Once, she'd flubbed her lines in *Fiddler on the Roof* because she'd spotted Jude in the front row. The woman looked just like her—dark, leggy, a little insecure, a little self-possessed—but by the time she realized her mistake, she'd ruined the whole scene. The director ordered the stagehands to remove her things from the dressing room before curtain. She blamed Jude. She blamed her for it all.

"I don't understand it," her mother said, when she announced that she was moving to New York. "Why're you going all the way out there? You can become an actor right here."

But she wanted some space from her mother too. At first, her mother refused to engage with Jude's claims. Then she tried reason. Do I look like a Negro? Do you? Does it make any sense that we could be related to her? No, it didn't, but little about her mother's life made sense. Where had she come from? What was her life like before she'd gotten married? Who had she been, who had she loved, what had she wanted? The gaps. When she looked at her mother now, she only saw the gaps. And Jude, at least, had offered her a bridge, a way to understand. Of course she couldn't stop thinking about her.

"I really wish you'd stop worrying about that," her mother told her. "You'll drive yourself crazy. In fact, I'm sure that's why she said all those things to you. She's jealous and wants to get in your head."

She'd answered Kennedy's questions, irritated but never angry. Then again, her mother was normally calm and rational. If she were to lie to her, she would do so as calmly and rationally as she did anything else.

In New York, Kennedy lived in a basement apartment in Crown Heights with her boyfriend, Frantz, who taught physics at Columbia. He was born in Port-de-Paix but raised in Bed-Stuy in one of those red-brown project buildings she passed by on the bus. He liked to tell her horror stories about growing up—rats gnawing on his toes, cockroaches gathered in a corner of the closet, the dope boys who lingered in the building lobby, waiting to steal his sneakers. He wanted her to understand him, she'd thought at first, but later she realized that he just liked having a dramatic backstory that contrasted with the man he'd grown up to be: careful, studious, always cleaning his horn-rimmed glasses.

He wasn't cool. She liked that. He wasn't one of the black boys she'd admired from afar, smooth boys slouched in beat-up cars or gathered in front of the movie theater, whistling at girls walking by. She and her friends pretended to be annoyed but secretly delighted in the attention from these boys they could never kiss, boys who could never call home. Oh, the little crushes she had on these boys. Safe ones, the way Jim Kelly sent a thrill through her. She'd perch on the arm of her father's chair during Lakers games just for a glimpse of Kareem Abdul-Jabbar in those goggles. Harmless crushes, really, but she knew better than to tell anybody about them. Frantz was her first black lover. She was his fourth white one.

"Fourth?" she said. "Really? What were the other three like?"

He laughed. They were standing in his faculty adviser's kitchen during a department party, drinking ginger beers. They'd just started dating then and she was overdressed—she'd worn a long skirt and heels, imagining herself in some glamorous 1960s movie, hanging on the arm of her bespectacled professor husband in a smoke-filled living room. Instead, she was crowded with a bunch of grungy thirtysome-things in a third-floor walk-up, listening to Fleetwood Mac.

"They were different," he said.

"Different how?"

"Different from you," he said. "All people are different, white girls too."

He was different from anyone she'd ever known. His native lan-guage was Creole, his English inflected by his accent. He had a nearly photographic memory, so when he helped her run lines, he always learned them before she did. They'd met at 8 Ball, the dive bar where she worked. Somehow, past the burly bikers crowded around high tops, past the tattooed girls feeding the jukebox quarters to play Joan Jett, past her own attempts to blend in, they'd noticed each other. She was still trying to find her first acting gig then, and nobody under-stood why she'd left Los Angeles to do so. But she liked the stage. In Los Angeles, every actor she knew was obsessed with breaking into Hollywood, because anyone with sense knew that Hollywood was where the money was. But that whole process seemed like a drag. Waking up at dawn, standing in front of a camera for hours, repeat-ing the same lines until some asshole director was satisfied. The stage was something else altogether—new every time, which terrified and thrilled her. Each show was different, each audience unique, each night crackling with possibility. The fact that there was no money in what she was doing was just a bonus. She was only twenty-four then, still romanced by the idea of her own suffering.

"I know that," she told Franz. "That's why I'm asking what they were like."

Soon she regretted asking when they began to run into his ex-girlfriends around the city. Sage the poet, who published long rambling essays about the female body that she still sent to Frantz for notes. Hannah the engineer, studying how to improve sanitation in poor countries. Kennedy had imagined a frumpy girl wading through sewage, not this perky blonde on the subway, perfectly balanced in her five-inch boots. Christina played the clarinet for the Brooklyn Philharmonic. At dinner, Kennedy stirred her creamed spinach while Christina and Frantz discussed Brahms. He was right, they were all different. She felt stupid for being surprised. Part of her had imagined that his other white girl-friends were altered versions of herself—her if she had, say, grown up in Jersey or decided, on a whim, to dye her hair red. But his taste in white girls was varied and she couldn't decide what was worse, to be the latest iteration in a series of similar lovers or to be radically different from the ones who'd come before her. Belonging to a pattern was safe, at least; to be singular was a risk. What was it, exactly, that Frantz liked about her? How could she ever hope to keep him interested?

"What if I told you," she said, "that I'm not white?"

She didn't plan to say this, it just came out. Frantz smiled, his beer raised to his lips.

"What are you, then?" he said.

"Well, not full white," she said. "I'm part black too."

She'd never said this out loud before. She'd wondered if saying it might make it feel more real, as if something innate would awaken inside her at the sound of those words. But the admission felt phony, like she was reciting lines. She couldn't even convince herself. Frantz squinted at her a moment.

"Ah, yes," he said. "I see it now."

"You do?"

"Sure," he said. "I know plenty of Negroes with hair as kinky as yours."

He was teasing. He thought she was kidding, and over time, it became a joke between them. If she was running late, he'd say that she was on colored people time. If she snapped at him, he'd say, "Easy there, sista." Soon it became a joke to her too. Jude, her mother's secret, all of it. She would know, she decided. You couldn't go through your whole life not knowing something so fundamental about yourself. She would feel it somehow. She would see it in the faces of other blacks, some sort of connection. But she felt nothing. She glanced at them across the subway car with the vague disinterest of a stranger. Even Frantz was, essentially, foreign to her. Not because he was black, although that, perhaps, underscored it. But his life, his language, even his interests were apart from her. Sometimes she stepped inside the little closet he'd converted into an office and watched him scribble equations that she'd never understand. There were many ways to be alienated from someone, few to actually belong.

HER MOTHER HATED FRANTZ. She called him uppity.

"And not for the reason you think," she said. They were sitting in the window of a café, watching all the people walk by. Her mother had flown out to visit her during her Thanksgiving break. Kennedy had insisted she couldn't take time away from work and auditions to visit home, but really, she just wanted her mother to see her New York life. She took a perverse delight in it, like she was a child dragging her over to see the drawing she'd scribbled on the wall. Look at the mess I've made! Her mother had tried her best not to react. She'd kept her lips drawn tight during the grand tour of the basement apartment. Nodded quietly as Kennedy took her by 8 Ball. But Frantz was the last straw, the one part of her unacceptable life that her mother could not ignore.

"And what reason is that?" Kennedy said.

"You know." There were two black women next to them eating croissants. Her mother would never say it aloud. "It's not that. I just don't like anybody who acts like him—"

"Like what?"

"Like his you-know-what don't stink."

She must have had the only mother in all of Brooklyn who was too polite to say the word *shit* in public.

"I don't know why you don't like him," Kennedy said. "He was perfectly nice to you."

"I never said he wasn't. But he walks around like he's the smartest person in the room."

"Well, he is! He has a PhD from Dartmouth, for God's sake. I always feel like a dummy around him."

"I just don't understand it. You never liked anyone like him before."

In high school, she'd dated boys in studded leather jackets who wore their hair long and greasy like the Ramones. Her first boyfriend could barely see without swiping long strands out of his eyes. She'd thought it was darling but it drove her father crazy. He imagined her dating, as all fathers do, boys who reminded him of his younger self, hair shorn, sharply dressed, career focused. Not these slouchy boys she brought home, always a little baked, shy of total irreverence but near it. She dated boys in bands that played music so terribly, she could not have endured listening if not for love. She'd dated a wrestler in college and watched him run around for hours draped in garbage bags, trying to drop weight. She could never love a man who cared that much about anything, she told herself later, but here she was, living with one who jotted equations on the bathroom mirror before he could forget them.

"Well, it was time for a change," she said.

Her bad-boy phase had ended. Her mother should have been relieved, but she only looked troubled.

"It's not because of that girl, is it?" she said.

They hadn't spoken about Jude in two years. But she hadn't left them. Kennedy knew, right away, who her mother meant.

"What're you talking about?" she said.

"Well, you never liked anyone like this before. Then that silly girl got into your head. I just hope you're not trying to prove anything."

She seemed so flustered, fingering the handle of her coffee cup, that Kennedy looked away. If dating Frantz had been some type of experiment, then it had failed terribly. Loving a black man only made her feel whiter than before.

"I'm not," she said. "Come on, let's go to the museum."

THE WINTER SHE SAW Jude Winston again, Kennedy starred in an off-off-Broadway musical called *Silent River*. She played Cora, the sheriff's rebellious daughter who longs to run away with a rugged farmhand. For months, she obsessed, more than normal, about getting sick. She drank so much hot tea with lemon that by February she could barely stand the smell of it and pinched her nose, gagging it down. She swallowed chalky zinc pills and triple-wrapped her neck in a scarf before stepping outside. She scrubbed her hands furiously after she climbed off the subway. She wasn't built for a New York winter under ordinary circumstances; landing her biggest role since she'd moved to the city certainly fit the bill of extraordinary. The night she got the call, Frantz took her out to dinner. She was giddy. He was relieved.

"I was starting to think," he said, but didn't finish. He was five years older than her, and age aside, he was a serious man who believed in serious pursuits. It was becoming increasingly apparent that her acting career didn't make the cut. At first, he'd seemed charmed. My California dreamer, he called her. He ran lines with her in the living room and met outside of auditions for recaps on the subway. But now, as he smiled plaintively across the table, she could see that he was less happy and more surprised, like a parent discovering that Santa Claus was actually real. He'd answered the letters and eaten the cookies and left the presents under the tree, but he'd never expected a fat man to come sliding down the chimney.

She worked harder in that musical than she'd ever worked at anything. She tacked bright flyers advertising the show on every storefront and lamppost she could find. She suffered the glares of neighbors when she practiced her songs in the stairwell, where the acoustics were better. In the morning, she soft-shoed across the bathroom tile, rehearsing the choreography as she brushed her teeth. When she wasn't rehearsing, she rested her voice. Nobody who'd ever met her would believe this but it was true: for weeks, she barely spoke at all. She'd left 8 Ball by then and started at a coffee shop called Gulp, near the theater. The shows took up her evenings, and besides, bartending was a chatty field. Pouring coffee required less conversation. On her breaks, she drank tea and talked to no one. At home, Frantz gave her a small whiteboard where she passed him messages. Dinner? Heading out. Your mother called. He seemed tickled by it all, as if he'd been roped into a piece of performance art.

You'd be amazed by how loud the city sounded when you'd decided to be quiet. She became jittery, as easily spooked as a horse. Even the sudden sound of the coffee grinder made her jump. But when Jude pushed through the door, Kennedy heard nothing, not the bell jingling, not the street noise filtering in with the chill. For three years, she'd imagined what she might say to Jude if she ever saw her again. Now Jude stood across the counter, but when Kennedy opened her mouth, nothing came out. She couldn't even whisper.

"I thought it was you," Jude said.

She was still lean and ropy, bundled up in a big white coat that made her skin shine darker. And she was smiling. She was goddamn smiling, like they were old pals.

"I saw a flyer with your name," she said. "We were walking by and I saw that flyer in the window and—wow, it's really you."

By the door, she recognized Jude's boyfriend—his curly hair longer, beard darker, but still, unmistakably, him. He lingered by the window, blowing warmth into his hands, his shoulders flecked with ice. She couldn't help it—she was surprised that they were still together. She knew his type—painfully handsome—and it wasn't the type to love a girl like Jude. Sure, she was striking in her own way, but a pretty boy like him would never fall for a girl who was difficultly beautiful. But here they were, still together and in New York. What on earth were they doing all the way out here?

"How've you been?" Jude asked.

She was acting casual, but nothing about their friendship had ever been pure coincidence. She no longer believed in the magic of accidents when Jude Winston was concerned. A white man in a gray coat stepped inside the café, and Kennedy waved him forward. If she was back in Los Angeles, she probably would have sworn at Jude. But here, cocooned in her self-made silence, she could only ignore her. Jude looked startled, but stepped out of line.

The man paid for his coffee and left. Then Jude slipped a scrap of paper onto the counter. "This is where we're staying," she said. "In case you want to talk."

SHE CALLED. Of course she called.

She knew she would even after she slipped the paper into her apron pocket. She didn't throw it away—that was the first sign. The second was the fact that she kept thinking about it. One tiny slip of paper wedged in her pocket that might as well have been a razor, digging into her side. It made no sense for a piece of paper to bother her this much, and twice during her shift, she resolved to rip it into tiny pieces. But every time she pulled it out, she glanced at Jude's small, neat handwriting. Hotel Castor, room 403, and the phone number. By the third time, it was too late. She'd already memorized the number.

After work, she stepped into the phone booth across the street and dialed. No one answered, and on the train she thought about calling again once she got home, but she didn't want Frantz to overhear. How could she possibly explain this to him? That a black girl, claiming to be her cousin, had mysteriously appeared in the city. He'd think she was joking again. She called the next morning, right before work, and this time, Jude answered.

"I'm not supposed to be speaking to you," Kennedy said.

Jude paused. For a second, Kennedy thought she didn't recognize her voice, then she said, "Why not?"

"Because," Kennedy said, "I'm in a musical."

"I'm sorry," Jude said evenly. "I don't understand."

"I'm not supposed to be speaking to anybody. I'm resting my voice."

"Oh."

"So whatever you have to say to me, just say it. I'm not wasting time going back and forth with you."

"I'm not here to fight."

"Then why the hell are you here?"

"Reese has surgery."

The whole time, she'd imagined all that Jude could possibly want. Revenge, after that nasty thing she'd said to her at the cast party. Money, like her mother suggested. Well, good luck with that. One look at her life and anyone could tell that she didn't have any. She could barely afford her rent. She imagined telling Jude this—a little ashamed, a little proud—but it turned out that she hadn't resurfaced in New York because of Kennedy at all. Her boyfriend was sick—dying, even—and here Kennedy was, assuming Jude was thinking about her. "You know what your problem is?" a director had told her once. "You consider yourself your most fascinating subject." She'd always thought everyone felt like a lead character onstage, surrounded by sidekicks and villains and love interests. She still couldn't tell which bit role Jude was playing in her life, but she wasn't even registering in Jude's.

"Is it serious?" she asked. "I mean, is he okay?"

"It's not like he's dying," Jude said. "But it's serious. Yes, I'd say it's serious."

"Then why'd you come all the way out here? There aren't any more surgeons in Los Angeles?"

Jude paused. "We're not in Los Angeles anymore," she said. "And it's a special sort of surgery. You have to find a certain type of doctor who'll do it."

She was being vague, which, of course, only made Kennedy want to know more. But she couldn't ask outright. It was none of her business, Reese's life or Jude's. This time, it seemed, their meeting was just an accident.

"Where do you live, then?" she said.

"Minneapolis."

"What the hell are you doing out there?"

"I'm in medical school."

In spite of herself, she felt a little proud. Jude was living the life she said she wanted, years ago. Still loved by the same man, on her way to becoming a doctor. And what did Kennedy have to show for all that time? A basement apartment with a man she barely understood, no college degree, a job serving coffee so that she could belt out songs in a half-empty theater each night.

"I'm glad you called," Jude said. "I didn't think you would."

"Yeah, well, can you blame me?"

"Look, I know things ended sort of strangely—"

Kennedy laughed. "Well, that's a goddamn understatement."

"But if you'd just meet me for ten minutes, I have something to show you."

Her mother had called Jude crazy. Maybe she was. But she was already reeling Kennedy back in. She could have hung up. She could have hung up right then and never spoken to her again. She could have tried to forget about her. But Jude was offering her a key to understanding her mother. How could she say no to that so easily?

"I can't right now," she said. "I'm at work."

"After, then."

"I have a show after."

"Where?" Jude said. "Reese and I will come. It's not sold out already, is it?"

The company hadn't sold out a single show yet, but still, Kennedy paused, as if she were thinking.

"Maybe not," she said. "Usually there are a few tickets left."

"Great," Jude said. "We'll come tonight. We've been wanting to see a real show while we're in New York City and all."

She sounded unbearably innocent, not like the steely, guarded girl Kennedy knew. She was almost charmed by it, but mostly, she felt like she'd found her sure footing again. She gave Jude the name of the theater and told her that she had to go.

"All right," Jude said. "We'll see you tonight. And Kennedy?"

"Seriously, I've got to go—"

"All right, I'm sorry. I just—well, I'm looking forward to it. Seeing you act again, I mean. I loved your last show."

She hated how good that made her feel. She hung up without saying good-bye.

Fifteen

In *Pacific Cove*, Charity Harris was the girl next door, meaning half the fans loved her and the other half found her a total bore. When she disappeared on a cruise ship during her final appearance, Kennedy even received fan letters rejoicing in her misfortune. At the time, it hadn't bothered her. She didn't care if fans loved or hated her, it was attention all the same, and nobody had ever felt strongly enough about a character she'd played to write her about it. Still, she'd hoped, driving off the studio lot, that this wouldn't be Charity's last scene.

"This is the soaps," the director told her. "Nothing's final but a cancellation."

Charity deserved a better end, she would drunkenly tell friends at bars, well into her forties, far beyond when it was appropriate for her to still care so much. Even if she couldn't hope for Charity's miraculous return—a fate that every actor killed off a soap dreamt about—she at least wanted Charity's story wrapped up neatly, some bullshit chyron about the girl leaving Pacific Cove, moving to Peru to raise llamas, she really didn't care what.

"But just disappearing?" she said once. "Into the ocean? And that's it? I mean, what the fuck."

"*Deserve* is a bullshit term," her yoga instructor boyfriend said. "None of us deserves anything. We get what we get."

Maybe she felt Charity was robbed because she'd been such a nice girl. A better girl than Kennedy, certainly, who had made her share of mistakes. She'd slept with two married directors, stolen money from her parents when she was too proud to ask for more loans, lied to friends about audition times so she would have a leg up. But Charity was sweet. She'd met the love of her life, show hunk Lance Garrison, when she was rescuing a drowning dog, for God's sake. Yet when she disappeared, Lance only waited half a season before he was making eyes at the detective's sultry daughter. Five years later, the two had a big wedding that broke a *Pacific Cove* ratings record—twenty million viewers, according to *TV Guide*, which included the wedding in its fifty top soap-opera moments of all time. The episode was even nominated for an Emmy! And in all the glowing reviews, no one even mentioned Charity, or the fact that the happy couple would have never found each other if Charity hadn't stepped onto that cruise ship, waving gleefully from the deck as she floated out into daytime television heaven.

Perhaps, even more than the lost job, she was peeved that she hadn't starred in a big soap-opera wedding. She was more upset about that than the fact that she never married in real life.

"I never play the girl next door," a black guest star told her once. "I guess no one wants to live next door to me."

Pam Reed smiled wryly at the craft-service table, popping a cherry tomato between her lips. She was a real actor, Kennedy overheard two grips saying. In the 1970s, she'd played a policewoman in a popular action movie franchise until the villain shot her in the third film. Then she'd been a judge on a network legal drama. She would play judges throughout the rest of her career, and sometimes Kennedy flipped on the television and saw Pam Reed on the bench, leaning forward sternly, her hand under her chin.

"TV loves a black woman judge," Pam told her. "It's funny—can you imagine what this world would look like if we decided what's fair?"

She'd played a judge on *Pacific Cove* that afternoon. Even between takes, she was intimidating in her long black robe, which was why Kennedy, reaching for a cluster of grapes, said the first stupid thing that came to her mind.

"I lived next door to a black family," she said. "Well, across the street. The daughter's name was Cindy—she was my first friend, really."

She didn't tell Pam that their friendship had ended when, in a fit of childish rage, she'd called Cindy a nigger. She still cringed when she remembered Cindy bursting into tears. She had, ridiculously, started crying too and her mother had slapped her—the first and only time she'd ever struck her. The slap confused her less than the kiss after, her mother's anger and love colliding together so violently. At the time, she'd thought saying *nigger* was as bad as repeating any swear word; her mother would have been just as upset and embarrassed had she hollered *fuck* in that cul-de-sac. But after Jude, Kennedy remembered the look on her mother's face when she'd dragged her into the house. She was angry, yes, but more than that, she looked terrified. Frightened by her own emotion or, more disturbingly, by her daughter, who had revealed herself to be something so ugly.

She never said the word again, not in passing, not repeating jokes, not until Frantz asked her to in bed. It was like a game, he'd told her, stroking her back, because he knew she didn't mean it. She didn't know why she was thinking of Frantz now. Saying that word to him was different than saying it to Cindy. Wasn't it?

Pam Reed just laughed a little, dabbing her mouth with a cocktail napkin.

"Lucky her," she said.

THE NIGHT JUDE WINSTON CAME to her show, Kennedy left her body onstage.

Any actor could tell you this had happened to him before—better actors had experienced it much earlier in their careers, she was sure. That winter night was the first time she truly knew what it felt like to step outside of herself. Singing felt like breathing, dancing as natural as walking. When she sang her duet with Randy the Farmhand—a lanky drama student at NYU—she felt, almost, as if she were falling in love with him. After the curtain call, the cast surrounded her with cheers, and part of her knew, even then, that it was the greatest performance she would ever give. And she'd only managed it because she knew that somewhere, in the darkened theater, Jude was watching.

In the dressing room, she changed slowly, the magic from the stage disappearing. Frantz would be waiting for her in the lobby. On Thursday nights, he came by after his office hours. He would tell her that she'd been good tonight, great even. He would notice a difference in her, might even wonder what had caused it. And there, waiting also in the lobby, would be Jude and Reese. What she hadn't expected was to find all three waiting together, Frantz grinning as he waved her over.

"You didn't tell me you had friends visiting," he said. "Come on, let's all get a drink."

"I don't want to keep everyone out," she said.

"Nonsense. They came all this way. Just one drink."

She barely remembered that numb walk to 8 Ball. She'd only chosen that bar because she knew it would make Jude uncomfortable.

And sure enough, as soon as they walked in, Jude glanced around the dim bar, overwhelmed by the punk music screaming out of the speakers. She gazed at the obscenities scribbled on the tabletops in permanent marker, the bikers crowding the bar, and looked as if she'd rather be anyplace else. Good, then no one would be tempted to stay longer. Stupidly, she hadn't anticipated these two parts of her life collapsing. She would see Jude after the show for a minute, the girl would show her whatever she planned to. She'd never imagined that Jude and Frantz might end up talking and discover that they both knew her. A friend from school, Jude must've told him, because Frantz kept asking what Kennedy was like in college.

"Baby," she said, "stop bugging them. Let's just drink."

"I'm not bugging," Frantz said. He turned to Jude. "Am I bugging?"

She smiled. "No, it's fine. It's just a little overwhelming, being here."

"We're not really big city people," Reese said. It was so folksy and charming, Kennedy could puke.

"I wasn't either," Frantz said. "I moved here when I was a boy. The city still does something to me, you know. Say, how long are you two in town? I'm sure Ken would love to show you around—"

"Let's get drinks first," she said. "Before we start planning tours."

Frantz laughed. "All right, already." He pushed out of the booth, nodding to Reese. "Give me a hand?"

The two men headed to the bar. Now Kennedy was alone with Jude for the first time in years. She'd never wanted a drink more.

"Your boyfriend's nice," Jude said.

"Look, I'm sorry for what I said, at that cast party," Kennedy said. "About you and Reese. I was drunk. I didn't mean it."

"You meant it," Jude said. "And you were drunk. Both things can be true."

"Fine, but is that why you're here? Is that why you're messing with me? I'm tired of all this."

"All what?"

"Whatever you're doing. This game or whatever this is."

Jude stared at her a moment, then reached for her purse.

"I had a feeling I'd see you again," she said.

"Great, you're a psychic." Kennedy could see the boys ordering at the bar, and it dawned on her that she hadn't even told Frantz what she wanted. A small intimacy but still remarkable, Frantz knowing what she wanted before she even asked for it.

"I didn't want to tell you," Jude said. "At the cast party. I didn't think you'd want to know. I only said something because I was mad. You said that thing to me and I wanted to hurt you. It wasn't fair." She pulled something white out of her wallet. "You shouldn't tell people the truth because you want to hurt them. You should tell them because they want to know it. And I think you want to know now."

She handed Kennedy a white square of paper. A photograph. Kennedy knew, before even looking, that it would be a picture of her mother.

"Christ, that took forever," Frantz said, sliding back into the booth with the drinks. "Hey, what's that?"

"Nothing," she said. "Scoot out, I have to hit the can."

"Ah Ken, I just sat down," he groaned, but slid over nonetheless, and she climbed out of the booth, clutching the photograph. She did go to the ladies' room, but only because she needed better light. Jude could have handed her a photo of anyone, for all she knew. For a second, she stood in front of the bathroom mirror, holding the picture against her stomach.

She didn't have to look at it. She could rip it up, and at the end of the night, she'd never have to speak to Jude again. Soon Reese would have his surgery, then they would leave the city for good. She wouldn't have to know. She could do that, couldn't she?

Well, you know what happened next. She knew too, even before she flipped the picture over. Memory works that way—like seeing forward and backward at the same time. In that moment, she could see in both directions. She saw herself as a little girl—eager, pestering, clambering to be close to a mother who never wanted her to be. A mother whom she'd never actually known. Then she saw herself showing the photograph to her, the proof that she'd spent her whole life lying. When Kennedy flipped the picture over, she could make out the figures of twin girls in black dresses, another woman standing between them. The photograph was old, gray and faded, but still, under the fluorescent light, she could tell which of these identical girls was her mother. She looked uncomfortable, like if she could have, she would have run right out of the frame.

Her mother had always hated taking pictures. She hated being nailed down in place.

"YOUR FRIENDS ARE NICE," Frantz said later that night, crawling into bed.

She'd barely spoken on the subway ride home. She wasn't feeling well, she'd told everyone after one drink, she'd better call it a night. In the bathroom, she'd slipped the photograph inside her waistband like when she was little, trying to sneak treats out of the kitchen. Except instead of a chocolate bar melting under the shirt, she felt the sharp corners poking at her the whole walk to the station. Part of her wanted Jude to think that she'd gotten rid of it. Flushed it down the toilet or something. Jude had looked disappointed as they'd said good-bye. Well, good. Let her feel disappointed. Who did she think she was, anyway? Disrupting her life a second time, and for all she knew, Jude could still be lying. She looked nothing like either girl in the picture or the woman standing between them, darker but still fair, a hand on each girl's shoulder. The three looked like a set, like they all belonged to each other. But Jude belonged to no one. And what about Kennedy? Who the hell did she belong to?

"We're not friends," she said. "Not really. I mean, they're just people I used to know."

"Oh. Well." He shrugged, then rolled over, kissing her neck. She squirmed away.

"Jesus, stop," she said.

"What's the matter?"

"What do you mean? I told you already, I'm not feeling well."

"Well, Christ, you don't have to bite my head off."

He rolled away from her glumly and turned off the light.

"I knew they weren't your friends," he said.

"What?"

"You don't have black friends," he said. "You don't like anybody black but me and we're not really friends, are we?"

In the morning, she called Hotel Castor again, but nobody answered.

She lay alone in bed, studying that faded photograph until she had to get to work. The twins, side by side in those somber black dresses. Her mother and not-her-mother, her grandmother between them. A whole family where her mother said there'd been none, and Jude, somehow, knowing all of this. Once, when she was thirteen, her mother had brought her to the mall to buy a new dress for her birthday. Kennedy was beginning to pull away by then, wishing she could have gone to Bloomingdale's with her girlfriends instead. But her mother was barely focusing on her. She paused in the middle of the shop floor, fingering the lacy sleeves of a black gown.

"I love shopping," she'd said, almost to herself. "It's like trying on all the other people you could be."

DURING HER LUNCH BREAK, Kennedy called the hotel room again. Still no answer. This time, she tried the front desk.

"The girl said they'd be at the hospital all day," the receptionist told her. "In case anyone called."

"Which hospital?"

"Sorry, miss, she didn't say."

Of course, what did she expect from some country girl who'd found herself in New York City for the first time? Of course she'd never considered how many hospitals were in Manhattan alone. She was irritated but flipped through the phone book to find the closest hospital to the hotel. The receptionist told her that she couldn't release the name of any patients, and Kennedy, hanging up, realized that she didn't know Reese's full name anyway. Still, she left work early and rode the bus to the hospital. At the nurse's station, she asked a tiny redhead to page a Jude Winston. She waited five minutes, the phone book page crinkling in her pocket, wondering if she'd have to work her way uptown until she found them. Then the elevator doors opened. Jude stepped out, frazzled at first then relieved once she saw it was only Kennedy.

"You didn't leave the hospital name," Kennedy said. "I could've spent all damn day looking for you."

"But you didn't," Jude said.

"Yeah, well, I could have." Jesus, they were already bickering like siblings. "It's a big city, you know."

Jude paused. "Well," she said, "my mind's all over the place right now."

It was exactly the type of thing her mother would have said—sly, meant to guilt her into submission.

"Sorry," she said. "Is he all right?"

Jude chewed her lip. "I don't know," she said. "He's still under. They won't let me see him. Since we're not family and all."

It occurred to Kennedy then that if she suddenly had a heart attack, right here in the hospital lobby, Jude would be her nearest relative. Cousins. They were cousins. But if Jude told a nurse this, insisting on the right to visit, who would ever believe her?

"That's absurd," Kennedy said. "You're the only one he has out here."

"Well." Jude shrugged.

"He should just marry you," she said. "Get it over with. You've been together long enough and then you wouldn't have to worry about bullshit like this."

Jude stared at her for a second, and Kennedy thought she might tell her to go fuck herself. She deserved it, probably. But Jude just rolled her eyes.

"You sound like my mother," she said.

THE PHOTOGRAPH WAS from a funeral, Jude told her. In the cafeteria, the girls sat across from each other at a long metal table, sipping lukewarm coffee, the photo lying between them. A funeral, she'd figured as much—the black dresses and all—but now she glanced back at the picture, those twin girls. Matching hair ribbons, matching tights. For the first time, she noticed one twin clutching the other's dress, as if she were trying to keep her still. She touched the photo, reminding herself that it was real. Needing it, somehow, to tether her in place.

"Who died?" she said.

"Their daddy. He was killed."

"By who?"

Jude shrugged. "Bunch of white men."

She didn't know what was more shocking, the revelation or how casually Jude offered it.

"What?" she said. "Why?"

"Does there have to be a reason why?"

"When someone gets killed? Usually."

"Well, there isn't. It just happened. Right in front of them."

She tried to imagine her mother as a girl, witnessing something so horrible, but she could only picture her eight years ago, standing at the end of the darkened hallway with a baseball bat. Kennedy had been a little drunk, sneaking back home after a party; she'd expected her mother to yell at her for breaking curfew. Instead, she was standing at the end of the hall, a hand covering her mouth. The baseball bat clattered on the wood floor, rolling toward her bare feet.

"She never talks about him," Kennedy said.

"Mine either," Jude said.

At the end of the table, an old Jewish man hacked into his sweater sleeve. Jude glanced over, fiddling with a candy wrapper.

"What's she like?" Kennedy asked. "Your mother."

"Stubborn," she said. "Like you."

"I am not stubborn."

"If you say so."

"Well, what else is she like? She's got to be more than stubborn."

"I don't know," Jude said. "She works at a diner. She says she hates it but she'd never go anywhere different. She'd never leave Maman."

"Is that what you call your grandmother?" Kennedy still couldn't bring herself to say *our.*

Jude nodded. "I grew up in her house," she said. "She's getting old now. She forgets a lot. She still asks about your mom sometimes."

An announcement crackled over the PA system. Kennedy added another packet of sugar to coffee she'd never finish.

"This is strange for me," she said. "I don't think you understand how strange it all is."

"I know," Jude said.

"No, you don't. I don't think anybody could possibly know."

"Fine, I don't know." Jude stood, tossing her coffee in the trash can. Kennedy scrambled after, suddenly afraid that she'd leave her here. What if she'd pushed Jude away and now Jude decided not to tell her anything more? Knowing a little was worse than not knowing at all. So she followed Jude onto the elevator, riding in silence to the fifth floor, then she sat beside her in the waiting room next to a wilting plant.

"You don't have to stay," Jude said.

"I know that," Kennedy said. But she did.

THE HOSPITAL RELEASED REESE that evening. When Jude wheeled him outside, Kennedy glanced up, startled to find the sky already cloaked in navy blue. For hours, she'd sat beside Jude in the waiting room, flipping idly through magazines, wandering down to the cafeteria for more coffee, or sometimes just sitting there, staring at that picture. She called in sick to her show. Admitted the flu had gotten to her after all. And in spite of every reason she had to leave, she stayed there in that quiet hospital room, until a brusque white nurse told them they could go. She thought about calling home. Frantz always tried to ring her before her shows, he'd worry if the understudy picked up. Still, she hailed a cab and helped Jude guide Reese inside. He was still a little loopy from the anesthesia, and the whole ride to the hotel, his head kept lolling onto her shoulder. Jude squeezed his thigh, and Kennedy glanced away. She couldn't imagine needing anyone so openly.

She could have said good-bye outside the hotel, but she climbed out too. She and Jude didn't speak. They each wrapped an arm around Reese's waist, and together they lugged him inside. He was heavier than he looked, and by the time they reached the elevator, her shoulders burned. But she still held on until they made it inside the hotel room and gingerly lowered him onto the bed. Jude sat on the edge of the mattress, pushing the curls back from his forehead.

"Thanks," she said softly, but she was still looking at Reese. That tenderness in her voice only meant for him.

"Well," Kennedy said. She should've left but she lingered in the room. Jude would spend a few more days in the city while Reese recovered. Maybe Kennedy could stop by the hotel again tomorrow. Surely Jude couldn't stay inside this dingy room all day, watching him sleep. Maybe they could go out for coffee or lunch. She could show her around the city so she'd be able to say that she did more in New York than see a mediocre musical and sit in a hospital waiting room. Jude walked her down to the lobby, and Kennedy slowly wrapped her scarf around her neck.

"What's it like?" she said. "Mallard."

She'd imagined a town like Mayberry, folksy and homey, women leaving pies to cool on their windowsills. A town so small that everybody knew your name. In a different life, she might have visited over the summer. She could have played with Jude in front of their grandmother's house. But Jude just laughed.

"Awful," she said. "They only like light Negroes out there. You'd fit right in."

She'd said it so offhandedly that Kennedy almost didn't realize it.

"I'm not a Negro," she said.

Jude laughed again, this time uneasily.

"Well, your mother is," she said.

"So?"

"So that makes you one too."

"It doesn't make me anything," she said. "My father's white, you know. And you don't get to show up and tell me what I am."

It wasn't a race thing. She just hated the idea of anyone telling her who she had to be. She was like her mother in that way. If she'd been born black, she would have been perfectly happy about it. But she wasn't and who was Jude to tell her that she was somebody that she was not? Nothing had changed, really. She'd learned one thing about her mother, but what did that amount to when you looked at the totality of her life? A single detail had been moved and replaced. Swapping out one brick wouldn't change a house into a fire station. She was still herself. Nothing had changed. Nothing had changed at all.

That night, Frantz asked where she'd been.

"The hospital," she said, too exhausted to lie.

"The hospital? What happened?"

"Oh, I'm all right. I was with Jude. Reese had surgery."

"What type of surgery? Is he all right?"

"I don't know." She'd never asked. "Something with his chest, it looked like. He's fine now. Just a little out of it."

"You should've called. I've been waiting up."

She would leave him. She'd always had a good sense for when it was time to leave. Call it intuition or restlessness, call it whatever you want. She'd never been the type to overstay her welcome. She knew when it was time to leave Los Angeles, and a year later, she would know to leave New York. She knew when she ought to be with a man for six weeks or six years. Leaving was the same, regardless. Leaving was simple. Staying was the part she'd never quite mastered. So that night, when she looked at Frantz in bed, his dark brown skin shimmering against the silver sheets, she knew that she wouldn't stay with him much longer. Still, she sat on the edge of the bed and slipped his glasses off, blurring right in front of his eyes.

"Would you still love me," she said, "if I weren't white?"

"No," he said, tugging her closer. "Because then you wouldn't be you."

WHEN SHE LEFT FRANTZ, she wandered a year, not telling anyone where she was going. Her musical had ended and she was beginning to tire of theater, although she'd stick around years longer, joining improv comedy troupes, auditioning for experimental plays. Acting seemed to be the one thing she never knew when to quit. Before she fled, she saw her mother one last time. They were sitting together in the backyard, sipping chardonnay by the pool. It was an unnaturally bright winter day. She was shocked by the warmth, shocked that there had ever been a time when she hadn't found the idea of a warm February day remarkable. She closed her eyes, sunning her legs, not even thinking about poor Frantz, huddled by their rattling radiator.

"I used to come out here in the mornings," her mother said. "When you were at school. I never had anything to do, but somehow, I was always floating out here, thinking."

It was a lovely day. Kennedy would remember this later, how she could have said nothing, could have lain out there in that sunlight forever. Instead, she handed her mother the photograph.

"What's this?" she asked, tilting her head to look at it.

"It's from your father's funeral," Kennedy said. "Don't you remember?"

Her mother said nothing, her face blank. She stared at the picture.

"Where'd you get this?" she said.

"Where do you think?" Kennedy said. "She found me, you know. She knows you better than I do!"

She hadn't meant to yell. She just expected her mother to feel something. She would show her a picture of her family and her mother would start to cry. Wipe away tears and finally tell her daughter the truth about her life. Kennedy deserved that, didn't she? One moment of honesty. But her mother pushed the picture back toward her.

"I don't know why you're doing this," she said. "I don't know what you want me to say—"

"I want you to tell me who you are!"

"You know who I am! This," her mother said, jabbing at the picture, "is not me. Look at it! She doesn't look anything like me."

She couldn't tell which girl her mother was pointing at, her sister or herself.

JUDE LEFT HER PHONE NUMBER on the back of the photo. For years, Kennedy didn't call.

She kept the picture, though. She carried it with her everywhere she traveled: Istanbul and Rome, Berlin where she lived for three months, sharing a flat with two Swedes. One night they got blitzed and she showed them the picture. The blond boys smiled at her quizzically, handing it back. It meant nothing to anybody but her, which was part of the reason she could never get rid of it. It was the only part of her life that was real. She didn't know what to do with the rest. All the stories she knew were fiction, so she began to create new ones. She was the daughter of a doctor, an actor, a baseball player.

She was taking a break from medical school. She had a boyfriend back home named Reese. She was white, she was black, she became a new person as soon as she crossed a border. She was always inventing her life.

BY THE EARLY 1990S, her acting jobs began to dry up for good. No director had much use for a blonde in her thirties who hadn't yet proven to be a star. She played a few older sisters on a handful of network shows, then a teacher or two, and then her agent stopped calling her at all. She felt too young to be washed up, but then again, she had ridden an improbable string of luck. Her whole life, in fact, had been a gift of good fortune—she had been given whiteness. Blonde hair, a pretty face, a nice figure, a rich father. She'd sobbed out of speeding tickets, flirted her way to endless second chances. Her whole life, a bounty of gifts she hadn't deserved.

She became a spin instructor for two years, the studio placing photos of Charity Harris on the flyer to attract customers. But she grew tired of sweating all the time, her legs twitching and cramping, and so, in 1996, she finally decided to go back to school. Not real school, she told everyone, laughing at the thought, but realty school. She'd sold ads for shitty products on daytime television for years, why couldn't she sell a house? On her first day, she sat awkwardly at the tiny desk, staring at the handout the teacher was passing down each row.

What Clients Value in a Real Estate Agent:
- Honesty
- Knowledge of the housing market
- Negotiation skills

She could learn most of this, she told herself, except for the first bullet point. She had been acting her entire life, which meant that she was the best liar that she knew. Well, second best.

IN HER FIRST YEAR at San Fernando Valley Real Estate, Kennedy sold seven houses. Her boss Robert told her that she had the Midas touch, but she privately called it the Charity Harris effect. She had the type of face that people vaguely remembered, even those who had never watched *Pacific Cove*. Everyone thought they knew her. And of course, the *Pacific Cove* fans always showed up to her open houses, long after the show had ended.

"I never thought it was right what happened to you," one woman whispered to her once in a Tarzana model home. She'd smiled politely, guiding the woman through the hallway. She could be Charity if they needed her to be. She could be anyone, really.

Before each open house, she felt like she was back onstage again, waiting for the curtain to rise. She tweaked the decorations, swapping out framed photographs of stock families. A black family became a white one, a soccer beanbag chair became a basketball, a horn of plenty tucked inside a cabinet in exchange for a menorah. A model home was nothing but a set, if you thought about it, the open house a grand performance directed by her. Each time, she stood behind the door, bowing her head, as jittery as the first time she had ever taken the stage, knowing that her mother would be out there in the audience watching. Then she put on a big Charity Harris smile, opening the door. She would disappear inside herself, inside these empty homes where nobody actually lived. As the room filled with strangers, she always found her mark, guiding a couple through the kitchen, pointing out the light fixtures, backsplash, high ceilings.

"Imagine your life here," she said. "Imagine who you could be."

Part VI

PLACES

(1986)

Sixteen

B y 1981, Mallard no longer existed, or at least, it was no longer called Mallard.

The town had never actually been a town at all. State officials considered it a village but the United States Geological Survey referred to it only as a populated place. And although the residents may have created their own boundaries, a place has no legal borders. So after the 1980 Census, the parish redrew town lines and the residents of Mallard woke up one morning to learn that they had been allocated to Palmetto. By 1986, Mallard had been scrubbed off every transit map in the area. For most folks, the name change didn't mean much. Mallard had always been more of an idea than a place, and an idea couldn't be redefined by geographical terms. But the name change confused Stella Vignes, who stood in the Opelousas train station, staring at the map for ten minutes before she finally waved over a young black porter and asked the best way to get to Mallard. He laughed.

"Oh, you must be from them old days," he said. "Ain't called that no more."

She flushed. "What's it called, then?"

"Oh, lots of things, lots of things. Lebeau, Port Barre. Supposed to be Palmetto but some folks still call it Mallard. Folks stubborn like that."

"I see," she said. "I haven't been back in a while."

He smiled at her and she glanced away. She'd traveled as plainly as she could, afraid to draw attention to herself. One simple bag, her wedding ring tucked inside. Wore her cheapest slacks, pinned her hair back like she used to, although now it was beginning to streak with gray. So she'd touched it up with a rinse before leaving, embarrassed by her own vanity. But what if Desiree dyed hers? She couldn't be the old twin. The thought terrified her, looking into Desiree's face and not seeing her own.

Like leaving, the hardest part of returning was deciding to. For months, she'd tried to imagine any other way, but she was desperate. She hadn't heard from her daughter since she'd visited from New York City with a photograph, and Stella found herself staring directly at her past. She didn't remember taking a picture at her daddy's funeral, but then again, she didn't remember much of that day. That itchy black lace scraping against her legs. A pinch of pound cake, spongy and sweet. A closed casket. Desiree pressed into her side. Her sister, somehow knowing what she wanted to say even if she couldn't.

In the backyard, staring down at that photograph, she fell just as silent. She knew, before she even opened her mouth, that she would lie, the way she'd always lied, but this time her daughter wouldn't believe her.

"It's like you're incapable of telling the truth," Kennedy said. "You don't know how to do anything but lie."

For months, she'd refused Stella's phone calls. Stella left messages on the answering machine, humiliated by the thought of smug Frantz listening to her beg. She had even spoken to him once or twice; he always promised to pass along her messages, but she couldn't tell if he was just pacifying her to free up the line. Then six months ago, Frantz told Stella that her daughter had moved out. "She's gone," he said, "and I don't know where. She just left one morning. Didn't even leave a forwarding address. There's still boxes of her things and she won't even tell me where to send them." He seemed more inconvenienced by the junk he was storing than the fact that Kennedy had abandoned him. Stella panicked, naturally, but weeks later, Blake received a postcard from Rome, written in their daughter's hasty scrawl.

Went to find myself, she wrote. I'm safe. Don't worry about me.

The language bothered Stella most of all. You didn't just find a self out there waiting—you had to make one. You had to create who you wanted to be. And wasn't her daughter already doing that? Stella blamed the dark girl, who'd stalked her daughter around Los Angeles, who'd tracked her, somehow, all the way across the country. The girl was determined to prove the truth to Kennedy and she would never give up. Unless. In her office, Stella stopped pacing, slumping against the door.

She knew what she had to do: tell Desiree to call her girl off. She had to go back to Mallard.

So when Blake left for business to Boston, she booked a flight to New Orleans. As the airplane descended, she wrung her hands, staring out the window at the brown flatness. She could always go back. Turn around, buy a ticket to Los Angeles, forget this whole foolish idea. But then she imagined that dark girl appearing, again and again, and she clutched the armrest as the plane rattled gently onto the runway. Now, in the train station, the lanky porter smiling at her, knowing somehow, she was sure of it, that she had returned from a place she had never imagined that she could leave. He pointed at a bus stop.

"Puts you down right outside Mallard," he said. "Have to walk from there, I'm afraid."

She hadn't ridden a bus in years. He nodded toward a pay phone.

"You could call your people," he said. "Have someone come get you."

But she wasn't sure if she had people anymore. Instead she said, "It'll be good to stretch my legs."

———

ONCE MALLARD WAS NO LONGER MALLARD, some joked that the name of the diner ought to change also to the name people had long been calling it: Desiree's. "Y'all goin by Desiree's" became so common a refrain that by the 1980s, there were children born who had never remembered a time when the diner had been called anything else. The town ignored the faded coffee cup on the roof still bearing Lou's name, which he didn't appreciate, but he was old now. He leaned on Desiree for everything; she was head waitress and manager, she hired and fired cooks, she changed the menu when she felt like it. She was the face of the establishment, framed, for years, within its black-and-white windows. Lou would leave the diner to her when he died, he'd always said, although Desiree said that she didn't want it.

"I got a life outside Lou's," she said. "I don't wanna be stuck in here forever."

But what was that life, exactly? Sometimes she didn't even know herself. Early, still coming and going. Her mother's unraveling memory. Her daughter, living across the country. She'd visited her in Minneapolis in the winter of 1985. The two had walked arm in arm down the slushy sidewalks, bracing themselves against the unexpected ice. She hadn't seen snow like this, real snow, in almost thirty years; on one corner, she closed her eyes, fat flakes falling onto her lashes. She was thinking of her own first winter in D.C., Sam taking her ice-skating downtown, laughing at her wobbling. The whole rink filled with young colored people like them, holding hands, the flashier skaters twirling and slicing across the ice. Even the Santa Claus swinging his bell on the curb was colored. She had never seen a Negro Santa before and stared so hard, she nearly lost her balance.

"It's supposed to snow all week," her daughter said. "I'm sorry, Mama."

"What you sorry for? You can't control the weather."

"I know, but—I wanted it to be nice for you."

She brushed ice out of Jude's hair. "It is nice," she said. "Come on, let's go."

Inside the grocery store, the lights glowed brightly and her daughter trailed behind, slowly pushing the cart. Desiree grabbed a bundle of celery. She'd offered to cook—insisted on it, really, having seen the sad state of her girl's cupboards. Nothing but cold cereal and canned food.

"I should've taught you how to cook," she said.

"I cook."

"Too many smart girls don't know how to keep a house anymore."

"Well, I do, and Reese cooks too."

"Oh, that's right. Y'all are—what's it you call it?"

"Modern."

"Modern," she repeated. "He's a nice boy."

"But?"

"But nothin. He seems sweet. I just don't understand why he won't marry you. What's he waitin for, the Grim Reaper?"

"Well, what about you?" Jude said.

"What about me?"

"And Early."

Desiree reached for a bell pepper, startled by the sudden seize of tenderness she felt just hearing his name. She missed him. Imagine that, grown as she was, still missing him. She'd called him after she'd landed in Minnesota. She'd never been on an airplane before, felt as brave as if she'd leapt across the face of the moon. She wished he was with her but he'd offered to stay at home with her mother. Desiree was beginning to realize that it could be dangerous leaving her alone.

"Oh, that's different," she said.

"How?"

"Y'all are young. Don't you wanna start a life together? Hand me that onion."

"We have a life together," Jude said. "We don't have to be married for that."

"I know, I just—" She paused. "I don't want you to be gun-shy. Because of what happened to me."

Desiree studied a bruised tomato, unwilling to look at her daughter. She didn't like to think about the fights her daughter might have seen, that brutal education in love. Jude wrapped her arms around her.

"I'm not," she said. "I promise."

FOR DINNER, Desiree cooked shrimp creole and rice in their tiny kitchen. She stirred the saucepan, gazing around the apartment at the mismatched dining chairs, the orange loveseat, Reese's photographs framed on the wall. He'd started freelancing for the *Minnesota Daily Star*. Small assignments, usually, like Little League games or business openings. On slow days, he worked bar mitzvahs and weddings and proms. Sometimes he wandered around for hours until his fingertips turned red, shooting the tentacles of ice freezing across a lake, or a homeless man huddled in a doorway, or a worn red mitten wedged in a bank of slush. He said that he hated the cold but he'd never been so productive. He'd sold one photograph for two hundred dollars. He wanted to save up to buy a house.

"I just want you to know I'm serious," he told her. "About your daughter."

And he did look serious, perched on the edge of the couch, wringing his hands, so serious that she could have laughed at his earnestness. Instead, she squeezed his arm.

"I know, baby," she said.

When she'd first moved back to Mallard, she never imagined

herself here, sitting on a used couch in Minnesota across from a man who loved her daughter. All week, she went with Jude to campus, staring out at the students trudging past, bundled to their eyes, and couldn't believe, still, that her daughter was one of them. Her girl had gone out into the world, like Desiree had done when she was young. A part of her still hoped that she had time left to do it again.

"It's foolish," she'd told Early when she'd called. "I don't have no business startin over. But I don't know. I wonder sometimes. What else is out there."

"Ain't foolish at all," he said. "What you wanna do?"

She didn't know, but she was embarrassed to admit that when she imagined leaving Mallard, she only saw the two of them in his car, driving a long road to nowhere. Just a fantasy, of course. She would never leave Lou's, not now, not while her mother still needed her.

Her last night in Minneapolis, snow thundered on the roof and Desiree cracked the blinds open, peeking outside. She was holding a coffee mug that Reese topped off with whiskey while Jude cleared the dishes. His photographs spread across the table, snapshots from their life in Los Angeles. Jude rested her hand on the back of his neck as he leaned forward, pointing out the different parts of the city he'd shot. The pier at Manhattan Beach, the Capitol Records building shaped like a spindle of records itself, a humpback whale they'd seen in Santa Barbara. The people they'd known, the friends left behind, shots of crowded rooms during parties. It was strange, seeing a city she had only watched on television, through her daughter's eyes.

"Who's that?" she asked.

She was pointing at one photo in particular, shot in a crowded bar. She wouldn't have noticed it at all if not for the blonde girl in the background, grinning over her shoulder, as if she'd just overheard a joke. Her daughter shuffled the picture back into the pile.

"Nobody," she said. "Just some girl we knew."

Later that night, falling asleep in bed beside her daughter, the boy-friend gallantly offering to sleep on the lumpy couch, a little embar-rassed as he carried over his pillow and blanket—as if Desiree didn't know what went on between the two of them when she wasn't under their roof, as if she didn't know what would probably go on the moment she left, between two people who were young and in love and so relieved to be freed of that old lady who kept asking when they would get married—she kept thinking about the blonde girl in the photo-graph. She didn't know why she was so struck by her. The girl just looked like California, or what she imagined it to be: slender and tan and blonde and happy. She thought about calling Early if it wasn't so late, if she wasn't going to see him one day later, if she wouldn't have been so embarrassed by the fact that she still wanted to call him in spite of all of that. And did you know Jude does things like this, she would've asked him, befriends white girls? It's a new world, ain't it? Did you know the world is so new?

By 1986, Big Ceel was dead, a fact that Early Jones only discovered reading the paper in Dr. Brenner's office. He was waiting with his mother-in-law, or, rather, a woman he had begun to think of as such, when he saw a photo of the man, pages deep into the *Times-Picayune*, below the headline LOAN SHARK FOUND DEAD. Stabbed, it turned out, over a card game gone wrong. Seemed fitting, in a way, that Ceel, a man who'd built a life on lending and collecting, would meet his end over money. At the same time, it seemed disgraceful, dying over such a small sum. Forty dollars, the paper said. Forty dollars, shit. Of course by then, Early knew well enough how little men were willing to die or kill for. He'd seen worse, more risked for less. Still, it stunned him to learn about Ceel's demise in such dispassionate black print, almost as much as it shocked him to discover that Ceel's government name was Clifton Lewis.

Oh, he realized. C. L. It dawned on him, closing the paper as Dr. Brenner called Adele's name, that, in a way, Ceel had been his oldest friend.

By then, he hadn't run a job for Ceel in three months. "I oughta throw you a retirement party already," Ceel had told him, in their last phone call. "You ain't that kid no more I first met. You lost your killer instinct." Early hung up, knowing that Ceel was just trying to goad him, knowing that Ceel still needed him, the old man telling Early, more than once, that he was the best hunter he'd ever had. Once, his insults might've worked. But now life was different. Early wasn't a kid anymore. He had responsibilities. A woman he loved. Her mother, whom he loved too, who had nearly burned the house down when she had turned on the stove to boil water for coffee, forgotten about it, and gone back to sleep. He had gone out to Fontenot's that day, bought a Mr. Coffee for the kitchen, taught Adele how to use it. But after that morning, she never made coffee again. When Desiree left to open Lou's Egg House, he woke up and made a cup for Adele. And if he was off working for Ceel, who would be home to do that?

For the first time in his life, he found a job, a real one, at the oil refinery. Now he went to work every day—like a proper man, Adele would have once said—in gray coveralls with his name stitched over the heart. Early Come Lately, his foreman called him, since he was the oldest roughneck in the crew. He worked mornings when Desiree closed, evenings when she went in early, seesawing their schedules so that Adele was never left alone.

One morning, he took Adele fishing down on the river. Swallows swooped overhead, rustling through the pines. Adele glanced over, tightening her sweater around herself. She wore her hair in two long braids now. Each morning Desiree combed her hair, or if she had to get to Lou's, Early did. She'd taught him how to braid one afternoon, demonstrating with pieces of yarn. He'd practiced, again and again, amazed that his fingers were capable of anything so delicate. He liked the mornings when he braided Adele's hair. She only allowed him to because she was forgetting, and he could forget, too, that she wasn't his mother.

"You warm enough there, Miss Adele?" he asked.

She nodded, gathering her sweater closer.

"Desiree said you like goin fishin," he said. "That true?"

"Desiree say that?"

"Yes'm. I told her we find her some fish to fry up tonight. Sound good, don't it?"

She stared up at the trees, wringing her hands.

"I ought to be gettin to work myself," Adele said.

"No, ma'am. You got the day off."

"The whole day?"

She was so surprised and delighted by the idea that he didn't have the heart to tell her that she hadn't gone to work in the past nine months. The white folks she cleaned for had been the first to notice her lapse in memory. Dishes ending up in the wrong drawers, laundry folded before it dried, canned beans chilled in the refrigerator while chicken rotted on the pantry shelf.

"Oh, I'm old," she'd said. "You know how it is. You just start forgettin things."

But Dr. Brenner said that it was Alzheimer's and it would only get worse. Desiree cried on the phone when she called to tell Early. He cut a job in Lawrence short to be with her. It'd be all right, he'd told her, rocking her, even though he couldn't think of anything more terrifying than looking into Desiree's face one day and only seeing a stranger.

"Are you my son?" Adele asked.

He smiled, reaching for his fishing rod.

"No, ma'am," he said.

"No," she repeated. "I don't have any sons."

She turned, satisfied, to the trees, as if he'd just helped her solve a riddle that was troubling her. Then she glanced at him again, almost shyly.

"You not my husband, are you?"

"No, ma'am."

"I don't have one of those neither."

"I'm just your Early," he said. "That's all I am."

"Early?" She laughed suddenly. "What type of fool name is that?"

"The only fool name I got."

"I know who you are," she said. "You that farm boy always hangin around Desiree."

He touched the end of her gray braid.

"That's right," he said. "That's exactly right."

WHEN THEY RETURNED to the house, there was a white woman sitting on the porch.

Early had caught two small speckled trout, delighting Adele, who'd watched them wriggle on his line. Now, heading back home, Adele humming, her arm looped though his, he spotted the white woman through the clearing and gripped her arm tighter. Once a woman from the county came by to check on Adele. Desiree was humiliated, some strange white woman wandering around her house to make sure that the living conditions were suitable.

"It must be suitable enough," she told Early, "she been livin here sixty years!"

He hated the thought of government workers poking around, as if the two of them were not capable of looking after one forgetting woman, but the visits came with the assistance. They needed money for the medicines, the doctor visits, the bills. Still, he wasn't too thrilled about meeting the county woman. No surprise what she'd think of him.

He patted Adele's hand.

"If that lady ask, we'll tell her I'm your son-in-law," he said.

"What you talkin about?"

"That white lady on the porch," he said. "From the county. Just to make it all go down easier."

She pulled away.

"Quit foolin," she said. "That ain't no white woman. That's just Stella."

In all the years he'd hunted Stella, imagined her, dreamed about her, she'd become larger in his eyes. She was smarter than him. Clever, twisting away each time he drew near. But this not-white woman, this Stella Vignes, looked so ordinary, he lost his breath. Not like Desiree—he wouldn't have confused the two, even as he drew closer, Stella clambering to her feet. She wore navy blue slacks and leather boots, her hair pinned into a ponytail. Pitch black, like she hadn't aged at all, unlike Desiree, whose temples began to streak silver. It wasn't just her clothes, though, but the way she held her body. Taut, like a guitar string wound around itself. She looked scared, but of what? Of him? Well, maybe she ought to be. He wanted to rage at her for every night Desiree fell asleep thinking of her, not him.

But Stella wasn't looking at him. She was staring at her mother, her mouth open like a trout gasping for breath. Adele barely glanced at her.

"Girl, come help us clean those fishes," Adele said. "And go get your sister."

Her mother had lost her mind.

Stella realized this, slowly, as she followed her down the narrow

314

hallway to the kitchen, where a strange man unloaded fish from an icebox. All the times she'd imagined what her mother might say if she came home—she would be angry, might even slap her across the face—she'd never pictured this: her mother a shell of herself, bustling around the kitchen as if the only thing on her mind were fixing dinner. As indifferent to Stella as if she'd been gone twenty-five minutes, not years. The strange man following after her, picking up a knife after she'd set it down, keeping her away from the stove, finally convincing her to have a seat at the table while he made her a cup of coffee.

"Are you Desiree's husband?" Stella asked.

He let out a low laugh. "Somethin like that."

"Well, who are you, then? What're you doing with my mother?"

"Why you actin like that, Stella?" her mother said, handing her a spoon. "You know this your brother."

He couldn't be the dark girl's father. He wasn't nearly as black as her, even though he looked grizzled and tough, like the type of man who might bully a woman.

"How long has it been like this?" she said.

"Year, maybe."

"Jesus."

"Girl, don't take the Lord's name in vain," her mother said. "I raised you better than that."

"I'm sorry, Mama," she said quickly. "Mama, I'm so sorry—"

"I don't know what you talkin about," her mother said. "Probably don't need to know. Start workin on that fish."

Her daddy had taught her how to gut a fish. She'd trounced alongside him in the river, water splashing up to her knees. Desiree marching up ahead, stomping so loud, Daddy said, that she'd scare all the fish away. They were his twin sprites, following him through the woods. The fishing part always bored Desiree; she wandered off, sprawling on her stomach somewhere making daisy chains, but Stella could sit with him for hours, so still, imagining that she could see through the murky water to every living thing swirling around her bare toes. After, he showed the twins how to clean the fish he'd caught. Lay it flat, slide the knife inside the belly, and then what? She couldn't remember. She wanted to cry.

"I don't know how," she said.

"You just don't like gettin your hands dirty," her mother said. "Desiree!"

"She at work, Miss Adele," the man said.

"Work?"

"Over in town."

"Well somebody ought to get her. She's gonna miss supper."

"Stella'll fetch her," the man said. "I'm gonna stay right here with you."

He wrapped an arm around her mother's shoulders, protectively. Protecting her from me, Stella realized, gently setting down the knife. She stepped out onto the front porch and stared into the woods. She did not realize until she was walking through the dirt that she had no idea where she was going.

THE FIRST THING to know about the Reunion, as it would later be called, is that there were no real witnesses. Lou's Egg House was always empty between lunch and dinner, which was when Jude phoned from the student union. Desiree loved those noisy calls, even though Jude always sounded harried, rushing off to a lecture or a lab. That afternoon, she was trying to coax Desiree to visit her again.

"You know I can't," Desiree said.

"I know," Jude said. "I just miss you. I worry about you sometimes."

Desiree swallowed. "Well, don't," she said. "You out there livin your life. That's all I want for you. Don't you worry about me. Mama'll be all right."

She didn't hear the bell jingle over the door until after she hung up the phone. It surprised her. The diner had been empty when she'd stepped into the back to answer the phone, except for Marvin Landry, who was never sober past noon, the war having done him, and that afternoon in particular, he was slumped in a back booth, a fifth of whiskey inside his jacket. He hadn't touched the turkey sandwich Desiree had left in front of him. He didn't even wake up when Stella Vignes stepped inside. He didn't see her pause in the doorway, glancing around at the peeling linoleum floors, the bursting leather stools, the bum snoozing in the corner. Didn't hear Desiree call from the back, "Be right out!"

He certainly didn't see Desiree backing out of the kitchen, retying her apron. She didn't notice him at all, because when she turned around, she was staring at Stella.

"Oh," Desiree said. That was all she could think to say. Oh. Less a word than a sound. She dropped her apron strings, the garment flapping uselessly against her. Across the counter, Stella was smiling but her eyes filled with tears. She stepped toward her but Desiree held up a hand.

"Don't," she said, choking back anger. Stella standing in front of her, appearing with no warning, no apologies, returning only after Desiree had finally let her go. Wearing that blouse that she would sometimes remember as the color of cream, other times the color of bone, a blouse that looked like it had never stained or wrinkled. Tiny pearl buttons. A shiny silver bracelet. No wedding ring, her hands tightening into fists the way they curled sometimes when Stella was nervous, and she was nervous now, wasn't she, she had never been nervous around Desiree before. But why shouldn't she be? All those

years, what had given her the nerve to show her face again? To expect
that she might be welcomed? Desiree's thoughts ran jumbled through
her head. She could barely follow them. And Stella's smile faded, but
she still took another tiny step closer.

"I mean it," Desiree said. Her voice low, threatening.

"Forgive me," Stella said. "Forgive me."

She was still repeating those words when she walked around the
counter. Desiree tried to push her away but Stella pulled and then they
were struggling, and then they were holding each other, Desiree exhausted, whimpering, Stella begging for forgiveness into her sister's
hair. And that's what Marvin Landry told everyone he saw when he
finally woke up: a turkey sandwich resting on a plate in front of him,
and a misted bottle of Coke, and behind the counter, Desiree Vignes
wrapped around herself.

SHE'S DIFFERENT NOW.

The same words passed through each twin's mind. Desiree, eyeing
how Stella held her knife and fork, barely gripping the metal. Stella,
noticing how boldly Desiree moved around the kitchen now. Desiree,
watching Stella rub the back of her neck, a gesture that seemed so wea-
ried, it startled her. Stella, listening to Desiree speak to their mother, her
voice soft and soothing. And all the while, to Adele Vignes, the twins
were the same as they'd ever been. Time was collapsing and expanding;
the twins were different and the same all at once. There could have
been fifty pairs of twins sitting at that dinner table, a seat for each person they had been since they'd spoken last: a battered wife and a bored
one, a waitress and a professor, each woman seated next to a stranger.

Instead, there were only the twins, Early sitting between them. He
felt, watching Stella primly cut her fish, that he didn't know Desiree

at all, that maybe it was impossible to know one without the other. After dinner, he cleared the dishes while the twins stepped out onto the front porch, Desiree carrying a dusty bottle of gin that she'd found in the back of the pantry. She'd brought it out even though she didn't know if Stella even liked gin, but Stella's eyes drifted to the bottle, then back to hers, and Desiree felt the thrill of a silent conversation. She smuggled it outside, Stella trailing after her.

"Don't y'all stay out too late," their mother called. "It's a school night."

Now they passed the bottle lazily between them, wincing through sips of that ancient gin, which had been a wedding gift from Marie Vignes. The Decuirs had been scandalized—what a present from your mother-in-law!—and somehow, the controversial bottle had been forgotten over the years. Desiree sipped, then Stella, the twins falling into an easy rhythm.

"You talk different now," Desiree said.

"What do you mean?" Stella said.

"Like that. Wut do you mean. How'd you learn to talk like that?"

Stella paused, then smiled. "Television," she said. "I used to watch hours of it. Just to learn how to sound like them."

"Jesus," Desiree said. "I still can't believe you did it, Stella."

"It isn't so hard. You could've done it."

"You didn't want me to. You left me." God, Desiree hated how wounded she sounded. After all these years, whining like a child abandoned on the play yard.

"It wasn't that," Stella said. "I met someone."

"You did all this for a man?"

"Not for him," she said. "I just liked who I was with him."

"White."

"No," Stella said. "Free."

Desiree laughed. "Same thing, baby." She took another sip of gin, swallowing hard. "Well, who was he?"

Again, Stella paused.

"Mr. Sanders," she finally said.

In spite of everything, Desiree laughed. She laughed harder than she had in weeks, years even, laughed until Stella, laughing too, snatched the bottle out of her hands before she knocked it over.

"Mr. Sanders?" she said. "That ol' boss of yours? You ran off with him? Farrah said—"

"Farrah Thibodeaux! I haven't thought about her in years."

"She said she seen you with a man—"

"What ever happened to her?"

"I don't know. This was years ago—she married some alderman—"

"A politician's wife!"

"Can you believe it?"

The twins, laughing, talking over each other again, churning their way through that bottle. Desiree, looking out for their mother, the way she'd done when they were teenagers smoking on the porch. She was a little drunk by now. She didn't even know how late it was.

"How'd you do it?" she said. "All those years."

"I had to keep going," Stella said. "You can't turn back when you have a family. When you have people that depend on you."

"You had a family," Desiree said.

"Oh, that's not what I mean," Stella said, looking away. "It's different with a child. You know that."

But what was different, exactly? A sister easier to shed than a daughter, a mother than a husband. What made her so easy to give away? But she didn't ask this, of course. She would have felt even more like a child than she already did, glancing over her shoulder to make sure her mother didn't catch her drinking.

"So it's you and Mr. Sanders—"

"Blake."

"You and Blake and—"

"We have a daughter," Stella said. "Kennedy."

Desiree tried to imagine her. For some reason, she could only envision a proper little white girl posed on a piano bench, her hands folded on her lap just so.

"So what's she like?" Desiree said. "Your girl."

"Willful. Charming. She's an actor."

"An actor!"

"She does little plays in New York. Not Broadway or anything."

"Still," Desiree said. "An actor. Maybe you can bring her next time."

She knew she'd said the wrong thing when Stella glanced away. A tiny look, but one that Desiree could still read. When their eyes met again, Stella's were full of tears.

"You know I can't," she said.

"Why not?"

"Your daughter—"

"What about her?"

"She found me, Desiree. In Los Angeles. That's why I'm here."

Desiree scoffed. How could Jude have found Stella? Her daughter, a college student, stumbling upon her in a city as large as Los Angeles. And even if she had, somehow, found Stella, her daughter would have told her. She never would've kept a secret like that from her.

"She didn't tell you," Stella said. "I don't blame her. I was awful. I didn't mean to be—I was scared, some girl showing up out of nowhere, saying she knows me. She looks nothing like you, you know that. What was I supposed to think? But she found my daughter. Told her all about me, about Mallard. Then she pops up again in New York—"

Desiree pushed off the porch step. She had to call Jude. She didn't care that it was late, that she was tipsy, that Stella was miraculously sitting on her front porch. But Stella grabbed her wrist.

"Desiree, please," she said. "Just listen to me. Just be reasonable—"

"I been reasonable!"

"She'll never stop! Your girl will keep trying to tell mine the truth and it's too late for all that now. Can't you see that?"

"Oh sure, it's the end of the world. Your girl finding out she ain't so lily white—"

"That I lied to her," Stella said. "She'll never forgive me. You don't understand, Desiree. You're a good mother, I can see that. Your girl loves you. That's why she didn't tell you about me. But I haven't been a good one. I spent so long hiding—"

"Because you chose to! You wanted to!"

"I know," Stella said. "I know but please. Please, Desiree. Don't take her away from me."

She bent over, crying into her hands, and exhausted, Desiree returned to the step beside her. She wrapped an arm around Stella's shoulders, staring at the nape of her neck, pretending not to see the gray hair threading through the black. She'd always felt like the older sister, even though she only was by a matter of minutes. But maybe in those seven minutes they'd first been apart, they'd each lived a lifetime, setting out on their separate paths. Each discovering who she might be.

IN THE BEGINNING, Early Jones could never fall asleep in the Vignes house. The comfort disturbed him. He was used to sleeping under the stars or cramped in his car or lying on a hard prison cot. Or before all that, piled on a mattress stuffed with Spanish moss, beside eight of his siblings, whose names he no longer remembered, let alone their faces. He was not used to this: a big bed and homemade quilt, the headboard carved by a man nobody talked about but who lingered still in all the furniture. At first, he would lie in bed beside Desiree, under a roof that did not leak, and chase hopelessly after sleep.

Sometimes he ended up pacing in front, smoking cigarettes at three in the morning, feeling as if the house itself had rejected him. Other times, he fell asleep on the porch and didn't wake up until Desiree tripped over him the next morning.

"He's like a wild dog," he'd heard Adele tell her. "You give him a nice bed, he still feel better sleepin in the dirt."

She wasn't wrong. He was a hunter, after all. He wasn't built for soft quilts and roomy chairs. He only felt like himself with his nose pressed to the trail. Which was why, the next morning, when he heard Stella sneaking out the front door, he followed her outside.

"Mighty early for the train," he said.

She jolted, almost dropping her little bag. She looked shamed that he'd caught her.

"I have to get back home," she said.

"Ain't right to leave like this," he said. "Without sayin good-bye."

"It's the only way," she said. "If I have to tell her good-bye, I'll never leave and I have to. I have to go back to my life."

He understood. In spite of himself, he did. Maybe that was the only way his parents could've dumped him. If they'd told him good-bye, he would've hollered, clinging to their legs. He would've never let them go.

"You need a ride?" he said.

She glanced toward the dark woods and nodded. He led Stella to his car. He offered to drive her, not out of kindness, but because Desiree loved Stella and that was how love worked, wasn't it? A transference, leaping onto you if you inched close enough. He drove Stella past the bus stop, all the way to the train station. She sat in the front seat of his beat-up ride, both hands clutching the bag in her lap.

"I never meant it to be this way," she said.

He grunted. He didn't want to look at her as she climbed out of his car. He didn't want to be the only one to tell her good-bye. He already knew then that he would lie to Desiree when he came home. Pretend he hadn't heard Stella inching across the hall. The same way he knew, when Stella slid her wedding ring into his palm, that he would never tell Desiree about it.

"Sell it," she said, not looking at him. "Take care of Mama."

He tried to hand the ring back to her but by then, Stella was climbing out of his car, Stella walking into the train station, Stella disappearing behind the glass doors. That diamond ring felt cold in his palm. He had no idea what something like that could be worth, and he wouldn't know for sure until weeks later, when he had it appraised. That bald white man staring at it through his magnifying glass, gazing back at Early warily and asking how he came by the ring again. Passed down through the family, Early told him. Like most truths, it sounded a little phony.

WHEN DESIREE WOKE that morning, she reached across the bed and felt nothing but air. She wasn't surprised, but she still cried out, touching the empty space across the bed. The night before, she had fallen asleep across from her sister, two women squeezed onto a bed that was far too small. Stella in her old spot, Desiree in the place she'd slept for years. For hours, they stayed up, whispering in the dark until their vision blurred, neither wanting to be the first to close her eyes.

A MONTH AFTER Stella returned to Mallard, her daughter finally called home and announced that she was moving back to California. Her thing with Frantz—and wasn't it just like her, to call a serious relationship a "thing"?—had run its course, she'd spent all her money in Europe, her heart wasn't in musical theater anymore. She offered up a few different excuses but Stella, listening, her heart in her throat, didn't care why. She didn't even care that her daughter hadn't said that she wanted to be close to her parents, that she missed them. She had gone home and now her daughter was coming home too. The two events were unconnected, of course, but in her mind, she bound them together, one return triggering the other. She canceled her afternoon class to meet Kennedy outside LAX. Then there she was, walking through the terminal, lugging a bulging suitcase. She was thinner now and she'd cut her hair, blonde waves falling halfway down her neck.

Stella pulled her into a hug, holding on to her for so long that the others waiting at the baggage carousel stared.

"Are you okay?" her daughter asked. "You look different."

"Different how?"

"I don't know. Tired."

She'd spent the past month unable to sleep through the night. Each time she closed her eyes, she saw Desiree.

"I'm fine," she said, grabbing Kennedy's hand. "I'm just so glad you're back."

"What happened to your ring?" her daughter said.

She almost lied. It scared her, how natural lying was. She almost told her daughter the same story she'd told Blake when she came home, bare-handed for the first time in twenty-odd years. How she'd taken off her ring at work to wash her hands, how she must have left it in the soap dish in the faculty bathroom, how she had hounded every janitor she could find but none could locate it. She'd seemed so distraught that he ended up comforting her.

"Oh it's all right, Stel," he said. "I think you're due for an upgrade anyway."

He was having the new ring custom made at her favorite jeweler. A lie procuring the first ring, a different one procuring the second. She could never be completely honest with her husband, but somehow, standing in the airport, she couldn't bring herself to lie to her daughter again. Maybe it was the exhaustion, or her relief that her girl was finally home, or maybe, reaching for the bulging suitcase, she knew that her daughter had running in her blood too. She would always feel that urge to escape tugging at her and never understand why, not if Stella didn't explain it to her. Her daughter, who would forever be the only person in her life who really knew her.

She gripped the suitcase handle, staring down at the worn carpet.

"I gave it to my sister," she said. "She needs it more than I do."

Kennedy stopped. "Your sister?" she said. "You went back there?"

"Come on, honey," Stella said. "We can talk in the car."

Traffic would be a nightmare. She knew this long before she inched onto the 405. Bumper to bumper, red taillights as far as she could see. When she'd first moved to Los Angeles, she'd found the traffic a little beautiful. All those people going places. She was frightened to drive on the freeway, but once she got the hang of it, she went for drives alone in the middle of the day for the peace of it. She liked studying the cloudless sky, the pale blue mountains up ahead. Her baby girl strapped in the backseat, babbling along with the radio.

"You can ask me what you'd like," she said, gripping the steering wheel. "But when we get home—"

"I know, I know," her daughter said. "I can't say anything."

"It hurts to talk about," she said. "You understand? But I want you to know me."

Her daughter turned away, glancing out the window. They weren't far from home but this was Los Angeles. You could cover a lifetime in eleven miles.

Seventeen

They named the dead man Freddy.

He was twenty-one, six foot two, one hundred eighty pounds, the victim of an enlarged heart. In their more morbid moments, the lab called him Fred the Dead. At the University of Minnesota, all of the medical students named their cadavers. It personalized death, the faculty said, it restored dignity to the undignified process of dying. To the undignified process of science. This was what people had in mind when they imagined donating their bodies to research: a group of twentysomethings in lab coats jokingly brainstorming names, each year at least one group so lazy they dubbed you Yorick and got on with it. Weirdly enough, naming Freddy made his body less intimate to Jude. It wasn't his real name. He'd lived and died a completely different man, one they would never know beyond the details inscribed on his chart. He'd barely lived at all, really, and now he would quite possibly live a more interesting life here on the slab in their basement laboratory.

Once she got past the smell, Jude liked working with cadavers. She didn't have to joke about them to mask her discomfort; she never felt sick at the sight of a dead body. Lectures bored her but she was rapt during labs, always the first to grab her scalpel when the professor asked for volunteers. People lived in bodies that were largely unknowable. Some things you could never learn about yourself—some things nobody could learn about you until after you died. She was fascinated by the mystery of dissections as well as the challenge. They had to search for tiny nerves that were impossible to find. It was almost like a little treasure hunt.

"That's gross, baby," Reese said. He always squirmed away when she came home smelling like formaldehyde. He made her shower before kissing him. He never wanted to be touched after the dead people. He'd always been more sentimental, at least she thought, until the afternoon that her mother called to tell her that her grandmother had died. She stood in her windowless office, holding the phone against her cheek. She was TAing that semester and had been given an office she rarely used. Nobody had the phone number except for Reese and her mother, in case of emergencies. She'd been so startled to hear her mother's voice that it hadn't dawned on her the only reason she might be calling.

"You knew she was sick," her mother said. She was trying to comfort her or maybe just alleviate her shock.

"I know," Jude said. "Still."

"It wasn't painful. She was smilin and talkin to me, right up until the end."

"Are you all right, Mama?"

"Oh, you know me."

"That's why I'm asking."

Her mother laughed a little. "I'm fine," she said. "Anyway, the service is Friday. I just wanted to let you know. I know you're busy with school—"

"Friday?" Jude said. "I'll fly down—"

"Hold on. No use in you comin all the way down here—"

"My grandmother is dead," Jude said. "I'm coming home."

Her mother didn't try to dissuade her further. Jude was grateful for that. She'd already acted as if notifying her of her grandmother's passing had been some inconvenience. What type of life did her mother think she was living that she couldn't interrupt with that type of news? They hung up and Jude stepped out into the hallway. Students buzzed past. A friend from the biology department waved his coffee at her as he ducked into the lounge. A weedy orange-haired girl tacked a green poster for a protest onto the announcement board. That was the thing about death. Only the specifics of it hurt. Death, in a general sense, was background noise. She stood in the silence of it.

WEST HOLLYWOOD WAS A GRAVEYARD, Barry said the last time he'd called. Every day, a new litany of the dying.

There were the men you sort of knew, like Jared, the blond bartender at Mirage with the heavy pour. He'd wink then tilt the bottle of gin into your glass, as if he were doing you a personal favor and didn't treat everyone to his generosity. His memorial was in Eagle Rock. There were exes or enemies like Ricardo, known as Yessica, a queen who'd beaten Barry at more balls than he would ever admit. He'd asked to be cremated and Barry had stood along the shore at Manhattan Beach while he was scattered into the ocean. Then the men you loved. Luis had just been admitted to Good Samaritan Hospital, and when Jude called, he kept talking about how a nurse told him that Bobby Kennedy had died there.

"Can you believe it?" he said. "I mean, a president died here."

She didn't have the heart to tell him that Bobby Kennedy was never president. He died running for office, a young man with promise.

"Not that young," Barry said, when she called him after. "He was in his forties."

"That's not young?" she said.

He didn't answer, and she wished she hadn't said anything at all.

On the weekends, she attended impassioned meetings held by activists who organized petitions and letter-writing campaigns and demonstrations intended to shame the government out of its indifference. She volunteered with a student group that handed out condoms and clean needles in downtown Minneapolis. She visited patients who had no family, brought them magazines and playing cards. She thought about death constantly, and still, only on the afternoon that her grandmother died did she find herself unable to touch the cadaver. It was silly, but she couldn't even look at him. She kept imagining her grandmother lying lifeless on a slab somewhere. Maman would never donate her body to research. She would hate the idea of strangers touching her, and besides, she was a Catholic who still believed that cremation was a sin. On Judgment Day, her body would be resurrected, so she needed to keep it intact.

"Just bury me in the backyard in an old pine box," Maman used to say. This was years ago, when her grandmother began to realize that she was sick. Her memories ebbing and flowing like the tide.

That whole year, Jude had read every book she could find on Alzheimer's disease. She studied the illness desperately, as if understanding it would make any difference. It didn't, of course. She was only a first-year student and she wanted to be a cardiologist, anyway. The heart was a muscle she understood. The brain baffled her. Still, she borrowed books from the medical library, reading all she could. Inside her grandmother's brain, protein fragments hardened into plaques between nerve cells. Brain tissue shrank. Cells in the hippocampus degenerated. Eventually, as the disease spread through the cerebral cortex, her grandmother would lose the ability to perform routine tasks. She would lose her judgment, control of her emotions, language. She would not be able to feed herself, recognize people, control bodily functions. She would lose her memory. She would lose herself.

"Don't you waste all that money on me," her grandmother had said. "I won't be around to see none of it."

She didn't care about the outfit she was buried in, what Scripture might be engraved on the headstone, which flowers adorned her. But no cremation, absolutely not. She was adamant about that. Jude never pressed her even though she didn't understand. If God could reassemble a decaying corpse, then why couldn't he reanimate ashes? But she didn't want to picture this either, her grandmother burned, flecks of bone and skin swirling in an urn. She left lab early.

At home, Reese stirred soup over the stove. He was shirtless, barefoot in jeans. He was always shirtless these days. You would've thought they were living in a cabana in Miami, not freezing in the north.

"You're gonna catch pneumonia," she said.

He smiled, shrugging. "I just got out the shower."

His hair was still wet, tiny beads of water dotting his shoulders. She wrapped her arms around his waist, kissing his damp back.

"My grandma died," she said.

"Jesus." He turned to face her. "I'm sorry, baby."

"It's okay," she said. "She's been sick—"

"Still. Are you all right? How's your mama?"

"She's fine. Everyone's fine. The funeral's Friday. I wanna fly down."

"Of course. You should. Why didn't you call me?"

"I don't know. I wasn't really thinking. I couldn't even look at the cadaver. Isn't that stupid? I mean, I knew it was a dead body before. What makes today any different?"

"What do you mean?" he said. "Today is different."

"We weren't really that close."

"Don't matter," he said, pulling her into a hug. "Kin is kin."

THAT AFTERNOON, in a Burbank makeup trailer, the telephone rang seven times before the hairdresser yanked it off the hook, then shoved it at the blonde sitting in his chair. "I'm not your personal secretary," he whispered loudly, handing over the phone. He didn't know why the talent—which she was, in spite of his own taste—didn't respect his time, why she was always late, why she didn't tell her stalker boyfriend, or whoever kept calling, to bother her later. She told him that she wasn't expecting a call but rose to answer anyway, hair half teased in a style that would mortify her decades later when she saw grainy clips from *Pacific Cove* on the internet.

"Hello?" she said.

"It's Jude," the voice said. "Your grandma died."

Stupidly, Kennedy thought first about her father's mother, who'd died when she was little, her first funeral. It was the *your* that threw her off, not *our* grandmother. Her grandmother, the one she had never met. Would never meet. Dead. She leaned against the counter, covering her eyes.

"Oh Christ," she said.

The hairdresser, sensing tragedy on the other end of the line, excused himself. Finally alone, Kennedy reached for a pack of cigarettes. She'd been trying to kick the habit. Her mother finally succeeded, now she nagged her about it all the time. Sometimes she told herself she'd quit cold turkey. She'd throw out every pack of cigarettes she owned. Then she'd always find loose ones hidden in her drawers, in the glove compartment of her car, tucked away for her future self. She felt like a junkie, really. Quitting was the only time she felt addicted. But she could quit later. Her grandmother had died. She deserved a cigarette, didn't she?

"You should really work on your bedside manner," she said.

On the other end of the line, she imagined Jude smiling.

"Sorry," she said. "I didn't know any other way to put it."

"How's your mom?"

"Okay, I think."

"Jesus, I'm sorry. I don't know what to say."

"You don't have to say anything. She's your grandmother too."

"It's not the same," she said. "I didn't know her like you did."

"Well, I still thought you should know."

"Okay," she said. "I know."

"Are you gonna tell her?"

Kennedy laughed. "When do I tell her anything?"

She did not tell her mother, for example, that she still talked to Jude. Not all the time but often enough. Sometimes Kennedy called her, left messages on her answering machine. Hey Jude, she said, every time, because she knew it drove her crazy. Sometimes Jude phoned first. Their conversations always went like this one—halting, a little combative, familiar. They never talked long, never made plans to meet, and at times, the calls seemed more perfunctory than anything, like holding a finger to another's wrist to feel for a pulse. A few minutes they kept their fingers pressed there and then they let go.

They did not tell their mothers about these phone calls. They would both keep that secret to the ends of the twins' separate lives.

"Maybe she'd want to know this," Jude said.

"Trust me, she doesn't," Kennedy said. "You don't know her like I do."

Secrets were the only language they spoke. Her mother showed her love by lying, and in turn, Kennedy did the same. She never mentioned the funeral photograph again, although she'd kept that faded picture of the twins, although she would study it the night her grandmother died and not tell a soul.

"I don't know her at all," Jude said.

THAT NIGHT, late in bed, Jude asked Reese to fly home with her.

She was tracing her finger along his thick eyebrows, the beard he hadn't trimmed in so long, she'd started calling him a lumberjack. He was changing, always. His jawline sharper now, his muscles firmer, the hair on his arms so thick that he couldn't walk across the carpet without shocking her. He even smelled different. She noticed every little change about him since they'd broken up, right before she moved to Minnesota. He didn't want to leave his life in Los Angeles. He didn't want to follow her to the Midwest, hanging off her like dead weight. One day, he told her, she would wake up and realize that she could do much better than him.

All spring, they'd broken up slowly, one piece at a time, picking little arguments, making up, making love, then starting the whole cycle all over again. Twice, she'd almost moved in with Barry; it was better to break up now than delay the inevitable, she told herself, but each night, she slept in Reese's bed. She couldn't fall asleep anywhere else.

That year, the first snow had arrived earlier than she'd expected, tiny flurries falling on Halloween. She'd stared out the window of Moos Tower, watching undergraduates scurry past in their costumes. She was thinking about her cowboy sitting on the couch in that crowded party and, again, tried not to cry. But that night, she found him outside her apartment door in a black knit cap covered in snowflakes, a canvas bag slung over his shoulder.

"Goddamn," he said. "I'm so goddamn stupid sometimes, you know that?"

At the university, she met a black endocrinologist willing to write Reese a prescription for testosterone. They had to scrimp each month to afford it out of pocket, but those street drugs would wreck his liver,

Dr. Shayla said. She was blunt but kind—she told Reese, scribbling onto her pad, that he reminded her of her own son.

Now, lying in bed across from him, Jude kissed his closed eyelids.

"What do you say?" she asked.

"Really?" he said. "You want me to?"

"I don't think I can go back there without you."

She'd fallen in love with him when she was eighteen. She hadn't slept a night away from him in three years. In a dingy New York City hotel room, she'd slowly unwrapped his bandages, holding her breath as cool air kissed his new skin.

ALZHEIMER'S DISEASE WAS HEREDITARY, which meant that Desiree would always worry about developing it. She would begin filling out crossword puzzles because she'd read in some women's magazine that brain puzzles could help prevent memory loss.

"You've got to exercise your brain," she would tell her daughter, "just like any other muscle."

Her daughter didn't have the heart to tell her that the brain was, in fact, not a muscle. She tried her best to help her with the clues while she imagined Stella out in the world somewhere, already forgetting.

JUDE WINSTON'S HOMETOWN, which had never been a town at all, no longer existed. And yet, it still looked the same. She stared out the window of Early's truck, which surprised her when he'd met them in Lafayette. She still expected the El Camino. "That car's older than you," Early said, laughing. "I had to junk it." He was wearing his refinery coveralls, which also struck her, Early in a uniform. He pumped Reese's hand and pulled her into a hug, kissing her forehead. His beard scratchy like she'd remembered it.

"Look at you," he said. "All grown up. Can't hardly believe it."

He still looked strong even though his hair was beginning to gray, silver creeping up his sideburns, threading through his beard. When she teased him about it, he laughed, touching his chin. "I'm gonna cut it off," he said. "Rather walk around babyfaced than lookin like Santa Claus."

"How's Mama?" she said.

He wiped his forehead, pushing back his baseball cap.

"Oh she all right," he said. "You know your mama. She tough. She'll push through."

"I wish I'd been here," she said. But she wasn't sure if she meant that. She'd never known what to say around her grandmother anyway. But she wished she could have been there for her mother, who was never supposed to endure this alone. There were supposed to be two women comforting her grandmother at the end, one on each side of the bed, one holding each hand.

"It's all right," Early said. "Nothin you could've done. We just glad to have you now."

She squeezed Reese's thigh. He squeezed hers back. He was staring out the window, lips slightly parted. She knew he missed this, not sundappled beaches or frozen city sidewalks but brown countryside rolling flat into acres of woods. The white shotgun house appeared, looking the same as she'd remembered, which seemed wrong since her grandmother would not be sitting on the porch to greet them. Her death hit in waves. Not a flood, but water lapping steadily at her ankles.

You could drown in two inches of water. Maybe grief was the same.

SHE SPENT THE EVENING helping her mother cook for the repast. Early went to finalize everything at the funeral home and brought

Reese with him. She stared out the kitchen window, watching both men climb into the truck, wondering what on earth they'd find to talk about.

"Y'all still happy?" her mother said. "He treat you good?"

Desiree wasn't looking at her, bent over the oven to pull out the tray of yams.

"He loves me," Jude said.

"That's not what I asked. That's two separate things. You think you can't ever hurt nobody you love?"

Jude chopped celery for the potato salad, feeling that familiar surge of guilt. Four years she'd known about Stella and hadn't said a word. She'd never expected that Stella would reemerge on her own, that one morning her mother would call her, fighting tears, and expose her lies. She'd apologized as much as she could, but even though her mother said she forgave her, she knew that something had shifted between them. She'd grown up in her mother's eyes, no longer her daughter but a separate woman, complete with her own secrets.

"Do you think—" She paused, scraping the celery into a bowl. "Do you think Daddy loved you?"

"I think everybody who ever hurt me loved me," her mother said.

"Do you think he loved me?"

Her mother touched her cheek. "Yes," she said. "But I couldn't wait around to see."

THE MORNING OF THE FUNERAL, Jude awoke in her grandmother's bed because, her mother told her, two unmarried people would not be sharing the same bed in her house. She was still trying to nudge them down the aisle, if a statement that obvious could be considered a nudge. She did not know that Jude and Reese had talked, once or twice, about marriage. They wouldn't be able to, not without a new birth certificate for Reese, but still they talked about it, the way children talk about weddings. Wistfully. Her mother thought they were hip intellectuals who considered themselves too cool for marriage. Which was better than her understanding just how romantic they were.

Jude carried clean sheets to her old bedroom, helped Reese make the bed, not even pointing out that her mother and Early were also unmarried, in the eyes of the law and the Church. She couldn't fall asleep until morning. She wondered, foolishly, if she might feel her grandmother's presence somehow. But she felt nothing and that was worse.

In the hallway, she turned, pinning back her hair, while Reese zipped her black dress.

"I could hardly sleep last night," she said. "Without you there."

He kissed the back of her neck. He was wearing his good black suit. Her mother had asked him to help carry the casket. She'd heard them talking last night in the kitchen while she brushed her teeth. Her mother told Reese that she considered him a son, wedding or not, but she hoped at least that he wouldn't make her wait forever to become a grandmother.

"I'm not sayin it has to be now," her mother was saying. "I know y'all both busy. But someday, that's all. Before I'm old and gray and can't hardly move around. You would make a good daddy, don't you think?"

He was quiet a minute. "I hope so," he said.

NEAR THE END OF HER LIFE, Adele Vignes had told Desiree stories about her childhood that were so vivid, Desiree wondered if her mother was confusing them with her soap operas. A girl she'd hated in school who'd tried to push her down a well. Her brothers dressed in all black to steal coal. A poor boy bringing her a carnation corsage for senior prom. She'd bring up one of these anecdotes in front of the television, where she sat watching her soaps each afternoon. The shows seemed like the perfect form for her. Each day, the stories inching forward, but at the end of the week, the world essentially unchanged, the characters exactly who they had always been.

The first time her mother called her Stella, Desiree had just helped her into her chair. She was searching for the remote in the couch cushions but stopped suddenly.

"What?" she said. "What'd you call me?" She was so confused that she'd sputtered, "It's me, Mama. Desiree."

"Of course," her mother said. "That's what I meant."

She seemed embarrassed by the slipup, as if it had only been poor manners. Dr. Brenner told them not to correct her mistakes. She said what she believed in her mind to be true; correcting her would only agitate or confuse her. And normally, Desiree didn't. Not when her mother called Early Leon, not when she forgot the names for ordinary things—pan, pen, chair. But how could her mother forget her? The daughter who'd lived with her for the past twenty years? The one who cooked her meals, eased her into the bathtub, slowly administered her pills. Dr. Brenner said that was the nature of the disease.

"The far stuff, they remember," he said. "Nobody knows why. It's like they're living their lives backward."

Here was the backward story: the present and its tedium receding, all those doctor visits, the endless pills, the strange man shining lights in her eyes, the television programs she could never follow, the daughter watching her, rising each time Adele lifted out of her chair, any time Adele tried to go anywhere. She found herself in the strangest places. She went out to take a walk and fell asleep in a field for hours until the daughter, crying, wrapped her in a blanket and brought her home. She was a baby, maybe. The girl was her mother, or her sister. Her face switched each time Adele looked at her. Once there had been two. Or maybe there still was, maybe every time she closed her eyes, a new one appeared. She only remembered the name of one. Stella. Starlight, burning and distant.

"Where did you go, Stella?" she asked once.

This was toward the end, or, rather, the beginning. She was waiting for Leon to come home from the store. He had promised her daffodils. Stella was sitting next to her, rubbing a powdery lotion into her hands.

"Nowhere, Mama," she said. She wouldn't look at her. "I've been here the whole time."

"You did," Adele said. "You went somewhere—"

But she couldn't think of where. Stella climbed into bed with her, wrapping her arms around her.

"No," she said. "I never left."

DESIREE VIGNES UP and left Mallard, people would say, as if there were anything abrupt about her departure. No one had expected her to stay past a year; she'd remained for almost twenty. Then her mother died, and she decided, finally, that she'd had enough. Maybe she couldn't live in her childhood house after losing both her parents, although their final moments could not have been more different. Her father died in the hospital, staring into the faces of his killers. Her mother had simply gone to sleep and not woken up. She might have still been dreaming.

But it wasn't only the memories that pushed her out. She was thinking, instead, of the future. For once in her life, looking forward. So after she buried her mother, she sold the house, and she and Early moved to Houston. He found a job at the Conoco refinery, and she worked at a call center. She had not worked in an office in thirty years. Her first morning, she shivered under the air-conditioning as she reached for the phone, trying to remember her script. But her supervisor, a thirtysomething blonde girl, told her that she was doing a fine job. She stared at her desk, shadowed by the praise.

"I don't know," she told her daughter. "It just seemed like time to move on."

"But you like it there?"

"It's different. The traffic. The noise. All the people. It's been awhile, you know, since I been around so many people."

"I know, Mama. But you like it?"

"Sometimes I think I should've left sooner. For you and for me. We could've been anywhere. I could've been like Stella, lived a big life."

"I'm glad you're not like her," her daughter said. "I'm glad I ended up with you."

At the call center, she sat down each morning to dial the lists of phone numbers. It wasn't easy work, her young supervisor told her on her first day. You have to be okay with rejection, people hanging up on you, cursing you out.

"Won't be worse than nothin folks have said to my face," she said, and the supervisor laughed. She liked Desiree. All the young girls did. Called her Mama D.

After her first week, she'd memorized the script, reciting it to herself when she sat on the bench outside the office, waiting for Early to pick her up. Hello Name—you were always supposed to personalize it—my name is Desiree Vignes with Royal Travel here in Houston. As a seasonal promotion, we're giving away three days and two nights of hotel accommodations in the Dallas-Fort Worth-Arlington metropolitan area. Now I'm sure you're thinking what's the catch, right? She always paused here, laughing a little, which either endeared her to the caller or gave him an opportunity to hang up. She was surprised by how often they stayed on the line.

"You got a sweet little voice," Early told her once, grinning at her across their porch.

But what seemed more likely is that people were lonely. Sometimes, she imagined cold-calling Stella. Would she recognize her voice? Would it still sound like her own? Or would Stella sound like a lonely person who wanted her to keep talking, just to hear another voice on the line?

ADELE VIGNES WAS BURIED on the colored side of St. Paul's Cemetery. Nobody expected any different. This was the way it had always been, the white folks in the north side, the colored folks in the south. Nobody complained until the year the eucharistic ministers at the white church that owned the cemetery cleaned tombstones for All Souls Day but only on the north side. When Mallard protested, the deacon did not want a fight, so he dispatched two grumbling altar boys with sloshing buckets to scrub the headstones on the colored side too. Jude almost laughed when her mother had told her—that was the solution, not desegregating the graveyard, just cleaning the headstones on both sides. A strong hurricane could flood the cemetery, the old caskets swinging open, filling with brown water. Some gravedigger rooting through the mud for gold watches and diamond rings, marveling over his good fortune, would step over bones, not knowing the difference.

At the cemetery, she watched Reese lift her grandmother, Early lined up across from him, four other pallbearers behind. Across the open earth, the priest blessed the body, his hand tracing the sign of the cross through the air, and like that, her grandmother was lowered into the earth. She rubbed her mother's back, hoping that she wouldn't turn around. She couldn't look at her face, not right now. During the service, she'd held her hand, imagining another woman sitting in that pew, Stella worrying her fingers along a strand of rosary beads, joining her sister in silent grief.

At the repast, the town gathered inside Adele Vignes's house, hoping to catch a glimpse of Mallard's lost daughter. She was in medical school now, they'd heard from her mother; half the room expected her to walk in wearing a white coat. The other half was skeptical, figuring that Desiree Vignes was exaggerating. How could that dark girl have done all those things Desiree said?

But they did not find her amongst the dead. She had slipped out the back door with her boyfriend, holding his hand as they ran through the woods toward the river. The sun was beginning to set, and under the tangerine sky, Reese tugged his undershirt over his head. The sun warmed his chest, still paler than the rest of him. In time, his scars would fade, his skin darkening. She would look at him and forget that there had ever been a time he'd hidden from her.

He unzipped her funeral dress, folding it neatly on a rock, and they waded into the cold water, squealing, water inching up their thighs. This river, like all rivers, remembered its course. They floated under the leafy canopy of trees, begging to forget.

ACKNOWLEDGEMENTS

Endless thanks to: my agent, Julia Kardon, for always believing; my editor, Sarah McGrath, for helping me wrangle this unwieldy book and challenging me to grow as a writer; to everyone at Riverhead but especially Team Brit, past and present: Jynne Dilling Martin, Claire Mcginnis, Delia Taylor, Lindsay Means, Carla Bruce-Eddings, and Liz Hohenadel Scott.

To every friend who has listened to me wail about the impossibility of writing a second novel, but especially Brian Wanyoike, Ashley Buckner, and Derrick Austin, whose support kept me sane. To my early readers Chris McCormick, Mairead Small Staid, and Cassius Adair, whose incisive and generous feedback encouraged and guided me. To all the librarians, booksellers, and readers who supported *The Mothers*. And lastly, to my family. I'm grateful for your love.

Bringing a book from manuscript to what you are reading is a team effort.

Dialogue Books would like to thank everyone at Little, Brown who helped to publish *The Vanishing Half* in the UK.

Editorial
Sharmaine Lovegrove
Sophia Schoepfer
David Bamford
Thalia Proctor
Catherine Burke

Contracts
Anniina Vuori
Amy Patrick
Megan Phillips
Stephanie Cockburn

Sales
Caitriona Row
Ellie Kyrke-Smith
Hermione Ireland
Hannah Methuen
Andrew Cattanach
Lucy Howkins

Design
Nico Taylor
Jo Taylor

Production
Narges Nojoumi
Nick Ross

Operations
Sanjeev Braich
Natasha Allen

Publicity
Millie Seaward

Marketing
Celeste Ward-Best